# THE FOURTH GUNMAN

*Also by John Lansing*

DEAD IS DEAD

THE DEVIL'S NECKTIE

BLOND CARGO

# THE FOURTH GUNMAN

## John Lansing

GALLERY BOOKS / KAREN HUNTER PUBLISHING

New York   London   Toronto   Sydney   New Delhi

Gallery Books
An Imprint of Simon & Schuster, Inc.
1230 Avenue of the Americas
New York, NY 10020

Karen Hunter Publishing
A Division of Suitt-Hunter Enterprises, LLC
P. O. Box 632
South Orange, NJ 07079

First Karen Hunter Publishing/Gallery Books trade paperback edition April 2018

GALLERY BOOKS and colophon are registered trademarks of Simon & Schuster, Inc.

For information about special discounts for bulk purchases, please contact Simon & Schuster Special Sales at 1-866-506-1949 or business@simonandschuster.com.

The Simon & Schuster Speakers Bureau can bring authors to your live event. For more information or to book an event, contact the Simon & Schuster Speakers Bureau at 1-866-248-3049 or visit our website at www.simonspeakers.com.

Manufactured in the United States of America

10  9  8  7  6  5  4  3  2  1

Library of Congress Cataloging-in-Publication Data is available.

ISBN 978-1-5011-8953-1
ISBN 978-1-5011-8952-4 (ebook)

*For my sister, Bobbi,*
*who continues to be an inspiration.*

# One

Luke Hunter sat hunched over a tight built-in desk in the cabin of a weathered thirty-six-foot catamaran docked in Marina del Rey. His fingers flew over the keyboard of a MacBook Pro. There had been one amber sconce illuminating the cabin before he broke into the vessel, but now the laptop computer was throwing more light than he was comfortable with. At two a.m., all was quiet on the dock, but Luke was running late and still had another stop to make before he could call it a night.

Luke's hair was short, brown, and unruly, his Italian eyes smoky, his beard dark and in need of a shave. His angular face was set with determination as he slipped a flash drive into the computer, tapped a few keys, and hit Copy, hoping to make short work of his theft.

The cabin was teak and brass, and well worn. Rolled navigational charts littered the cramped workspace but didn't intrude on the comfortable living quarters and the bunk that occupied the bow of the catamaran.

Luke spun in the chair, unraveled specific charts on the bed, snapped photos with his iPhone, and stowed the maps back where he'd found them. He had a theory as to why so many of the charts were focused on the waters in and around the Farallon Islands, off the coast of San Francisco, and hoped the computer files would corroborate his suspicions.

He took pictures of the scuba tanks, masks, flippers, spear-gun, and weight belts which were stowed aft. The galley was diminutive but efficient. A few potted succulents and fresh herbs on a shelf above the sink lent a feminine touch to the nautical surroundings. Nothing of interest there.

Luke heard the screech of the rusted security gate which led from the parking lot to the yachts and immediately shut down the computer, pocketed the flash drive, and closed the lid, tamping out the light.

He hoped it was just another liveaboard moored at the same dock, returning home after a night on the town. But he spun in place, laced his hands behind his head, and stretched out his legs, facing the teak steps that led from the stern into the cabin, ready to talk his way out of a dicey spot if necessary. It would be un-comfortable but doable. He set his face into a gotcha grin, ready to go on the offensive. It wouldn't be the first time he'd been caught with his hand in the cookie jar.

The boat rocked slightly, the slippered footfalls nearly silent as a woman made her descent into the body of the vessel. Silk drawstring pants hugged her willowy frame as she stepped off the wooden stairway and seemed to suck all the air out of the cabin.

Roxy Donnelly had straight red hair that kissed her collar-bone and parted in the middle, and a light feathering of freckles on her cheeks and chest. Her hazel eyes bore into Luke's, assessing the situation. She came to a conclusion and—without speaking—told him everything a man wanted to hear from a woman.

Roxy was backlit, her figure silhouetted in a diaphanous white blouse. Luke could see she was braless, and his heart quickened. Her nipples rippled the fabric, and sparks spread to Luke's chest and down to his groin. As he became aroused, he found himself at a loss for words. No mafioso cracking wise, only deep breathing trying to hide his visceral reaction to the danger of her unexpected arrival. The cabin seemed to become tighter still, if that was possible, until Roxy broke the silence.

"I knew you were smarter than you looked." If she was aware that Luke had raided her computer, she gave no indication or surprise at his presence. "You saw the schedule, Trent's on call."

She stepped closer and Luke found himself on his feet. "I made the schedule," he said.

Roxy stepped so close their noses touched. He could feel her breath. The light scent of perfume was intoxicating. She reached down and touched his erection, stoking the fire. "I know what you drink, but I don't know how you like it."

"Any way you serve it," Luke said, his voice deep, throaty, and bedroom. He knew he should hit the road but stood transfixed.

Roxy took his hand, squeezed it, and led him to the queen-size bunk in the rear of the cabin. "Get comfortable."

She stepped into the galley, poured two glasses of Scotch, neat, kicked off her slipper shoes, and glided barefoot to the bed, handing Luke his drink. They clinked and each took a deep sip, never breaking eye contact.

Roxy set her glass down, slowly unbuttoned her blouse, and shrugged out of it, revealing sheer perfection. A dancer's body. Compact upright breasts, a narrow sculpted waist, and a sapphire-pierced belly button. She tossed the blouse onto the chair Luke had been sitting in, leaned over him, and unbuckled his belt more roughly than he would have expected.

Luke might have received a reality check, but by the time his cell phone buzzed in his pants pocket, they were hanging over the chair.

"You're not upset?" he said, more a statement of fact.

"You should've called first, but it was inevitable. It was perfect the first time. We work too hard for no pleasure. Roll over, I'm good with my hands."

No argument from Luke, who pulled off his gray crewneck and tossed it on the chair. He eased onto his stomach carefully.

Roxy was fully engaged. She lit a candle, then raked his back with her fingernails, the brief contact from her nipples as she leaned over him burning a trail from his neck down to his waist. As she straddled Luke, he felt her heat and let out a husky groan.

Roxy started on his lower back and slowly worked her way up his spine, compressing with thumbs and forefingers every third vertebrae until she reached his neck.

"You are good," he murmured.

By the time Luke realized cold steel was pressed against the back of his head and not her thumbs, he was dead.

The explosion of the hammer striking the .22 round in her derringer created a blinding electric flash behind Luke's eyes. The bullet rattled around his skull, tearing up brain matter, until his world turned pitch black.

Roxy jumped off the bed, grabbed a plastic garbage bag out of the galley, pulled it over Luke's head, and cinched it around his neck to catch any blood evidence. She picked up her cell and called Trent.

"We've got a situation," and Roxy gave him the rapid-fire shorthand version while she rifled through Luke's pants and billfold, her voice devoid of emotion. Her body vibrated uncontrollably as adrenaline coursed through her nervous system. She dropped Luke's keys and willed her hands to stop shaking as she placed his cell phone and the flash drive next to her laptop. "I'll clean things up on the home front, you keep your ears open and get a feel for the play at your end. Stay on shift—Shut the fuck up and let me talk!" And then in a tight whisper, "I killed a man, okay? I've had better nights. Okay, okay, but only text if you sense movement in our direction." Roxy was unraveling. "You won't hear from me again until, until, shit, Trent, until I call you."

Roxy snapped out the light and walked over to the door—she tried to still her breathing as she sucked in the thick sea air and listened for any movement on the dock. Water lapping against hulls and nylon lines clanking on aluminum masts were the only early-morning sounds. If not for the dead body lying on her bunk, it would almost be peaceful.

Roxy got down on her hands and knees and scrabbled around until she came up with the keys she'd dropped. She sat on the edge of the bed and made a mental list of what she had to accomplish. Sucked in a breath, nodded, and went into action.

Roxy pulled the duvet cover over Luke's body and changed into jeans and a black T-shirt and black running shoes. She grabbed a pair of thin cotton gloves and shrugged into Trent's oversize black hoodie.

She rifled through the junk drawer and pulled out a roll of blue painter's tape, took a credit card and the cash out of Luke's wallet and added it to her own, and ran out of the catamaran, locking the door behind her.

———

Roxy pulled the hood over her red hair and slipped on the gloves as she ran up the dock and out through the chain-link security gate.

There was a smattering of cars in the lot, and Roxy started hitting the button on the remote-entry key for Luke's car but got no response. She knew Luke drove a black Camaro but was at a loss. She spun in place and felt like she was going to explode. She turned off the emotion, knowing that if she didn't fly right, she was as good as dead.

She jogged over to the next lot that was half full and tried the key again. Nothing. Roxy fought to suck down the bile and panic that threatened to overwhelm her. She ran up and down three rows of cars. Still nothing. She pounded toward the apartment complex across the street.

Roxy heard the ding before she found the car.

Luke had parked in the open lot that serviced the channel on the other side of the road. Mercury-vapor security lamps provided ambient light. Roxy checked the license plate and went to work.

She pulled out the tape and ripped off a small strip, turning a 1 into a 7. She tore off two smaller strips and changed a second 1 to a 4. She repeated the task on the front plate and dove, flattening herself on the rocky macadam surface, as a car drove up the street.

A black-and-white rolled onto the lot, its tires crackling over the uneven surface. The cop car did a silent drive past her aisle, slowed, then moved up to the far end of the lot, turned left, and back out onto the street.

Time seemed to stand still, but the pounding of Roxy's heart reminded her that the clock was ticking and daylight would be her enemy. She grabbed a handful of dirt from the ground and wiped it onto the license plate with one eye peeled for the cop car. She did the same with the rear plate, obscuring some of her handiwork. After the cop car made its final pass down the street and disappeared onto the main drag, Roxy jumped behind the wheel of the Camaro, adjusted the seat and mirror, put on a pair of dark glasses, and rumbled out of the parking lot.

---

It took sixteen minutes to get from the marina to long-term parking at LAX. The black Camaro had black-tinted windows, and when Roxy pulled into the lot, hit the button, grabbed a ticket, and waited for the electronic arm to rise, she had her hood pulled tight, her dark sunglasses in place, and her head tilted down. If there had been a security camera at play, all it would've recorded was the top of a dark hoodie.

The lot was huge. Roxy motored to the far end and parked between two large SUVs that all but swallowed Luke's low-slung muscle car. She checked the glove compartment to see if there was anything worth taking, or revealing as to Luke's true purpose, snooping in the wrong place at the wrong time. She found the car's registration and proof of insurance and pocketed the documents in the hope that it might slow the inquiry sure to follow. She hit the button that opened the trunk, readjusted the driver's seat, locked the doors, and exited the vehicle.

A salmon glow pulsed above the horizon, a warm-up for the main event. The adrenaline had worn off, and Roxy was so tired she could have slept standing up. What she saw when she looked in the trunk got her heart pounding and her head spinning again. A large leather satchel on wheels, filled with cash. More cash than Roxy had ever seen in her twenty-seven years on God's planet. It was Mafia money. The weekend's take from the illegal gambling yacht where she bartended. She zippered the bag and slammed the trunk shut. She didn't need any more heat than she'd already generated.

Roxy took a few steps away, spun back, opened the trunk, grabbed the satchel, and started wheeling it down the long row of cars toward the shuttle that arrived every fifteen minutes. She'd take the short ride to Tom Bradley International Terminal, where she planned on using Luke's credit card at a McDonald's to create a paper trail.

Inherent problems were created by taking the Mafia's money, but leaving it would have been a major fuckup. A man on the run would never leave without the cash.

———

Two black stretch limos roared into the parking lot at Long Beach Shoreline Marina, adjacent to the *Bella Fortuna*. Doors flew open, and eight men exited the vehicles, ran across the lot, and pounded up the yacht's gangplank, disappearing into the body of the luxury craft.

A somber Frankie-the-Man stood at the railing on the main deck and looked down as Vincent Cardona stepped out of the lead car and walked slowly up the gangplank. The two men locked eyes for what seemed to Frankie like an eternity before Cardona boarded the ship.

Heads would roll, and Frankie instinctively rubbed his neck—his was at the top of the list.

———

The yellow cab let Roxy off at the Admiralty Club in Marina del Rey. She paid the driver with cash and waited until he was gone before walking next door to the Killer Shrimp Diner, where she was a regular and knew the kitchen was open twenty-four/seven. She peeled off her sunglasses, pulled the hood back, and shook out her startling red hair.

Roxy forced herself to eat scrambled eggs, bacon, and buttered toast, generating an alibi with her own credit card receipt. She paid up and rolled the satchel, laden with cash, down the sidewalk and the half-mile trek to her catamaran as the sun breached the Santa Monica Mountains behind her.

# TWO

Twenty-four hours had passed since the death of Luke Hunter, and the weather had turned nasty. The sea was whitecapped, the crescent moon blanketed by a thick marine layer. A perfect night for what Roxy and Trent had to accomplish.

A perfect night to dump a body.

Trent was piloting the catamaran, heading south toward the San Pedro Channel and powered by the auxiliary engine. He knew the depth of the basin was good for at least 2,250 feet. He'd studied the charts, set the GPS, and they were just a few minutes from their destination.

Trent looked right at home, almost regal, standing behind the wheel of the craft that bucked, rolled, and cut through the waves, never veering off course. He was a Saudi national and a U.S. citizen, raised in the States from the age of eight, so he had no discernible accent. He was twenty-eight years old, with a boyish open face, a buffed physique, a swarthy complexion, buzz-cut brown hair, and gray eyes that could set Roxy's heart thrumming. A finely inked tiger ran the length of one muscled forearm, the tattooed claws drawing red blood.

Roxy stepped out of the cabin and carefully made her way behind him, wrapped her arms around his six-pack, and leaned her cheek against his back, trying to still the beating of her heart.

Trent gave her hand a firm squeeze before grabbing the wheel with both hands. "You're a brave woman, Roxy," he shouted over his shoulder, fighting the howling wind. "A warrior."

The moment he announced they were approaching their destination, the GPS gave off a shrill cry. The night was black; there were no other boats in the area, no container ships navigating the channel. It was time to get to work. He shut off the engine, locked the wheel, and lowered himself into the cabin, followed by Roxy.

Luke, head still covered with the plastic garbage bag, was dressed in nothing but his briefs. He'd been rolled onto the cabin floor; his body lay on top of the duvet cover.

Trent grabbed two fifty-pound diving belts from their scuba gear and carried them up to the main deck. Roxy handed a twenty-five-pounder through the hatch. Trent ran back down, wrapped Luke's body tightly in the blanket, and, with Roxy's help, dragged his deadweight up the stairs and onto the aft deck behind the wheelhouse.

Trent pulled back the duvet and fastened one belt, cinched it tight around Luke's waist, and then made short work of the second. He grabbed the twenty-five-pound belt, wrapped it twice around Luke's neck, and secured it. Postmortem lividity had turned Luke's back, buttocks, and legs a blackish-purple where the blood had settled.

Trent pulled the duvet taut, rolling Luke's body over, and ripped a cut from top to bottom on the garbage bag so it would disengage after splashdown and be dragged out to sea. He worried it might fill with air as the corpse decomposed, and drag the body to the surface.

Roxy steeled herself as she looked down at Luke. His face was bone-white, his eyes devoid of color, just a thick opaque film. If there was one life lesson she had learned from her father, it was to meet trouble head-on. Never roll over, never look back, and never run. She swallowed her rising bile and choked, "Do it."

Trent grabbed both ends of the blanket and muscled Luke's body with 125 pounds of lead weights off the stern of the catamaran, tossing the duvet into the chop behind him.

Roxy and Trent stood shoulder to shoulder as they watched Luke float for a second and then slip below the water's surface; they were confident he was permanently buried at sea and they could move forward with their plan.

# Three

Retired Inspector Jack Bertolino was sitting in the nosebleed seats at Klein Field at Sunken Diamond, Stanford University's baseball stadium, in Northern California. The sun was blinding, the sky ultra-blue, the wisp of cirrus clouds as white as cotton. The old-growth pepper trees surrounding the field swayed in the light breeze, carrying the scent of eucalyptus and fresh mowed grass and taking some of the heat off the early September afternoon.

Jack had his eyes closed behind his Ray-Bans, taking in the sounds of the college baseball game, now in the eighth inning, being played in the stadium below. His hair was dark brown verging on black, with strands of silver feathering the temples, and worn long enough to threaten his collar. His angular face was weathered from years doing undercover narcotics work on the streets of NYC, and his tan only served to accentuate the scars from hard-fought battles. A bump on his otherwise straight Roman nose, a gift from a crack dealer, buffered some of Jack's innate intensity. At six-two and big-boned, Jack had a tight fit in the stadium seating, but the sound of the hard ball slamming into leather, the crack of the bat, the umpire's barked calls, and the emotion of the crowd made it a perfect day. Took him back to his youth playing the game on Staten Island, where he had raised his son, Chris.

There was a chance Chris was going to pitch for the first time since the attempt on his life had shattered his throwing arm nine months earlier. Jack wouldn't have missed seeing his son in action again for the world. It hadn't been an easy recovery for the young man, physically or mentally, and Jack tried to keep his own emotions in check. He didn't want his heavy feelings to pull Chris down.

Jack was jolted out of his reverie as a trim man wearing a light-weight gray suit and dark aviator sunglasses, with zero body fat and white brush-cut hair, banged against his knees as he moved down the aisle, finally dropping into the seat directly to Jack's right.

An attractive, serious woman wearing an equally professional gray pantsuit, with a jacket cut large enough to accommodate her shoulder rig and 9mm, made her way up his aisle. There was something about a woman and a gun that was a turn-on for Jack. Or maybe it was her shoulder-length auburn hair that shone as bright as her mirrored sunglasses. She head-tossed her hair off her face as she took the seat to Jack's left, feigning interest in the game.

Jack wasn't surprised by the untimely visit; he had made the feds on his flight from LAX and been waiting for them to play their hand.

"To what do I deserve the honor?" he said, his eyes lasered on the game as the Ohio State Buckeyes headed for the bench and the Stanford Cardinals ran onto the field. Chris had been in the bullpen warming up for the past twenty minutes but remained sidelined; the game was tied three to three at the top of the ninth, and it seemed unlikely he'd be called to play.

"I couldn't do it," the female FBI agent said, her eyes never leaving the field. Jack didn't respond, so she continued, "Come to the game if it were my kid. Too much pressure." Her voice carried an easy strength, and she wasn't going to be deterred by his silence. "Especially with all your boy has been through," letting Jack know he had no secrets from the FBI.

Ohio pounded a ball toward the left-field fence. The batter shot by first and was held up on second by the third-base coach.

It never surprised Jack how much the government knew about civilians' lives, but his son was sacrosanct. And he knew if he spoke right away, he might not be able to control his growing anger at the personal violation.

The male agent, picking up on Jack's energy, took off his glasses and proffered his hand. "Special Agent Ted Flannery." He looked to be pushing fifty but had the body and vigor of a thirty-year-old. "Sorry for the intrusion, Jack, but we've come to ask for your help." Flannery's hand hung in midair until it became clear Jack wasn't going to respond. Undaunted, the agent went on, "You've had a good relationship with the FBI throughout your career, Jack, and beyond. It's been duly noted and appreciated, and because of your recent history, you're in a unique position to be of service."

"What do you need?" Jack asked, giving away nothing.

"Vincent Cardona," the female agent said, answering his question. "You visited his home in Beverly Hills on the seventh of May. You were on Cardona's payroll, hired to find his daughter, Angelica Marie, who'd been kidnapped. An altercation occurred. You slammed Cardona up against the wall, Peter Maniacci drew

down on you, and Cardona's cousin Frankie, with two other gunmen on his heels, ran out of the kitchen, ready to shoot you dead
if ordered."

"You wired the house?" Jack asked.

"Cardona's too smart for that. He does a sweep once a week.
No . . ." She paused for effect. "The fourth gunman was an FBI
agent."

The level of intensity in her tone wasn't lost on Jack. She had
referred to her agent in the past tense, but there was something
more. Something unspoken, Jack thought.

Ohio thundered a ball over the fence for a two-run homer.
Jack's body tensed as the coach walked onto the field, huddled
with the pitcher and catcher, and signaled toward the sidelines.

Chris Bertolino, number 11, ran out onto the mound and
tossed a few back and forth with the catcher as the field was
cleared and the game resumed. At six-two, Chris was as tall as
Jack, but lean and rangy with sandy brown hair, a gift from his
mother's side of the family.

Jack raised his hand to his lips, and the feds let him concentrate on the game. They knew Bertolino wasn't a man who could
be pressured, and understood the personal significance of this
moment.

Chris sucked in a deep breath, nodded to the catcher, and unloaded. His first pitch flew high on the outside. Ball one.

His second pitch went wide. Ball two.

The third pitch was hit. A sizzling line drive caught by the
shortstop. First out.

The catcher walked out to the mound, whispered a few words
to Chris, and resumed his position behind home plate.

Chris nodded, his game face on. If nerves were at play, he

showed nothing to his opponent. He wound up and fired a fast-ball. Strike one. He denied the first two signals from the catcher and threw a second blistering pitch. Strike two. The crowd in the stands started to get loud. Chris tossed a slider, wide. The batter reached, fanned for the ball, and came up empty. Strike three.

The stadium erupted as the second batter stepped into the dugout and tossed his helmet in disgust.

The crowd started chanting and Jack's stomach tightened.

The lanky Buckeye leadoff batter made a big show of whipping his bat to loosen up before flashing a dead eye toward Chris, hocking a loogie onto the red clay, and stepping up to the plate.

Chris smoked a fastball.

The batter swung and made contact. The ball took a short hop and was plucked up by the second baseman, who threw Ohio out at first.

The crowd leaped to its feet as Chris led the team off the field, having stopped the flow of blood.

Jack let out a long, even breath, trying to slow his beating heart.

Chris never made it to bat. The first three Stanford starters were struck out in succession.

Stanford lost the game five to three, but it was a personal triumph for Chris, and Jack wished he were alone to savor the moment.

"I've got to get down to my boy," he said to the female agent, who seemed to be in charge.

"Our agent disappeared three weeks ago," she said, clearly unwilling to relinquish the moment. "He was deep undercover, and we believe he was on to something major. He never checked in, never filed a final report."

"You should call in the cops."

"We won't jeopardize the case we've built against Vincent Cardona."

"I've been down that rabbit hole," Jack said, ending their impromptu meeting. "Don't want anything to do with the man." He stepped past the woman.

"Jack," she said. The undercurrent in her voice, a sadness, struck a chord and turned him in place. She reached out with her card and looked up to lock eyes with him. "Liz Hunter. Think about it, Jack, and call me. Any time." And then, "We could use your help."

Agent Hunter wore light makeup on her clear tanned skin. She couldn't have been over thirty, but her wide forehead was etched with fine worry lines. The hazards of the job, Jack decided. Her cheekbones were high and strong, her figure athletic, her slender, elegant neck tilted slightly to make her point. Jack found himself wondering what her eyes looked like.

"Why should I get involved?"

"The missing agent is my brother."

Jack nodded, took the card, turned, and made his way down the steep concrete steps toward the Cardinals locker room.

# Four

Jack asked Chris to pick out the restaurant. Anything, any taste he wanted, this was his night. Though Jack had a hunger for Italian, he found himself staring at a plate of black rice, fried tofu, and mixed seasonal vegetables. Steamed. He was already on his second glass of wine, trying to stay involved in the conversation that Chris's new girlfriend, Elli, was dominating.

Elli was a petite nineteen-year-old with a cute figure. Blonde hair, blonde eyebrows so light they almost disappeared. A UCLA junior who had classic California beauty with aqua-blue eyes the color of a backyard swimming pool.

There was nothing small about her opinions, Jack thought as she extolled the nutritional and health virtues of said food. Jack wasn't buying into the rhetoric or the food philosophy, but to each his own. As long as Chris was happy and on the straight and narrow, who was he to complain.

And Chris was happy for the first time in months, and that warmed Jack's heart. His son had proved himself in front of three thousand fans that afternoon and come out of the crucible without any scars. The coach had promised he'd make it into next week's game with UCLA, and Chris was riding a well-deserved high.

The biggest surprise of the evening was having Jack's ex-wife join the dinner via FaceTime. He couldn't catch a break. So here Jeannine was, leaning against the salt and pepper shakers, her face beaming on the small cell screen, agreeing with the young vegetarian. Kindred spirits, Jack thought wryly.

Chris rolled his eyes, signaling to Jack that he thought the whole FaceTime thing was goofy but didn't know how to say no to his mom.

"So, you've given up meatballs, Jeannine?" Jack asked, trying to keep the sarcasm to a minimum.

Elli turned the iPhone so Jeannine had the pleasure of looking at Jack while responding.

"I'm a woman of mystery, Jack. More than you'll ever know."

Elli's laugh was abbreviated by Jack's cutting glance.

"Jeremy has been off red meat for at least a year now," Jeannine went on, unfazed by how strange it was to be a virtual face on the dining table beaming in from twenty-seven-hundred miles away. "His cholesterol is down to a hundred and eighty. And I hardly miss it. You look like you could use a few more vegetables in your diet, Jack. Your skin tone is off."

"I blame Apple" was all he could think to say, hoping he didn't sound defensive, and then got pissed off that he cared.

Jeremy was his ex-wife's live-in boyfriend. That is, living in the house Jack had built with his own sweat equity while he was a rookie undercover cop providing for his family and clawing his way up through the ranks of the NYPD.

Jack lost the house in their contentious divorce settlement, and although he was happy his son had been raised in the family home, it rankled him that Jeremy was seriously entrenched there. And yet he was pleased that the man provided a firewall between him and his ex. The couple had a falling out a few months earlier, and Jack had manipulated his son into getting the lovebirds back together. He almost felt guilty.

After a twenty-three-year marriage, Jeannine could read Jack's discomfort like no other and was enjoying herself. Their officious waiter saved him from further scrutiny when he reminded the table that no cell phones were allowed in the restaurant.

"Send my best to Jeremy," Jack said.

"Would you like to say hello?"

Jack fought the urge to toss the cell phone into the fountain and said, "Food's getting cold." He turned the phone back toward the kids before Jeannine could go in for the kill.

Everyone said their goodbyes and thankfully hung up.

"That was fun," Elli said to Jack.

"A joy."

Chris laughed and Jack's face creased into a grin.

"Would you like some more Brussels sprouts, Jack?"

"No, I'm good, Elli, thanks. Getting full," he said, referring to his half-eaten plate. "Don't like to fly on a full stomach."

"So, what're you gonna do, Dad? Take the case?"

"What do you think I should do?" Jack tossed back.

"It's her brother and all. If it was our family . . . I'd reach out to her," Chris said. Jack thought his son sounded like a cop and wasn't sure he was entirely comfortable with that.

"I think you should take the case, Jack," Elli said, insinuating herself into the conversation. "It sounds exciting. And no matter how they show the Mafia on TV and in the movies, they are evil, pure and simple."

Jack was loath to admit he finally agreed with something the young opinionated woman had to say. He wasn't crazy about mix-

ing it up with Vincent Cardona again, but he'd already decided
to call Agent Hunter in the morning and let her bring him up to
speed on the case. "I'll give it some serious thought," Jack con-
ceded as he checked his watch and placed his credit card on the
table.

————

Jack walked up the polished floor of the Delta terminal at San
Francisco International Airport for his flight back to LAX and his
home in Marina del Rey. He held his carry-on bag in one hand
and a half-eaten Quarter Pounder with cheese in the other. Jack
polished off the burger, dropped the wrapper in the trash, and
dashed to his gate seconds before the door closed behind him.

# Five

Liz Hunter gazed out the window on the seventeenth floor of the Federal Building at 11000 Wilshire Boulevard in Westwood. If she looked past the solid block of steel, and brake lights, and exhaust fumes that was the daily logjam on the 405, she could see all the way to the Pacific Ocean. The impressive view did little to lighten her mood.

She turned back to Jack, who was seated at a long mahogany conference table across from Agent Flannery. Her eyes were a muted blue verging on gray. Aloof but attractive, he thought.

The two agents wore their buttoned-down gray suits, just like the legion of FBI agents he'd passed in the hallway. Liz wore a starched white blouse, open at the collar, that wasn't revealing in a prurient way but couldn't deny her figure. Jack, wearing a navy sport jacket over his California uniform—black T-shirt and jeans—worked to suppress his interest and keep his eyes focused on Liz's face.

"He should have stayed at J. P. Morgan," Liz went on, bringing Jack up to speed on her brother's history. "He graduated second in his class at Cornell and was drafted his senior year. Accounting major. He'd be a partner by now, knocking off a six-figure salary with a house on the North Shore of Long Island."

Jack had heard the *if only* story many times before. Her brother, Luke, needed the pump. Didn't want to make empty deals, wanted to make a difference. The NYPD was filled with idealistic men and women who broke their parents' hearts when they dropped out of law school and entered law enforcement.

"I was already in the service. We were . . . competitive. Sibling rivalry."

"A wife, kids?"

"Good God, no. It's bad enough that I haven't told my parents. Not yet, not until I have an answer."

"How did he get hooked up with Vincent Cardona?" Jack asked.

Flannery took the lead. "Cardona's been a person of interest for many years. He was impossible to get a handle on. To infiltrate. Luke had the look, had the attitude. We changed his last name to Donato and embedded him through Cardona's cousin, Frankie-the-Man."

Jack knew Frankie well. As well as you could know 350 pounds of scary.

"Frankie's got relatives in Boston who are on our payroll. The Galanti brothers. They traded Luke's entrée for working off time."

There were two main ways of getting a confidential informant to do your bidding, Jack knew from personal experience. Money and working off prison time. Jack's associate Mateo had been a top earner for the cartels before Jack busted him. He'd become Jack's CI and worked off a twenty-year prison sentence.

"The backstory we documented," Liz said, "had Luke arrested

for embezzlement at a boutique brokerage firm. He spent twenty-six months at a low-security prison that catered to white-collar criminals. Mustered out and wanted to move west. Frankie did the background check and Luke got the thumbs-up."

"And he's been undercover for . . . ?"

"Eighteen months."

"A long time."

Liz nodded. "Worked himself up to a position of trust. He was doing taxes and giving financial advice to a few of the guys and caught Cardona's eye, and he decided to exploit Luke's expertise."

"What was he working on?" Jack asked.

Flannery stood. "We're not at liberty to reveal that."

"Let me see the file."

"No can do, Jack."

Jack jumped to his feet. "You follow me to Stanford, you ask for a favor, and you don't trust me enough to show me his file. Your missing brother's file?" he fired at Liz, his voice rising in intensity.

"It's not about trust, Jack," she said, trying to keep the emotion out of her voice.

"What's it about?"

"Protocol," Flannery snapped as if it didn't need to be said. "And bottom line. And time in. Two years and a half a million in overtime. Washington isn't willing to jeopardize that. Reaching out to you goes against my better judgment. It appears I was correct."

Jack walked out of the room. Flannery flashed dark eyes at Liz, who followed in Jack's wake. She caught up with him in the hallway as he banged the elevator's down button.

"It's not me, Jack. Some of the higher-ups grudgingly agreed to my suggestion. But they're concerned about your loyalties. Your having worked for Cardona before."

"It's a double-edged sword," Jack agreed. "But you vetted me before you flew up north. You know better." The elevator dinged, the doors swished open, and Jack stepped in. He turned, hit Lobby, and locked eyes with Liz as the doors swooshed closed. There was nothing left to say.

---

Jack suffered traffic on the way back to the marina and was in a piss-poor mood by the time he arrived home. And so he did what he always did when he was frustrated, angry, and wanted to throw down on the first asshole he ran into.

He put on a tomato sauce.

Jack set a well-worn pot on the stove and slow-heated some extra-virgin olive oil. He pulled out his wooden cutting board, indented in the middle from years of knife cuts, and prepped the garlic and onions, then tossed them into the pot. As soon as the oil began to sizzle and the fragrance filled the loft, Jack started to relax.

Jack had maintained an ambivalent relationship with the feds throughout his twenty-five years in narcotics. He was smart enough to know that in his specialty—cartels and money laundering—you sometimes had to share intel. Give to get. There were times when the only way to infiltrate a Colombian cartel was to work with the feds, who had deeper relationships south of the border.

As far as drugs on the mainland, the NYPD knew where all the bodies were buried, where all the drug and money-laundering houses were operating, and all the significant players. And Jack was willing to share information that had taken years to develop in order to take down some of the top players. The cartel king-pins. He gave to get and put tons of cocaine and millions of the cartel's cash on the table.

Life was too short to put up with bullshit from the feds, Jack thought as he opened two cans of San Marzano tomatoes and hand-squeezed them into the garlic and onions, translucent now and just starting to brown.

He grated fresh pepper, tossed in a pinch of red pepper flakes, added sea salt, stirred, and admired his handiwork. The color, the fragrance, the taste . . . a simple red sauce never disappointed. Life should be that easy.

Jack stepped out onto his balcony to cut some fresh basil from one of his pots, looked down from his fourth-floor perch, and there she stood, mirrored sunglasses reflecting the late-afternoon sun, staring up at Jack.

Liz Hunter.

In her buttoned-down suit, glossy auburn hair blowing back off her face in the marina breeze, standing tall, holding a leather briefcase, and looking every inch the federal agent she was. Jack couldn't have called the expression on her face contrite, but when she raised her eyebrows in a question, he decided to give her a shot and see what she had to say for herself. He waved Liz toward the front door and buzzed her in.

———

"Nothing personal, Jack. We were all on camera. It was just your basic video liability clause. A little insurance," Liz explained while she took in every square inch of his loft and nodded her approval. "If things go wrong, Washington can deny culpability. Claim you're a lone wolf who strayed beyond the terms of our agreement."

"You're a good actor," Jack said as he tore off rough pieces of basil and dropped them into the sauce.

"Goes with the territory."

"You want a glass of wine?"

"Love one. Jesus, you cook, too?"

Jack wondered what she meant by the *too*. "Goes with the territory," he said, letting it slide and popping the cork. "Better than therapy. Show me what you brought."

Liz took a seat at the dining table and opened her briefcase as Jack poured two glasses of red. He gave the sauce a stir before moving behind Liz to look over her shoulder at the photographs and thick files she laid out on the table.

"How long's he been gone?" he asked.

"The date's fluid. He didn't connect with his liaison on the twenty-eighth. His normal schedule was once a week, but it wasn't set in stone. He had a few days' leeway on either end if things got uncomfortable."

"And was it? Uncomfortable?"

"He was onto something new. Wasn't sure, and he wasn't ready to talk about it. We were drawing a blank, and then a week ago we found his car at LAX in a long-term parking lot. The plates had been altered and weren't matched on the first go-round. The only prints in the car were my brother's."

"Could he have gone rogue?"

Liz barked a laugh. "No offense, Jack, but my brother's a straight arrow. It's all about the takedown with him. Another notch on his belt. Another scumbag off the streets."

Her use of present tense wasn't lost on Jack, and he hoped her assumption was correct. "Give me the CliffsNotes version and we'll go from there."

"Here's Luke with Vincent Cardona, Peter Maniacci, and Frankie-the-Man, Cardona's cousin, enforcer, driver, and body-guard. All men you're acquainted with."

"You don't look related."

"Irish father, Italian mother."

The photograph had been taken at a great distance with a telephoto lens. It showed the group walking up the gangplank of an ultra-high-end yacht. The kind of ocean-going vessel you'd see docked in the French Riviera during the Cannes Film Festival.

"Cardona's new revenue stream, the *Bella Fortuna*." Liz pulled schematics of the ship's architecture out of her briefcase and opened it on the table for Jack. "It's a joint venture in an illegal gambling boat. There's a heliport, a pool, staterooms for eight, and a liveaboard crew of twelve. Only a vetted, elite group of men and women is allowed to sit at their tables. Referrals only. Private club. They fly in from all over the world. Taiwan, Italy, Russia, China, no buy-in, and there's no limit to the play."

"Where's the boat moored?"

"In Long Beach. Cardona's a silent partner, and Luke became his eyes and ears on board. Kept track of the money, on the look-out for cheats and employees who might have their hands in the till. Their schedule is fluid depending on bookings and weather. Some of the patrons embark from Long Beach; some are dropped off in the club's personal water taxi or private yachts; and some chopper in. Luke became Cardona's bagman: he'd deliver the Mob's take at the end of the weekend."

"Who's the front man?"

"A woman named Caroline Boudreau. Old-money family from Louisiana. Fell on hard times, borrowed from the wrong people, and came up with a business plan to pay off their debt."

"Why didn't they set up shop on the Gulf Coast?" Jack asked.

"Too much competition. The Mob would be cutting into their own profit margins. And the jet-setters love L.A."

"How did Vincent Cardona get in the mix?"

"Cardona's been doing so well at the Chop House in Beverly Hills, he seemed like the perfect fit to run the gambling enterprise. At least that's what the East Coast families decided. It's not legal, but they could fudge with the private-club designation. On the face of it, the downside isn't formidable. You're not looking at a heavy sentence. The upside is astronomical."

"Nail him for money laundering, you'll put a crimp in his lifestyle."

"That's what we couldn't discuss at the office. That's what my brother was setting up. Take a look at the files and get back to me tomorrow, let me know what you decide. I'll be your liaison."

"You think that's wise?"

The flash of fury behind her gaze answered the question. Liz handed him her card with a private number penned on the back. "That's good twenty-four/seven, Jack. Don't worry about waking me, I haven't slept through the night since Luke went missing."

Liz stood, snapped the briefcase shut, and started for the door. "Are we good here?"

"I'll let you know in the morning. I've got two associates—"

"Mateo and Cruz are already budgeted." And answering Jack's unspoken question, "We're the FBI, Jack. One of the perks of being in the government's employ."

Liz studied Jack for a flaw in her judgment. Not finding one, she slid on her mirrored sunglasses and walked out the door, leaving her full glass of wine on the table. Jack knew he'd passed muster, but wasn't sure how he felt about making the commitment.

The way the feds had it set up, he and his team would take all the risk and all the liability without any of the protection. He walked over to the pot of sauce, tasted a spoonful, tossed in another pinch of sea salt, and turned down the heat.

———

"El Jefe," Mateo said to Jack, his face splitting into a wide grin. "I hope this late-night call will give me an excuse to fly to Los Angeles."

"That'll be your decision to make, my friend. How're things?"

"Every night I witness the moon rising from my balcony and not a jail cell is a blessed event."

Mateo lived in a twenty-seventh-floor penthouse condo with a view across Biscayne Bay to the bright lights of South Beach and the downtown Miami skyline.

Jack gave Mateo the rundown of the case, as he now understood it. Iceberg tips, but enough, he hoped, to pique his associate's interest.

"What do I need to bring?" was Mateo's answer.

He never disappointed, Jack thought, pleased. "A tuxedo, a few suits, hell, just fill a few suitcases. You'll be rubbing shoulders with high rollers."

"I know some players in town. I might be able to get us a seat at the table without going directly to the well," Mateo said. "And speaking of Vincent Cardona, I know you were relieved to be free of the man."

"I didn't say I wasn't conflicted, but having the door open puts me in a unique position."

"And maybe an opportunity to see that beauty, Angelica?"

Angelica Marie Cardona had the ability to raise Jack's blood

pressure. He'd developed an emotional attachment while working on her kidnapping case, but he'd never acted on his impulse.
"She's twenty-three. Hell, she could be dating my son."

Mateo took a sip of his Gray Goose rocks, his eyes creased
into a smile.

"You saved her life, Jack. She'll be loyal to you until the day
you die, as I will, Jefe. I'll book a flight."

———

Jack took a sip of cab and stared at the picture of Luke Hunter
standing next to Vincent Cardona. Luke wore the feral gaze and
narrow tailored suit of a young gangster. And Cardona, who was
pushing three hundred pounds of beefy muscle, couldn't have
been mistaken for anything but a gangster.

Jack debated whether to face the lion and run the abridged
version of his investigation past Cardona. Might save him some
grief in the long run. Jack was fully aware the Mafia never gave
without getting. He could call in the favor but knew damn well
there'd be hell to pay on the back end.

As expected, the FBI had been thorough in running down
all the leads in Luke's disappearance without showing their hand
or alerting the cops. Nothing of interest had been discovered in
his apartment; it had already been ransacked and picked clean by
Cardona's men the night of his disappearance. His closets were
full, his suitcase empty. There was no indication of what he'd been
researching that had him excited.

Luke's only personal relationship of record in his eighteen
months on the job was with a waitress at Wolfgang Puck's place
in the downtown Ritz-Carlton. But it was an on-again/off-again
affair. Neighbors reported screaming matches in the wee hours

between the two. Jack wondered what that was about. The woman had already been interviewed by an associate of Cardona, and then by one of the feds posing as a PI. She'd admitted to a vague understanding of Luke Donato's career path in Cardona's crew, and had denied any knowledge of his whereabouts. She didn't seem too broken up by his disappearance. Said it was par for the course in her line of work. Jack would give her another try.

There was a detailed list of everyone who crewed the yacht, with addresses and thumbnail sketches and bios. Luke also provided names, financial status, and brief histories of the whales, the high rollers who dropped hundreds of thousands at the ship's illegal gaming tables.

Jack was leaning toward interviewing Peter and Frankie-the-Man before approaching Cardona. He might be able to shake something loose with Peter, get a leg up on the case. He didn't expect much from Frankie, who might already be in the hot seat after having vouched for Luke, but he'd give it a shot. If it was an inside job, and if they'd discovered his cover and taken him out, why would they interview the girlfriend?

Eighteen months was a long time to be undercover, and the tease of big money might have been enough to lure Luke Hunter over to the dark side. It wouldn't be the first time, Jack thought as he took a sip of wine and closed the file.

Jack decided to wait on Vincent Cardona. He wanted to get a feel for the operation and the players before he showed his hand. If Luke had taken a flier and they were searching for him, Cardona would do the right thing, or what was most beneficial to him. He'd give Jack a free pass on the yacht to question his men and the crew. The man owed him that much.

Hmmmm. Jack would probably get to see Angelica in the

course of the investigation. Not a negative. He'd thought about calling her on occasion. Gone as far as dialing her number but disconnected before it rang through. Jack knew nothing good could come from dating the daughter of a Mob boss.

Jack reminded himself he was old enough to be her father. He walked over to a full-length mirror and thought, Hell, I don't look old enough to be her father. And then he looked at the deepening lines around his eyes and the battle scars etched across his face and did the math a second time.

# Six

"Ten grand to play the tables? That's some major hubris, Jack," Agent Hunter said into the phone, a chill in her voice.

Jack couldn't argue the point, but he wasn't going to play cards on his own dime. Not if the feds wanted his help.

The convertible top was down in Jack's sterling silver Mustang, Ray-Bans firmly in place, black T-shirt, jeans, dark hair whipping in the breeze. He glanced at Cruz Feinberg, his young technical genius, who was riding shotgun and listening to the conversation on the car's Bluetooth system with rapt attention. Cruz had been moody ever since the disposition of their last case, and Jack was waiting for the right time to broach the subject.

Jack said, "It's pocket change for those players. Me, not so much. Mateo was able to set up an invite for tomorrow night. The only way I'm going to get an unbiased read is if the crew thinks I'm one of the players. Have it wired to my account by midday tomorrow, and I'm on board. I'm playing catchup, Liz, and I can't score with one hand tied behind my back."

"Do you even know how to play cards, Jack?"

"I've been leading with a poker face most of my life."

"Not the same thing."

"I've been known to play a few hands. And Mateo paid for his college tuition counting cards at the blackjack tables in Medellín."

"That's comforting, Jack," she said with clipped sarcasm.

"And Liz, if Cardona isn't involved with your brother's disappearance, I won't share any intel I discover on the periphery of the investigation that the FBI might find incriminating. I won't jeopardize the lives of my men."

Agent Hunter didn't argue the point. "Stay on mission, Jack. I'll work on Flannery to open the vault. Try not to lose his money."

"Later," and Jack clicked off.

He glanced at Cruz, a grin planted on his satisfied face. The two men fist-bumped. Cruz was Jack's newest associate. His mother was Guatemalan, his father a Brooklyn Jew who'd founded Bundy Lock and Key. Cruz took after his mother: five-nine, dark-skinned, angular face, and at twenty-four could still pull off his black spiked hair. He had intelligent brown eyes that saw more than your average millennial's.

"You're a badass, Jack," Cruz said.

"I do what I can." Jack took a moment and then dug in. "What about you? You've been curiously silent the past few weeks. You want to talk about it?"

Cruz stared out the window, struggling with his emotions. "I keep thinking about Nick, afraid he'd bleed out on my watch. I had a gun in my hand, and I was prepared to kill Toby Dirk if I had a clean shot. I don't know how I feel about that."

The shootout on the backside of Catalina Island with the Dirk Brothers, a gang of ruthless killers, had been bloody, vicious, and deadly. Narcotics detective Nick Aprea, Jack's good friend and only ally on the LAPD, had taken a bullet that tore up his shoulder. He was still in rehab, lucky to be alive.

Jack felt a pang of guilt placing Cruz in physical danger, but knew it went with the territory. Cruz had lived through one hell of a baptism by fire. Jack remained silent, knowing that would draw Cruz out, let him vent, get to the young man's truth.

"Taking a life . . . I don't know how you do it, Jack, and I don't want to know."

"Fair enough. You've experienced more than your share of violence in the past few months. It has an effect, Cruz. It affects all of us. I'd be worried about you if it didn't. But understand one thing . . . under extreme duress, you rose to the occasion and saved Nick Aprea's life. One of the good guys. You were ready to take the life of a killer to save a hero. You just have to decide whether you have the stomach for the job.

"And know that if you hadn't been thinking on your feet when Sean Dirk teed off on the back of my head, and been there to pull me out of the Venice canal, I would've been toast."

"I thought I was gonna have a heart attack," Cruz said, grinning.

"Thankfully you didn't, and I'm here to talk about it. That's two in a week. Two notches on your belt, and I'm forever in your debt no matter what you decide. Now, I'll do what I can to keep you out of harm's way, but I can't promise cases won't spin out of control." Jack let that sink in, and then, "Give it some time, Cruz. Give it some thought, talk to someone you trust, and let me know what you want to do moving forward. Whatever you decide, I'll always have your back."

"I trust *you*, Jack. I'm not going anywhere—not today, anyway. I just wanted you to know what I was thinking about, you know . . . what I was feeling."

"That's a good thing."

Both men settled into the ride and took in the vastness of the Pacific Ocean and the approaching Long Beach Harbor.

---

"What I'm looking for are photos of anyone and everyone who gets on or off the boat," Jack said to Cruz while they walked along the Long Beach Shoreline Marina. "And then we'll put names with the faces."

The *Queen Mary*, now a hotel and tourist destination, was permanently docked across the inlet. The retired world-class luxury liner was all but swallowed up by the sheer density of the harbor beyond, with its cranes, cargo ships, and acres of multicolored containers moving goods to and from the Far East.

"Crew, vendors, clients," Jack went on. "If Luke ripped off the Mob, he might not have been working alone. If his disappearance was tied to a case, and not financially motivated, we need to get a handle on who or what was piquing his interest."

"I can do that."

"Good."

Jack and Cruz walked around the periphery of the marina and its 1,624 slips filled with a sea of recreational boats, finally reaching their destination, where the super-yachts were moored. The two men were stopped in their tracks by the size, beauty, and style of the gambling yacht Vincent Cardona's syndicate now controlled.

The *Bella Fortuna*. It wasn't a new craft but classic in its retro design, a throwback to the romance of the thirties, with sleek art deco styling. It had a heliport on the bow and an infinity pool aft. It was the kind of ship dreams were made of.

If Vincent Cardona was successful in his new venture, dreams would also be crushed. Chapter One in the Mafia handbook.

Jack understood that he was walking a tightrope. If he discovered Cardona was good for the death of Luke, he and his team would be in mortal danger.

If he discovered Luke was alive and, in finding him, put Cardona's business in jeopardy, they would all become targets.

"I'll talk to the harbormaster and see about renting a slip while we're working the case. You can set up shop on my boat, and we'll keep you out of the picture."

"Works for me," Cruz said.

# Seven

*Day Four*

Jack cleaned up well. He wore a black Armani tux; his dark hair was brushed back and fell over his crisp white collar. The small crescent scar under his right eye could intimidate, and straightened only when he smiled. He wasn't smiling now.

He looked right at home among the wealthy patrons trying to take his money. Jack sat in front of the spotless green felt of the central poker table with a view of the grand salon and the eye candy the wealthy men in the room collected. Their young "friends" and trophy wives plunked silver dollars into the slots with studied abandon. These weren't your typical Vegas high rollers; these were international movers and shakers.

Jack had been in his share of high-end political situations in his twenty-five years in narcotics, but purely bottom-line; he was out of his pay grade here. He wasn't intimidated, just aware, and knew if he lost the ten grand, it was Agent Liz Hunter who would feel the sticker shock. But to judge from the number of red, blue, and black chips stacked neatly by his right hand, it was clear Jack was more than holding his own. A glass of cabernet sat untouched. He concentrated on the hand being played, and his lively brown eyes gave away nothing.

The pot held eight thousand dollars, chump change for his opponent, not so for Jack, playing with the FBI's money. The Indonesian man who sat directly across from him was in his late thirties, slim with a tight physique, and wore a charcoal gray Tom Ford suit. He was the only other player with a stake left in the game and stared Jack down, trying to divine the cards he was holding. Jack held his gaze, amused, and tossed eight black thousand-dollar chips clinking onto the soft felt, doubling the bet. The man looked at his hand, back at Jack, ran his hand through his dark brown hair, clucked, and then tossed his cards on the table in disgust. These men might be rich, Jack thought, but they hated to lose. And Jack loved taking the man's money as he buried his cards in the deck—the man hadn't paid to see what he was holding—and added the winnings to his growing pile of chips. He glanced across the room and gave an imperceptible nod to Mateo.

---

Mateo, dressed to the nines, stood at the bar talking with Caroline Boudreau, the owner of the yacht, who appeared to be leaning on his every word. Mateo, firmly in his element, had that effect on women, but wondered if it was Caroline Boudreau who was playing him.

Boudreau was just shy of fifty but looked a good fifteen years younger. Her shoulder-length hair was a lustrous chestnut with subtle streaks of blonde. She wore a gown that shimmered in the discreetly placed pin spots accentuating her well-endowed figure. Boudreau's laugh was easy, with a musical lilt. Probably the only thing easy about the woman, Mateo thought. She exuded style and had the visual power to intimidate—and used it to great effect.

Roxy, who was tending bar, poured a Grey Goose on the rocks and placed it in front of Mateo the second he put down his empty, and then stepped back to give the couple the illusion of privacy. She hand-combed her red hair behind one ear and listened to every spoken word.

Mateo looked like a young Antonio Banderas, and his rakish swagger was known to loosen tongues. That was the plan. Jack would get a feel for the players, as long as his luck held out, and Mateo would work the room.

Caroline, who didn't miss a trick, picked up on Mateo's connection to Jack. "Don't take this the wrong way, Mateo—Mateo is your real name?"

Mateo didn't take offense. "It is," he said with pride and a South American flourish.

"I think you can understand the problem I'm having."

"I wasn't aware we were having a problem."

"We don't generally entertain law enforcement at our tables." She made the statement without any rancor. All business now.

Roxy's face remained placid as she picked up a champagne glass and checked for water spots.

Mateo flashed his most endearing smile. "My dear friend no longer wears a badge, Caroline. You've got nothing to be concerned about. I wouldn't think of disrespecting you, your business, or Philip Casnoff, who personally extended himself in making our introduction."

"It's not me you have to be concerned with," she said, glancing across the room. "It appears your friend is being summoned."

Peter Maniacci approached the central poker table and tapped Jack on the shoulder. "Mr. Bertolino, there's an urgent call for you on the foredeck."

Peter's black sideburns were cut to sharp points, like daggers. His dark eyes had dark circles under them and made him look older than his thirty-five years. He was scarecrow-thin but always armed and dangerous. You could put him in a high-end narrow-cut black suit, but he still looked like a neighborhood thug.

Jack looked past Peter as Frankie-the-Man filled the doorway that led to the outer walkway of the yacht. His humorless porcine eyes were trained on Jack. At 350 pounds, he carried many bulges, but the automatic in his shoulder rig spoke the loudest.

Jack excused himself from the table, and as soon as he stood, Peter slid into his seat. "I'll play the next hand," Peter informed the table.

Jack's jaw tightened and flexed. "Gentlemen, this call might take a while. I hope no one minds if I cash out." And then, "I'm sure you'll take care of that for me, won't you, Peter?"

Jack wasn't asking, and Peter gathered up the chips.

————

"Let's go for a ride, gentlemen," Frankie said, his voice a rasp of broken glass. Jack and Mateo complied and walked down the floating gangplank to the water taxi idling below.

"How're things?" Jack asked the big man.

"Been better. How's Miami, Mateo?"

"Living the dream, my friend."

Frankie-the-Man didn't know how to respond to that level of

optimism, so he grunted and dummied up. A skill set he'd per-
fected. And then, "Vincent would appreciate you stopping by the
restaurant tomorrow around eleven."

"Will do."

The pilot of the water taxi eased away from the *Bella Fortuna*
and pushed the throttle forward. Water rooster-tailed behind the
sleek mahogany runabout as the men settled in and watched the
shoreline lights glisten in the distance while they sliced through
the water, heading back toward Long Beach Harbor.

# Eight

*Day Five*

Vincent Cardona sat hunched over his bar on the second floor of the Beverly Hills Chop House. He was sporting a hangover, a five o'clock shadow at eleven-thirty in the morning, and a burgundy and gray Nike workout suit that did little to hide his girth. A cup of coffee rippled steam, mingling with his half-smoked cigarette in an ashtray bearing his restaurant's logo. Cardona stubbed out the cigarette, folded the copy of *The New York Times* he'd been reading, and slid it down the bar toward Peter Maniacci, who was chowing down on a plate of corned beef hash and scrambled eggs. Peter grabbed the paper and buried his head in it.

Jack stood stiffly next to Cardona, nursing a cup of coffee, black. Cardona appeared lost in dark contemplation. When he snapped out of it, the big man focused his lidded eyes on Jack and let out a final breath of smoke. His eyes crinkled into a deadly grin reaching for friendly.

"So, Jack, you must be a fuckin' mind reader. I was thinking about giving you a call on this very matter. And then you show up on my yacht last night, unannounced."

"You don't say."

Cardona nodded. "What are the odds? You're looking for Luke Donato. I'm looking for Luke Donato. You've told me the why but not the who."

"I provide anonymity for my clients. When we worked together, did I talk out of school?"

"Point taken. Trust and all that. So, my guys have come up with zilch in their search. And you've proved to be very adept at finding people."

"How is Angelica?"

Cardona's dark eyes narrowed. "Good, she's good, Jack." He shook his head and raised his heavy brow in lieu of a thank-you, changing the subject. "I'll tell you this much . . . Donato disappeared with the weekend bankroll. A ton of cash."

"How much?"

"Four hundred and seventy-five grand. My clientele, heavy rollers all." Cardona blew over his coffee and still burned his lip. "And I trusted the prick. I even liked him," he said, flashing daggers toward Frankie-the-Man, who slouched in a red leather booth trying for invisible but finding it impossible to hide 350 pounds of Italian horseflesh.

"And the heist might not be the sum total," Cardona growled. "I got people rechecking the books. Doing forensic fucking accounting. The accountants are stealing me blind."

Jack had heard enough. "I need access to your people, Vincent, to your boat, to your crew."

Cardona's eyes widened in surprise. "Jack, no offense, but what you got is a boat, what I got is an oceangoing vessel. You hear that, Peter? Jack, here, referred to my super-yacht as a boat."

Jack owned a used twenty-eight-foot Cutwater cabin cruiser

that he docked in Marina del Rey. This wasn't the first time Cardona had dissed his modest slice of heaven.

Peter shook his head, feigning outrage at Jack's ignorance on the subject. He was a bad actor.

Cardona was on a roll. "The sharing of information is a two-way street, Jack. You know how it works. Here's what I can live with. I'll open the doors for you. Get tongues wagging. And if you deliver Luke back into the fold, no questions asked, I pump a hundred large into your business."

"Not interested in your money," Jack said without missing a beat. "You're not my client."

Cardona didn't take offense. "C'mon, Jack, I know you can work out the details. Back in the day you were a laundering genius."

Jack gave Cardona his deadeye. "On the other side of the transaction."

"Okay, Jack, so you wear the white fucking hat on this one. Big fucking deal. So, what's in it for me?" Cardona said, face reddening, anger rising, cutting to the chase. He pulled out his Marlboros and tamped the pack against the bar, then against the edge of his flexed fist, lipping a single cigarette into his mouth.

"If I don't find Donato one way or another, the cops are eventually gonna be called in. I don't think that would be advantageous to your bottom line. If he's dead, and there's a good possibility that's the case, and I don't find the killer, you will become a person of interest. Again, that won't be good for your bottom line or your personal health."

"I'm trying awfully hard not to take offense here, Jack, because of our history. Because of our history," Cardona hammered, "I'll cut you some slack. And what if you find Donato alive?"

"Then I give that information to my client, and you get to

live your life unimpeded. You can't be a suspect in a murder that wasn't committed. And I won't share any information of a personal or professional nature that I uncover during the investigation with my client or the LAPD. You have my word on that."

Cardona's eyes turned so steely they could chill a polar bear. "You know, it's a dangerous game you're playing here. He didn't just rob *me*."

Jack imagined Cardona was suffering blowback from the families back east. He really didn't give a shit. "I'm aware of your complications. I'll keep you in the loop, but if Donato's alive, I won't lead him to slaughter."

Cardona lit a match, took a hit off the cigarette, and chased it with a sip of coffee. He swallowed, then blew out a plume of smoke while his lizard brain did the analytics. He slid a white envelope that contained Jack's winnings from the previous night. Jack pocketed the money without counting it. He was up eighteen grand.

"Sorry about the inconvenience, Jack. Frankie wasn't aware you were on the guest list." Finally, "Don't fuck with the clientele, Jack. They're sacrosanct."

"Unless one of them was in business with Donato."

Cardona's face turned a deep shade of red at the mere implication, and then, "I'll give Caroline Boudreau a call. She'll be accommodating."

Jack nodded to Cardona, glanced over at Frankie-the-Man, who looked miserable, and raised his thick brow in a no-harm-no-foul sort of way, then headed down the carpeted stairs to the first floor and out into the garish Beverly Hills sunshine.

Before the heavy wooden door had closed, Peter was off his stool, snapping his 9mm into his shoulder rig, hustling after Jack.

Jack walked briskly up Canon Drive and ducked into an antique shop for a five-count. Just as expected, Peter powered by with a worried expression, throwing furtive glances up the block and across the street, coming up empty. Jack stepped out behind him, and the two men were walking in tandem before Peter knew better. He sensed Jack before he saw him and kept his eyes straight ahead, trying to save face and failing.

"Yo, Mr. B . . . you gotta teach me how you do that."

"Peter, how was Paris?"

While Jack was rescuing Angelica Marie Cardona, who'd been held captive by an international sex-trafficking ring, Peter had become a minor celeb when he took down one of the sheik's men escaping with a stolen Cézanne. A French national treasure. It earned him a trip to Paris and an audience with the president.

Peter pulled out his cell phone and showed Jack. "They gave me a medal."

"No kidding."

"And I came back with a souvenir." Peter pulled up a picture of a young, stacked beauty.

"What does she think you do for a living?" Jack asked.

"Don't have a clue. She doesn't speak a lick of English. And my French . . ." Peter raised his hands in defeat.

"So how do you communicate?"

"In the French way. We're like Adam and Eve, only I'm the apple."

Jack laughed as the men crossed Brighton Way and sat down next to Mateo, who had commandeered an outdoor table on the patio at Il Pastaio and was nursing a double espresso. Peter shook hands with Mateo and showed him the picture of his most recent acquisition.

"You're a fortunate man," Mateo said.

"Yeah, life's looking up." Peter tucked his phone away, exposing his 9mm. Then he discreetly pulled his jacket down, covering the gun but making his point.

The men ordered bottled water, Jack and Mateo ordered the fresh pasta the restaurant was famous for, and Peter begged off, having filled up on his late breakfast.

"Tell me about Luke Donato," Jack said.

"My take?"

Jack nodded and dipped some Italian bread into the dish of olive oil and balsamic the waiter had delivered.

"Good guy, generally speaking. I think he decided to bankroll himself on money that didn't belong to him and hit the road. Bad move to steal from thieves. We never forget."

Jack knew that if Luke had siphoned off enough money to start a new life, he'd always be looking over his shoulder. And with his résumé and pedigree, it didn't have the right feel. Jack wouldn't discount the possibility, but his cop radar told him he was working a murder case, a body reclamation job, and not a missing person.

"Who did he hang with?" Jack asked. "Did he date?"

"He mostly stayed to himself but flirted with everybody. Caroline Boudreau, the woman who runs the boat. She's a looker, huh?" he directed at Mateo, who nodded. "And Roxy, the bartender, but I don't think she took the bait. She's got a thing going with the yacht's engineer. And then there was one of the chefs . . . hell, between you and me, anything in a skirt. Young guy looking for some fun. No one blamed him until he disappeared with the cash."

"How about Frankie-the-Man?"

"What about him?" Peter asked tightly.

"He looked on edge. More so than normal."

"Okay, this stays at the table."

Jack and Mateo nodded as the waiter set down the plates of pasta. Peter stayed silent until the waiter had spooned some Parmesan onto the fettuccine Bolognese and walked back into the dining room.

"Luke came in on Frankie's coattails. Frankie's feeling some heat from the boss and maybe the higher-ups. The kid was good with numbers, started doing everyone's taxes, and he jumped ahead of a few guys on the crew. A few ruffled feathers there."

"Anyone in particular?"

"He got into a scuffle once with Rusty, but nothing major. Donato was better with the books than he was with a gun. We had an incident, and Rusty thought Donato was a little slow to participate in the action, if you know what I'm sayin'."

"I think maybe Luke was a little too good with the numbers and left Frankie holding the bag. My guess, Frankie'll do what he can to help you 'cause it'll go a long way to helping himself. That and the good work you did on the Angelica front. Nobody will forget that, Jack. I won the medal, but it should've gone to you."

Jack evaded the compliment. "So, you gonna be tailing us?"

"Pretty much so, yeah. What can I say? This is my new cell number," he said, handing off cards to Jack and Mateo. "You get in a jam, give a ring. I'll never be too far away. Mangia." And Peter got up from the table and strolled up Canon with the ease of a white shark trolling for seal.

# Nine

WP24, Wolfgang Puck's Asian fusion restaurant, was located on the twenty-fourth floor of the Ritz-Carlton. It boasted spectacular views of the downtown skyline. Lights were twinkling on and the mirrored buildings stood in stark contrast against the cloudless, darkening sky. The sun had just dropped below the horizon and the pale ascending moon was opaque, tangerine, and full.

"I need this job," Miranda said through red lips pulled tight against even white teeth. Her perfect skin, the color of mocha. "You should have called before dropping by."

"Would you have talked to me?" Jack asked.

"Order something and I can give you a few minutes."

"A glass of cabernet."

Miranda's brown eyes flared. She turned with attitude, her stylish braids fanning wide as she strode toward the bar. Her gravity-defying six-inch stiletto heels made the walk muscular and impressive.

The rooftop deck was filling with young, well-heeled men and women from the financial district. Brokers, real estate agents, hipster wannabes, showbiz types, and models, all looking to hook up after a tough day in the Los Angeles trenches.

Miranda was back with a glass of wine and a setup of mixed olives, cloth napkin, and silver. And a cup of coffee for herself. She sat across from Jack and blew the steam over her cup. "I've got a ten-minute break."

"I'm just trying to get a handle on Luke, what he was all about, what he was capable of," Jack said without preamble. He took a drink of the cab and raised his eyebrows in appreciation.

"Well, he was dating me. What does that tell you?"

"That he had good taste," Jack said without blinking. Not enough to melt the thaw but maybe enough to crack the door open. "Did you spend most of your time together at your place or his?"

"Mine. It's out of the way. I was never sure if he was worried about running into an old girlfriend, members of his crew, or the police. His line of work, he had an erratic schedule."

"His employment . . . it didn't bother you?"

"I work in a club where the martinis are twenty-five bucks, dinner's a month's rent . . . I don't know why I'm telling you this. I feel like I'm talking to a damn priest." But she didn't stop talking. She looked at the well-dressed patrons, her eyes hardened, and she continued. "I never could differentiate between mobbed-up guys, showbiz muscle, hip-hop gangsters, MBAs who'd steal you blind, and self-made men and women who'd step over people like me to get to the top."

"L.A.'s a confusing place," Jack said in agreement, wanting to keep her on track.

"Luke . . ." She paused, searching for the words. "Well, he was one of the good guys even if he was a wiseguy. We didn't talk about his day-to-day business; he thought the less I knew, the better. I didn't argue the point. After an eight-hour shift in these heels, I didn't need the aggravation. We shared a few laughs, he was good in the sack, and he's been paying my rent for the past six months. I was finally starting to get ahead. He'll be missed. I'm rooting for him."

"So, you think he's alive?"

"He's smart. I get an email from Belize, I'll turn in my cocktail tray and jump on a plane."

"What about the late-night screaming matches that were reported by neighbors?"

"Effing busybodies. I'm very vocal, okay? And Luke knew how to push my buttons." Miranda looked up, swiped a tear from her eye as the manager crooked his finger in her direction.

Jack saw the action, pulled out his credit card and his business card, and asked her to call him if Luke got in contact or she had any thoughts, anything, that might be helpful. "If he does get in touch and wants to stay hidden, I'll respect that. My client just wants to know he's alive."

When Miranda returned with the check, she had penned her phone number on his receipt. He smiled when he saw the total. Twelve dollars for the olives and twenty-three for a glass of Clos du Val.

Jack signed for the check, left Miranda a crisp twenty on the tray, and steeled himself for the sea of headlights he was about to confront on I-10 west and the trip back to Marina del Rey.

---

Heel-toe, heel-toe, four miles per hour on the 10. Jack went over the facts as he knew them. Luke Hunter was missing, along with $475,000. If Agent Liz Hunter really knew her brother, it seemed unlikely he was in the wind. More likely a shallow grave somewhere or buried at sea. Jack would enlist the feds to check the financial statements and credit card receipts of the entire crew of the *Bella Fortuna*. All that money wouldn't be easy to hide, and the temptation to spend would be large. It was thin but a starting point.

He planned on dividing and conquering the crew. Get some-one talking off campus. Jack was being given carte blanche with Vincent Cardona's blessing, but if he didn't come up with an answer soon, the East Coast families would be paying him a visit. He'd alert his team to keep an eye out for trouble.

Jack knew he should put in a call to Agent Hunter and keep her up to speed. Her boss was probably worried about the ten grand. He planned to return the seed money and play on the house.

Jack sighed as he looked across two lanes of traffic and caught sight of a '78 green Plymouth Fury in his side mirror. The aging muscle car crept past Jack in the fast lane, doing five miles an hour. The driver slid low in his bucket seat and averted his face, but his black sideburn, cut to a sharp edge, gave the driver's identity away. It was Peter Maniacci, and his car was locked in tight.

Jack saw an opening and cut hard across a lane while horns blared and expletives hurled. He did a tire-burning exit onto Robertson Boulevard, hung a tight left off the freeway, and a right onto Venice, heading for home.

He hadn't noticed the Plymouth following on the trip down-town, and he'd been on the watch. He'd have Cruz check the Mustang's undercarriage for bugs. Peter was getting a little smarter, but not smart enough.

Jack laughed out loud, thinking about the panic filling Peter's car. He hoped no pedestrians had suffered in the process but was satisfied he'd inflicted a little anxiety and pain on his tail.

---

Jack decided to deal with the bug himself. He pulled his right tires up onto the curb in front of his building and found the GPS tracker in thirty seconds, attached to the side of his gas tank. As he slid out and brushed the knees of his jeans, the bass rumble of a Harley turned him toward Bruffy's Tow and Police Impound, located across the street from Jack's building.

J.D. owned the business and helped Jack out on occasion. He was a man of few words, but the deep lines that creased his face like knife slashes told the story. And despite the faded jailhouse tats and weathered skin, his hazel eyes still had a youthful intensity.

He pulled up next to Jack's Mustang and spoke over the bap-bapbapbapbapbap of the Harley's idling engine. "Jack."

"J.D., heading to Vegas?"

"Damn, Jack, you know me better than my old lady. Yeah, I'm like an old fucking clock. Leave Thursday night to beat the heat. Two hundred milligrams of Viagra in my pocket, three grand I can lose, and my main squeeze waiting in a suite at the Hard Rock."

"Sounds like a plan."

"What can I do you for, Jack?"

J.D. was nobody's fool, and his ability to read people was uncanny. Jack handed him the GPS bug Peter had planted. J.D. looked it over.

"Can you toss it out in the desert just shy of Vegas?" Jack asked.

"Done." And then, "You got one dark sense of humor, my friend."

"If you can't laugh . . ." Jack said, letting J.D. complete the thought.

"Watch your back, Jack." J.D. slipped the Fat Boy into gear

and thundered down Glencoe Avenue, setting off car alarms in his wake.

Jack grinned as he eased his car off the curb and into his building's parking structure.

———

"You've got interesting friends, Jack," Agent Liz Hunter said, leaning against her government-issue gray Ford sedan. She might have been smiling behind her mirrored sunglasses, but Jack wasn't sure and didn't much care. He was tired of people appearing unannounced. He did wonder what she meant by *friends* in the plural, but let it go.

"What can I do for you, Liz?"

"Check in on a regular basis. You know the drill, Jack. What's your gut tell you?"

"Too early to speculate." Jack popped open the trunk of his car, pulled out a thick envelope, and handed it to Hunter.

"Flannery will be relieved," she said.

"I live to make him happy," Jack said, bone-dry.

"I'm sorry, Jack. I won't push, but . . . I've got to do something. It's my brother. You of all people should understand."

Hunter was referencing the reason Jack had worked a case for Vincent Cardona in the first place. Cardona had provided information that helped Jack take down the Colombian cartel boss who had tried to kill his son. He'd owed a blood debt to the mobster and paid in full.

"Stay in touch." Agent Hunter yanked the car door open. She stopped to still her beating heart, back ramrod-straight, lips pulled tight against her teeth.

"Liz."

The agent turned, face stony.

"When your brother disappeared, so did a half a million of the Mob's money. Check the bank statements and credit card receipts for the entire crew. I'll get a list of the vendors, their drivers, and shoot them over tomorrow."

Liz nodded, afraid that if she spoke, she'd reveal too much emotion.

"Good," Jack said, "and I'll be better at keeping you in the loop, but I need room to move. I'm three weeks behind the eight ball."

"Consider it done."

Jack turned and was stopped with "Jack." Liz took off her mirrored sunglasses. Her eyes were guarded, but Jack could read the pain. "Thank you." Hunter jumped into her car and turned over the engine.

Jack headed toward the lobby as Liz powered out of the lot.

————

The elevator dinged open, and as Jack rounded the corner, he was stopped in his tracks by the sheer mass of Frankie-the-Man, standing uncomfortably in front of his door.

"I hope you didn't scare my neighbors."

"I made nice."

Jack wasn't sure if Frankie's nice was normal people's nice, but took the big man at his word, keyed the door, and let Frankie in.

"Vincent told me I should bring you up to, ah, my speed, or you know, fill you in where I can be of help. Nice place, I wouldn't have thought it was, ah, your, ah, kind of . . . Nice place." And Frankie left it at that.

"Can I pour you a glass?" Jack said as he headed for the bar, opened a bottle of Benziger, and poured one for himself.

"Rough day, huh?" Probably the only sensitive words the man had ever uttered to Jack. "And yeah, you got vodka?"

Jack pulled the bottle of Grey Goose he kept in the freezer for Mateo and poured a double for Frankie.

Frankie knocked the shot back with a flick of his meaty wrist. Jack poured again, set the bottle down on the kitchen island, and waited for the big man to speak.

"So," Frankie said as if he were midsentence. "The night in question, I walked Luke down the gangplank to his car that was parked out front, engine running as per usual. I always let him do the heavy lifting, 'cause it was his job, am I right? And he heaved the weekend's take into the back of his Camaro, slammed the trunk, same as always, no attitude, nerves, whatnot."

"Did you see anybody else in the parking lot? Anything out of the ordinary?"

"Empty. Pin-drop silent. Regular. So, Luke, he cracks wise about going to Vegas and bettin' it all on red, and the prick peels out before I can read him the riot act for even fuckin' around. As far as I know, he's headed for the drop-off."

"But he never arrived."

"You're fuckin' brilliant, Jack," Frankie said, and then sucked back his anger, realizing he was the one under a microscope. "Whatever," he said, more to himself than to Jack. "So, if Luke's not dead, he will be, I'll see to it myself, but Jack, here's the thing, I ain't feeling it. I'm feeling plenty of other things. Like shit for one. But I'm not feeling him, like, in the wind. Something's off. Something's not right here."

Frankie walked over to the kitchen island, grabbed the bottle, and poured himself another heavy round.

"What's your take on his girlfriend?" Jack asked.

"Who the fuck knows. I'm not pickin' up any scam in her. She works for a living is all's I can see. Hot, but a worker bee. But Luke, fucker must be hung like a water buffalo, 'cause he was ruling the roost. Reminded me of me, back in the day."

Jack wondered what day, on what planet, Frankie-the-Man was talking about, but let it slide.

"Luke had his pick of the litter, everyone wanted a piece of him."

"That might piss off some of the guys. You know, getting first pick and all. Getting to the front of the line."

Frankie rolled that notion around, wondering how much honesty would sink his fat ass, but knowing that if he didn't rely on Jack, he was already a dead man.

"Rusty had a bone to pick. Who knows?" Frankie tried to sound noncommittal as he gave up his best bet.

Jack went with the flow. "Guy gets pissed off enough, maybe sets up the competition to take the fall. Disappears that guy and makes off with the cash. You pull that off clean, it's a win-win."

"Like I said, who knows? I ain't tellin' anyone what to do, but if it was in that someone's interest to get to the bottom of this thing, I'd say maybe you should look into it."

"Thanks, Frankie."

Frankie understood an exit line when he heard one and started for the door. "Jack, I'm lookin' bad here . . . I got guys waitin' to crawl over my back. You need anything . . ."

Jack nodded, no sympathy felt, and left the big man walking toward the elevator, harboring thoughts of doom.

# Ten

The *Bella Fortuna* looked like a precious gem in the distance, floating gracefully on the calm waters of the Pacific. The ship's underwater lights created a halo the color of Capri's blue grotto sea cave, Jack thought. His helicopter circled once and then set down for a soft landing on the bow of the ship. Jack was late to the party, and Mateo had called in a favor.

Jack stepped from the chopper, ducked below the spinning rotors, and watched as the pilot lifted off, back toward terra firma and Long Beach Harbor. He straightened his tux, hand-combed his hair, and grabbed the proffered glass of champagne from the cocktail waitress who was there to greet him.

"Welcome back, Mr. Bertolino. We've been expecting you."

"Thank you"—Jack glanced at the nametag—"Doris," and, to the muted, crooning voice of a young Sinatra, he followed the trim woman into the main cabin. Mateo was seated at the central poker table and, to judge from the formidable stack of chips, doing quite well. He nodded imperceptibly, no eye contact; Jack chalked it up to his focus on the game.

There was a slight turnover in gamblers, but he recognized some of the same players he'd taken money from the night before. Jack's attention was drawn to a woman standing by herself, dropping silver dollars into the slots with youthful abandon. The woman turned as if her name had been spoken, and Jack's blood pressure spiked. Heat rose up his neck, burning his cheeks and ears. He felt schoolboy-foolish at his reaction.

Angelica Marie Cardona.

A natural-blonde beauty who radiated strength. Tall, athletic, porcelain skin, and like her namesake, an angelic face. But her green eyes had witnessed more of life than any twenty-three-year-old deserved, and Jack could read her emotional scar tissue. Still, Angelica was the total package. The kind of damaged soul a foolish man would jump out of a plane to protect or, in Jack's case, his Cutwater cabin cruiser at twenty-eight knots.

She was also Vincent Cardona's daughter.

Angelica never broke eye contact as she walked toward Jack, grabbed a glass of champagne, stepped up, and brushed his lips with a kiss, the same way she had on Jack's dock the last time he'd seen her. Angelica slid her arm through the crook in Jack's, and they walked past the bar and out of the main room toward the aft.

Their reunion wasn't lost on Caroline Boudreau or Rusty Mannuzza, a thin man with feral eyes and a cruel smirk who stood at her side, overseeing the gaming tables. Rusty was wound too tight, and it was clear there was no love lost between the two. He pulled a cell from his pocket and punched in a number as he disappeared out of the main salon and strode toward the bridge, where the captain piloted the ship and multiple security screens were located.

Caroline's brow furrowed slightly as she watched Roxy pouring a Manhattan and missing the cocktail glass. She appeared uncharacteristically edgy, Caroline thought, and wasn't sure if it was the spill or Jack and Angelica's presence, but Roxy wiped the bar and then her expression clean. Caroline chalked it up to her bartender's perfectionism and watched as Mateo added a stack of chips from the center of the green felt table to his growing pile. She decided it might be fun to take a closer look at the rakish Colombian.

---

Vincent Cardona's Chop House was in full swing. Standing room only at the bar, while the piano man belted out show tunes. But Cardona, who had just fielded a call from Rusty, was purple with rage. He stepped into his office, threw back a shot, and dialed a number.

"So where did you say Bertolino was headed?" It was his quiet, deadly voice.

Peter Maniacci was leaning against his green Plymouth, parked in the middle of the desert. He had contemplated calling the boss, dreaded the conversation, and wasn't surprised when his cell trilled. The I-15 freeway could be seen in the distance. A solid ribbon of red taillights pointed toward the bright lights of Las Vegas, creating a white crown on the horizon. The night sky was alive with star fields, and the craters of the moon could be seen with the naked eye. All of it lost on Peter, who knew he'd been suckered and was in deep shit.

"Boss, he must have found the bug on his car. That's all I can come up with. I don't know how it ended up out here—"

"Where are you?" Cardona said cutting him off.

"I'm standing in the middle of bumfuck, a half hour shy of the Strip, and I don't know where the hell the prick is."

"He's on the ship," Cardona hissed.

Peter rubbed his temple with his free hand; he knew there was no reasonable response. Bertolino had done it again.

"Did you hear what I said? He's on the fucking yacht. And guess who he's with?"

Peter remained mute.

"Not too good at this game, are you? He's with my daughter." Cardona let that sink in. And then, with the slickness of a python, "But hey, I bet you're tired. Why don't you keep going and get a room for the night. Play a few hands, have a few drinks."

"Really?" Peter's cell connection pixilated, and he wasn't sure what he had heard.

"Yeah, yeah, really, and tomorrow, you prick, you keep fucking driving to New York, and you can tell the East Coast families where their money is and where the thief is hiding."

"I'll be back in three hours."

Cardona hung up.

Peter clicked off his phone. "Fuckin' Bertolino," he raged at the moon. He pulled out his 9mm. He wanted to kill someone, shoot something, but he was the only douche standing in the middle of the desert. And so he emptied his clip, blowing the pulpy arm off an ancient, protected thirty-foot saguaro cactus.

Peter jumped into his car, did a dust-raising U-turn, and sped back toward the I-15 south and a world of hurt.

———

"You've got a new scar," Angelica said, tracing Terrence Dirk's near-lethal attack with a delicate finger. It was Dirk's brutal jab to Jack's forehead that had broken the skin over his right eye. Eighteen stitches that left a reminder.

"I'm starting to feel like a junkyard dog. How about you? You look terrific."

"But?" she said, killer eyes creasing into a smile.

"How're you doing?"

"I'm doing okay. It feels empowering not to need my father's money."

Angelica had been kidnapped and imprisoned for over a month while rich, politically connected men negotiated her value as a sex slave. The story had gained international notoriety when a YouTube video surfaced of Angelica being held captive in a glass-enclosed prison, tearing up a monologue from *Cat on a Hot Tin Roof.* Jack broke the case and saved her life. The story garnered international coverage, and a Hollywood producer paid them both handsomely for the film rights.

"I wouldn't be alive to collect the windfall if you hadn't come into my life."

"That's a good thing," Jack said, trying to slow things down, and waited for Angelica to continue.

"There's no easy answer, Jack. Some days I'm cool. Therapy helps. I'm back at the Strasberg Institute, taking scene study. And some days I still feel like I'm drowning. Less and less, so I guess I'm pretty good. All things considered."

"All things considered, you look like you're doing great."

"I started to call you a thousand times."

"I dialed your number," Jack said, not knowing why he was opening that door. Where were his governors? No good could come of taking their relationship any further.

"I know the math is holding you back," she said.

Why the hell did she have to be so damn smart? Jack thought, pissed that he was careening the wrong way down a one-way street. He had work to do, and Angelica was the last person who should be on his mind. He wondered if Cardona knew where his daughter was.

"My father doesn't know I'm here. Well, he probably knows by now. But he wants me to be happy. He's worried about me."

And Jack was worried the young woman was reading his mind. He cleared all thoughts and became mesmerized by the beauty of her knowing smile. They took a drink of champagne at exactly the same moment and Jack choked back a laugh.

"Do you know why I'm here?" he asked.

"Luke's disappearance."

"Any thoughts? Any ideas where he might be?"

"I didn't have too much contact with the man. He was an enigma."

"How so?"

"Just a feeling I got when I was around him. He was guarded. Like someone in my acting class might be. Afraid to reveal too much of himself. Dad said he was good at what he did. Didn't seem the type to take the money and run. He had too much class for that. An uncommon trait in Dad's crew."

Mateo walked through the door and ambled over, hand outstretched to greet Angelica.

Jack excused himself, saying he had business to attend to and they would continue their conversation at a later date.

Angelica understood Jack was on the clock and let him off the hook with "Count on it."

---

Jack stood with Caroline Boudreau on the heliport at the bow of the ship. The lights on the mainland glittered in the distance and a light ocean breeze buffeted their hair. Caroline's stature and elegance could dress up a string of pearls and screamed old-world money. Her Southern accent was lyrical; her eyes were engaging and used to great effect, putting members of the opposite sex at ease or anywhere else she pleased. But none of it held sway over Jack. He was there to do a job and wasn't going to stop until he found Luke Hunter. Dead or alive.

"We threw big parties," Caroline said, pulling a strand of hair off her face. "The biggest, swankiest, hippest, most decadent parties in the French Quarter. And that's saying something. Paul Prudhomme catered from his restaurant, K-Paul's, and the Learjets would fly in from Europe and beyond. It was quite the spectacle."

"What did your father do for a living?"

"My father was one of the original jet-setters," she said by way of answering. "They did a *Life* magazine spread on him and a few of his intimate friends back in the early sixties."

"So, he didn't work?" Jack asked.

"He didn't have to. Oh, he dabbled, dabbled in real estate. Played the market. But we were living off the accumulated wealth of a hundred successful years of commerce. We believed it would last forever. There was no reason not to."

"How did your father get hooked up with the Mob?"

"It was something about the swagger of the made men. Kind of like you. That machismo you give off. They'd come to parties, turn heads, dominate the conversation, and rich men cowed to them. My father got sucked in and started to emulate them. Thought they were friends, thought he had it under control. The man foolishly thought *he* was in control."

Jack had heard it all before. But he wanted to keep Caroline talking. "Where did it go wrong?"

"Franklin was better at spending than creating or even holding on to his fortune. The banking crisis of 2008, the recession, almost took him down for the count. The housing bubble, when it finally burst, crippled him. His properties started to fall like dominoes. He leaned on his 'friends' to shore up the dam. They were only too happy to lend a hand. And then they started squeezing.

"Franklin became depressed. Fond of saying he'd rather be dead than poor. And when his philandering dick became smaller than his growing vig, he took the path of least resistance."

"How did he die?"

"A bottle of Macallan 25 and a silver-plated .38. The man always had style."

Jack was impressed with Caroline's brutal honesty. "What about your mother? Brother? Sisters?"

"No, no, and no. Mother died of breast cancer the summer of '85, and I was an only child. And, as you can imagine, spoiled rotten.

"The big surprise came when our lawyer read the will. I was left with a frightening IRS bill. After consolidating the family's holdings, I was told in no uncertain terms that I was still in major debt to the Mafia.

"The *Bella Fortuna* was my only asset. And pushing fifty, throwing parties was my only marketable skill set."

Caroline probed Jack's eyes to see if he was being judgmental. She got his poker face.

"I'm not ashamed," she said with a bit too much attitude. "It was how I was raised. All I knew."

Jack remained silent, and Caroline got defensive. Her voice, brittle. "So sue me. It was a match made in greed, and I cut a deal with the devil.

"I have a five-year plan, and all things being equal, I hope to find myself free and clear and able to buy my partners out with enough set aside for a comfortable retirement."

Jack knew that was never going to happen. It wasn't the way the Mob operated. Once they had their hooks in you, they would suck you dry and leave you bleeding on the side of the road. Or at the bottom of the ocean. He was pretty sure Caroline, when she woke up at two o'clock in the morning, was aware of that.

"Or I'll marry into the life I've grown accustomed to," she said, flashing a smile that could open a miser's wallet. "One of my high rollers."

"Sounds like a plan."

"Don't condescend, Jack. You don't wear it well."

"Okay."

"It was a compliment."

Jack didn't have a response to that.

"Do I have something to be worried about?" she asked, in full recovery now. As if she could change Jack's answer by willing it so.

"Not if you're honest with me, Caroline. My only interest in this case is finding Luke Donato. You're underwater financially, and an infusion of cash could change your life. Did Luke ever approach you about cutting a side deal? Skim the profits, cook the books, and guarantee you the success you deserve? If he was dirty, it's a move that would make sense."

"No," she snapped, not happy with the direction the interrogation was taking.

"Talk about your relationship," Jack said, easing up before he pushed Caroline away. "Your take on his disappearance and his relationships with the crew. I know nothing happens on your yacht without your scrutiny."

"I'll take that as a compliment, Jack. I run a tight ship. Luke worked for Vincent Cardona, but he was a mystery."

"How so?"

"He had the look, but he outclassed the rest of his crew. If he wasn't young enough to be my son, I would've . . . But it was pure business between the two of us. A fun flirt. He made me feel young."

"Was he dating anyone in particular?"

"Luke knew how to play women. If he wasn't on Vincent's payroll, I would have hired him myself. He was good for business. But no, no one on the crew. No one that I was aware of, and I would've known."

"What do you think happened?"

"He disappeared, and so did the money."

"How much are we talking about?" Jack asked, testing Caroline.

"Four hundred and seventy-five thousand, give or take. What do they say . . . follow the money, and you'll find Luke."

"Not enough for a new start," Jack said, running the numbers in his head. "If that's what he was after. He could've done better staying the course."

"I agree, and that's why I'm so concerned. It wasn't a big enough bankroll to change his life . . . but more than enough to take his life."

"I'll want to go over your list of the crew. Get your insight on every member. Work history, past history, dreams, affairs, anything you discovered while working shoulder to shoulder training these people."

"Are you going to interview my people on board?"

"Some, but they might talk more freely on their own turf," he said. "A list of phone numbers and addresses would help. And then I'll need a copy of the security tapes the night Luke disappeared. In fact, three months before and the weeks since his disappearance, see if it shakes something loose."

"Why three months?" she said, keeping the resistance out of her voice.

"If he took the money, it didn't happen overnight. I need to see his movements on board, who he connected with, who he snubbed. I'll also need a client list for the same time period. I won't tap that well unless it becomes imperative."

Caroline's eyes darkened, the defensive mama bear worried about killing her golden goose. But Vincent Cardona had anointed Jack, and she knew better than to say no.

"Hold for a second," she said, pulling out her cell. "Trent, can you meet me on the bridge? I need help downloading the digital files of the security tapes. The last three months should do it. Thanks, hon." And then Caroline put on the happy face. The transition was seamless. "I'll have a full package for you in the morning. You go over the lists, check out the tapes, and I'll make myself available. Anything I can do to help. Now, why don't you take a look around, have a few laughs; I have to make sure my clientele is being cared for. Rich men are like children. They get needy their last night out."

Jack waited until Caroline walked back into the main salon and checked the players sitting at the poker table through the bay window. The Indonesian gentleman Jack had taken for a few thousand the night before was at the table, sitting in the same seat. Superstitious, Jack thought, and it wasn't working. A rather large Russian was adding a tall stack of black chips to his winnings. Good for ten grand, Jack thought. The redheaded bartender was pouring drinks, and he decided to head in her direction. Bartenders generally had a finger on the pulse of the room.

Jack paused when he saw Mateo escorting Angelica down the gangplank to the waiting water taxi. She turned before boarding, caught Jack's eye, and broke into a mischievous smile that he felt in his chest. Their conversation would be continued.

———

As Jack started toward the door, Rusty Mannuzza stepped out of the salon like a bantam rooster, blocking his entrance.

"Jack, I like your style. She's a little young for you, no?"

"Rusty, you're on my list, we need to talk."

"Jack, you do what you gotta do, but stay outta my way, huh? I've got a business to run."

"That was quick."

"Meaning?" Rusty challenged.

"You appear to be the only man who benefited from Luke's disappearance."

"Don't go there, Jack. It wouldn't be a smart move. I got the skinny on you from my cousin. My Staten Island cuz. Said he ran into your mother at Tucci's Deli."

Rusty was playing a dangerous game, but Jack wasn't biting.

"Think you're a big shot, Jack? Why don't you stick to cradle robbing? I'm sure Mr. Cardona will have something to say about that."

"Where were you the night Luke disappeared, Rusty? Say about two a.m."

"Bangin' your mother."

Jack's arm snaked out and grabbed Rusty by the throat. He spun the wiry man around and muscled him backward over the banister, out of sight of the players in the salon. Rusty's face reddened as he fought Jack's grip and fought to breathe.

"I had a cat named Rusty," Jack said, voice low. "He always landed on his feet. You won't be so lucky."

Jack released Rusty, who staggered, gasped for air, and contemplated pulling his gun, then wisely vetoed what would have
been his last move. With blazing eyes and a strained rasp, "You're
a dead man, Bertolino." Rusty straightened his tie, buttoned his
tight-fitting jacket, and strode past the gamblers, up the stairs,
disappearing onto the bridge.

"You make friends everywhere you go," Mateo said, walking
up the hallway, a big grin on his face.

"It's a gift."

"Cruz called. Rusty's Jag's set up with GPS. He's got it synced
to my iPhone and his. At least we'll know the route they take for
the dropoff. See if anything sparks."

"Good work. Get some sleep when you're done and we'll
compare notes in the afternoon. How's the action?"

"I was down ten, and I made twenty on the last hand. The
man in the gray suit, Indonesian, name's Sukarno, a bad player, a
worse loser."

"I took a few dollars off him last night."

"I want to get back to the table and salt his wounds. Not getting much from the heavy rollers except their money."

"What about the Russian?"

"The bear? Methodical but angry. He's knocking back
hundred-proof Stoli like Kool-Aid. The more he drinks, the more
he wins."

"You think he's Russian Mafia?"

"It wouldn't surprise me, but I don't think the affiliation would
sit well with Cardona, no? These players have to be vetted."

Jack didn't disagree. "I'll run the list by Agent Hunter in the
morning. See what they've got on him."

"I'll fill you in later, boss." Mateo headed for his seat at the central table and was greeted by a smiling Doris with a fresh Grey Goose on the rocks. The Russian raked a stack of black chips off the felt and Jack made his way to the bar.

---

Jack felt a hot flash of pain streak down his back, grabbed a water bottle from a silver ice bucket, and chased a Vicodin with a sip of spring water. Roxy stayed busy, respecting Jack's privacy until he shifted his focus to her.

"What did you do to Rusty?" Roxy asked, her eyes creasing into a smile as she poured Jack a glass of cabernet.

Jack was impressed the woman had memorized his drink of choice. "A slight attitude adjustment," he said without anger.

"I don't think it took," Roxy said, laughing as she spun a napkin and set Jack's wine on top of it. "He's more dangerous than he looks, Jack," she said on a more serious note. And then, "Ask away."

Jack grinned. "I'm that transparent?"

"We all know why you're here. We've all been prepped. There are no secrets on a yacht this size. We all eat, sleep, and work together. It's much too incestuous for secrets. The boat hasn't been the same since Luke's disappearance. He was a big flirt but a ton of fun. He made all the girls feel special, and he didn't piss off the guys. Well, most of them," she said, shooting a glance toward the bridge.

"Were you working the night he disappeared?"

"I was cleaning up my station and checking inventory when he walked out the door. It was business as usual until the next morning, when my phone rang off the hook. Mr. Cardona's men asked the same question, and I gave the same answer."

Jack took a sip of wine and watched as Mateo tossed his cards onto the felt while the Russian's big hand raked in another pot. Jack didn't micromanage his men but hoped Mateo wasn't losing his way, or their winnings.

In the silence, Roxy tried to repress the vision of Luke's naked body bucking as she fired the .22 round into the back of his head.

"Are you seeing anyone on board?" Jack asked, jolting her back to now. "A relationship?"

"I am, Mr. Bertolino," Roxy said in a teasing, flirty manner. In control again. "His name is Trent Peters, and he's the ship's engineer and brilliant at all things mechanical. He was on board all night. There's a skeleton crew on hand when we're dockside, and he was on call that night and the next."

"Any ideas? What's the gossip on board? The prevailing theory?"

"It's fifty-fifty he made off with the cash or was killed for the cash. And from my way of looking at it, he's either dead or as good as dead. We're all aware who we work for"—Roxy leaned in to Jack conspiratorially—"and mobsters have long memories."

"Shot of Stoli?" Doris requested with smiling eyes, breaking the moment.

"If you'll excuse me," Jack said, leaving his wine behind while Roxy poured and Doris headed back toward the Russian and a big tip.

———

Ava Gould, short blonde hair with electric-blue highlights, looked up from the sushi-grade tuna she was expertly cutting into sashimi. The kitchen was larger than Jack would have imagined, and the ornate plate of mixed fish, artistically presented and grand.

"Ah, the PI," Ava said with a knowing smile that made Jack

like her on the spot. "Are you hungry? I can make you a plate, or if you wait, the spread will dazzle you in the dining room in fifteen."

"I'm good. Thanks. Just nosing around, getting a feel for the place."

"And for the natives?"

Ava had a slight New York accent, the familiarity of which relaxed Jack.

"One in particular. MIA."

"Oh, I loved that man."

"Past tense?"

"Luke," she said, staring into space before arranging the slices of tuna like a fanned deck of cards around a mold of wasabi and ginger. "I would have covered that man in gravy and eaten him alive if I'd had the chance."

Jack laughed.

And then wistfully, "If I were a betting woman, I'd be upstairs playing instead of down here slaving, but I'm not feeling him."

"Not feeling him how?"

"I don't think he's alive. The man wasn't a thief. He was in the wrong line of work. I'm generally a good judge of character, and I didn't pick up any negative vibes. I trusted him. Left my bag open on the counter, you know, like you do around family."

"Was he seeing anyone?"

"You mean was he doing anyone." Not a question.

"That's what I mean," Jack said, grinning.

"I think Doris hit the jackpot a few weeks ago. She took a twenty-minute break and hit the floor like she'd just returned from two weeks in Hawaii. We were all jealous as hell."

"Who's we?"

"The rest of the female crew, and oh yeah, Ramón."

Ava cut slices out of half a lemon until it resembled a flower, then set it on the platter. She seemed to be struggling with something, and Jack let the silence work its magic.

"I was talking to Luke," she said, "and probably making a fool out of myself. Par for the course. Rusty walked past and said, 'Keep it in your pants.' To me, it wasn't a request. I thought Luke was going to take him off at the ankles."

"Why do you put up with it?" Jack asked without judgment.

"Do you know how much a line chef makes on the mainland?" She opened the fridge. "I make triple. We call it hazard pay for keeping our mouths shut and our heads down." Ava pulled out an oversize cut-glass bowl of shrimp cocktail that she set in the middle of the platter and barked, "Ramón!"

A young, attractive Hispanic man arrived, perked up when he saw Jack, and expertly picked up the tray of fish, batting his lashes as he headed out the door.

"Incorrigible," Ava said with an understanding smile.

"Did you sense anything unusual his last night on board?"

"Didn't see much of him, but he was beautiful as always."

Jack handed Ava his card. "If anything else occurs to you, anything he might have said or someone else might have said, any suspicions, any time, day or night, give me a call."

"Will do," Ava said, taking off her apron and melting into a chair as if the thought of Luke's disappearance sucked the lifeblood out of her. "If I'm right, find out who did this, huh?"

"Count on it."

———

"We've gotta push the schedule forward," Roxy said to Trent, who was lying in bed on their catamaran, propped up on pillows, with his hands laced behind his head. The amber sconce washed the cabin with soft light. His lids were at half-staff, his face relaxed.

Roxy was sitting at the built-in desk, glaring at her laptop, her face lit by the screen, wearing nothing but one of Trent's oversize T-shirts. She was enmeshed in a Google search. "Trent, goddammit, this isn't good." No response. "This is bad." Nothing. "Bertolino is no one to fuck with. He presents himself one way, but he's a killer."

Still no response.

"Get off your ass and read the goddamned articles! He was a decorated heavy hitter on the NYPD."

Trent swung his legs off the bunk, poured a glass of wine, and stood behind Roxy, who was clicking on different stories reporting Jack Bertolino's history.

"Caroline said he was manageable," Trent said, setting down his wine. "Give him what he wants and he'll move on. I'm not feeling any pressure. We have airtight alibies for the night in question—"

"What the hell are you talking about," she snapped, "with this *night in question* bullshit? Do you mean the night I killed a Mafia associate?"

"Keep your voice down."

"Fuck you!" she screamed. Knowing Trent was right pissed her off all the more. Frustrated, she complied, continuing in a harsh whisper, "The night I was alone on the cat *without* an alibi? That night?"

"Your work timeline and the onboard security video exonerate you. There's nothing to tie you to Luke. We go when the Chinese tanker docks. That's our schedule."

"I hate it when you're so damn calm and there is nothing reasonable to be calm about, you know that?"

"I do know that," he said without rancor. "And I still love you. Do you want to know why?"

"No," she said, on the edge.

"I forgive your emotional outbursts because you excel in every other department." Trent ran his hands down Roxy's breasts and gently pulled off the T-shirt. "Let's calm you down some, and then we'll deal with scheduling," he lied, knowing the schedule was set in stone.

Roxy stood, took a deep breath, and grabbed Trent by the back of his neck and pulled him in. They locked lips and, as their heartbeats quickened, rolled onto the bunk and got down to something they both excelled in.

# Eleven

The sun sat firmly in the azure sky, throwing an early-morning glow over Long Beach Harbor while Cruz sipped coffee in the cabin of Jack's Cutwater cruiser. He glanced through a side window at his unobstructed view of the *Bella Fortuna*, put down his cup, and snapped a series of photographs as Trent broke the surface of the water at the magnificent ship's aft. The digital camera, set on a tripod with a telephoto lens, brought Trent's image up close and personal without jeopardizing Cruz's cover, obscured through row upon row of aluminum masts and rigging.

Trent peeled off his mask, pulled one of the boat's underwater cameras out of a mesh bag that hung by his side, set it carefully on the dock next to a toolbox, and adjusted the strap on his scuba tank. He muscled to a seated position on the dock, his fins dangling over the side.

Roxy walked down the gangplank, sat next to him, shared a sip of her hot coffee, and started talking. The couple glanced over their shoulders mid-story, as if they felt eyes on them. Satisfied they were alone, they continued the conversation, which appeared to be of a serious nature, Cruz thought.

A white van with a colorful Tequila Herradura logo painted on the side panel pulled dockside. Cruz snapped a few shots of the driver, who made short work of offloading a shipment of liquor while Roxy followed the deliveryman up the gangplank and into the yacht's main salon.

Trent pulled his mask over his face, engaged the mouthpiece, and disappeared below the water's surface with a replacement camera to finish his repairs.

———

Jack was on the bridge of the *Bella Fortuna* with Caroline, who wore a tight-fitting purple and black workout suit. The woman took great care of herself, Jack thought. It made good business sense. He was already impressed with her work ethic, the illegal gambling business notwithstanding. Caroline had found time to make notes on the list she handed Jack, along with the digital security tapes. He planned on cross-checking her work with the FBI's files in case she had skin in the disappearance of Luke.

The *Queen Mary*, looking resplendent with Long Beach Harbor looming in the background, could be seen through the yacht's windshield, over the *Bella Fortuna*'s intricate computerized wheelhouse and electronic dashboard. The high-tech instrument panels looked like something out of NASA control central. Multiple security screens populated the mahogany-paneled wall in the rear of the cabin, exposing every room, corridor, gambling table, deck, Jacuzzi, and landing platform on the ship. They even covered the bottom of the craft, where Trent could be seen doing his repairs. A single dark screen snapped on, revealing a close-up of Trent's face as he smiled and mugged for the benefit of his boss. On another screen, Roxy could be seen at the bar in the main salon, checking

off the cases of liquor delivered against her order sheet. The only
areas that escaped the intrusion of the digital high-def cameras
were the staff's sleeping quarters, the eight staterooms, and the
community bathrooms.

"Caroline, do you remember if Rusty was on board the night
Luke disappeared?"

"I'll check the schedule, but it's not likely."

It seemed like Caroline was being politic and resistant to saying more.

"I don't get the feeling Rusty's a good fit," Jack said, giving her
an opening.

"To put it mildly. And it was oil and water between the two
men. I hear you've met."

Jack smiled. "We had words."

"You know how to turn a phrase, Jack."

Jack excused himself from Caroline, having decided to take
a walk around the ship while all was quiet. She couldn't say anything but yes. Jack walked down three levels in the bow of the
craft to keep himself out of Roxy's field of vision, then made his
way toward the stern and the engine room.

Caroline's eyes narrowed as she tracked his path on the security screens, wondering how in the world Jack had learned to
navigate his way around her ship so quickly.

---

The engine room was warm, and there was a slight buzz of the
auxiliary power generator that kept all the electrical, cooling, and
heating systems alive while the yacht was docked.

The room was spotless, the turbine diesel engines massive,
and one would need a technical degree to keep the system run-

ning smoothly. Jack was impressed. He walked over to the only desk in the room and did his thing. There was a bookshelf stacked with technical manuals, books on sailing, physics, computer science, a biography on Edward Teller. Nothing struck a chord. Jack couldn't help himself and as he pulled open the center drawer—

"Anything of interest?" Trent said, walking through the doorway, tone crisp but not angry as he stowed his scuba gear and toolbox in a gray metal locker. As he hooked his weight belt in the locker, his mind flashed on the twenty-five-pounder he'd wrapped around Luke Donato's neck before sliding him off the stern of the cat. He cleared that image from his mind and turned as Jack introduced himself and proffered a hand, which was accepted.

"Sorry for the intrusion," Jack said, sliding the drawer closed.

"No worries, I'm sure it goes with the territory." Trent grabbed a towel and hand-dried his hair. "What can I help you with? I know why you're here. We all know why you're here."

"I'm at a total loss," Jack said, keeping it light, pissed that he'd been caught with his hand in the desk. "I get who Luke Donato is—I mean, I understand his function on the boat, but I've got no traction as to why he'd run off with the kitty, knowing he'd be on the run for the rest of his life. Any ideas?"

"I don't have much contact with the powers that be. I'm a systems man. No one wants to see me unless something doesn't work. And then I better be able to fix it."

"My guess is you need a degree for this level of technology?"

"Graduated with a master's in engineering from UCLA. Started working at JPL, the Jet Propulsion Lab, and got lost in the Mensa crowd. And then I got hit with wanderlust. I grew up sailing with my family and decided to shift focus and landed here."

"You must have spent some time with Luke at the command center."

"Again, only when a camera was down, or engine trouble, or electrical. You know, a boat this age . . . Then it was up to me to sleuth why a system failed and find a solution. Small talk was all we shared. Nice enough guy, didn't really know him personally. And not to put too fine a point on it," Trent said, instinctively lowering his voice, "the more distance I keep from my employers, the better."

"Do you mind explaining?"

"I think you know what I mean." Trent turned his back to the camera and pressed his index finger against his nose, bending it sideways: the universal sign for the Mafia. "And the less said, the better my chance of keeping the gig."

Jack changed the subject. "How did you come to be hired? I don't think they advertise on Craigslist."

"I signed on as engineer on a hundred-and-seventy-one-foot sailing ship. Circumnavigated the globe twice. One of our ports of call was an island in Indonesia. Met a guy who had a penchant for super-yachts and liked to gamble big-time. We hit it off, shared a common background in tech, he made the connection for me, and as they say, the rest is history."

"How did he make his money?"

"Technology wonk. So, anything else?" Trent said, shifting the conversation. "I want to get out of this wet suit and clock out. It's been a long week."

Jack decided not to push any further.

Trent had prepped himself for this interrogation. He knew that the more truth he told, the better his lies would be, and he hoped he hadn't opened a can of worms.

"Do you have the rest of the week off?"

"Some well-deserved R and R."

"Are you staying in town? I mean, can I reach you if I think of anything else?" Jack felt a slight pause.

"Roxy and I might be taking off for a few days, but you can always reach me on my cell." Trent jotted down the number on a yellow Post-it and traded it for one of Jack's cards.

"Thanks for your time. If you think of anything at all that might point me in the right direction, you can reach me twenty-four/seven."

"Cheers," Trent said.

Jack left the engine room, and Trent's eyes went from gray to ball-bearing steel.

---

Jack swung his Mustang out of the lot and circled around to another parking structure to protect Cruz's cover. The tension on the yacht had been so thick that the sun spilling on Jack's face felt like a million bucks. And then when he stepped foot on his cabin cruiser, his blood pressure dropped a few notches and his smile came easier.

"I could get used to marina life," Cruz said as Jack came into the cabin. "There's coffee on the stove."

"All's quiet?" Jack asked, pouring a mug.

"It was a busy night, slight activity this morning, but most of the crew is gone, and the clientele who were left took off as soon as the *Fortuna* docked. It looked like a funeral procession, with the line of stretch limos. I got some interesting shots of Cardona's crew leaving with the weekend's receipts. There's some trouble on the reservation."

Jack's cell rang. He checked the screen and clicked on. "Miranda, hello."

Luke's girlfriend sounded like a different person, more relaxed, minus the attitude. "I don't know if it's anything," she said. "But I was cleaning my apartment and about to throw a pile of Luke's magazines into the Dumpster. There are some doodles, numbers that don't mean anything to me, scrawled in the margins, and I thought you might want to take a look. Now that I think about it, he also used my laptop a lot, and I don't know, but there might be something there."

Jack felt the first spark of excitement that came when there was a possible break in a case. It could be nothing, but it was well worth the trip to Hollywood. "Sounds good. Text me your address, and I'll run over if that's convenient . . . Great, I'll see you in forty-five."

Cruz knew from the tone of Jack's voice something was up.

"I've got to make a stop in town, why don't you shut down, catch some shut-eye, and we'll meet up at Hal's around five and compare notes. Good work wiring Rusty's car."

"Piece of cake."

"I'll leave a message for Mateo and have him join the party." And Jack headed down the dock.

————

The El Palacio was a permanent fixture on Fountain Avenue. Built in the thirties, the white stucco Spanish-style apartment complex still had remnants of old Hollywood elegance, but the L-shaped courtyard looked tired now, the fountain dry. The glory days, when it was filled with the youthful optimism of studio actors and actresses, a shadow of the past.

Miranda's one-bedroom apartment had white walls, high ceilings, hardwood floors, and a newly renovated kitchen and bath. "The place used to have four- and five-bedroom two-story apartments. An actress got murdered in one of the units back in the forties. The new owner chopped the hell out of the place to turn it into a moneymaker. Who can blame him," she shouted from the kitchen. Miranda was stacking dishes into the dishwasher, wearing a blue work shirt, jeans, and pink UGGs. She dried her hands and walked into the living room. "Sure I can't get you anything?"

"You've done more than enough." Jack was flipping through the stack of magazines piled on a small desk next to a laptop, and a shoe box containing Luke's toothbrush, hairbrush, and shaving gear.

"I couldn't find anything on the computer, but I'm not savvy like that. I've seen on TV that a search can be done. If you're interested and you promise you'll get it back to me, I'll lend it to you. But if you break it, you own it."

"Deal."

"You want to pick up some lunch on the Strip? I'll take you to one of the new hot spots."

"I've got to move on this, Miranda. We can get coffee when I drop the computer off."

"Coffee, huh?" Knowing it was a nice kiss-off. Well, she was okay with nice. "Luke told me to take ten percent of my tips every week and pay myself first and then the bills. He set me up with an index fund. Said it might not look flashy, but in a few years I'd feel really smart. I could sure use some of that."

Jack wasn't sure if Miranda meant more smarts or more money, but he felt her pain.

"What kind of gangster does that?" she asked.

Jack couldn't answer her question, not yet. He placed the magazines in the shoe box, picked up the computer, conveyed his thanks, and headed for the marina.

---

Jack was sitting in his favorite booth at Hal's Bar & Grill: in the back of the room, with a clear view of the dining and bar areas. The bar was separated from the main room by large metal sculptures, and the walls were tastefully hung with contemporary pieces from the thriving Venice art scene.

Arsinio, waiter extraordinaire, was setting down drinks in front of Mateo, Cruz, and then Jack. Cruz was showing the men his surveillance shots on his laptop. Arsinio knew better than to interrupt a business meeting and made himself scarce.

"I cut out the chaff, and well, you'll get the picture," Cruz said, narrating the sequence of photographs. "Rusty checking his watch, Rusty back on board. Now it's Frankie-the-Man checking his phone and then checking his watch, now belching, I think. Rusty down the gangplank, looking pissed. And here we go. Peter Maniacci pulls to a stop. Peter jumps out of his ride. Rusty gets in his face, gives a two-fisted blow to Peter's chest. Peter pushes back. Both men start for their guns, and Frankie pulls his first and quiets the natives."

Jack can't help himself and emits a gruff laugh.

Cruz continues, "Then Rusty goes back on board; Rusty appears in the next shot wheeling the weekend receipts. Here's Frankie hefting the leather satchel and heaving it into Rusty's trunk. Rusty fires up his car, Frankie slides in, shotgun, the car bends under his weight." Cruz looked up to see if he'd gotten a laugh. Nothing. He pushed on. "And Peter follows in his Plymouth. A few minutes later, you can see Mateo's rental car on the surface road."

"Where was the drop?" Jack asked Mateo.

"Both cars pulled into the alley behind Cardona's restaurant. I waited down the block about a half hour and then followed Rusty, alone now, to his condo in Westwood. I left Peter and Frankie at the Chop House to fend for themselves."

"There was another series I thought might be of interest," Cruz said, scrolling through photographs and then turning his laptop so Jack and Mateo could weigh in. It was the sequence of Trent and Roxy sitting dockside while Jack was on the bridge of the *Bella Fortuna*, talking to Caroline.

"Good catch, Cruz," Jack said. "They look jumpy. I wonder what that's all about. So here's the play: Trent referenced an Indonesian high roller who was his entrée to our gambling boat. Mateo, I want you to check out your poker buddy and see if the man is one and the same.

"And Cruz, I want you to take a look at Miranda's computer, see if you can pull up any of the websites Luke frequented. And check out the numbers and doodles scrawled in the margins of these magazines. Could be something, could be nothing. When I get home, I'll dive into the onboard security tapes and see if anything catches my eye. Let's reconvene in the morning and compare notes."

# Twelve

Angelica Marie Cardona was standing outside Jack's door, holding a single red rose in pale delicate hands, looking even more angelic than Jack remembered. And then he looked into her eyes and saw a totally different woman. Jack bent to brush her cheek, and Angelica grabbed the back of Jack's hair and pulled his mouth onto hers. Jack was erect before coming up for air. He keyed the door with one hand and ushered her in with the other.

Angelica tossed the rose onto the kitchen island and jumped into his arms, her legs wrapped tightly around his waist. Her mouth buried in his neck, then his ear, and now his mouth. Jack moved the few steps to the bed and stripped off the duvet cover with one hand. The only thing he wanted to get tangled up in was Angelica.

Angelica pulled his black T-shirt over his head and threw it across the room. His hands flew over the top three buttons of her silk blouse, pulled it over her head and onto the floor. He slowed his breathing and pulled off her jeans, revealing a flowered silk thong. His breath came in fits and starts now as he kicked off his jeans and she pulled his briefs down and one-handed them over his feet, slowly moving back up his body, running her lips against his flesh, her teeth and tongue against his erection. Jack couldn't breathe now and mumbled, "We really . . . should . . . slow down."

Angelica moved up to his mouth and pulled back a centimeter. "Go as slow as you want, Jack. But don't stop."

Jack rolled Angelica over on her back and moved from her lips to her stomach to her sex, down her thigh to her pink manicured toes. Angelica wrapped her legs around his neck, and Jack complied. The sounds emanating from Angelica's throat were primal, deep, and passion-filled.

Jack lifted her up and they found each other, dissolved into each other, seated, rocking, staring, eyes wide open. The room fell away and Angelica's gaze turned smoky, the picture abstract, their breathing, and heartbeat, and power in sync. Deep and ragged and wet.

Angelica disengaged, got up on her knees, and presented her breast and her nipple, red from their friction. She squeezed him hard, rolled, and Jack entered her from behind. When Angelica turned and their eyes met, Jack understood sexual bliss. He felt her tightening, pulsing against him, around him, and gave himself to the moment. Angelica spun and he held fast and their bodies collided and rolled, and they came together. She was smiling and tears spilled, but Jack didn't discern pain. He just drew her closer and trusted that Angelica's were tears of joy.

---

Angelica was towel-drying her blonde hair, and Jack watched her in the mirror, transfixed. He was dressed in clean jeans, bare-chested and barefoot. She was dressed in her jeans, also bare-chested and barefoot.

"Don't take this the wrong way, Jack, but you look like a

schoolboy. Battered and bruised, but with your shit-eating grin, definitely a schoolboy." She shook out her silk blouse, unbuttoned the front, and slid into it with the grace of a dancer.

Angelica's coarseness was unexpected and disarming, Jack thought. "No offense taken. Wine?"

Angelica nodded, ran her lips across Jack's, and he walked past, conjuring baseball scores to stifle his arousal. Angelica knew the effect she was having and smiled at herself in the mirror, left two buttons discreetly undone, and followed in his wake.

"I want you to let yourself go, Jack."

"If I'd gone any further, the cops would be knocking on my door." Jack popped the cork and poured two glasses of red. He handed one to Angelica and clinked it with his.

"You know what I'm saying." And he did. They both took a sip and Jack again ruminated how this young woman, *young* being the operative word, could read minds. "There are no guarantees in life," Angelica went on. "Surprises, but no guarantees. You taught me that."

"Who are you? And are you hungry?"

"I didn't come here to eat, Jack."

"You've made that perfectly clear."

Undaunted, Angelica was going to speak her mind. "Let the past go. One day at a time, Jack. If I sound like a fortune cookie, cool. Let me be your good luck."

It sounded easy enough, but Jack wasn't sure he could submit. His cop radar was picking up distress signals. Their relationship created complications beyond belief. Angelica was what his uncle called an old soul. Wise beyond her years. That was the upside. But her family tree had poisonous roots, and Jack wasn't sure Angelica had the cure.

Angelica took another big sip of wine, slipped on her sandals, and took Jack by the hand. "Walk me to my car? My uncle flew into town, and I've been summoned for a late family dinner at the Chop House."

Jack let go of the timing implications of the East Coast family flying into town, and walked Angelica down to her car, parked in front of his building.

Angelica jumped into her Lexus convertible, powered the top down, and turned her head toward Jack, lips slightly parted. Jack leaned in and planted a tender kiss on her perfect lips. She nodded her approval and executed a U-turn. Jack heard Miles Davis drift from her car's stereo as she headed for Washington Boulevard. Definitely an old soul, Jack thought, which brought a smile to his face as he watched the red taillights recede and walked back into his building.

———

Angelica's car and the lovers' goodbye kiss filled Peter's long-distance lens. Satisfied that he had documented their assignation per Cardona's orders, he lowered the camera, turned over the engine of his new follow car, and pulled away from the curb.

Before being jobbed by Bertolino and humiliated in front of the boss, Peter might have had second thoughts about invading Jack's privacy. He didn't think it was relevant. But now he didn't give a shit.

———

Peter's car, a new black Toyota RAV4, pulled away from the curb and followed Angelica's car down Glencoe. Special Agent Ted Flannery lowered his camera and let the scene he'd witnessed play out, percolating in his analytical mind, coming up with four distinct possibilities as to how it could affect the efficacy of his case. If Luke had taken the money and run, Flannery was sure there was more than the initial total Jack had reported. If he was dead, Flannery would make sure Cardona was put away and the L.A. Mafia dealt a fatal blow. If Jack was consorting with and not investigating the target, he'd be sharing cell space with Cardona. Let's see how well he does on the inside. The thought would have made Flannery smile if he hadn't been livid at the thought of a rogue FBI agent on his team and how it would damage his otherwise stellar career trajectory.

And then a smile did crease Flannery's stiff lips. He was rethinking his initial strategy and had come up with a move that would be either a game changer or a career ender.

———

All conversation ceased as Angelica Marie Cardona entered the private dining room at the rear of the Chop House. With the arrival of the East Coast family, it was a full table, with one empty seat calling her name. It was between her godfather, Mickey Razzano, who was the capo for one of the five New York Families; and her aunt Lucille, who was Cardona's sister and Mickey's wife.

"Well, I'm glad you could make time for your family," Vincent Cardona said through a forced smile.

"Hi all, welcome," Angelica said, kissing her father deferentially on the cheek and taking in the cast of characters.

"Are you preggers?" Lucille rasped, yanking Angelica her way and planting a wet kiss on her cheek. "Lemme look at choo."

"Aunt Lucille!" Angelica found herself at a rare loss for words but couldn't hide the red moving unceremoniously up her face to her ears.

"You look beautiful! What, Vincent, c'mon, she has that glow. What'd I say?" Lucille had no shame.

Cardona spared his daughter direct eye contact, used to his sister's social blunders, but his tight grin told the story.

Angelica, angered at her lack of control, and her aunt's implication, and the invasion of her privacy, walked around the table of twenty-five, diffusing the energy, kissing cheeks and shaking the hands of uncles, aunts, first cousins, extended family, and their Mafia associates. Rusty made a show of ignoring her presence while whispering conspiratorially into her first cousin Jimmy's ear. Jimmy winked slyly and held on to her hand a moment too long, reminding her of extended-family Sunday meals in New York City as a child. Angelica, bristling, knew she was most certainly the topic of her cousin's conversation.

Conspicuously missing from the family reunion were her father's men, Peter and Frankie-the Man. Frankie was being blamed for the hire of the missing Luke Donato, and Peter was probably tailing Jack. Angelica chastised herself for stepping into the middle of her father's business. She'd be more careful in the future.

Show tunes were being belted from the piano bar, while the clatter of dishes and silver drifted into the private room, riding the wave of high energy from patrons laughing, eating, and drinking in the main dining room of the Chop House.

Angelica took her seat next to Mickey, a wiry man in his sixties with bluish circles under his stony brown eyes, thin salt-and-pepper hair and mustache, and an attitude that could snuff out a candle.

"You look good, Uncle Mickey."

Mickey's eyes pierced and took her in thoughtfully before speaking. This man, her uncle through marriage, held the power of life and death over his soldiers. And, ultimately, her father.

"No, you, you look beautiful. I feel younger just sitting next to you. The family is proud, taking care of that business the way you did. Right, Vincent?"

Cardona nodded seriously, conflicted over his brother-in-law bringing up such a personal subject at his dinner table. It was disrespectful. But then his eyes crinkled into a genuine smile of pride as he was reminded how close he had come to losing his daughter, the love of his life. It was also a reminder of Jack Bertolino, the man who had risked his life to save her. Jack was a complication, a thorn in the side, no doubt about it. And Vincent wasn't sure he could ever call the debt paid in full. But it wouldn't stop him from taking care of business.

"You made us all proud," Mickey went on, not knowing when to stop, invoking murmurs of agreement from around the table.

"Thank you," Angelica said politely as a waiter appeared at her side, saving her from further discussion. He offered a bottle of Italian red and a California chardonnay. Angelica chose the Barolo. The waiter nodded, poured, and the table seemed pleased with her selection.

"To family," Angelica said, raising her glass. "Salute!"

The entire table echoed, "Salute!"

As glasses clinked, a cadre of waiters entered carrying plates filled with New York steaks, sausage and peppers, fresh asparagus, eggplant parmigiana, and a large bubbling tray of lasagna.

The conversation was momentarily stifled as cigars glowed

in ashtrays and grunts of approval took center stage at the feast set before them. Voices grew louder as the wine loosened tongues and reached a crescendo as the party began in earnest.

---

Mateo strolled confidently up the gangplank of the *Bella Fortuna*, dressed to the nines in upscale casual, a chilled bottle of Dom Pérignon under one arm and a killer smile on his face as he took in the vision standing on the deck.

Caroline Boudreau.

A light breeze played through her hair; her chiffon dress buffeted gently as she opened the gate and welcomed Mateo onto her playground. "He came bearing gifts," she said with approval.

"My mother taught me well."

"In all honesty, a young man such as yourself, I was surprised you weren't already engaged for the evening."

"My only regret," Mateo said, walking Caroline into the main salon, empty and dimly lit, his hand resting comfortably on the perfect curve of her waist, "was that you beat me to the call."

"It was out of the ordinary," and her eyes crinkled into a coy smile, "but I'm learning in life that time is precious." After giving the statement some thought, "And the proper course of action is whatever we choose to make of it. If I'm not mistaken, you've proved me correct."

"You flatter me," he said, and he stepped close and took in her lightly perfumed scent; his lips lightly brushed hers, met no resistance, and completed the task. "Champagne?" his deep voice crooned, library-soft.

"I'll grab two glasses, and we can relax on the main deck and take in the night sky. If it gets too cold, we've got the entire run of the ship."

Mateo had an inkling that the night was going to be anything but cold, and they would eventually retire to the warmth of the fine woman's cabin.

"Promise me one thing," Caroline said, one-handing two champagne flutes from the bar, "no business tonight. Tell me about Medellín, your mother, your life, but no business."

"Okay, no business." And he flashed his killer smile.

That seemed to satisfy. Caroline took Mateo by the hand, and they strolled in the night air like lovers on a first date.

---

Jack sat at the desk in his office and screened the security tapes from the *Bella Fortuna*. He played them in real time and fast-forwarded when there was nothing of interest. He started with the night of Luke's disappearance. Jack had a good handle on the crew, names, faces, and was interested in the high rollers who occupied the gaming tables.

He rewound every time Luke made an entrance or exit. He could follow most of the agent's movements as he strolled from one camera angle to another. Luke looked like an affable guy, controlled strength, no attitude with the crew. The crew's attitude toward him when he'd walk away from a conversation was one of clear attraction from the women and deference from the men.

At the end of the night, the camera followed Luke past the bar where Roxy was taking inventory, down the gangplank wheeling the leather satchel containing the money, where he was met by Peter and Frankie-the-Man. Luke placed the money in the trunk of his Camaro and pulled out of the lot. Jack stayed on that camera and saw no one in the camera's field of vision follow the car as it disappeared into the night along with its secrets.

There was no sign of Rusty Mannuzza the entire night. That didn't mean he couldn't have hijacked Luke on the road.

Jack's eyes were glazing over, and his back was starting to cramp. The adrenaline rush from the perfect sex had left the building. He downed a Vicodin, took a sip of wine, and straightened in his chair. He was viewing a segment from a month before Luke's disappearance. The *Bella Fortuna* was out at sea. Luke could be seen walking from the bridge through the main gaming salon. Ramón was covering the bar, and Roxy was probably on a break, Jack surmised. The cameras followed Luke down two flights to C deck, where the crew's bunks were located; with a subtle glance over his shoulder, Luke ducked into one of the cabins.

Jack stayed on the one camera, took a sip of wine, and fast-forwarded the digital tape, being mindful of the time code. Fifteen minutes passed in seconds, and when the timer hit twenty-seven, the cabin door swung open and Jack hit Play. Luke stepped out. A sly grin on his face morphed into business mode as he strode up the hallway and mounted the stairs.

It wasn't the only thing he'd mounted, Jack thought as he stayed on the single camera for another five minutes, expecting to see Doris exit the room, as reported by Chef Ava.

Jack let out a surprised "Huh" as he watched Roxy step into the hallway, straighten her dress, shake out her red hair, and walk past the stairwell Luke had taken, wisely choosing the stairs in the bow of the yacht. Jack rewound and replayed the sequence, noting the time on the digital tape.

Jack had nothing against a woman playing the field and being discreet, but Roxy's lie of omission was too perfect, especially when the missing person case was turning into a murder investigation. Jack decided to pay Roxy a visit in the morning.

He pulled up the photos Cruz had taken during his surveillance, and stopped on the sequence of Roxy and Trent sitting dockside. Except for the shots of Rusty and company, the other crew members departing the ship looked bored, tired, and happy to be on solid ground.

Roxy and Trent's glances over their shoulders looked guarded. Concerned. It might be nothing, but Jack was going to take a second pass interviewing the pair before shifting his focus to Rusty, who occupied first position in his mind. The man had motive, means, and opportunity and was meaner than a caged grizzly. Rusty had known when Luke was leaving the yacht, where he was delivering the money, and had held a possible vendetta against the newbie who'd jumped in front of him in the chain of command.

Jack sent a copy of the tapes to Cruz to get a second set of eyes on the yacht's crew and wealthy patrons, and continued his search.

He took another sip of wine and dialed a number. It was picked up on the first ring.

"Agent Hunter. I hope it's not too late."

"What can I do for you, Jack?"

"I need a favor. I'm looking through Luke's personnel files, and I've got a few questions, a couple of red flags. Could you do a deeper probe of Roxy Donnelly and Trent Peters? Backgrounds, personal history, banking records. And Cardona's man Rusty Mannuzza. Especially his last two months' banking and credit card statements."

"Why the interest? What do you have?"

"Nothing in particular. I got into a dustup with Rusty on

board last night. He's already filled Luke's position and isn't un-happy about the field promotion. He had means and motive. And something about my interview with the other two, who are an item, doesn't entirely jibe. It's all preliminary, but the sooner the better would be appreciated."

———————

Agent Hunter was in her condo, lounging in baggy sweats, sprawled out on an overstuffed blue paisley couch, a half-eaten frozen pizza and a bottle of Heineken her only company. Her de-meanor was guarded. "I'll get on it first thing, Jack. And thanks for keeping me in the loop."

Hunter clicked off the call and pulled up an email Ted Flan-nery had sent. It was a series of close-ups of Jack leaning into Angelica Cardona's convertible. The kiss and Angelica's reaction looked postcoital. If Jack was playing the FBI, she knew her career was as good as over. That didn't feel right to her. If it was just a foolish transgression, it could still jeopardize their case, and the fault would lie at her feet. The flash of anger, colored by a twinge of unexpected jealousy, was a shock to her system and filled the empty room. She had to keep her emotions in check and get a life, or things could fly out of control.

# Thirteen

*Day Seven*

Roxy was a brunette now, matching the photo and alias on her doctored license that she handed the officious TSA officer at John Wayne Airport. She was traveling with a carry-on and placed her laptop, handbag, and shoes into the plastic tray, then her luggage onto the rollers. She stepped onto the painted footsteps at the base of the metal detector, holding her breath before being waved through.

Trent had rented a Ford Explorer, taken off the night before, and would be waiting when she landed. They made it a general rule never to fly together. If the plane went down, they wanted the survivor to be alive and well and able to complete the mission. If Trent thought it was overkill, he didn't let on when Roxy laid down the law. He was double-parked outside Arrivals as Roxy walked through the doorway, wheeling her carry-on and dodging raindrops as she tossed her bag onto the back seat, jumped into the four-by-four, and planted a kiss on Trent's cheek. He was all business as he put the Ford in gear, hit the wipers, and merged with traffic before the airport cop who was headed in their direction could get close enough for an ID.

---

Jack arrived in Long Beach with a care package of bagels, lox, and the works for his team. He called ahead and told Cruz to put on a pot of coffee. Mateo would be arriving in moments: he said he didn't have far to travel, and Jack intuited his meaning.

Jack stepped onto his transom and down onto the deck of his cabin cruiser, interrupting Mateo's sparring with Cruz, whose eyes were bloodshot and his bedroom hair spiking in crazy directions.

"You looked like a *GQ* ad, that's all I said. No offense meant." But Cruz couldn't contain his youthful grin. "You still do."

Mateo, dressed in casual finery from his late-night date, turned to Jack. "You see what I have to put up with, El Jefe? The night has eyes. There's no privacy in this life anymore."

Enjoying his associate's discomfort, Cruz needled, "You stepped into my world, my digital frame. I was on the job, man. If you want to change places, I'd be more than happy to fill in for you."

Mateo chuckled good-naturedly. "In your dreams, son."

"You do look relaxed," Jack said pointedly as he knifed cream cheese onto an onion bagel. Cruz jumped up and made a plate while Mateo poured three cups of coffee. "Anything to report?" Jack asked, not wanting to pry, but what the hell. Jack knew if there was anything related to the case, Mateo would be forthcoming, but if it was social, the man didn't kiss and tell, and Jack respected that.

"I promised Caroline we wouldn't discuss business, but when she opened the door, I stepped through. The Indonesian player's name is Sukarno Lei. And it was his recommendation that got Trent hired on as engineer. Caroline said the man was brilliant. I left it at that, but I'll do a follow up. Find out where he made his money."

"All right, he told the truth. Anything else?"

"I had other things to attend to, Jefe. So, what's on the agenda?"

"I have a call in to the feebs. They're going to do a deep-background check on Rusty, Roxy, and Trent.

"Cardona's New York family is in town, there was a big dinner last night at the Chop House. They'll be second-guessing Cardona's operation. I want you to stay put, Cruz, and keep an eye out for any and all movement on board.

"And Mateo," Jack went on, "I want you on Rusty like WD-40. You followed the weekend cash to the Chop House; maybe we'll get lucky and see where it lands. They can't run a half a mil through the restaurant's books week in, week out."

To Cruz, "You find anything of interest on the security tapes?"

"Okay," he said, wiping cream cheese off the side of his mouth and pulling out a yellow pad. "First of all, and I know you caught this, but Luke got it on with Roxy." Jack nodded, Mateo set down his coffee, and Cruz went on, "Which means she lied on your first interview. Or fudged the truth."

"Lie of omission," Mateo said.

"But obfuscating," Cruz added.

"You're too smart for your own good," Mateo chided.

"Right. I caught something else," Cruz directed at Jack. "Three nights ago." He had his laptop set to a specific timeline. He turned it to face the men and hit Play. "Keep an eye on the Russian. Now watch Doris set a drink in front of Mateo, and watch the Russian glancing up as Doris leaves the table."

"He won that hand, if memory serves," Mateo said.

"He did, and now look at the same scene from camera two's

point of view. Mateo sat down and Doris was there with his drink; as she turned, she glanced at Sukarno, who checked his cards and waved her off. Doris smiled and blinked." Cruz hit Pause, and the frame froze on Doris with her eyelids at half-mast. "Subtle—not a wink, just a blink, we do it all the time, just a normal physiological response, but the timing is suspect. Sukarno placed a bet, Doris walked away, and the Russian doubled the pot."

"Sukarno folded," Jack said.

"Nothing fancy, nothing high-tech," Cruz said, "but I think the Russian is a cheat, and I think Doris is on the take. I found two other hands where she dropped off a Stoli to the Russian, filled other drink orders, and he won the hand. She moves quickly, almost sleight of hand, always smiling. I think she's a player."

"I told Jack the more he drank, the more he won, but I missed the play," Mateo said, giving it up to Cruz.

"Good work," Jack said. "Go over the tape and see when the Russian disembarked on the night Luke disappeared. If Luke was on to their scam and exerting pressure, Doris could have supplied the intel about the cash receipts. They are solidly persons of interest. I'll take care of Doris. See if her checking account balloons when the Russian's in town."

"You are the man," Mateo directed at Cruz, and drained his coffee.

Cruz blushed under the weight of the praise, tried for nonchalance, and failed. Mateo and Jack enjoyed the moment at his expense.

"I'm going to run," Mateo said. "I'll check in later. What are you up to?" he asked Jack.

"I'm going to pay a visit to Roxy if she's still in town. Trent floated the possibility of a road trip. If she's here, I'll see if I can shake her up. If not, I'll find something to shake up."

Mateo and Cruz didn't doubt him for a second.

-------

The rain had subsided, but the air was brisk in Oakland, the sun making occasional appearances between angry gray-and-white cumulus clouds. Trent wasn't happy with the unscheduled stop. They were operating on a tight schedule, and mistakes wouldn't be tolerated. But this was Roxy's game, and if it freed her to stay on mission, so be it.

He pulled curbside in front of a nondescript three-story tan stucco nursing home. It was no more than a way station for the severely injured and infirm waiting to die, he thought dispassionately.

Roxy pulled off her brunette wig, shook out her red hair, adjusted her makeup in the rearview mirror, and jumped out. She held the door to the lobby open for a bundled, skeletal man being wheeled by an attendant for his fifteen minutes of vitamin D before she disappeared into the lobby.

-------

Trent punched a number into his throwaway phone. "We're in Oakland. ETA, about an hour. Have some personal business to attend to. Is the submersible on board?" He reflexively slid down in his seat as a black and white rolled past his location. "Sukarno!" Trent snapped. "I logged twenty hours in Baja with the same make and model. I can thread an effing needle with it." Trent didn't take kindly to being second-guessed at the eleventh hour. "Good. Yes. I brought the cash. I brought the camera. No worries. The captain gets a hundred K up front and a hundred on the back end. I'll call you when we're settled."

Trent clicked off, pissed at the intrusion, and averted his eyes from the depressing human warehouse.

His personal cell trilled and he picked up without checking the caller ID. "Yeah? . . . Hey, Jack, what's up?" Trent forced a smile he hoped would color his voice. "I told you we might be taking a trip. Yeah, Baja."

"I'm thinking of taking a run down there myself," Jack said. "Do a little fishing when the dust settles. Where do you stay?"

"Las Ventanas al Paraiso."

"Sounds fancy."

"Our guilty pleasure. I'm staring at the Sea of Cortez as we speak."

"How long you there for?"

"Three days max, but I could spend a month. Life on the yacht gets claustrophobic."

"Is Roxy close by?"

"I told her to spoil herself. She's taking a day of beauty at the spa. You want a return call?"

"Not necessary, I'll keep my powder dry."

Trent bristled at Jack's choice of words. "No worries, I'll have her ring you up when we're back in town."

Trent clicked off, his tight smile ice-cold. He powered down the window; the damp air still smelled like ozone. He sucked in a few deep breaths and closed his eyes.

He was drawn back in time to an island resort in Jeddah on the Red Sea. He was eight years old, standing in the crystal-clear aquamarine water. His toes played over the pure white sand, which was rippled by the rhythmic lapping of waves, and time stood still.

He felt the warmth and perfection of his mother's smile as she sat on a colorful blanket, waving to him from shore, and the safety of his father's gaze. The family had spent two weeks at the seashore every year as far back as an eight-year-old's memory could serve. It was where the entitled class went to relax. Splashing in the water, browning in the sun, learning to swim—it was pure perfection.

And in one instant, on one night, in an upscale neighborhood filled with boutiques and coffee shops, the three of them sharing a fabulous meal on Tahlia Street, an Al-Qaeda suicide bomber rocked his world. Trent remembered falling through space, and when he landed, both his parents, along with twenty-eight other innocents, were dead.

Young Trent spent a month in the hospital and then was shipped across the globe to live with his uncle's family in a blue-collar, ethnic neighborhood in South Philadelphia. His uncle was a strict disciplinarian and his aunt, frugal to a fault. Tight with her purse strings, tighter with her affection. There were only so many smiles his aunt could muster, and they were saved for her own children. Trent was treated like the stepchild he was, and the warmth and social standing that had been his birthright were a distant memory.

---

Roxy made small talk with the admissions nurse in the lobby of Rush Street Care. The administrator pulled out her father's files and ran a finger down the last few pages, speed-reading.

"No discernible changes. Blood pressure stable, heart rate solid. With severe stroke victims, that isn't always the case."

"Has he spoken?"

"No. And I don't want you to fret, but it's not likely. We don't see too many miracles here. We do our best to make things as comfortable as is humanly possible. The fact that you make an effort to visit from time to time is the miracle. That and the checks you send. Thank you for staying on top of his care."

"Is he awake?"

"He drifts in and out. He still understands. How much? We're not really sure. But I occasionally get eye blinks when I engage him. Two for yes, one for no. Why don't you go see him?"

Roxy walked down the worn hallway, averting her eyes from the open doorways, trying to tamp down the instant nausea caused by the antiseptic smell of the dying and her all-consuming rage. She reached the end of the hallway, steeled herself, and entered the room.

Her father was lying in a hospital bed, eyes closed, face drawn, skin almost opaque. His arms were crossed over his chest; ugly raised scars ran parallel with the length of his arms, a reminder of multiple suicide attempts. Sadly, he had failed again. This time the massive stroke that followed were the gods laughing at his expense, Roxy thought, as she swiped at her hot wet eyes. It left him with a strong heart and mind and the inability to move or truly communicate. An occasional yes or no with a blink or two, the nurse had said. His life reduced to a single bed, a single chest of drawers, and two framed pictures. Scuffed linoleum, mint-green paint in need of freshening, floral curtains, and dust motes that drifted haphazardly, illuminated by the slanted shaft of light bleeding through the window.

One of the photographs was her father with his grinning youthful face sticking out of an MI battle tank during Operation Desert Storm, waiting to roll into Baghdad. He looked vital and attractive and so damn young. He'd believed in a cause he thought righteous. It had been a heady experience for about six months. And then two years later, he was back home, and the PTSD reared its ugly head.

The second photograph was Roxy in uniform. She mustered out of the service when her father hit the skids back in the States. She blamed the United States Army for turning its back on the father she loved. And slowly but surely, as she'd witnessed her father sinking into oblivion, becoming a shell of a man, her fury blossomed.

Roxy stood over her father and kissed him on the cheek. His eyes were closed, not responding to her touch. "I'm here, Daddy," and then Roxy's roiling emotions shut her down. Overwhelmed, she sucked in a ragged breath and whispered, "I miss you so much. Are you in there? Are you dreaming? I hope sweet dreams."

Roxy closed her eyes, and her father was seeing her off at the airport. He looked tired, she thought, having already suffered deep bouts of depression. The VA filled him with prescription drugs, but he hadn't slept through the night in months.

She'd found a double brown bag hidden behind the lawn tools in the garage, overflowing with empty Myers's rum bottles. He'd pull a Coke from the second fridge out in the garage, spill half of it in the compost heap, and fill the rest with dark rum. Breakfast of champions. Thought he was getting away with something. Roxy kept his secret, a drunkard's dream.

But on that humid morning, his eyes had been clear and filled with pride, his daughter in uniform traveling to Fort Hood and then a six-month deployment to Afghanistan. Her father had held her face with both rough hands and squeezed a bit too hard. They smelled of Marlboros and raked leaves. She didn't mind and held on to that scent, their connection.

If there was one piece of wisdom he'd imparted before she went off to war, it was to meet trouble head-on. Because it sure as hell would be coming her way in the desert. No use delaying the inevitable. Never roll over, never run, but never look back. Little did she know that her true battle wouldn't come from behind enemy lines.

Roxy opened her eyes and whispered to her father. "I've found a way to rage against the machine. To get even . . . for you, for me. Just know, if I don't visit for a while, I don't want you to worry. You're in good hands. If you can hear me, I want you to keep a good thought; payback is going to be a motherfucker. Know you are loved, Master Sergeant Fred Donnelly."

Roxy kissed him again and walked to the bureau, straightening the photographs.

Her father's eyes snapped open and blinked once. Roxy didn't turn back as she walked out of the room. Her father blinked once again, and again, and then again as the blue vein on his temple throbbed, and his milky eyes reddened, and tears welled and escaped his personal prison.

————

Trent leaned over and pushed open the passenger door. He let Roxy engage her seat belt. "I know it hurts. Any change?"

"He's a shell . . . you could have come in."

"He gets agitated when I'm in the room."

"Bullshit."

Trent turned over the engine and pulled away from the curb. Roxy stared into the side mirror until the building that warehoused her father was swallowed up in the flow of traffic.

Trent spoke in even tones, not wanting to set Roxy off but wanting his point to stick in case her commitment wavered. "Another story about the Afghan interpreters on NPR. Thirteen thousand waiting for visas. Supported the troops and now living with death threats." He let his emotions free, anger now coloring his speech. "Interesting that nobody's talking about the twenty-six thousand civilian deaths. They're just shadow people, collateral damage. The cost of war."

Trent drove with one eye on the road and one eye on Roxy. He saw her face morph from emotional to warrior's steel.

"We're late," he said, running a yellow light, narrowly averting an accident.

---

The eighty-foot trawler had rust spots on the rust. The captain's wizened face was crustier than the steel skin of his fishing boat. It wasn't pretty, but the stalwart diesel engine cut smartly through the rough chop.

Roxy stood on the bow while Trent, in the wheelhouse, unfolded his navigational chart and shared the coordinates of their trip with Rafi, the wiry Indonesian captain. Rafi had been paid handsomely to keep his mouth shut and not question their destination, or the need for the state-of-the-art underwater submersible that was canvas-wrapped and hanging from the heavy metal winches hooked off the boat's stern.

Roxy wiped salt spray from her cheek and stood resolute with her mission. She felt reasonably secure as she glanced back at Trent, knowing he'd be risking his life in a few hours, and felt a hint of melancholy as the San Francisco skyline bled into the Golden Gate Bridge and disappeared, the cloudy gray sky melding with the gray water obscuring the horizon.

No turning back.

# Fourteen

Jack had the top down on his convertible as he pulled to a stop in Marina del Rey. Roxy's address was a P.O. box, but his call to Caroline Boudreau had directed him to slip 375—on the opposite side of the marina from where Jack docked his own boat—and the catamaran Roxy and Trent called home.

Not bad, Jack thought as he took in their comfortable cat. Slip fees were cheaper than rent, and if you got bored, you could pull up anchor and change the scenery.

One of the nice things about the marina midweek: there were very few people around. Jack jumped the chain-link security fence, winced at the stabbing pain that shot down his back on landing, and ambled along the dock with his compact evidence bag like he belonged. He walked to the end to make sure he was alone, then backtracked, stepped onto the catamaran, picked the lock as if he had the key, and shut the cabin door behind him.

Jack checked his watch and gave himself fifteen minutes. In and out before he blew his cover. The interior of the catamaran looked homey and lived in, he thought as he took in the compact space.

But something was out of kilter. And when he started looking in the desk drawers, he realized everything was too clean. No loose papers or bills, no clothes draped around the living space; the bed looked like something out of a magazine. The duvet cover was pristine. No computer or laptop in any of the drawers. The top of the desk gave off a sheen, as if it had just been sprayed with Pledge.

He found two passports in the bottom drawer, along with a few nautical maps of the waters off the marina and surrounding areas up and down the West Coast, from Vancouver to Baja. He pulled out his cell phone and took photos of the maps and the passports: Roxy was dressed in military uniform; Trent had more stamps, which coincided with the brief summary he'd given of his world travels. Jack slid the maps and passports back into place and continued his search.

He pulled sticky tape out of his evidence bag and went over the pillows, sheets, and shag carpet next to the bed. He bagged them and stepped into the head. He checked inside the medicine cabinet, and again, just your average over-the-counter meds, potions, and shaving gear. Trent had the upper shelf, Roxy the bottom. Jack pulled hair samples out of the shower drain and the wastebasket and moved to the galley.

He pulled out the empty plastic garbage bag in the kitchen to see if anything had fallen underneath and came up empty. He checked the compact fridge and the small freezer. No cash, no drugs, a couple bottles of chardonnay, nothing out of the ordinary.

It was clear from the clothes jammed into the built-in closet that Roxy and Trent were tight on space. Nothing in pockets, shoes, and suitcases. They must've been traveling light, Jack thought.

He made one last pass around the kitchen, and wedged between the counter and the stove was a tight packet of brown paper bags for recycling. He rifled inside each bag, came up with two receipts that had been left behind, and pocketed them to check out later. In the aft of the cabin were a few articles of scuba gear, but no tanks, masks, weight belts, or flippers. Maybe Trent left his gear on the *Bella Fortuna*.

Satisfied that his search had been thorough, Jack glanced out the side window for the all-clear, stepped out, and locked the door behind him. Walking up the dock, he was greeted by one of the slip owners, who smiled warmly and thanked him for opening the locked gate.

"Were you visiting Roxy and Trent?" the old gent asked without suspicion. When Jack raised his brows, "I saw you stepping off the cat," he explained.

"I'm in the market for a used catamaran. My broker said there was one for sale but sent me to the wrong slip. He texted 375 instead of 1375."

"I do that all the time. Technology," he said, chuckling. "Well, enjoy your day."

"You, too, sir," Jack said, feeling a twinge of guilt for lying to the old guy.

Jack jumped into the Mustang and took the long route out of the lot. Just in case.

———

Roxy walked over to the bulky canvas-wrapped object, about the size of a Jet Ski. She unsnapped the fasteners, revealing a high-tech bright yellow one-man submersible with a large claw in the front, dual headlights, and a curved windshield to cut effortlessly through water.

They dropped anchor fifty miles west of San Francisco, in a national marine sanctuary near the Farallon Islands.

Roxy and Trent muscled a large lead container into a side compartment of the submersible and secured the latch.

Trent, in full scuba gear, padded to the side of the craft, stepped onto the running board, then turned and dropped backward, splashing into the ocean.

Roxy signaled the wheelhouse, and a loud rattle cut through the pounding surf as the captain lowered the amphibious craft into the dark water.

Trent uncoupled the machine, engaged the engine, and let the craft idle until the boat's lines were hauled up and out of the way. He gave Roxy a thumbs-up, pulled half of his body toward the front of the craft, gripped the steering mechanism, and put the mini-sub into gear, slipping below the water's surface. The yellow glow of the headlights faded as the water's depth swallowed man and machine, the only sign of life the compressed air escaping Trent's regulator and bubbling to the surface.

Two years of planning were coming to fruition, and the moment was so charged Roxy felt immune to the cold wind fanning her hair and reddening her neck, cheeks, and ears, or the glare of the captain, wondering what he had signed on for. She denied any possibility of failure and warmed to the prospect of success.

————

There was something mystical about being underwater, weightless, floating unencumbered, Trent thought as he checked the coordinates on his watch and slowly spiraled down toward the sea floor. If the dump site wasn't located at the two-hundred-foot depth, then the ocean cratered at six thousand feet, and the mission would be aborted. He'd done his research, his due diligence, but was ready to work a grid pattern if his numbers were off by even a few degrees.

The water was murky; the headlights cut two channels of light, enough to take care of business if the tides hadn't shifted the underwater graveyard he was seeking. The sound of his breathing and the hum of the craft's motor were elating.

Trent skimmed the ocean bottom like a manta ray, startled a school of sea bass, and checked his coordinates again. He nosed the craft up a slight rise and then dove deeper. Sea grass swayed at 250 feet. A massive school of anchovies swarmed as one organism in a circular pattern, creating an undulating fabric of silver lit by the headlights, obstructing his vision, and then parted like an opening-night curtain.

What they revealed spiked Trent's blood pressure. The sound of his beating heart rivaled the tank's breathing apparatus and the submersible's whispering props as it cut through the deep silent water.

A nuclear waste dump site.

Federal records showed that from 1946 to 1970, nuclear waste was regularly dumped in the Atlantic Ocean and at dozens of sites off the coast of California. A product of the all-but-forgotten legacy of the Cold War, and Trent had stumbled upon that product when he was employed as an engineer at JPL, NASA's Jet Propulsion Laboratory.

Trent paused to slow his heart rate and raked his headlights across an acre of fifty-five-gallon steel drums in different states of disrepair from years of saltwater corrosion.

Trent put the engine into neutral, let the submersible settle on the ocean floor, and got to work. He pulled out a dosimeter used to measure radiation emitted from spent fuel rods and waded into the haphazard grouping of corroding metal drums. Some of the containers were leaking, and he knew that over the years the water had dissipated their potency. The meter emitted a light buzzing sound.

He swam a short distance to one container that looked to be airtight and as pristine as forty-six years underwater allowed. He ran the dosimeter around the circumference of the lid and startled as it gave off a harsh, extended rasp.

Trent swam back to his submersible and set it down in front of the target metal drum. He slid out and vise-gripped the sides of the lid open, leaving it intact. He muscled the shielded containment box out of the body of the submersible and let it settle in the sand next to the drum. He unlatched the thick lead top and swam back to the craft.

Operating on pure adrenaline, Trent hovered above the steel drum. The mechanical claw on the front of the submersible yawned open and delicately closed on the lid. Trent finessed the levers and as he tried to lift the heavy metal lid the claw slipped off. Once, and then again he missed his mark. Trent tamped down the growing panic, forced a state of calm and concentration, and on the fourth try, the claw closed on the edge of the lid and pried it up and off, raising a cloud of sand where it landed. Trent, elated when he saw the contents, soldiered on, no time or oxygen to spare.

He floated directly above the drum and used the mechanical claw to pull out the first bundle of fuel rods, gingerly placing it in his own container. The nuclear fuel rods were long slender zirconium metal tubes housing pellets of fissionable material. One centimeter in diameter, the tubes came bundled together to increase their efficacy.

Beads of sweat rolled down Trent's forehead and stung his eyes as he went back, manipulating the mechanical claw until he had a second bundle securely placed in his lead-lined box.

Trent switched on the GoPro underwater camera, shot the nuclear waste in the containment strongbox, then panned across the entire dump site, which looked eerily like a cemetery from hell. He then nudged the box's lid closed, latched it, and set the submersible on the rippled sandy bottom.

Trent ran the dosimeter around the secured lead box, relieved that the meter registered safe levels of radiation. He strained to secure the locked case in the body of the submersible, and wasted no time putting the engine into gear and arcing up and away from the steel drum, now leaking its deadly contents. Trent powered forward, building to five knots as he rose to the safety of the water's surface.

———

The sound of a hardball cracking against a baseball bat usually calmed Jack's world. Not this time. His son was standing at the mound in UCLA's Jackie Robinson Stadium, and the batter had hit it high and long over the left-field wall. It looked like it was drifting foul, but no such luck.

Chris's girlfriend, Elli, yelped, "Shit!" Jack could relate.

Chris sucked it up as the batter and the man on first scored. He had his game face on, but Jack could feel the pain. The game had been tied two to two, and now the Stanford Cardinals had to make up a two-run deficit. That was if Chris could make it out of the inning without giving up another run. The catcher pulled off his mask and ran up to the pitcher's mound and conferred with Chris, trying to keep him focused.

The Bruins and the Cardinals were both members of the NCAA Division Pac-12 conference. Stanford, UCLA, and USC had won more NCAA championships than any other conference in history. The rivalry was fierce and making the roster, being chosen to pitch, was no small feat.

UCLA had two men out, and Jack was power-eating his salted peanuts, trying to calm his nerves. The manager of the UCLA team put in a pinch hitter, a beefy lefty with powerful arms and a record to back them up. He was a senior and being scouted because he was that good.

Chris denied the first two signals from the catcher. He nodded on the third, wound up, and fired a sliding fastball. The batter swung and hit nothing but air. Strike one. The Stanford fans roared. Jack was on his feet, crunching peanut husks underfoot.

Chis threw the next two pitches for balls.

Jack swigged his beer and drained it without thinking.

Chris denied one signal and accepted the second. He took his time, pulled from his depths, and threw a blistering fastball.

The batter stepped in and swung from his heels. The line drive rocketed at Chris, who stood tall, lifted his glove, and snatched it out of the air. The sound of the ball smacking against leather was like heaven on earth.

Jack went airborne, pumping his fist, and watched with pride as Chris jogged to the team's dugout.

He looked down at Elli, who was taking her hands off her eyes. She looked up sheepishly. "I get too nervous."

Jack let out the breath he'd been holding. "I know what you mean. I know exactly what you mean. He did good."

Jack saw two Stanford pitchers warming up and wasn't sure Chris was going to make it to the top of the seventh. The Stanford team went down in order, and Jack feared the manager was going to try and stop the bleeding.

Elli audibly groaned when the manager signaled the bullpen and a lanky blond headed out to the mound and tossed a few warm-up pitches while the rest of the team took the field.

It was all part of the game, Jack understood. But it never felt good when it happened to his son.

Stanford lost, four to two.

Chris tried to put on a happy face as he met up with Jack and Elli. And Jack said he understood when Chris begged off dinner. Jack hugged his son and was surprised when Elli, who stood a foot shorter than Jack, gave him a low bear hug. They had shared an emotional moment, and Jack returned the hug before heading back to the marina.

---

The night sky was black, the star field dynamic, and the cratered half-moon the only light on the horizon. Rafi, the Indonesian captain, stood at the bridge. Coordinates were set and the trawler was running on autopilot. Trent and Roxy sat at a scarred wooden table sharing a bottle of chardonnay, physically trashed from the dissipating rush of the day. Rafi excused himself with a smile and broken English and stepped out, leaving Trent at the helm to keep an eye out for passing freighters.

Roxy finished her wine and, as she poured a second glass, said, "He's been gone too long."

Trent grabbed a fishing knife off the table on his way out the door, and Roxy took his place at the helm. He ran silently toward their temporary cabin, which had been locked. The door was open a crack, and he could see the corner of the containment box and Rafi holding one of the radioactive bundles in his bare hands.

Rafi's head swiveled as he listened for a sound. All clear, he thought as he placed the fuel rod back into the lead box and quickly closed the lid. As he threw the latch, Trent kicked the door open. Startled, Rafi straightened.

Trent buried the razor-sharp blade into the captain's neck, just above his spine, and pulled the door closed. He could hear a dull thud as Rafi slammed onto the containment box and rolled to the ground.

Trent ran back to the bridge, saying, "We've got a situation," which Roxy read as "The captain is dead."

Trent grabbed his level-A protective suit out of his backpack and stepped into it. "Text Sukarno: we'll need a cleanup crew before we hit the dock." Roxy jumped into action, helped fasten the airtight suit, and then went for her phone. Trent ran out looking like a crazed techie on a hazmat team.

He grabbed a gaff from the trawler's stern. The six-foot pole with a sharp hook on its end was used to land big fish. It would now be used to dispose of Rafi.

Trent opened the door to the cabin and saw the captain, dead on his back. His jaw slack, open mouth exposing brown and broken teeth, face frozen in surprise. Blood spatters painted the top of the lead containment box.

Trent hooked Rafi's foot with the gaff and pulled him out onto the deck. He caught his breath, pulled the knife from the captain's neck, and rolled the slight man over the side of the trawler to splash down into the dark water below.

Trent dragged the heavy box onto the deck and used the gaff to pull his wet suit, his phone, and Roxy's change of clothes out of the cabin before snapping off the light and shutting the door. He tossed the weapon, electronics, and all of their contaminated personal belongings overboard along with the gaff. He grabbed a hose off the fishing table on the aft and carefully sprayed himself down. Then he went to work on the container and his bloody footsteps on the deck.

Trent stepped cautiously out of his white protective suit, threw it overboard, and watched it billow, float, and then get sucked into the water, disappearing like an apparition in the trawler's foamy wake.

# Fifteen

Jack walked out of the coffee shop with two cups, black, and headed up Abbot Kinney toward Mateo's stakeout position.

Mateo had followed Rusty into Beverly Hills, where he was joined by the East Coast crew, Cardona, Peter, and Frankie-the-Man. The coffee klatch in the Chop House lasted all of forty-five minutes, and he snapped a photo of Rusty wearing a satisfied smirk and walking toward his car with a heavy leather satchel. Mateo smelled money and followed Rusty into Venice, where he disappeared inside a pop-up store near the sushi joint Wabi-Sabi. He hit Jack with a 999 text and his location, a block from the intersection of Palms and Abbot Kinney with a clear view of the location.

Jack slid into Mateo's rental, a black seven-series BMW, and burned his hand passing the scalding coffee. "Hot?" Mateo asked. "I did a walk-by, and it looks like they're selling hand-crafted soaps."

"Must be a lot of dirt in Venice to afford the rent on this street. I think the shop's heavy, and we know where Cardona cleans some of his cash."

One of Jack's specialties on the NYPD had been taking down money-laundering cells. He and Mateo, who worked as his confidential informant, had taken the cartels for millions of dollars. They'd set up shop, launder a million dollars to prove their bona fides, and then set up a sting and confiscate the next two million without anyone being the wiser. All the while digging deeper into the cartel's hierarchy.

"There are three of them inside," Mateo said. "Rusty's girlfriend met him curbside when he pulled up. There must be a back room, because when I did the walk-by, Rusty and his squeeze were nowhere to be seen, and there were no customers to block my view. Just one cute woman working the cash register. Why do they always get beautiful women to count the cash?"

"Because they can," Jack said.

"That's his Jag in front. I'll bet it's registered to his woman."

"Stay on him—" Jack was cut short as two gray government-issue sedans roared past and skidded to a stop in front of the shop. Two more cars sped down Palms, one car blocked the intersection, and an agent jumped out and ran to the back of the building, while the second unit slid around the corner and came to a chattering stop. Two more vehicles peeled off of Venice Boulevard and blocked the egress out of the pop-up store.

Eight FBI agents deployed, weapons raised, swarming the shop.

"What the hell," Jack said as his cell phone beeped a text message from Agent Hunter, the only person he'd talked to about his issues with Rusty beside his team. And then a second 911 text alerting him of the impending raid. Perfect setup, he thought, trying to keep his anger in check, and ignored both texts. "This is going to come back to bite me in the ass."

———

"Oh my God, Rusty, I fucking warned you . . ." his girlfriend squealed as shouted voices alerted them the FBI were on the premises.

"Shut up," Rusty hissed as he threw the lock on the door to the storefront and grabbed the bag of cash out of her hands.

The locked door exploded off its hinges as Rusty bolted out the back.

The panicked gangster was stopped in his tracks, staring down the gun barrel of a federal agent. Rusty dropped the bag of cash, raised his hands, assumed the position, and as the agent pulled out his cuffs, the gangster juked and ran straight into the fist of a backup agent who had circled up Palms. The first agent yanked Rusty off the pavement, threw him against the bricks, opening a gash on his forehead, and patted him down, pulling a 9mm out of Rusty's shoulder rig.

The second fed picked up the leather satchel and the two agents muscled the bleeding man down Palms, jerked him around the corner, and joined the rest of the team inside the store as the growing crowd on Abbot Kinney took selfies and video of the arrest.

———

"Should I drive?" Mateo asked.

"I want to see who else shows up when they report in."

No sooner had Jack spoken than another gray sedan turned off Venice Boulevard and pulled to a silent stop in front of the store.

Special Agent Ted Flannery stepped out of the car. Tailored suit, mirrored sunglasses that raked up and down Abbot Kinney, looking at the stunned shopowners, the tourists snapping pictures, and the growing traffic jam. Looking for anything out of the ordinary before disappearing inside the storefront.

"I'm taking off," Jack said, his voice deadly calm, fighting to control his emotions until he'd played out all the possible ramifications of the raid and was rational enough to plan his next move. "I want you to stay put, see if anybody else was in the back room of the shop. I'll catch you later." He stepped out and blended with the crowd, away from the action.

---

Jack was sitting at a picnic table on the side of a taco stand on Lincoln Boulevard near Whole Foods, finishing off the first of three seafood tacos, when a shadow crossed his plate. He didn't look up.

"At least one of us has an appetite," Agent Hunter said, getting no response. "I tried to warn you."

"Timing was suspect."

"Look, Jack," she said, and took the bench opposite him. "I know this looks bad, but think it through—what would I have to gain by making your job tougher?"

"Well, Liz, some people can't deal with the truth."

"I can't live without it."

"Then who told Flannery that Rusty was on my radar screen? That he took over Luke's position on the *Bella Fortuna*?"

"Jack, we've been on to Rusty for a year and a half. Luke got caught in a hijacking that went bad. The driver of the sixteen-wheeler was armed and open-fired on the crew. Rusty shot the driver dead and Luke drew his weapon but didn't fire. Rusty smelled a rat and never got over it. And when Luke got the nod from Cardona to move up the ranks, things went from bad to worse."

"So you've got him on two counts. Murder two—manslaughter, maybe—and money laundering."

"We'll save the shooting for the one-two punch. See if we can turn him."

"I'm not optimistic," Jack said, "but you never know. The Mafia code of silence isn't what it used to be."

"Now I'm going to share something that could mean my career if it came to light that we spoke on the subject." No response from Jack. "This is where you reassure me I don't have anything to worry about."

"You need something to drink?" Jack asked instead.

"They don't serve what I need."

Jack's humorless expression and raised eyebrows told her to continue.

"Ted Flannery was surveilling you. Outside your building last night."

Jack did a slow burn.

Liz Hunter soldiered on. "He has photos of you leaning into Angelica Cardona's convertible, kissing her goodbye." Hunter let that sink in before dropping the other shoe. "And he wasn't the only one interested in your personal life. Cardona's man Peter Maniacci was in a black RAV4. He also captured the moment. The prelude to the kiss must have been something, Jack, because you were oblivious to your surroundings, and you don't do oblivious."

Jack took the two uneaten tacos and dropped them into the overfilled garbage can. He took a sip of soda, his eyes searing into Agent Hunter's. "So the FBI is again worried about my loyalties."

"That's a piece of it."

"And Vincent Cardona knows, and I'm thinking he's second-guessing giving me carte blanche on his gambling boat."

"That's the other piece. I'd watch my back, and I'll understand if you want off the job."

"Why did Flannery drop the hammer on Rusty? He had to know it would muddy the play."

"He didn't see it that way. Rattle their cage and keep you on your toes. He's worried. He's not saying, at least to me, but if it turns out Luke was dirty, Ted's career stalls, and I'll be shipped to a storefront office in Montana. This way he can squeeze Rusty and leave Cardona intact. Shake up the play with you in place to decipher the pieces."

"A dangerous game."

"Like I said, watch your back."

Jack took a swig of Diet Coke and rolled that around. Finally asking, "What is it you want?"

"It hasn't changed for me. I need to know what happened to my brother. And I want you to come out of this alive. My number is still open to you twenty-four/seven. Don't be shy. I'll fill in as many blanks as I can and run interference with Ted when necessary." Liz handed Jack a hefty manila envelope. "Here's everything you asked for. Let me know what else I can do."

"I need to know what you find in Rusty's apartment and his girlfriend's. My hands are tied while he's in custody, and there's going to be blowback with Cardona's crew."

Agent Liz Hunter stared at Jack for an extended beat, slid on her mirrored sunglasses, and walked to her car.

There was something about Hunter that got under Jack's skin. He made a mental note to take her advice and keep his eyes wide open; he worried that he might be losing his edge. The Vicodin, wine, and sex last night. He'd gotten too loose and might have jeopardized the case. It wouldn't happen again. He vowed to cut back on the wine.

The peace Jack usually felt sitting on the deck of his boat eluded him. Flannery had moved a piece on the chessboard at Jack's expense, jeopardizing his team in the process. It was an ego-based decision, provocative and dangerous. Jack was on high alert as he read through the intel Agent Hunter had provided.

Cruz was stationed in the cabin, eyeballing the *Bella Fortuna*. Jack had been sure there'd be action from Cardona's family after the news of Rusty's arrest hit the airwaves, and just as Mateo stepped onto the boat, Cruz shouted from the cabin, "They're here."

Cruz snapped digital photos as two town cars pulled to a stop near the gangplank. Frankie-the-Man jumped out of his car and opened the back door for Cardona and Mickey Razzano. The second car's doors swung open and Peter, cousin Jimmy, and two of Uncle Mickey's bodyguards stepped out. Their car dipped from side to side as the two beefy gunmen slid out, hand-ironed their sport jackets, and followed their bosses. There was a chill in the air as Caroline Boudreau met the men at the top of the gangplank, welcomed them aboard, and led them into the main salon.

Cruz joined Mateo and Jack on the deck of the cabin cruiser after Cardona's men boarded the yacht.

Mateo flashed a tight grin. "I received a text from Caroline a few minutes ago telling me she was having visitors and it might be wise to keep a safe distance."

"You're a player," Jack said.

"We all have our areas of expertise."

Jack tried but couldn't work up a grin. He knew he had to face the lion and let her rip. "Gentlemen, I fucked up big-time. Angelica Cardona paid me a visit the other night. That wasn't the fuckup. But when I walked her to the car and kissed her good night, I missed Peter Maniacci and Agent Flannery. They both captured the moment on film, and I missed it. It may be why Flannery dropped the hammer on Rusty, and there will be blowback from Cardona."

"Give yourself a break, Jack," Mateo said. "That is one hell of a woman."

"I second that," Cruz said.

Jack rifled through his reports, trying to get his train of thought back on track, thankful for these men. "I got Trent's backstory when I questioned him on board. He didn't mention being forced to leave JPL. It seems that high-clearance, classified documents disappeared on his watch, but culpability couldn't be proved. The feds never tied him to any wrongdoing, but he was given his walking papers, and he fell off their radar screen. That's when he made a career change and hit the open seas. Love to know what kind of documents went missing."

"He was right on, describing Sukarno and his link to the *Bella Fortuna*," Mateo said. "Sukarno Lei is a technical genius. His start-up technology company was grossing a hundred mil when the guy was in his early twenties. Two years after the company went public, he sold out to a Chinese conglomerate for a half a billion in cash and stock options worth twice that. He made the *Forbes* list of highest earners that year. Bought the island he was born on in Indonesia, spends his time there, and travels the globe. And as we both know, he's fond of gambling and hates to lose but does it prodigiously, thank you very much."

"Okay, Trent gets points for that," Jack said. "Now, Roxy appears to have had sexual relations with Luke. The only shipboard tryst we've uncovered to date. We don't know if Trent was aware or, if he was, what that means. It could be nothing, but if he discovered the affair, it's motive enough for a jealous man to commit murder."

"A crime of passion," Mateo added knowingly, as if he'd made a few quick escapes himself.

Jack flipped through the files and grabbed one. The men could see a black-and-white photo of Roxy stapled to the top. "It says she spent a year in Afghanistan as a signal support communications expert. High marks from her superiors, and then mustered out under suspicious circumstances. The army is typically vague about it, but her commanding officer states personal family problems and leaves it at that."

"Maybe someone died?" Cruz said.

Jack shook his head. "Possibly, but that generally isn't enough. You might get a couple weeks' sick leave for family care or bereavement purposes, but not a full discharge. I'll ask when she's back from Mexico. Anything interesting in the Russian's background?"

"His name's Vasily Barinov," Cruz said. "Not clear if he's mobbed up. Only thirty hits on Google. His father was a Russian oligarch in the nineties. Made millions selling oil futures and bought his own company while Boris Yeltsin was in power and oil was king. Everything was sweet until Putin took over. Young Barinov, who'd taken the reins of the family business, wasn't a big fan of Putin, and the feeling was mutual. It looks like Barinov was one step ahead of the sickle, got out of town with a bag full of cash, his head on his neck, and never looked back."

"Good work, Cruz. This is where I give you the opportunity to walk away."

"What?" Startled by the question.

"You are a major asset to our organization, but the play has changed, and if you want out, I'll understand. There's no losing face; I told you I'd do my best to keep you out of the thick of it, and I'll always have your back, but things are getting dicey."

Cruz gave that a moment's thought and his face broke into a tough grin. "I'm firing on all cylinders, Jack. Past couple of days I've been giving it a lot of thought, meditating on it, and I don't know of any other position or career that would give me that . . . that thing. I'm good to go. I'll let you know if I'm in over my head."

"Excellent."

Mateo nodded his approval.

"Then here's the deal: I want you to keep your head down. Nobody knows you exist. Agent Flannery poked the hornets' nest, and I don't want you to get stung."

"No need to ask me twice," Cruz said, never one to take Jack's advice lightly.

"Goes for you too, Mateo. There's at least one member of the ship's crew who knows we're working the case together," Jack said, not so subtly referencing Caroline Boudreau.

Cruz barked a laugh and got *the look* from Mateo.

"The New York family is here to nose around," Jack continued. "One of their men disappears with half a mil, and we appear on-scene uninvited. I mix it up with Rusty, he gets arrested three days later, and the Mob loses a second bag of cash. They're not happy, and Flannery put us directly in their line of fire. They're gonna want to know who our client is, and Cardona might not have the juice to keep them at bay even if he's so inclined. If they discover we're on the FBI's payroll, we're as good as dead. Let's keep our cell phones charged and close at hand. Any sign of trouble, text 999. And let's all keep one in the chamber."

# Sixteen

Jack was sitting in his usual booth at Hal's Bar & Grill, across from narcotics detective and his only real friend on the LAPD, Nick Aprea. Nick tossed back a shot of Herradura silver, licked salt off his fist, and bit into a lime with studied grace, never breaking eye contact. "So, you're working for the enemy again." Statement of fact.

"I'm working for the FBI."

"Semantics. You're sleeping with the enemy."

"His progeny." Jack took a bite off a perfectly cooked cheeseburger, and chased it with a sip of cabernet.

Nick was drinking his dinner and picking at a plate of fried calamari as Arsinio dropped another shot of poison in front of the red-eyed detective. "Thank you, Arsinio."

Jack watched Nick replay the ritual, knowing he was in store for more pearls of wisdom and a shit storm of honesty.

"Welcome to my world." Nick's eyes creased into a sly smile.

Jack knew he was referencing his own young wife, who still blamed Jack for the bullet to the shoulder Nick had taken on Catalina Island, and the shootout with Toby Dirk. But Nick wasn't done talking.

"You'll lose some weight, you'll lose some sleep, but you'll grin a hell of a lot more."

"A reasonable trade-off," Jack said, hoping he was getting off lightly, but knowing better.

"You'll lose all credibility with the cops, except for moi and a few old cronies. You can't talk about your client or they'll be picking your bones out of a landfill."

"Fuck 'em, except for you and my short list of supporters."

"Yeah, not like your life's been a bed of fucking roses. You've been shot at, punched out, clubbed, and that's just the past few months."

"You're the only one at the table who's been shot."

"Tou-fucking-ché, hombre."

"You're mixing your cultures."

"The more I drink, the more I start speaking in tongues." Nick turned slightly in the booth, and Jack could read the pain that Nick would never admit to. Arsinio read the body language and hurried over with a fresh dish of limes and another shot of tequila. "So, why so tight-lipped about the case?"

"I'm serving two masters, trying to protect my guys and keep my eyes on the prize. My only focus is finding out what happened to Agent Luke Hunter, aka Luke Donato, and the bag of cash. And I really don't give a damn about the money."

"It's finding Luke, dead or alive. And from what little you told me, there's a good chance he's meat."

"I'm glad you haven't lost any of your sensitivity."

"Goes without saying."

"How's the shoulder?"

"Only hurts when I'm on the crapper."

Jack set down his cheeseburger.

"Fucking rotator cuff," Nick went on. "Doc says I'll be a hundred percent in a few weeks."

"About time."

"So, I'll take the DNA samples and run them by Molloy. It's gonna take a while. The ME's office is backed up worse than I am with these pain meds." Nick chewed a forkful of calamari. "I get Luke's brush, where you got it and all, but where did you pick up the hair samples? I don't think you said?" He bobbed his fork at Jack like a divining rod.

Jack gave his good friend the eye-roll non-answer while sliding the shoe box with the hairbrush and DNA samples across the booth.

"Fuckin' Bertolino," Nick said good-naturedly. "Good luck presenting it in court if we find a match."

---

Trent was on the backside of Curtis Tech. One of the few universities on the West Coast still operating a nuclear program. At two in the morning the night air was cool and damp, but Trent didn't feel a thing. He was operating on pure adrenaline.

Sukarno had provided the map and the connection to Carl Flagell, who worked in the lab. The two men were standing in an empty parking structure behind the building that housed the reactor.

Carl had stringy black hair, a gaunt face, sunken eyes, and a long, sharp nose that his face was still waiting to grow into. He smelled of marijuana, and his mellow unnerved Trent, who questioned Sukarno Lei's judgment call. He wasn't confident that this was the right man to facilitate the job.

Carl rolled up a heavy-duty industrial cart, and both men

muscled the heavy lead box out of the back of the Ford Explorer and onto the metal cart. Two aluminum briefcases and a wooden crate followed that.

"How is Sukey?" Carl said, pushing the cart toward the back door of the building.

"Who's Sukey?" Trent said, trying to keep the impatience out of his voice. He needed this process to go without a hitch or the entire plan would fall apart.

"Hah." Carl laughed. "It's what I call Sukarno at the poker tables. Gets him riled and off his game. I took him for thirty grand at Bellagio."

"Then why are you doing this?"

"I'm two seventy-five large into my bookie. My bookie's a made man. He promised to cut off my right hand if I didn't deliver the cash with said hand."

The Mafia connection was almost poetic, Trent thought as they entered the lab and rolled into a still, silent space. The walls were white, the room filled with major electronic components, a world-class cyclotron, and a thick Plexiglas wall fronted by a massive block of concrete.

"Take the robotic arms for a spin while I set you up." Carl rolled the cart through a side metal doorway and could now be seen pushing the cart to a position on the other side of the Plexiglas wall. He made short work of centering the cart, turning on a dosimeter, and joining Trent, securing the metal door behind him.

"That's ten-feet-thick thirty-ton blocks of concrete that'll shield the radiation emitted from your fuel rods. The robotic arms mimic your movements and deliver more power, more strength, than your own hands. Knock yourself out, you've got two hours." And Carl left Trent to his own devices.

Trent preferred to work alone.

Sukarno had provided a replacement level-A protective suit for Trent and enough military-grade C-4 plastic explosives to sink the *Queen Mary*. The icing on the cake: the radioactive cloud that would umbrella death or nuclear contamination over a five-hundred-yard radius, depending on wind direction.

Trent had learned the law of attraction in his physics class at UCLA. Like attracts like. For every action, there's an equal and opposite reaction. What goes out comes roaring back like a locomotive. Sukarno Lei was the living embodiment of that simple theory. It was clear from their first meeting that he was the mentor Trent had been searching for his entire life.

Both men were motivated by the almighty dollar. And if all went according to plan, Trent would walk away from the terrorist attack a very wealthy man.

And then along came Roxy. She was the purist of their small cell. She had all the right stuff. Military-trained and an anger quotient off the Richter scale. What motivated her was payback for her father. That and a little misunderstanding with her commanding officer while she was serving in Afghanistan. Roxy called it rape, the major called it consensual. He let her muster out with an honorable discharge; she accepted and vowed revenge.

Trent didn't feel a moment's guilt keeping Roxy out of the financial arrangement. With the detonation of the bombs and shutting down Long Beach Harbor, he'd be delivering on his promise to Roxy: revenge against the United States government. Roxy would be seriously pissed when she discovered a financial payoff was part of the equation, but Trent was confident he could finesse her after the fact. Everyone would get satisfaction if all went according to plan.

Trent jumped to his feet and put on the protective gear, making sure the seals were airtight. It might have been overkill, but he wasn't taking any chances.

The original protective container was on a metal workstation, next to the two opened briefcases, lined with thick sheets of lead. Trent laid down fitted sheets of C-4 and molded indented pockets into the claylike material with his robotic hands, to snug the pellets that would be extricated from the fuel rod bundles. One bundle for each briefcase.

Trent had assembled the bomb components back at his own storage facility before embarking on the trip north. He tamped the electric blasting caps into the malleable explosive material. He had already clipped the detonating cords and soldered them to the timers, and from the timers to cell phones. He snugged the entire device into the C-4. A call placed to the cell's number would engage the timer. When the predetermined time was reached, it would create a charge from the lithium battery and the blasting cap would detonate, setting off the explosives.

Now the hazardous work began. Trent was sweating in his suit, his work quick, methodical, and thorough.

He unclasped the lid of the containment box from the trawler. The dosimeter's raspy beep echoed in his hood, reacting to the deadly radiation levels. Trent's clear plastic faceplate started to fog. He fought to still the wild beating of his heart but never stopped working. One mechanical hand lifted a bundle while the other snapped off the top that bound the rods together. He turned the bundle upside down and dropped the pellets onto the C-4 and snugged the uranium oxide into the claylike explosive. He repeated the same procedure with the second briefcase. He placed another precut sheet of C-4 over both mechanisms, tamped the malleable material tight, and swung the lids down, locking the bomb with the heavy-duty clasps.

The dosimeter's beep silenced, and Trent's breathing returned to normal. He placed both cases in the original lead container and slammed the heavy lid shut.

Trent pulled his arms out of the robotic sleeves, ripped off the constricting headgear, gasped for air, and wiped the stinging sweat from his eyes.

He picked up his cell phone and called Sukarno. "Done," he said before clicking off and stepping out of the white suit.

---

The men finished loading the cargo, and the rear of the SUV dipped under the weight. Carl Flagell still had work to do. Part of Sukarno's deal called for Carl to dispose of the fuel rod casings.

Trent pulled out a satchel containing three hundred thousand dollars and handed it to Carl, who rifled through the stacks of hundreds, then, satisfied, closed the bag and fist-bumped Trent.

"I don't know you," Carl said. "You never met me. Take off, and put some miles between us ASAP."

Trent pulled silently out of the lot.

Carl walked back toward the lab, reached up above the doorway, pulled an argyle sock off the security camera lens, and disappeared into the lab.

Trent didn't snap on his headlights until he hit the highway and then drove the speed limit to the twenty-four-hour diner where Roxy waited for their trip back to L.A.

# Seventeen

*Day Nine*

Jack called Doris and explained he'd be ten minutes late for their planned meeting at Starbucks on San Vicente in Brentwood. It was a busy location, and Cruz arrived ten minutes early to set up and snag a table.

When Jack walked into the air-conditioned room, he saw Doris leafing through an *L.A. Times* in the rack. She turned as the front door pinged and flashed a thousand-watt smile. The tables were all occupied with laptop writers, out-of-work actors, and real estate agents. Doris offered to go somewhere less crowded, but on cue, Cruz vacated his table. Jack grabbed it, offering a seat to Doris and taking her drink order. Doris started texting the moment Jack ordered their coffees, and Cruz moved to the condiment counter. He appeared to be reading emails on his laptop but was busy hacking Doris's phone.

By the time Jack handed her an iced caffè mocha across the table, Cruz had downloaded her online banking statements and a list of recent phone calls.

141

"Can you believe what happened to Rusty?" Doris said, her eyes bright and conspiratorial.

"Sometimes bad things happen to bad people," Jack said, grinning.

Doris smiled back, assuring Jack that they were on the same team, and: "What have you found out about Luke? It's all anybody's talking about."

"What are they saying?"

"That he's sitting on a beach sucking down piña coladas, or dead."

"You're a smart woman. I know you've got the pulse of the crew, what's your theory?"

"Hmmmm, the jury's still out. I hope he's okay, he's really sweet"—and Doris leaned into Jack, lowering her voice—"for a gangster."

"Can I ask you a personal question?"

"Okay."

"Did you have a personal relationship with Luke?"

"You mean . . ." Jack raised his eyebrows and nodded. "Well, will this stay between us, we're not supposed to," and she continued without Jack's answer, "once, one time. He walked me to my car, and one thing led to another, and . . . we did it in my car. It wasn't easy; I drive a Prius. But it was hot."

"Just the one time?" Jack asked. And Doris nodded wistfully. "Tell me about your job, do you like it, do the clients treat you well?"

"They're the best. Just the best. The tips are through the roof. I almost have the down payment for a condo."

"Anyone in particular?"

"We're not supposed to say, but have you seen the Russian

playing poker? Mr. Barinov? When he's in town, I do very well. But then I'm very good at what I do. I understand the needs of my clients and work my tail off to be of service."

"That's a rare trait," Jack said, knowing her statement could be taken two ways. "I've seen you in action, and you are very good at your job."

"Thank you, Jack. Anything else? I've got a lot to do before we hit the open seas again."

"No, thanks for your time. If anything comes up that might help with my investigation, give me a call, and if I think of anything, I'll be in touch." Doris was good, and Jack almost had second thoughts about her connection to Barinov.

"Sounds like a plan," Doris said. She gave Jack's cheek a peck and tossed her empty into the wastebasket.

"Doris," Jack said, waving her back. She bounced over, high on youth, and caffeine, and money in the bank. "Sit down, one more thing. The way it works here is I give you time to be truthful, and then if I see a problem with your story, I get truthful."

Doris's smile dimmed a few watts. "Okay? What do you mean?"

"I know you're good at what you do."

"I told you that just now."

"You did. But the more you serve Barinov, the better he plays, and the more he wins. Understand?"

"He's Russian. The vodka relaxes him," she said, the schoolgirl veneer cracking.

"And here's the deal. I know you understand deals, because I've seen you on the security cameras. The more he drinks . . ."

"The better he plays . . ."

"Because . . ."

"I might get a bit excited when I see a hand where I know he

can win. But I don't say a word. I promise. When he wins, he tips."
Doris was red-faced now.

"This will stay between you and me if you start telling me the
absolute truth."

"But—" she squealed.

Jack cut her off, leaning in close. "Did Barinov ever ask you
about scheduling, money transfers, end-of-weekend deliveries?"

"Am I going to lose my job?"

"If you don't tell the truth, and if Barinov is tied to Luke's disappearance, it could mean jail time."

Doris's eyes went wide, filled with tears, and Jack handed her
a Starbucks napkin.

"We have you on tape, on multiple occasions, signaling Barinov after you delivered a drink. You *are* very good at what you do.
But in slow motion, your eye blinks become more pronounced,
and the odds of the Russian winning a hand every time you drop
off a drink gives good luck a bad name."

"Don't tell Rusty."

"Talk to me about Rusty."

"He was always in my face, asking if I was fucking Luke. His
words. Checking my tips. Invading my personal space. Please don't
tell him. He's dangerous."

"Rusty is out of play for the time being. It's Vincent Cardona
you have to worry about. Do you think Barinov could have killed
Luke Donato and taken the money?"

Doris was crying again, and Jack handed her another napkin
but didn't break eye contact.

"No, if I thought that, I couldn't live with myself. So my tips
got padded when he won. I'm a single woman in a cutthroat town.

I've got a few good years to cash in. I'm a glorified cocktail wait-ress, for Christ's sake."

"How did it work?" Jack asked, not moved by her story.

"Nothing was spoken, nothing was agreed upon, but it worked once or twice by accident, and then it shouted loud and clear at the end of the second night when the tip envelope was passed. If you bust Barinov, you bust me."

"Let's let it ride."

"What do you mean?" The crocodile tears instantly dried as she felt a possible reprieve being floated. Hell of a trick, Jack thought.

"You keep your job, you let Barinov play without cheating, and I'll do my job. If you have anything at all that can help me, you're on my payroll now. What did I just say?"

"I'll be your eyes and ears on board, and you'll let me keep my job." Doris's voice was cold, her speech clipped, as she accepted her new reality.

"Don't squander the opportunity."

Doris stood on shaky legs, walked out the door, and ran to her car.

Cruz joined Jack at the table after watching Doris pull away from the curb in her blue Prius.

"I've got everything we need," Cruz said. "I'll cross-reference the phone calls with our contact sheet and dissect her banking habits, but she's dirty. I'll have specifics for you later in the day. What did you think?"

"Doris is a cheat; she's also a terrific actress. She's dirty but thinks it's a venial sin and doesn't understand that if Rusty had caught her instead of us, the sin could have been mortal."

Trent's storage facility was a high-end affair on Jefferson Boulevard. No homeless patrons getting high, crashing for the night,
and leaving the grounds at first light. This was where the wealthy
came to store their treasures when their collections outgrew their
estates. Money was no object because Sukarno signed the lease
and was footing the bill.

Trent's unit at Security Storage was three hundred square feet,
a well-stocked workshop rather than a storage room. Although he
would be storing a weapon that, if detonated on these grounds,
would shut down the facility and the buildings fronting Playa
Vista for many years to come.

Trent was moving quickly. Morning traffic had caused a delay
on the 405, and the facility opened at eleven. He wanted to be
in and out before management arrived. He slid out the lead case
that contained the dirty bombs, easing it onto a pneumatic dolly
whose wooden surface was flush with the bed of the Explorer.
Trent unlocked the wheels and rolled it into his unit, closing the
door behind him.

————

Jack was on his way to the marina and a surprise visit to Roxy on
her catamaran when his cell chirped. He hit his Bluetooth as he
powered through a yellow light at Twenty-sixth. "Yeah?"

"You sound relaxed, Jack."

"Vincent, how are you?"

"Well, I'm trying not to feel disrespected here. I open up my
business to you at great personal risk, and I don't hear word one."

"No disrespect meant. There's not much to report."

"You've been on the case, what, over a week now? I know for you that's a lifetime, Jack. Tell you what, I'll see you here for an early lunch. If I don't . . . well, let's not go there, huh?"

———

Jack made his way past the silent piano toward the men at the bar, who also sat in silence. The air was charged. Cardona was perched on a stool at the end, where he had a view of the room. He nodded tersely in Jack's direction. The older man sitting next to him was mopping egg yolk off his plate of over easy with rye toast. He glanced up at Jack's presence; predatory eyes painted him up and down.

"Jack, long time."

"Hey, Mickey. You still have that '70 Caddy with the fins?"

"Sweet ride," he said, not answering the question. Mickey made it a rule never to give a cop a straight answer. That way it could never be used against him in a court of law. "Jack here went to school with my son, Paulie. Played baseball together in high school," he said to Cardona, who was unaware of their connection and not happy to be hearing about it for the first time. "Tossed papers on our stoop, he was spot-on. Let's hope he hasn't lost his touch."

Jack didn't think the warning merited a response.

"So what do you got?" Cardona said, placing his espresso cup on the bar with a crack.

"Not much of substance. I'll keep you in the loop when I have something real."

"So, you're a gumshoe now, huh, Jack? How's that going for you?" Razzano asked.

"It has its moments."

"You still look like a cop. How does that work, Jack? You grow up in the neighborhood; you look like a neighborhood kid. You join the force; you look like a cop. He could've come to work for us. We offered back in the day," he said to Cardona, who took in these revelations about Jack with narrowed eyes.

"The same way you join the family," Jack said. "You look like a thug."

Mickey didn't blink, but his body coiled like wrapped steel. One of his gunmen slid out of the booth with amazing speed, stopped by Mickey's headshake and Jack's body language.

"All right, all right, all right, let's fuckin' get down to business," Cardona said in his ham-fisted way of bringing civility to the proceedings. "Whatta you got on Donato? Whatta you got on Rusty? In that order, Jack."

Jack chose his words carefully. "Can we go somewhere with a little privacy?"

Mickey nodded to the booth, and both of his men complied by leaving the room.

"This is based purely on conjecture at this point. But I don't think we're going to find Luke Donato alive. I've interviewed everyone on the *Bella Fortuna*, and Donato was well liked. In fact, there wasn't a woman on board who didn't want to jump his bones, not that that's germane. I'm picking up loyalty and expertise from the guy. And the yacht itself is a winning proposition. It doesn't make sense—unless your accountants have turned up something I'm not aware of—that he would rabbit for a half a million dollars. We know the Mafia has a long reach and a longer memory. He wasn't a *cafone*."

"Where does that leave you?" Mickey asked, some of the rage having dissipated, but the slight not forgotten or forgiven.

"Hunting for the murderer."

"And Rusty?" Cardona asked, his face rigid, his eyes probing.

"You're not gonna like what I have to say, and I plan on walking out of here in one piece."

"Jack, what you say here stays here, between us. Right, Mickey?"

Mickey rolled his forefinger in a let's-move-it-along gesture.

"As far as I can see, Rusty's the only man on your team who's gained anything from Luke's disappearance. Take that any way you want. I don't have proof of wrongdoing yet, it's just a fact of life. And he's not good for morale on the boat."

"There he goes with the boat again," Cardona said to Mickey. "He's calling our super-yacht a fuckin' boat." No response from Mickey.

"Now let me get back to doing my job, and I'll keep you in the loop."

Cardona looked a question at Mickey, who said, "Who's so interested in Donato that they'd hire a high-price PI such as yourself?"

"I don't talk to the police about your business, and I don't talk to anybody about mine. I'll call you when I know something."

Jack turned and walked past the piano and down the stairs.

"What da you think?" Cardona asked Mickey.

"He's got a wise fucking mouth on him."

"Goes without saying, but he gets the job done. Let's wait and see."

"This is on you, my friend."

Cardona was well aware that his life stood in the balance.

# Eighteen

Jack put in a call to Roxy that went directly to voicemail. He decided to take a ride to the marina and see if anyone was home. She and Trent were both scheduled to work on the *Bella Fortuna* the next day, and Jack wanted to get Roxy by herself without the distraction of the workplace or prying eyes when he played hardball.

He pulled to a stop when he saw Trent, with a Nike sports bag slung over his shoulder, pulling his scuba gear out of the back of an Uber van. The side door was open, and Roxy stepped out, grabbing her luggage, and one of Trent's weight belts. Her eyes caught Jack's arrival, and he wasn't feeling the love.

"You want me to give you a hand?" he asked as he walked up.

"Jack," Trent said. "You are tenacious."

"My middle name. How was the dive?"

"Some of the clearest water in the world. Pure heaven."

"Hey, Jack," Roxy said, interrupting, "I was going to call when I got settled in."

"Thought I'd save you the dime. Traveling light?"

"It's the only way to go. Carry on and save time," Roxy said.

"Makes sense. Why don't you drop off your gear, and let's you and me take a walk."

"You can come aboard," Trent said, accommodating.

"You know how it works, I do better one-on-one."

"No problem," Roxy said. "Let me splash some water on my face. I'll be back in five."

Roxy followed Trent onto the catamaran and stepped down into the cabin.

Jack made note of the Uber van's plate number and formed a strategy for his interview, deciding to take off the gloves. He was relieved that the old gent he'd met after breaking into the catamaran didn't appear to be around.

_____

"He's trouble. I told you, goddammit," Roxy said, brushing her hair with violent strokes and then checking her makeup.

"Just relax, and Jack will, too. He's got nothing. Your timeline is your alibi. You look great, just go out and be accommodating. You'll do fine."

Roxy gave herself one last look in the mirror, grabbed a hat and sunglasses, and forced a smile that morphed into sincere warmth.

"That's my girl."

_____

Jack and Roxy walked along the sidewalk that overlooked the marina, heading toward the main channel, where the bright pastel buildings comprising Fisherman's Village could be seen in the distance. White mainsails floated by on stylish trimmed yachts. The screech of gulls soaring on the thermals and the snapping of steel lines against aluminum masts were hypnotic.

Roxy looked relaxed, floppy hat, red windswept hair, oversized Emma Stone sunglasses, good for hiding emotions, Jack thought.

"You didn't get much sun," he said.

"Red hair. I don't tan, I roast. I spent most of my time in the spa on a massage table."

"I find it's good to get away. It makes me more appreciative of what I've got when I return. And hey, this isn't half bad," Jack said, referring to the beauty of the marina. "Living on a boat. I can relate. My boat gives me a sense of peace."

"And freedom," Roxy agreed.

"Was Luke ever on your boat?"

"What? What are you talking about? Why would he be? And no."

"Simple question, had to be asked."

"Are you trying to set me up, Jack?"

"Just trying to get to the truth. You didn't out-and-out lie the first time we spoke. Well, in a court of law, they call it the lie of omission."

Roxy stopped in her tracks and faced off against Jack. "What the fuck do you mean?"

Jack caught his first glimpse of the woman who'd made it through basic training at the head of her squad. He also glimpsed a flash of crazy he hadn't seen before.

"You forgot to mention the affair you had with Luke on the *Bella Fortuna*."

Roxy was good at hiding her emotions but couldn't stop the blush from enveloping her light skin. Her silence was damning. She took a deep breath, searched for a response, and started walking again. "I wouldn't call it an affair. It was dangerous and exciting, and obviously, I should have waited more than five minutes before I left the cabin. It was one time, and Trent doesn't know it happened. We tried to be discreet, and it appears we failed. Who else knows?"

"It doesn't have to go any further than me if you're straight."

"Jesus, Jack, you know how to fuck up a beautiful day."

"I'll add that to my résumé."

"What do you want?"

"Your story. I know you were in the service, and I know you scored high marks from your superiors. And then you mustered out before completing your tour of duty. What happened?"

"That's classified information, Jack. I don't see what it has to do with Luke Donato's disappearance."

"Probably nothing, but once I have a full picture, I can cross you off my list. That's how it works."

"Am I really a suspect?"

"Everyone's a suspect until I find Luke. Or Luke's killer."

Roxy pulled off her sunglasses so Jack could see the whites of her eyes and read her sincerity. "This is personal, and painful, and I've never talked about it to anyone but Trent." Jack let his silence spur her on. "My father fought in Desert Storm and came back home with PTSD. The army was callous about mental issues and dealt with serious emotional problems by giving the damaged men and women bags full of pills. And that's when they could get in to see a doctor. Dad started drinking, fell into a severe depression, and committed suicide while I was overseas.

"I came home and scattered his ashes. I was furious. I blamed the army for my dad's death, and they *were* culpable. I put up enough of a fuss that they let me muster out without a dishonorable discharge. I floated around for a while and ended up on the *Bella Fortuna*. My relationship and my job . . . they're both important to me. And I'd appreciate it if you would be a man of your word. I've lost enough in my lifetime."

"Your secret's safe with me."

Roxy locked eyes with Jack, trying to divine whether he was telling the truth. Seemingly satisfied, she put her glasses back on, adjusted her hat, and: "No more surprises, Jack."

"No more lies, Roxy."

———

Roxy keyed the security gate as Trent said his goodbyes to the old gent who owned a boat on their dock. The old guy waved to Roxy as he headed toward his sailboat.

"What was that all about?" Roxy asked.

"Bertolino was on the cat while we were out of town. Told Ron he was in the market for a catamaran and his broker gave him the wrong slip. Why lie to the old man unless you've got something to hide?"

"Was he in the cabin?"

"All Ron saw was him stepping off the transom."

"Shit! Shit. Let's see if anything's missing or been messed with."

"The man's trouble," Trent said as he followed Roxy into the cabin.

"Do you think?" she snapped, not sure how much of her conversation with Jack she was going to share, but the growing knot in her gut felt malignant.

"We'll bounce it off Sukarno, let him weigh in."

Roxy rummaged through her drawers and cabinets and came up empty. Everything seemed to be in place. She pulled a bottle of chardonnay out of the fridge, poured a full glass, and took a heavy sip. "If Jack doesn't back off, we'll let Sukarno force the issue."

———

Jack stepped off the elevator on the fifth floor of the Sunset Vine Tower. Knocked on the door and stepped into Angelica Cardona's arms. He pushed the door closed with his foot, pulling her tight. He felt like a teenager again, and it took a while to come up for air.

"Now, that's a proper hello, Mr. Bertolino."

Jack handed her the bottle of Benziger cab and took in his surroundings. The sun had dropped below the Hollywood Hills, canyon homes' lights had blinked on, the night sky was a rich slate blue, and the view from the floor-to-ceiling windows encompassed the fully lit downtown skyline.

"Very nice," he said as Angelica poured him a glass from an open bottle on the kitchen island.

"I hope you're talking about me and not the view."

Angelica's loftlike apartment had clean modern lines. The kitchen was gourmet, the island gray Caesarstone. Angelica's shabby-chic furniture softened the hard edges.

"You, of course. It smells like heaven in here, and you look nothing like my aunt Delores."

"I've picked up a few tricks along the way. The sausage is cooked fresh, the meatballs made today, and the lasagna noodles are perfectly al dente. If all goes according to plan, we'll be eating in an hour."

"I could get used to this." He touched his glass against hers, and they both took a sip, their heartbeats settling to normal.

"Count on it." Her eyes crinkled into a sly smile, and Jack's pulse raised a few notches.

What a woman, he thought. There was something about living on the edge that had kept Jack in the field when he worked undercover. It made him feel alive, and was something he'd missed the past few months. That and the scent of a woman. But the last thing he wanted was to hurt this wonderful vision. As if reading his mind again, Angelica turned to Jack and broke the ice.

"Even though there's nothing I'd rather do while we're waiting for the lasagna to bake than drag you into the bedroom and jump your bones . . ."

"You wouldn't have to drag me. No dragging needed."

"We should talk a few things out, if that's okay."

"Good idea."

"I am perfectly clear that you're a cop. Okay, retired, but still a cop."

"And you are the daughter of a Mafia crime boss."

"That's the answer right there. The one you've been worrying about for days now. You just answered your own question, Jack. I'm the daughter. He's my father. He's family, but I'm not in 'the family.' I'm not a Mafia princess; I'm not a princess. I'm my own woman. Intelligent, independent, and free to make my own life choices, and it's what I intend to do. Stop worrying. You know in your heart I'm right. You're looking at me through other people's eyes, Jack. I deserve more than that. And so do you."

Jack took a moment before responding. "I'll be damned if you don't make me feel like a million bucks. But . . . it will be complicated, it already is, and things could go very wrong very quickly. I'm on a case that possibly pits me against your father's family. There may be no overlap; there might be no culpability in Luke's disappearance; but it's possible. I don't have the answers yet, but I won't stop until I get them. And if it goes south on me, I don't want you caught in the middle."

"Let's take a flier, Jack. Let's have some fun, and you do what you do best."

"What's that?"

"Make love to me," she said, smiling. "And then find Luke Donato."

Jack put his drink down. Angelica did the same. She set the timer over the oven, turned the gas off the pot of sauce on the stove, and they walked hand in hand into the bedroom.

# Nineteen

*Day Ten*

It was midmorning before Jack left Angelica's apartment. He was driving with the top down, listening to KNX Newsradio, and feeling good, optimistic, and hell, damned good. Nick Aprea was right. He'd lose sleep but wake with a smile on his face.

There was a news story about Virgin America's airline, and it gave Jack pause. There had been something disconcerting about his run-in the day before with Roxy and Trent. He called Agent Hunter, who picked up on the second ring.

"How's it going, Jack?"

"Do you need a passport when you're flying to Mexico these days?"

"You're right: why waste words on social niceties?"

"Sorry. I'm good, thanks."

"You sound chipper." Liz wondered if she'd come off defensive.

"I am—"

"Yes, you do need a passport. Ever since the State Department implemented the WHTI."

"Don't tell me."

"And you thought the feds had an acronym fetish." She put the glimpse of a smile back in her voice. "It's the Western Hemisphere Travel Initiative, why?"

"Then I need a favor," he said, evading the question.

"Jack—"

"Roxy Donnelly and her boyfriend, Trent Peters, claim to have been in Baja the past few days, and I know their passports were still in L.A.

"I showed up unannounced yesterday as they were stepping out of an Uber van, and the only luggage they carried for a three-day trip was a sports bag and a carry-on. That might fly when you're eighteen, but I'm not picking up a hippie vibe from either of them. Could you run two cell calls for me?"

"How do you know they were traveling without passports?"

"Good question."

"Jesus, Jack, text me the numbers and the time of your calls and I'll get it done." Now she knew she sounded snarky.

"Greatly appreciated, Liz. And do you have Vasily Barinov on your radar?"

"What's the interest?"

"He's a high roller running a scam on the gambling boat, and if Luke was on to him, it would give him motive. He was big in the Russian oil game in the nineties, but *was* might be the operative word. If he's hurting for cash and cheating at cards, half a million American would go a long way to getting him healthy again."

"I'll plug him into the system and get back to you."

"What's the word on Rusty?" Jack asked. Liz paused, roiling Jack's gut. "Don't tell me you're cutting him loose."

"I was going to fill you in when the ink was dry, but he lawyered up, and his legal team filed for a 1275 bail hearing before he was even processed. Turns out his mother owns the family home on Staten Island outright, and she's guaranteed a secured bond, using her house as collateral. It'll take forty-eight hours to go through the system, but he'll make bail, and we'll have to cut him loose."

"What about the hijacking?" Jack asked, his good mood spent.

"We may convene a grand jury, but Flannery doesn't want to drop the hammer on Cardona just yet, and Washington is in agreement. We have too much skin in the game to take him down piecemeal. I'll give you a heads-up before Rusty leaves the building."

"Thanks, Liz."

She hung up without saying goodbye.

Jack turned from news to a jazz station and cranked up the volume.

———

"Four series of numbers, nine top to bottom." Cruz was seated at the desk in the cabin cruiser, showing Jack his ideas about Luke's doodles in the margins of the magazines left in Miranda's apartment.

"Any thoughts?" Jack asked.

"If I put them side to side, could be a combination lock, numbers to a safe. I checked out the Powerball, but there were six, including the Power number. This doodle here that turns into a man's head after the first four numbers: could be an N. Hard to say. And after the forty-five, the period that turns into a curlicue, not a clue. If I plug in *north* after the first sequence of four, then the period could be degrees and might be maritime coordinates. I get a GPS hit near a marine sanctuary out in the Pacific. Nothing that makes any sense."

"What about Miranda's computer?"

"Nothing of relevance, unless he was shopping at Nordstrom or Overstock.com. Most of the hits were restaurants, clubs, and travel plans."

"Where were they looking to travel?"

"Baja, Hawaii, Indonesia, some wildlife preserve, I think it was called the Farallones."

"Too bad." Jack rang up Agent Hunter again. "Hi, Liz, what did you find in Rusty's apartment? And what's the status of his girlfriend, and the other woman who was working the front of the shop?"

"We cut the worker loose. If she didn't wear slip-ons, she'd be running around barefoot. And Cory, his girlfriend, is struggling to make bail. She's part of the business and can't provide legitimate pay stubs to corroborate how she pays her rent. There's a sixty-thousand-dollar Jaguar in her name, and we found twenty thousand in cash in her freezer and five in a spare handbag. She's being advised to dummy up from the same lawyer who's handling Rusty's case, but might be more forthcoming after a few days in lockup.

"You're going to love this—Rusty's condo has a ceiling panel that houses his air-conditioning unit. It also held fifty grand in vacuum-wrapped hundreds. When I dropped the bomb on Rusty, he didn't blink. Says he lost faith in the banking system during the Wall Street bailout. And get this, he said his financial adviser told him to keep a year's cash reserves in case of another market downturn."

"Christ. And how much was confiscated at the store?"

"Thirty grand, with Wells Fargo deposit slips from the previous week for twenty-five. So he's good for laundering charges."

"Just chump change. They must have been giving the Abbot Kinney location a test drive. No way to link the cash to Luke or the *Bella Fortuna*?"

"No, and nothing in either condo ties them to my brother."

"I'll stay on it, thanks."

"Jack . . . you're doing good. You're asking the right questions," and Hunter clicked off, not comfortable handing out compliments.

Jack understood her growing sense of dread. Each day that passed without an answer turned the case into a murder investigation. She never admitted out loud that her only brother might be dead and not MIA. But Jack knew that was exactly what she was feeling. It was a numbers game, and Luke's cards were stacked against him.

———

"The medical examiner's office is behind the eight ball," Nick Aprea said to Jack, as he banged the bottom of a ketchup bottle with his big hand. The guys were sitting in their regular booth at Hal's grabbing lunch. "Molloy said he'd get to it when he could get to it. I said, 'Look at it with a magnifying glass, Sherlock.' He didn't appreciate the literary reference but slid your samples under a microscope and compared them to the hair pulled from the brush."

On the fourth whack, Nick buried his fries under a mound of red. He ate a mouthful and washed it down with a longneck Dos Equis dark. Jack waited, knowing if he even sighed, Aprea would go into a laughing jag and continue the torture.

"I told you she'd be good for you." Nick said, changing the subject to Angelica. "You are exercising control. You're more relaxed. Very impressive."

"Nick."

"Hah!" came out like a bark. "Molloy said it wouldn't stand up in court, but he thinks there's a clear match. You got your red sample and two different browns. One of the browns, the longer of the two samples, matched the hair taken from Luke's brush."

"Huh."

"Eh? What does it tell you besides the guy was randy, which you already knew, and the woman was hiding their affair, which is typical?"

"I nailed her yesterday, and she withheld information again. No, she pulled off her sunglasses, stared me down, and bald-faced lied."

"Don't take this the wrong way, Jack, but you're just a PI. She don't owe you squat. You need a badge. The better to scare people with."

"Thanks for the career advice," and Jack went silent. He grabbed his wallet and pulled out the receipt he had taken from the wastebasket in the galley of the catamaran. He unfolded it and read.

"What?"

"Huh. When I was, uh, looking through the window of Roxy's catamaran, I happened to notice that she had a new cover on the bed. It had that new-fabric smell."

"And you sussed that out through the glass?"

"Yeah, and check out what I found stuck to the bottom of the garbage can."

Nick grabbed it. The game was more fun when he was running it. "Bed Bath and Beyond. Duvet cover, three hundred dollars."

"And look at the date. If I'm not mistaken, it's about two days after Luke and the money disappeared."

Nick took a bite of his cheeseburger and a swig of beer, knowing where Jack was going. "Maybe she was having her period and bled on the old cover. Couldn't get the stain out and bought a new one before her boyfriend saw it."

"You could be right about a bloodstain."

"It's a stretch."

"Something to think about." Jack grabbed the receipt and filed it back in his wallet. "That's all I'm saying. Thanks, Nick. Let me know when the DNA results come in."

"No problem, pard."

And Jack was out the door.

---

From a distance, the *Queen Mary* sat proudly in the afternoon sun. As Roxy got closer, she saw the old broad was aging. White paint flaked and peeled like the skin of a surfer who'd forgotten sunscreen. Roxy took note of pairs of security cameras covering the entrance to the ship on all exterior decks.

Roxy stepped off the elevator on the fourth floor, walked up the gangplank, and entered the wood-paneled Promenade Deck. She was a brunette again, wearing dark glasses and a tailored silk pantsuit, carrying a gray Coach bag, looking like she was embarking on a transatlantic trip. The fact that the ship was permanently docked in Long Beach Harbor did nothing to shatter the illusion. She was overdressed, but the tourists who stood in line for the tour paid her no mind.

She walked down the uneven hardwood flooring of the wide promenade and didn't readily see any interior cameras. She found one at the far end, but again, it appeared to be covering people entering the aft of the ship and not the long promenade. She checked out the ladies' room: no visible cameras.

Roxy walked up a flight of stairs at the aft of the ship and exited on the sun deck. The wind was blowing off the Pacific, but the warm sun on her face calmed the nerves that nagged at her the closer they got to D-day. She stepped onto a wooden gazebo and took stock of the location.

The *Queen Mary* was surrounded by a moat, a protective stone security wall constructed like a rock jetty. A Carnival Cruise ship was docked off the ship's aft. And a large waterway separated the *Queen* from the Long Beach Shoreline Marina, where the *Bella Fortuna* was moored.

In the distance Roxy saw the sea of skeletal cranes that jutted like Erector-set models in Long Beach Harbor, off-loading huge container vessels filled with materials shipped from around the world.

On the port side, R Deck, second floor, were two gaping doorways where supplies, fresh seafood, flowers, alcohol, and assorted vendors' goods were delivered to the ship. It gave her a second option, if needed.

Security was light but ever present. The crew and waitstaff were relaxed, and that made Roxy feel confident she could carry out her mission.

Their terrorist plot was two-pronged. Roxy's job was to secret one of the dirty bombs on the *Queen Mary* and engage the bomb on a time delay.

Sukarno would notify the major television networks.

When the Coast Guard and first responders were alerted that the *Queen Mary* was under attack and deployed, all hell would break loose. They wouldn't have the manpower to cover the cell's main target: a Chinese tanker heading for the Port of Long Beach, which housed the second busiest container port in the United States.

---

Jack was in a holding pattern and getting antsy. The *Bella Fortuna* was leaving port in two days, and he didn't have any answers about Luke's disappearance. He was waiting on DNA results from Nick and a phone trace from Agent Hunter. If Luke was still alive and he had inside help from Roxy and Trent, they might have met up in Baja.

It was worth a try, Jack thought as he looked out the window of the Boeing 737 and marveled at the aqua-blue Pacific and then the crystal-clear water of the Sea of Cortez. The plane made a hard tire-squealing landing. Jack unbuckled his seat beat, stood up, and grabbed his carry-on luggage from the overhead bin before the jet lurched to a stop.

He laughed to himself, knowing what Agent Flannery's reaction would be to the eight-hundred-a-night ocean-view junior suite's invoice he was going to submit to the FBI for reimbursement.

Jack checked into his room, tipped the bellman, and got down to business. He started at the concierge desk, where he struck up a conversation with Tim, whose name was etched on a silver nameplate prominently placed on the expansive white lacquered desk. Tim was a slender man in his thirties who was as stylish as the hotel and very accommodating.

"So, just one night, Mr. Bertolino?"

"Some friends of mine were thinking of coming down for a few days. We had tentative plans to meet up. Roxy Donnelly and Trent Peters. But they look like a no-show."

"Oh, yes, a terrific couple," Tim said. "But they haven't been here in a few months. In fact, if memory serves, the last time they were here was December, over the holidays."

"I was sure they said they were flying in."

"I would have known. Let me pull them up on the computer."

He tapped a few keys. "No, their last visit, as I said, was December twenty-third through the twenty-seventh."

"Too bad. I was looking forward to spending time. It's almost impossible to coordinate schedules." Jack pulled a photo of Luke Donato out of his pocket and slid it across the glossy desktop. "Have you by any chance seen this gentleman?"

"Why do I feel like I'm talking to the police? And it's against corporate policy, I'll have you know," Tom said in a mock scolding voice.

Jack discreetly passed two crisp twenties to the young man, who made the cash disappear like a sleight-of-hand magician.

"In all honesty, this man, Luke Donato, has gone missing. I've been hired by a distraught family member to discover his where-abouts."

The concierge glanced from the front desk back to the photo. "No, I would have remembered if he stayed at our resort."

Jack raised his eyebrows in a question.

"He's my type," Tim said without attitude.

Jack slipped another twenty across the desk. "Would you mind giving me a list of the other hotels in the general area? And if you could recommend a restaurant, I'd appreciate it."

"No problem, Mr. Bertolino. We do everything we can to make our visitors' stay at the Las Ventanas al Paraiso a pleasurable one."

Jack didn't doubt him for a second.

———

The moment Jack's taxi pulled away from the resort, Tim scrolled down a contact list on the computer, pulled out his cell, and punched in a number.

"Miss Donnelly, this is your favorite concierge at Las Ventanas. I'm fine, darling, thanks. I just wanted to let you know that a Mr. Bertolino checked in to the resort this afternoon and was hoping you were also arriving today. No? Okay, I just thought you might be interested. It was no problem at all. I always take care of my clients."

---

Six resorts and eight bars later, Jack had come up empty. He was eating at the open-air bar at an Italian restaurant overlooking the Sea of Cortez. The water was like nothing Jack had ever seen before. A blue so light, it seemed fluorescent. He polished off a Caesar salad, a plate of scampi, and a side order of spaghetti aglio e olio. The bartender came over during a lull in the service and refilled Jack's glass with cabernet. Jack was never one to worry about wine pairings. He drank what he liked.

"How long you in town for?" the bartender asked as he made Jack's dishes disappear under the bar.

"I leave in the a.m. Sorry to go."

"It's one hell of a spot."

Jack looked at the bartender, early forties, relaxed attitude, looked like he had job security, great window on the world. Jack almost envied him.

"I'm looking for an old friend and coming up empty." Jack slid the photograph of Luke across the bar.

"Luke Donato," the bartender said, brightening. "Great guy. Great tipper and a real good guy."

Jack straightened on his stool. "Have you seen him lately?"

The bartender gave that a moment's thought. "Can't say that I have. But he usually comes in with a nice gal. African-American. Good-looking."

Jack took a drink of wine. The bartender was referencing Miranda. "Have you ever seen this couple?" and he showed him the photograph of Roxy and Trent sitting dockside in front of the *Bella Fortuna*.

"Oh yeah. Good people."

"Ever see the two couples together?"

"Are they in trouble or what?" His tone wary.

"No, but Luke is MIA, and his family's worried. I'm just trying to get a handle on his whereabouts."

The bartender relaxed, topped off Jack's glass again, and said, "No, can't say I ever saw them as a foursome. We get so many coming through. But I think I would've remembered, you know, if I saw them together."

The bartender moved to his station and started filling orders.

Jack looked at this new wrinkle. Just because the bartender hadn't made them as a foursome didn't mean it didn't happen. Luke could've met up with Roxy on the side. Still, half a million split two or three ways wasn't enough for a man like Luke Hunter to go on the run.

But it might have been enough for two worker bees staying in an eight-hundred-dollar a night resort to kill him.

———

Jack was taking advantage of the infinity pool looking out over the tip of Baja. The view encompassed the Pacific and the Sea of Cortez, and Jack thought he could get used to this part of the world. There was no light pollution, and the night sky was spectacular. Jack's cell rang, breaking the mood. He swam over to it, dried his hands on the plush cotton towel, checked the incoming, and answered. "Liz. What's the word? You're working late."

"No rest for the weary. I got the coordinates of the phone calls you requested. They didn't land south of the border."

"I know."

"Do tell." Liz sounded put out.

"I'm in Baja. They're not. Where did they ping?"

"Oakland. We narrowed it down to a two-block radius. A mix of retail and suburban neighborhoods. Not upscale. Maybe they lie as a matter of course and they're visiting a friend, who knows. I just texted you the coordinates."

Jack's cell pinged. "Got it."

"Did you get anything else? Or are you barhopping?"

"I've got the pool to myself. Don't be jealous because it's un-believably beautiful."

"I'm glad one of us is relaxed."

"But here's the deal. Luke was down here with his girlfriend. I'll give Miranda a call in the morning and check out the dates, see if they overlapped. I'll take a run over to their hotel, show them the photo of Roxy and Trent, see if there's a connection."

"That's something, Jack."

Jack felt the change in Hunter's demeanor in his gut.

"I'll stay on it, Liz, and call when I land at LAX."

"Do that, Jack. And you deserve a moment's downtime."

"Let's see how you feel when I turn in the invoice." And Jack clicked off.

# Twenty

*Day Eleven*

Jack came up empty at Luke's hotel in Baja. None of the staff could connect Luke to Roxy or Trent. He decided to make a stop in Oakland before heading back to L.A. He'd canvass the two-block area where Trent had answered Jack's cell call. He might get lucky and, more important, be able to work in a dinner with his son.

Jack emailed Roxy and Trent's photo to Luke's girlfriend, Miranda, and then dialed her number as the plane was taxiing to the gate. Miranda drew a blank, and her dates in Baja didn't jibe with Roxy and Trent's. A big fat dead end.

"We didn't see anybody in particular," Miranda said. "Spent most of our time in the pool, the bar, and the bedroom. It was so romantic, and it's the kind of place where everybody respects your privacy. It was all very upscale and delicious. I miss it and I miss him."

"I'll have my associate drop off your laptop. We didn't find anything out of the ordinary."

"Too bad." And then, "Hey, I've got to run. The traffic downtown is . . ." Her voice dropped off the line.

"Are you there?" Jack asked to fill the silent void.

"I don't get the feeling Luke is still alive. It's sad."

Jack let Miranda have the final word and clicked off. He was angry and decided to rattle a few cages of his own until he came up with an answer.

———

"What did I miss?" Jack asked Mateo on speakerphone. The scenery blurred as his cab sped over the Bay Bridge toward Oakland. The water was slate gray, reflecting the ominous cloud cover.

Mateo and Cruz were working on board Jack's cabin cruiser. "Caroline is hunting for bear," Mateo said. "The New York family is on the *Bella Fortuna* with their accountants, auditing her books and holding her feet to the fire. She says there's nothing to hide, but it's taking its toll."

"There's no upside partnering with the Mob."

"She's learning the hard way."

Jack had little sympathy for Caroline Boudreau. She made her own life choices and was paying the price. He just hoped Mateo wasn't swimming in shark-infested waters. Come to think of it, he had the same hope for himself.

Cruz saw an opening and chimed in. "I made a list of all the businesses in that two-block radius of the cell towers, and not being sure what I'm looking for, I don't know what I've got. I just copied you."

Jack's cell dinged. "Got it."

"When you take a look around, you might spark to something. If not, you could ask her. Roxy's lies are stacking up, am I right? She might tell you the truth to throw you off your game."

"She's a player, all right. I'm not sure truth is in her vernacular."

I'm thinking an end run might serve us better. Let her live the lie, and not show our hand."

---

"Everything else is good to go," Trent said from the cabin of the catamaran. "No hitches. Roxy thinks we're better off just booking a cabin for two nights on the *Queen Mary*. Less complicated, fewer moving parts.

"The only potential storm front is the PI." He looked up at Roxy, who was impatiently listening to one side of the conversation.

"Give me the phone," she demanded. Trent waved her off. Roxy's hand snaked out like a cobra, grabbed the throwaway cell from Trent, and turned her back on him.

"The clock is ticking, Sukarno, we need this handled. And I don't mean next week. That might be too late, and I don't know about you, but I'm not keen on spending the rest of my life in a military prison because Bertolino thinks he fucking knows it all. I need to be assured we're on the same page."

"Bertolino is now my problem," Sukarno assured. "Your performance has been beyond reproach, and I don't want you worried at this stage in the game. Everything will go accordingly, and the result will be historic."

"Okay," Roxy said, nodding and catching Trent's angry gaze.

"Let me get off the phone and make plans," Sukarno said, his voice sugary.

"And throw the burner away," she said, not appeased by his manipulating tone of voice. "A new phone every day until D-day."

"Let me speak to Trent." The goodwill spent.

Roxy handed the phone to Trent and poured a glass of chardonnay.

"So we're good?" Trent said.

"If you're man enough to handle your woman. She's on edge, and we need total concentration. There's no room for histrionics. Send me the information you have on Bertolino, car, license plate, address, family, everything. I'll take care of things on my end, you keep your house clean."

"We're spotless, Sukarno. Let me know when it's done." And Trent clicked off.

"Really?" Trent said. "You rip the phone out of my hands when I'm doing business?"

"It took you too long to make your point. Jesus, you make me crazy sometimes."

"Women don't talk to powerful Indonesian men that way. They don't like it," he spat out in a snarky staccato.

"Fuck Sukarno, and fuck you," she fired back. "I'm more man than both of you. So, suck it up. Sukarno wouldn't have a clue if it weren't for us. Anyone can write a check. We've proved ourselves in the field. It's time for Sukarno to man up."

---

Sukarno Lei hung up the phone. The vein on his temple throbbed. He walked to the wet bar of his downtown penthouse, poured himself a stiff cognac, and tossed it back, waiting for the burn in his throat to cool his fiery anger. He had men in place for tasks like this—a simple phone call could have the man eliminated, but the timing felt wrong. It was too close to D-day, as Roxy had dubbed their operation.

If his new partners weren't up to the task, he had a fallback position. He could unload the dirty bombs on the black market for a small fortune. But the amount would pale if all went according to plan. And Sukarno was greedy. And vindictive. That was what propelled him to success in the competitive world of cutting-edge technology. It was how his father and his teachers had trained him.

Sukarno was an entrepreneur. He'd sold his tech start-up to Hua Yong Corp., a Chinese conglomerate, for five hundred million in cash. But it was the stock options that cemented the deal.

When it came time to exercise his options and cash out, the Chinese government's interference and the conglomerate's manipulation had cut his stock price in half. Sukarno had been livid. He didn't like to lose. He did like exacting revenge.

The Hua Yong container ship was headed for Long Beach Harbor with a full load of computer parts and high-tech components. Sukarno's plan was to ransom the conglomerate for safe passage. He'd provide video proof of the nuclear fuel rods and the dirty bombs. A shadow broker would be engaged to handle the negotiations. The money would then be wired to a protected Bitcoin account.

Sukarno's ultimate fuck-you to the Chinese pencil pushers would be to detonate the bomb anyway. He'd short their stock on the Shanghai Composite, which was guaranteed to tank when the story leaked, and double his profit.

———

Jack stopped at a corner coffee shop. Kill two birds, he thought. He ordered an iced Americano and a tuna wrap. The barista had never seen Roxy or Trent. Jack scarfed down the sandwich and hit the road.

It was a tired Oakland neighborhood. Two- and three-story shops painted in fading shades of blue, gray, and tan were snugged next to apartment buildings, restaurants, and bars. One block off the main drag, it was entirely residential. Jack stuck to where the action was and hit one retail shop—on Cruz's list—after another with no success. He got attitude from an ex-hippie who hated cops, and more than a few life stories from bored shopowners happy to have a friendly face to talk to. There was a used-record store, a bookstore, a few antique shops, and a bakery where he bought a glazed doughnut and received another blank stare and a definite no.

Jack crossed the main drag and stopped in the middle of the crosswalk, turning a 360 to get a feel for the entire area and a clue as to why Trent had chosen this neighborhood to make a stop. A three-story faded tan stucco building sat on the corner lot, just beyond the two-block radius. Rust stains haloed the leaking downspouts. It looked like an assisted-living residence or a hotel of some kind. An elderly man navigated a walker out onto the sidewalk and straightened his back, trying to find his balance. Jack dodged oncoming traffic and strode in his direction.

The front wheels of the man's walker squealed, and the rear tennis balls scraped against the broken concrete. Jack had his answer before he reached the man. A discreet painted sign over the door read: RUSH STREET CARE. He nodded to the man, who stopped to catch his breath.

"Nice day," Jack said. Master of small talk.

"They're all perfect."

"I can't argue that. Wonder if you could help me?"

The old man thought for a second. "I could try."

Jack liked the old guy. He pulled out the picture of Roxy and Trent and held it up for the man to view. "Have you ever seen these people?"

The man's eyes crinkled slightly. "Yes and no."

"Interesting answer," Jack said.

"Yes to the woman, no to the man."

"Was she visiting someone on the premises?"

"Well, she's too young to be admitted," the man said, enjoying his own observation. "What else would she be doing here? I don't know if you've noticed, but this isn't exactly the Taj Mahal."

"Do you know who she was visiting?"

"Can't say that I do, can't say that I do. Just a hello in passing. Hallway manners."

"Well, thank you sir. I appreciate your time."

"You better, cause it goes like a bleeping rocket."

The two men took a moment to contemplate that nugget of wisdom. Jack excused himself and walked into the lobby of Rush Street Care.

———

Jack put on his most ingratiating smile and approached the admissions nurse, seated behind a gray metal desk with a computer and a single pink carnation in a clear glass vase. The woman, who wore her salt-and-pepper bun pulled tight, smiled politely and asked if she could be of service.

"As a matter of fact, you can. I'm an associate of Roxy Donnelly's. I was devastated to hear the news and offered to stop by if I was in the area." Keep it loose, and mine for gold.

"Well, how nice are you? Our patients don't get many visitors. Most family members drop their parents off, and it's the last we see of them. Roxy has been very good about visiting her father, but he's not very good company, as I'm sure you're aware."

He was now. "I was in the area and thought it might be nice for him to hear another voice."

"It would be," she said so sensitively that Jack felt a wash of guilt.

"Roxy was just here, I think she mentioned."

"Three days ago, your paths just crossed."

"Damn, it would have been nice . . . Oh well . . ."

"Fred's down the hall on the right, room eighteen. He won't speak, but he might blink if he's awake or if you can engage him. Two for yes, one for no."

"Thank you," and Jack walked down the hallway, trying not to look into open doorways and intrude on the privacy of the elderly patients who called the facility home.

Jack approached room 18 and knocked on the door, not expecting an answer. He waited a silent moment and entered. Mr. Donnelly was lying on the hospital bed, eyes closed, breathing softly, and from the look of him, drifting somewhere between life and death. His skin looked as fragile and opaque as parchment paper. His arms were folded across his chest, revealing massive scars that ran lengthwise up both arms. The man had been serious about dying, Jack thought. It didn't work out according to plan.

There were two framed photographs on the only piece of furniture in the room. One had an inscription that read *Master Sergeant Fred Donnelly,* under a picture taken in an M-1 battle tank. He looked to have the world by the balls, Jack thought.

The other was a photo of Roxy, full of youthful promise and optimism. It must have been the beginning of her six-month deployment in Afghanistan, before it all went south on her. Jack now understood that she had told him half-truths. What he didn't understand was why she'd lied about her father being dead. What was she trying to hide or protect? Jack decided not to wake the man. He didn't want to inflict any more pain than the master sergeant already endured.

Jack stopped by the front desk. The nurse read his discomfort. "It's not easy," she said.

"Does the VA pay for Fred's care?"

"Oh, no. That dried up years ago. If it weren't for Roxy, Fred would've been warehoused at one of the lower-end VA facilities. It's all out of pocket, but we give personalized care here. We treat everyone as if they're part of the family. Whether they have the ability to understand or not."

"Thank you."

"Who should I say stopped by?"

"I'd rather it came from me. More personal."

"I understand. You have yourself a great day."

"I'll do what I can," Jack said, and headed out the door. The gray sky had cleared some, and slashes of blue were breaking through the cloud cover. The visit to Master Sergeant Fred Donnelly had reminded Jack how fragile life could be. He needed to spend some time with his son, and called for an Uber.

---

Quattro, the northern Italian restaurant in the Four Seasons Hotel, was on University Avenue in Palo Alto, a short walk from Stanford. When Jack offered, Chris surprisingly jumped at the opportunity. Even more surprising was his choice of entrée. Jack pointed out the vegetarian offerings and ordered the grilled octopus for himself, but Chris ordered the wagyu beef tenderloin.

Jack kept the surprise off his face as he watched his son decimate sixteen ounces of steak. There was a lesson to be had here, but other than being smart enough to keep his mouth shut from time to time, it evaded him.

"So you have a Russian millionaire, who cheats at the table," Chris said, pointing a forkful of rare beef in Jack's direction. "And he might be hurting for cash, clear motive, or he might just hate to lose. Or he might purely get off on the act of cheating. Like that rich actress who got caught shoplifting in Beverly Hills. Plenty of money but lives for the thrill.

"And then you have one of Cardona's guys who hated Luke's guts—and yours—who has plenty of motive and knew the route Luke would take for the money drop-off." Chris took a breath and a large bite of steak, washing it down with a sip of Peroni beer.

"And then there's Roxy," Jack said, taking a sip of his Brunello.

"Here's my gut feeling on her. If it was you lying in that hospital bed, stroked out, with someone to point at, someone to blame, I'd likely kill that someone. Or want to," he corrected, emphasizing *want*, and Jack exhaled.

"How did you feel when I was in the hospital and you knew who put me there?"

"I wanted to take the man down."

"And what did you do?"

"I took the man down."

"Exactly! But who does Roxy have to blame? Luke? For what? I'm not feeling it. Sounds like the government, from what she said. If that was the true part of the half-truths she's been spouting, why lie about her father being dead? And I have no idea where Trent fits in to the equation."

"They have expensive tastes, and paying for her father's health care can't be cheap. And if Trent discovered their affair . . ."

Chris nodded and rolled that around some and, with the ego of a twenty-one-year-old, discounted it with a headshake. "If the Russian is connected, my money's on him. A simple line. He was overextended, set Luke up with one of his soldiers, who took him out, grabbed the half mil, and he's hiding in plain sight, rubbing their face in it, playing at their tables."

Jack decided he'd do a one-on-one with Vasily Barinov. But it was the subtext of Chris's analysis Jack was struggling with. "You sound like a cop," he finally said, fighting for nonjudgmental.

Chris didn't deny it. "Did you ever hear the story about the shoemaker's son?"

"No."

"It was in a book on Transcendental Meditation that Elli gave me. It basically said that if you're a shoemaker's son, you should be a shoemaker. It's in the blood. It frees you up to do more important things with your life."

Jack wasn't comfortable with the direction the conversation was heading but reminded himself to keep his big trap shut and let Chris reveal his intention in his own time. He took an extremely healthy sip of red and waved the waiter over for another glass.

Chris grinned, self-satisfied, and knocked back some more beer. "God, this steak tastes great. Thank you."

Jack didn't take the bait.

"Go ahead." Chris smirked. "You're dying to ask."

"What does Elli have to say to the meat eater?"

"Aha!" Chris said, enjoying himself. "I don't flaunt it. I told her the doctor was afraid my ligaments wouldn't mend correctly without the extra protein."

"A white lie." Father and son commiserating.

"Right. And I eat chicken and fish when I see her. She didn't buy the argument but let it go. She's really intelligent, and uh, well, it's a good fit and worth the sacrifice."

Jack's heart was full with the pure love he felt for his son. They had lived through more than a few rocky years, and he was thankful to be on the other side of the trauma.

Both men dug in to their entrées and enjoyed a moment of well-deserved, comfortable silence.

---

"No, I wouldn't say it's purely a booty call," Jack said, standing on the balcony of his loft. He watched the landing lights on a string of approaching jets cut through the midnight-blue sky and disappear into the glow of LAX in the distance. He'd arrived home, showered, shaved, poured a glass of cabernet, and decided to throw caution to the wind.

"What would you call it, Mr. Bertolino?"

"Two consenting adults who enjoy each other's company and can't get enough of a good thing."

"And what time is it?"

Jack's face split into a grin. "Almost eleven."

"And is this the first time you've called me in two days?" Angelica asked coyly, enjoying the moment.

"I believe it might be. I just got home and thought—"

"It's a booty call, Jack," she said, cutting him off.

"Busted." He laughed. "Whatever you say, Angelica."

"I say get your booty over here before I change my mind."

"Traffic's light, I'll see you in a half hour."

---

Jack was cruising on the 405, the ragtop down, the air cool, and he was feeling no pain. He hit the gas and took the turnoff east on the I-10 toward La Cienega and the bright lights of Sunset Boulevard.

Jack was so caught up in the anticipation of the sexual liaison to come that he didn't feel two predatory SUVs tracking him up the freeway and closing the distance.

One car split left into the fast lane, and the other hit the gas. Jack glanced in his side mirror, and what looked like a flame caught his peripheral vision but didn't readily compute. He slowed his Mustang to sixty as the black SUV pulled alongside, threatening to swerve into his lane. A passing motorist had Jack locked in. As he hit the horn, the SUV's window powered down, and a man in dark sunglasses hurled a flaming bottle into the rear of Jack's convertible and sped away.

The Molotov cocktail exploded on impact.

Fire inundated the back seat of the Mustang. Black smoke trailed the car like a jet's contrail.

Jack hit the brakes; the second SUV slammed the edge of the Mustang's bumper, executing a perfect pit maneuver before speeding down the freeway.

Jack went into a fiery death spin at sixty miles an hour. With flames and choking smoke billowing, the other cars on the freeway gave him a wide berth as he fought to correct the Mustang's rotation.

After four stomach-churning, tire-squealing revolutions and his life flashing before his eyes, Jack skidded to a stop on the shoulder, leaped from the vehicle, the back of his jacket ignited. Two strides and the concussive explosion lifted Jack off his feet and slammed him face-first onto the gravel. He rolled, then rolled again, extinguishing the flames, jumped to his feet, and peeled off his smoldering jacket.

A secondary explosion buffeted Jack back a step. He was oblivious to the traffic that bunched up on the I-10 as passing cars slowed to view and shoot video of the carnage that would make the late-night news.

Oily smoke curled skyward; the flames illuminated Jack's face. Rivulets of blood dripped down his gravel-cut cheek. His narrowed eyes were darker than the smoke as he watched his Mustang burn to the ground.

# Twenty-one

Angelica Cardona leaped from her car in the driveway of the family home in Beverly Hills. She keyed the heavy front door and slammed it behind her.

Frankie-the-Man hoofed it out of the kitchen and met her in the hallway. He could tell she was steamed, and he knew why. "What can I do you for, Angelica?"

"Where's my father?"

He nodded his melon head toward the back of the house. "Gym."

Angelica pushed past the big man and stormed down the hallway, her boots clicking angrily on the burnished hardwood.

———

Vincent Cardona was dressed in Nike's finest, working up a sweat on one of two treadmills in front of the television in the pool house. The sixty-five-inch screen was set on CNN. The sound was muted and Cardona was reading the crawl. He kept his eyes on the television as his daughter stormed into the room and slammed the door.

185

"I didn't have nothing to do with it."

"Dad?!"

"Listen to what I'm tellin' you. It wasn't my play."

"Is Rusty still inside?"

Cardona was trying to calm himself down, so his response was too slow in coming. Angelica walked to the front of the treadmill, her angry eyes bearing down on her father. She kicked the power button off, and Cardona almost stumbled as the machine lurched to a stop.

"Is Rusty still inside?"

Cardona stepped off the machine, grabbed a towel, and rubbed down his face and neck. "Yeah. Few more days is all."

"Could he have had anything to do with Jack's accident?"

"That would be off the reservation. I'm looking into it, but I don't think so."

"What about Uncle Mickey?"

"He'd have to clear it with me first. I woulda heard."

Angelica went to the fridge and pulled out two bottles of water. She handed one to her father and opened the other, her hands trembling and her throat dry. She took a large swallow. Her father did the same. Her voice lost the edge as she chose her words. "Have I ever asked you for anything?"

"No. You're stubborn like that. Always have been. How do you think it makes me feel?"

"This isn't about you, Dad."

"No, no, I get it." Cardona flopped down in the overstuffed sofa in the spalike workout room. "C'mon, sit down, take a load off."

"Here's my deal."

"Oh, Christ."

"Don't *Oh, Christ* me. Listen to me. I want you to keep Rusty on a tight leash. Let Jack do his job and it'll be a win-win. If Jack has any more trouble and I hear it's generated by you, we are going to have major problems."

"Is that a threat?" he asked without rancor.

"No, Dad. Just reality. I appreciate everything you've done for me since my abduction. You've been very good. But I want you to hear me. I don't need any interference in my personal life."

Cardona listened to his daughter, who reminded him more and more of his late wife. He hadn't really thought about it. Maybe it struck a nerve that he kept tamped down, and he thought maybe that was where it should be kept.

"Jack was lucky to make it out of the car alive," his daughter said. "Lucky he didn't burn to death. The man who saved my life, and I'm worried that my father sanctioned the hit."

"You know, you're hurting my feelings. I've done plenty of stuff to piss you off, stuff I'm culpable for, but you know what I've never done? Never once?"

Angelica's face gave away nothing.

"Lied to you." Cardona gave that a moment to penetrate his daughter's anger. "And when you walked in here just now, what did I say? First thing out of my mouth."

"You had nothing to do with it."

"Thank you. So, is Jack in the hospital?"

"In and out. A few stitches, a few burns. His back's messed up. The last we spoke, he was downtown giving a statement to the cops."

Cardona didn't like the sound of that but let it slide. "You're right. Man lucked out. Would've been a hell of a way to go." And Vincent Cardona had spent more than his share of time contem-

plating how he would go down. If Jack pointed his finger in the
wrong direction, it could be him taking the fall sooner than later.
It was the only reason his brother-in-law was in town. Fuckin' East
Coast family. "I'd ask if he were still on the case, but I know better."

Vincent Cardona would stay on top of the situation. And if
Jack had to go, so be it. Vincent might have to pull the strings, but
he wouldn't be pulling the trigger. And his daughter, Angelica,
would just have to deal with it. It went with the bloodline. He left
her with a parting shot: "What if you'd been in the car?"

---

Mateo picked Jack up downtown at the Los Angeles Police Department Headquarters, where he'd spent five hours giving his statement to the cops and another three speaking to FBI Special Agent
Ted Flannery and Agent Hunter. Jack didn't have much to share,
and no one believed him for a second. Jack chose not to speculate
on his aggressors, couldn't provide a positive ID of the man who'd
thrown the Molotov, and was too preoccupied by the flames to get
a license number.

Jack's face and the flaming Mustang were looped on all the
network media outlets, and his cell was ringing off the hook.
After alerting Angelica, his son, and Mateo that he was safe, he
turned off his phone.

The feds escorted him out of the building. Flannery stepped
close, invading Jack's personal space. "You're off the case."

Jack glanced at Hunter, whose mirrored sunglasses betrayed
nothing.

"Stay focused, Jack. I'm in charge here, and I'm pulling the
plug. You haven't accomplished anything of substance, and I'm
not going to be held responsible for keeping you alive."

Jack had suffered more than enough crap in the past twenty-four hours. He was pissed off and dirty, and his back was in mind-numbing pain. He clicked into street mode and wanted to knock the arrogant agent on his ass.

Flannery assessed the situation and took a half-step back.

Jack geared into low talk. "If you think I'm going to walk away after someone tried to burn me alive, you're delusional. I'm done when I say I'm done. Try and interfere with my investigation, and I'll tell Cardona and the East Coast family who my client is. You can explain two wasted years and a missing agent to Washington from your desk in Juno."

Jack turned on his heel and jumped into Mateo's Beemer, idling at the curb. The seven-series peeled away from police head-quarters and Jack never looked back.

———

Roxy came out of the catamaran's bathroom dressed for work, towel-drying her hair. Trent sat shirtless on the bunk, surfing the morning news channels. He stopped on Channel Seven, where the screen filled with the image of Jack Bertolino standing stoically next to his burning vehicle on the edge of the freeway. Two fire trucks arrived, along with an EMT wagon and three black-and-whites. The news chopper's camera pushed in tight on Jack's tense face, then pulled back to show the first responders deploying. Fire hoses blasted amid the swirl of black smoke and ebbing flames. The chopper banked high and wide; the camera settled on a solid ribbon of white and red lights snarled in both directions. The rubbernecking traffic on I-10.

The anger in the cabin was palpable. Trent knew better than to engage when Roxy was on one of her tears.

"I've got to get to work," Roxy said without emotion. "I'll start a misinformation campaign on board. Someone overheard Rusty threatening to kill Jack after they got into that scuffle. I'll leak it to Ava and it'll be all over the ship in a half hour. Hopefully, Jack's hands will be full for a few days, and it might give us enough time to preserve our schedule."

"Makes sense." From Trent's point of view, the schedule was locked.

"And if we can make Rusty think Jack has him targeted, it might push him so far over the edge that he'll choose to take Jack out of play permanently."

"I'm due on board at eleven. I'll stay below, keep my nose out of the fray. You work your magic."

"And don't ask me again if I'm okay, because I'm not. You handle Sukarno, because I might drown the bastard and cut our losses. If he doesn't make a show on this trip, it might look suspicious. I get the feeling he's worried about me because I showed some emotion, but it's Sukarno who could take us down. He's your man, handle him."

"Sukarno is not a problem. He's our exit card."

"And he fucked up! Bertolino knows we weren't in Baja," she screamed.

"Keep your voice down," he hissed, walking to the stairs and peering up and down the dock. He sucked in a deep breath and in measured tones soldiered on. "And his attempt to slow Bertolino down was smarter than killing him outright and having the cops swarming the ship. Don't be shortsighted." Trent gave her a moment to ease the tension. "We're fine, we're on schedule, and we're near completion. If you need me, if you need anything, send a text on the safe phone, and I'll get back to you. But calm down."

Roxy answered Trent by striding into the bathroom and slamming the door.

---

Jack, Cruz, and Mateo were now gathered around the dining room table in his loft.

"So who wants me dead?" Jack asked, draining half a bottle of water, his throat sand-dry. The right side of his cheek was bruised and swollen, a butterfly suture stained with dried blood, tight on his left eyebrow. His back, a solid sheet of hurt. The doctors said his shoulders would peel but not scar; the hair on the back of his head was singed, and the rank smell pissed him off royally.

Mateo snorted a laugh. "Hey, don't take this the wrong way, boss, but your list of enemies is growing exponentially with the cases you close. Goes with the territory."

"Let's stay current," Jack said, his eyes crinkling into a grin, happy to be alive. "I've got four, five maybes."

"Who's your first choice?" Cruz asked. "First person who came to mind when you stood there watching your beautiful car melt into the rock."

"I *was* fond of the Mustang . . . Rusty," Jack said with a voice as raspy as the asshole's name. "I appear on-scene, he gets popped. That's what he's thinking, sitting in a jail cell, and it's not far from the truth. We've got Flannery to thank for that blunder. Rusty, he's number one."

Murmurs from the guys.

"The East Coast family," Mateo said. "They don't want anyone sniffing around their bottom line. And they're here because we're on-scene."

Jack didn't disagree. "I interjected a seed of doubt about Rusty's possible involvement in Luke's death, but it doesn't have legs. If the prick has a good alibi for the night Luke disappeared, they'll circle back to me, try and finish the job."

"What about the Russian?" Cruz asked. "Doris could've run to her sugar daddy after our sit-down."

"The Molotov cocktail has the Russian Mob's stench all over it," Jack agreed. "I'll call Hunter, if she's still in our corner, and get the research I requested on Barinov ASAP. I'll corner him on the *Bella Fortuna* and have a one-on-one."

"Roxy and Trent," Mateo tossed in, as if they should be moved to the top of the list.

"I'm still ambivalent. I could file her lie about Dad being dead under none of my business. And they're not aware I'm eighty percent on Luke's DNA being on her catamaran, and doing a full-court press to get the answer. Not sure they have the connections to order a hit even if they look good for Luke's murder and have the means to pay for one. We could be looking at two different motives here.

"Hate to say it, but the person who has the most to lose, businesswise, with me snooping around, is Caroline. She's in bed with some very unsavory characters." Jack threw a glance in Mateo's direction, and Cruz stifled a laugh. "Let me amend that," Jack cracked a smile, "she's in business with the Mafia and has a black book full of wealthy clients with the money and networks to make people disappear. If she loses the *Bella Fortuna*, she loses everything."

Mateo didn't blink an eye. There was no question where his loyalties lay. Everybody was a suspect until the killer was in handcuffs.

Jack went on, "That takes care of me. Who killed Luke? Who

had the motive and the means? They could have shot me dead on the freeway. Why go through the drama?"

"To slow you down," Mateo said.

"Scare me off. We're getting close, but I feel like I'm spinning wheels."

"Why don't you take the rest of the day, boss?" Mateo advised. "I'll be your eyes and ears on board. Mix it up with the crew. You've already been to hell and back."

"I'm going to close my eyes for a few hours, put on my tux, water-taxi myself onto the *Bella Fortuna*, and see who's happy to see me. Why don't you embark with the yacht, keep your ear to the ground, and work your way onto the bridge with a view of the video screens when I arrive. We might see more than anyone planned on sharing. First reactions. I'll play it from my end, hit all of my suspects. Cruz, I want you back on my boat and ready to hit 999 if there are any surprises coming our way."

"Let's get the scumbag who tried to kill you, Jack," Cruz said. "Even if it's a woman."

Mateo nodded through a dangerous grin.

Jack looked at his men, toasted them with his bottled water, and knocked back his Vicodin and Excedrin.

———

"If we're seen together, I'm as good as gone," Agent Hunter said. "Fifteen years of my life in the toilet. No pension, no savings, no letter of recommendation."

"You could walk away from the case."

"Would you?"

"Not if it were my blood."

"Here's my new number." Hunter handed Jack a handwritten

card. "I took a page from the bad guys' handbook, a throwaway phone. It'll keep Flannery at bay. He'll be watching my every move and computer keystroke. You should do the same, because he put in a requisition to go up on your phones."

"What do you have for me?"

"If the Russian didn't kill at the tables the night Luke went missing, he might've killed Luke for the weekend's receipts. His checking account and savings ballooned the day after Luke disappeared."

Jack took a moment in deference to Agent Hunter's admission. This was the first time she had verbalized the real possibility that her brother was dead.

"I'll get the numbers from Caroline and get back to you."

"Thank you, Jack."

"A little too early for that. Watch yourself."

# Twenty-two

The *Bella Fortuna* looked brilliant silhouetted against the black sky. A natural white pearl floating in a halo of blue created by the yacht's underwater spotlights. Faint music and laughter could be heard in fits and starts over the thrum of the water taxi. Picture perfect, Jack thought.

Unless the killer was on board.

———

Peter Maniacci stood at the top of the *Bella Fortuna*'s gangplank in a stylish green sharkskin suit, with all the grace of a Walmart greeter. He ran his eyes over Jack's bruised face and clucked. The nonverbal meaning was *Eh, you fuck with me, you get fucked*.

"So much for having my back," Jack said.

"Blame yourself. I've been reassigned."

Jack stopped in his tracks. "Let's not forget why I'm here, Peter. Any idea who wants me gone?"

"The list hasn't changed, Jack. But it's growing."

"Comforting." And Jack stepped into the main salon filled with beautiful people and lively action. The card tables were standing-room-only, and the slots were humming, ringing, and flashing.

Doris was the first of the crew to see Jack, and her eyes widened as she dropped off a drink to the Russian and scooted back to the bar.

Jack ignored Roxy, giving Mateo a moment to gauge her reaction on the security screens as he walked through the salon. He moved toward Caroline Boudreau, who was stationed across the room with a bird's-eye view of the tables. She looked elegant and self-satisfied. Business was good, life was looking up. And then she saw Jack.

His tux was pressed, his hair a little ragged over the collar after his run-in with the Molotov cocktail. Except for the bruises and the butterfly suture that added a rakish note, he turned heads as he stepped up to Caroline.

"Jesus, Jack. You make quite an entrance."

"Good evening to you, Caroline. You're looking well."

"Nobody expected to see you tonight."

"I try to stay light on my feet. But I'd like to stay on my feet. Any ideas? What are the drumbeats telling you?"

"Jack, Jack." She turned away from the room and gazed out the portside window. "The ocean wreaks havoc on the yacht's chrome. If the crew doesn't stay on top of things . . ."

"Gets rusty. Spreads like a cancer."

"You said it, I didn't."

"Who was banging the drum?"

"Doris. She couldn't wait to dish. Don't give her a hard time, she's harmless, and the men appreciate her."

"How did Vasily Barinov do the night Luke disappeared?"

"He almost broke the bank. I was relieved when he cashed out."

"Do you remember what time he left?"

"Not to the minute. But his car was waiting when we docked. He took off about an hour before Luke. I was happy to see him go. He's been on an ungodly winning streak lately."

"Some people have all the luck. Any issues with the audit?"

"I lost my appetite and five pounds. But that's all. Everything else was solid to the last dollar."

"Good for you." And Jack meant it. "Where's Mateo?"

"On the bridge with the captain and Frankie-the-Man, watching the tables on the video screens."

"I'm going to circulate and share the joy."

"Go get 'em, champ."

---

Jack circumnavigated the salon, got a feel for the old faces, and made note of the new players. There was an empty chair at the main poker table, and Doris was conspicuously missing, replaced by Ramón. Jack headed down to the B Deck and picked up his pace as he entered the dining room.

The room was empty except for Vasily Barinov, who was crowding Doris against the wall, his body language predatory.

"Mr. Barinov."

"Take a hike," the man said without turning around.

Jack thumped him on the shoulder with the heel of a hand, and Barinov spun with the speed of a Russian bear and threw down.

Jack grabbed the ham fist headed for his face, muscled it back, locked it in place with his other forearm, and dropped to one knee. The big man grunted in pain and fell heavily to his knees on the plush carpet to keep his wrist from snapping.

Doris bolted away from the wall, wide-eyed. "Jack, stop!"

Jack pushed his elbow against Barinov's windpipe and, with

his full body weight, leaned in. The Russian's eyes bulged. Jack hissed at Doris, "Get Frankie-the-Man. Now!"

Doris ran out of the room.

"Here's how this is going to play," Jack continued. "Open your mouth except to answer my questions, and I toss you to the wolves."

Barinov nodded.

Jack pushed away, stood, and took a step back. Barinov heaved his girth up, rubbed his wrist, and cleared his throat as he walked to the bar and poured himself a double Stoli.

"I have you on camera cheating at the poker table."

The Russian flicked his sausage fingers in a *who gives a fuck* gesture. Jack answered the challenge. "The mobsters in America, like in the motherland, take umbrage at anyone caught stealing at their tables. They have convincing ways of guaranteeing it never happens again. I'm sure you understand your position here."

Barinov knocked back the chilled vodka, assessed his situation, and poured himself another. He tossed that back.

"What do you want?" The man's accent was thick. His attitude, old-school.

"Lay off Doris. She's out of the gambling business. And then I need to know your moves, moment to moment, from the time you left the boat until first light, the night Luke Donato disappeared along with half a million dollars."

"I know nothing about Luke except who he worked for."

The past tense wasn't lost on Jack. He heard quickening foot falls behind him. Instead of seeing Frankie entering the dining room, Jack locked eyes with Rusty Mannuzza. The bantam cock himself, wound so tight he almost vibrated off the carpet.

"What the hell are you doing, Jack? Bracing our clients?" Rusty's hand was sliding toward his shoulder holster.

"Back from the dead." Jack grinned, twisting the knife.

Barinov stepped away from the bar. "Rusty, how was lockup?"

Rusty, who wanted to shoot Jack in the heart, couldn't stop the red from invading his face. He lit up like a Christmas bulb.

"We were having a discussion," Barinov added amicably, stepping between the two men. "Man talk. I tell you what." Barinov, who dwarfed Rusty, snaked his heavy arm around the mobster's neck and exerted some pressure. "Why don't you call the water taxi and alert my driver that I'm headed his way. I'll settle up with the cashier and surprise my wife."

The Russian pulled out a card and handed it to Jack. "Call me any time, Jack, and we'll finish our conversation. I look forward to it. I have some ideas you might find interesting."

Rusty was torn but allowed himself to be led out of the dining room by Vasily Barinov. Money talks.

Jack walked to the bar and poured himself a full glass of red. He pulled a Vicodin out of his pocket, dry-chewed it, and downed the bitter powder with wine. His back spasmed and his head pounded. Just another day at the office.

———

Doris found Jack at the bottom of the landing on B Deck. She kept her face averted from the camera and leaned in. "Thank you, Jack. I owe you. I don't know how I can ever repay you," but her eyes and proximity told a different story.

Not that Jack was immune to female flattery, especially in his bruised and burned state, but he had no interest in the unspoken offer. "Any thoughts on who came after me?"

Doris's eyes lit up as she mouthed, *Rusty*. Pleased she had something to share.

"What makes you think so?"

"Someone overheard Rusty saying he was going to kill you. You know, after you pushed him around."

"Who heard the exchange, and who was he talking to?"

"Don't know. I got the information from Ramón."

"Good work. Keep your ears open."

"Will do," and Doris ran up the stairs to the main salon and replaced Ramón on the floor.

——————

Jack caught Ramón before he could retreat to the kitchen.

"How are you feeling, Mr. Bertolino? God, it must have been awful."

"Been better."

"The camera likes you, though. I saw you on Channel Eleven."

"I appreciate that. Anything you want to share with me? Any speculation? Thoughts on who might want me *dead*?" Jack punched the word to keep Ramón on track.

The young man startled. "I did hear something."

Jack's silence goaded him on. "I heard Rusty say he was going to kill you. And make you pay for cold-cocking him."

"Really, you heard Rusty threaten my life?"

"I didn't actually hear him, but . . . I can't betray a confidence."

"That's noble, Ramón, but it's my life we're talking about here."

"I could get fired."

"I could get dead."

That seemed to carry some weight.

Jack flashed his most sincere eyes. "Your secret will be safe with me."

"Chef Ava." He whispered as if it pained him.

"And you think Ava overheard the conversation?"

"I don't know, really." Ramón looked guilt-stricken.

Jack nodded okay, letting him off the hook, and Ramón all but ran down the hallway.

———

Jack was numbed by fatigue, the hypnotic motion of the *Bella Fortuna*, and the jazz emanating from the hidden speakers in the hallway. He waited until Ramón exited the kitchen, balancing a platter of hors d'oeuvres, before walking in. This part of the investigation was like playing musical chairs. Eventually, the one person who had originated the gossip would be left standing with the truth or the fabrication. Ava's story was even more intricate than Ramón's. Rusty had been heard talking with Frankie-the-Man. After he shot Jack, execution-style, he was going to bury him at sea.

After a few lively give-and-takes, Ava finally admitted to hearing all the dirty details from Roxy and apologized for not calling him. She'd heard the story only after he made the evening news.

Jack decided to hit Frankie up next. If he corroborated the story, Roxy was off the hook. If not, Jack, would have to get to the bottom of why she was lying at Rusty's expense. With Rusty's short fuse and sociopathic inclination toward violence, it was a dangerous game to be playing.

———

Frankie-the-Man had replaced Peter at the top of the gangplank. He was lighting a new smoke off the burning embers of his last Marlboro. The big man looked morose. A real mood killer. Jack thought about the rich clientele disembarking the water taxi, ready to win fifty grand, and coming face-to-face with Frankie Downer.

"Hey, Frankie."

"Jack, I'd ask you how goes it, but I saw you tussle with Barinov on the security screens and I caught your freeway act on the tube. Don't you ever take a day off?"

"Someone tries to kill you, it's a great motivator."

"Still, you look like shit."

"Good to know. So, Frankie, there are rumors swarming like African killer bees. Did you happen to have a conversation with Rusty last week after our dustup? The meat of the discussion was Rusty's intention to blow up my shit and go Neptune Society on my body."

Frankie took a deep drag and blew the smoke out of his nose. He snorted. "Fuckin' women, they do love to gab. Never happened. I woulda let you know. I need you to solve this Luke business for me. You're no good to me dead."

"When's the next water taxi?"

"Forty-five minutes or so. After they drop off the Russian."

"What's your take on Barinov?"

"He's mobbed up. Plays it straight, but you didn't make it in Russia without protection. My guess, it followed him to L.A., where they have a presence."

This was the most articulate conversation Jack had ever had with Frankie, and he was impressed. "This a feeling or fact?"

"Remember when we were kids trying to cop weed? You could always tell who was a pot smoker. He didn't have to be high or wearing a tie-dyed shirt, you just knew."

Frankie was in a rare talkative mood. Jack thought he'd exploit the occasion. "What does the East Coast family think about Rusty's bust?"

"They think he's a jamoke, but wanna know the how and the

why. Just remember, desperate men do fucked-up things, Jack. And that's all the way down the line."

"You think he set me up?"

"I think he's going to." Frankie sucked the flame down to the filter and flicked the dead butt into the black ocean. "Your deal on the freeway . . . too much flash for the Italians."

"Thanks, Frankie."

———

Roxy watched Jack cross the room and had a glass of cabernet waiting for him on the bar. "I aim to please."

"So I hear."

Roxy's eyes crinkled into a dark smile, and Jack witnessed that flash of crazy again. "Do you always walk around with a target on your back? You're the only person anyone's talking about tonight. You pushed Luke off the twenty-four-hour news cycle."

"It's a gift."

"Let's hope one that keeps on giving. You seem to be ruffling someone's feathers."

"Any ideas?"

"Not a one. Hey, your boyfriend's back."

Jack turned in time to see Rusty stomp through the main doors, glare at Jack, and head up to the bridge.

"Have a good night," and Jack left Roxy with a twenty-dollar tip and her thoughts. Jack was certain her dreams would be rocky tonight, if she slept at all.

# Twenty-three

Jack pulled off his overcoat and tossed it on the kitchen island. He hurt too much to shrug out of his tux jacket and kept it on. He poured himself a Scotch and eased into his black leather chair. It was where he went to get quiet. To think. The burns on his shoulders radiated a solid sheet of pain. The Vicodin muted the throbbing but not enough. His face was tender, he was dead on his feet, but his mind was racing, and so here he sat.

It was an easy leap to make, Rusty for his attempted murder. Too easy. And Roxy should have seen that. Desperate people make rookie mistakes. It had taken Jack all of thirty minutes to discover where the drumbeat had started that shouted Rusty Mannuzza's name. So the question was, why the desperation?

Jack had caught her in one lie that she was aware of. Her affair with Luke aboard the *Bella Fortuna*. Unless the concierge in Mexico or the nurse up north had alerted her that he was on her trail. That was a distinct possibility but didn't answer the desperation question or lead to a definitive conclusion regarding Luke's death. Could it be as simple as the money trail?

He grabbed a yellow pad and pen, took a sip of Scotch, and started making a list of all the known facts related to Roxy and Trent's case.

He knew from the hair samples that Luke had been on board the catamaran. Roxy had denied it. Lie number two. Jack also found the receipt for a new duvet cover that was purchased two days after Luke's disappearance. If she'd killed him on board, and he'd bled on the bedding, she would have had to replace the duvet to cover her tracks. It was purely circumstantial but interesting.

And where was the body? What gossip had she used as Rusty's story? After he shot Jack, execution-style, he was going to bury him at sea. A reasonable scenario, but did she steal from real life? Jack had nothing to back it up with.

Trent had lied about being in Baja when he and Roxy were actually in Oakland. Number three. What was he doing with scuba gear in Oakland? And on the road for three days with only carry-on luggage. Roxy had been visiting her father and not at a cemetery. Lie number four. And the couple spent enough time at a luxury resort to be favored clients. That, along with supporting her father in the assisted-living facility, was clearly above their pay grade. More questions than answers.

Trent had lied about being fired from the Jet Propulsion Lab. Number five. Jack made a mental note to find out what classified papers had gone missing and created the cloud of suspicion leading to his dismissal.

Jack's son, Chris, had made an offhand statement about a possible motive for Roxy: he thought if she were harboring any ill will, it would be directed against the United States government. Roxy had said as much to Jack when he'd busted her for sleeping with Luke. She blamed the army for turning its back on her father's PTSD. Treating him with addictive drugs that had caused his suicide. That was her story, and Jack believed her.

There was no linkage Jack could find between the United States Army and Luke's disappearance. But there was something percolating just below the surface.

Jack texted Cruz, asking him to do a search of news stories from the Bay Area for the dates Roxy and Trent had been up north. Trust the impulse.

Jack thought about having another sip of Scotch and drifted off.

---

The skies opened up as a major storm assaulted the Pacific. Pounding rain, lightning, gale-force winds, and a choppy sea forced the *Bella Fortuna* to cut short the weekend trip.

Jack was unaware of the storm cell, or anything else, and woke from a dead sleep to an insistent, irritating rapping on his front door. He stretched his back as he crossed the expansive concrete floor and pulled the door open. His irritation dissolved as he looked into Angelica's green eyes, which were ringed in gray and matched the rain clouds.

She gave him an appraising once-over and delivered an emotionally charged kiss. Happy he was alive.

Jack could feel the warmth of her breasts burning through his shirt and was equally happy to be alive. Angelica pulled back breathlessly and handed him a brown bag she'd brought along.

"They're warm," she said.

"I know."

"The bagels, Jack."

"That's what I was talking about."

She swatted his arm playfully and walked in. "I called but kept getting your voicemail. I was worried and thought I'd make sure you were still among the living."

"Barely," and Jack locked the door behind her.

"Formalwear at breakfast. You are one class act."

Jack shrugged carefully out of his tux jacket and hung it on the back of a dining room chair. He grabbed the coffee beans and made short work of brewing a pot.

"I can see the damage to your face, how're the burns? And don't tell me you're fine."

"I'm fine."

Angelica caught the unmade bed, the yellow pad, pen, and one finger of Scotch in a glass, all grouped on the glass side table next to his leather chair. "And that's why you slept sitting up? The doctor told you to take it easy for a few days."

"Are you scolding me?"

"No, but you are one stubborn man."

"Guilty as charged. I get it from my mother's side of the family."

"Why don't you shower, and I'll make some breakfast . . . and keep the water off your back."

"Sounds like a plan." Jack unbuttoned his tux shirt and tossed it on his bed.

"Jesus, Jack. It looks awful." The bandages across his shoulders were stuck to his skin, and the ointment had bled through the gauze.

"And it looks better than it feels."

"Do you want me to change the dressing?"

"Doc said to give it three days, and they'll do the dirty work at Saint John's."

Jack's computer dinged and his Skype screen trilled. He was going to let it go unanswered but saw it was Chris and accepted the call. His son's worried face filled the computer screen.

"God, you look like shit, Dad. What the hell?"

"And hello to you, too."

"Are you hurt bad?"

"No."

"Yes, he is," Angelica said, walking into Jack's office. "Your father's a stubborn man."

Chris was taken aback for a moment, looking at this young, beautiful woman. "Hi . . . I'm Chris."

Angelica leaned over Jack's bare shoulder in a familiar way that shouted *relationship*. "Angelica. Pleased to meet you, Chris."

"Likewise."

The morning was full of surprises, and Jack wasn't sure he was up to the task.

"Was it Rusty?" Chris asked.

"Jury's still out, but I don't think so."

"What about—"

"Chris." Jack cut him off. "I'm dead on my feet, son. But I'm not dead. Let me call you later."

"Oh, okay."

"And thanks for checking on me. I really appreciate it."

"Okay, nice meeting you, Angelica." His son grinned and clicked off.

Angelica's smile tightened and the energy in the room chilled some. "Did you cut off the conversation because you didn't want me to hear about the case?"

"I don't think so. I ended the conversation because I didn't want to talk about the case. And because you're here and I didn't want to be rude."

Angelica wasn't sure she bought Jack's story. "Because your confidences are sacred. I'd never share them without your approval."

"I believe that. I appreciate that. But while I'm working a case and bogged down in conjecture, innuendo, and gut feelings, it isn't fair to a potential suspect or an innocent party to divulge that information with anybody until it's set in stone."

Angelica decided not to disclose the conversation she'd had with her father regarding Rusty. Jack seemed to have reached the same conclusion, so why rock the boat? "You're a smooth talker, Bertolino. I think I believe you." But she wasn't convinced. Jack had obviously discussed the case with his son. She understood the conflict of interest with her father and her father's business and chose to let it ride. "Now, about that shower. When you're clean and relaxed, call if you need help drying off."

That was an offer he was going to take her up on.

----

The meeting with Sukarno took place in his high-rise penthouse. Trent arrived first, Roxy a half hour later in her disguise.

Sukarno had new passports, identity cards, birth certificates, driver's licenses, credit cards, and enough cash for Roxy and Trent to grease palms for six months.

He handed Trent a uniform, hard hat, and laminated card hanging off a blue nylon cord. It was worn by the dockworkers and gave Trent top-level security clearance, allowing him unlimited access to Long Beach Harbor.

Roxy was given a printout of her reservations at the hotel on the *Queen Mary* using her new identity. She would be planting the first of the dirty bombs in her suite. At the specified time, she'd engage the bomb's timer, which was set on a forty-five-minute delay, text Sukarno that the mission was a go, and head for the rendezvous point.

Roxy thought of her father as she played the moves in her

head for the hundredth time. She couldn't stop the pictures from flashing. Her father in his vegetative state and the slurred voice of her commanding officer in Afghanistan. A social dinner turned ugly. The major had 150 pounds on Roxy and used his weight to pin her down, rip off her panties, and rape her. Now she was a card-carrying member of the squad, he had said.

There would be a heavy cost to America's reputation worldwide if their attack was successful, and that kept Roxy motivated. It wouldn't bring her father back or assuage her night sweats, but payback was going to be one hell of a bitch.

Trent's mission had more moving parts, and his location was harder to access. He had to ascend the farthest crane in Long Beach Harbor, eliminate the crane operator, and plant the second dirty bomb.

Sukarno would give the go-ahead to his shadow broker, Gregory, who would email the digital film of Trent's underwater expedition to the nuclear waste site, his gathering of the spent fuel rods, and the building of the dirty bomb, to three major news stations. A letter would accompany the film, alerting the media that a dirty bomb had been secreted on the *Queen Mary* in Long Beach Harbor and was ready to detonate.

The damning film, along with a separate letter, would also be delivered to the Chinese conglomerate that owned the tanker, *Hua Yong*, and its billion-dollar cargo. The Hua Yong Corp. was the same company that had bought Sukarno's technology business and manipulated his stock options, costing him millions.

A ransom demand would accompany the film, information Roxy was not privy to: one hundred million to guarantee the safety of *Hua Yong*'s cargo and container ship docked in Long Beach Harbor waiting to be unloaded. Five million to Gregory, twenty million to Trent, and seventy-five million to Sukarno. The money would be delivered to the men's Bitcoin addresses.

Once the money was wired, confirmed by the Bitcoin network, and dropped into their "wallets," the digital currency would immediately bounce to a "mixer" to further remove traceability by distributing the digital cash to a number of new addresses. The three men were the only people in the world who possessed the private keys giving them access to their personal accounts.

Instead of disengaging the bomb and fulfilling the promise of safe harbor for the Chinese tanker, Sukarno would give the go order to Trent.

With the Chinese tanker docked, Trent would trigger his bomb's timer with his cell phone, giving himself enough lead time to exit the harbor, and join Sukarno and Roxy.

The team would make their way to a waiting chopper and a short ride to Santa Monica Airport, where Sukarno's Learjet would be fueled and ready for their trip to Indonesia.

While the FBI, Coast Guard, Long Beach Bomb Squad, LBPD, SWAT, and Homeland Security descended on the *Queen Mary* and the panicked evacuation taking place, the first bomb would detonate.

Minutes later, the second bomb would blow.

Carried on the waves of the explosion, an umbrella of nuclear poison would rain down on the Chinese tanker, rendering her billion-dollar cargo useless for fifty years. All commerce at the Port of Long Beach would be disrupted for months while the EPA cleaned and contained the radioactive fallout. The economic effect on the United States would be staggering.

The attack, historic.

———

Jack walked past Oakland's Harborside pot club and got a contact high on his way to the Almar Marina. It appeared that the Motel 6, located directly behind the club, wasn't seeing a lot of action because the clientele was drifting out onto the street, hungry for johns. Jack would canvass the girls after he got a look at the boat in question.

Jack walked past the marina facilities, with power and water hookups, down the dock until he came to an older fishing trawler draped in yellow police tape.

The Oakland Marina was a solid mix of commercial fishing boats, cabin cruisers, sailing yachts, and liveaboards on vessels of every make and means. It wasn't high-class and had the earthy feel of a marina that had been in business since the early eighteen hundreds.

An old man, as weathered as the splintered dock, wearing a black watch cap and navy peacoat, limped toward Jack with a sense of purpose. "My fuckin' arthritis is kicking in" were the first raspy words out of his mouth. Jack could relate: the air was so thick with moisture, it could've been mistaken for rain.

"Evening," Jack said.

"Interesting, isn't it?"

"How so?"

"The captain was glowing like a dragonfish when they pulled him out of the water. Got caught in a net. Vietnamese fisherman thought he'd made a score. All he got was old Rafi, deader 'n a doorknob."

"You knew Rafi?"

"I know everybody."

"What'd he look like?"

"Wiry Indonesian fella. Missing some teeth."

"His name was Rafi?"

"He had a fancier name, but no one could pronounce it. Likable sort. He did some fishing, did some salvage. You gotta diversify to make a living at it. He made the papers. I talked to the bulls that were on the case."

"What did they have to say?"

"The boat was clean as a whistle. No prints. Nowhere? How's that possible?"

Jack had read the article Cruz emailed him from the *East Bay Times*. The captain had been stabbed in the back of the neck, severing his spine. But if the knife hadn't taken him, he would have died of radiation poisoning. The hospital hadn't seen anything like it in recent memory, and nobody could answer where he had come in contact with radioactive material.

Trent traveled with his scuba gear, and the time frame seemed to match their trip north. There was something about the story that had piqued Jack's interest enough to trust his instincts and take the short flight back.

"The cops were here," the old man went on, happy to have Jack's company. "The feds, the Coast Guard, and more. Everyone asking the same questions. Nobody had any answers. We live and let live down here. Nobody paid the captain any mind when he took off, or asked any questions when he didn't return."

"Where was the boat found?"

"Run aground five miles down the coast. How'd it make it down there without prints? That's what I'd like to know."

Jack was thinking the same thing.

"They towed it back yesterday, and the crews went over it in spacesuits and whatever. More action than we've seen around here in maybe ever."

"So, you didn't see what day he took off?"

"Not what time, but my check comes on Tuesdays, and when I went to cash it, the slip was empty."

That was the same day Jack had the phone conversation with Trent. Jack pulled out the photograph of Roxy and Trent. "Have you seen these people around?"

The old man grabbed the photo out of Jack's hand and held it an inch from his face. "Good-looking gal. Never seen her. I'd remember. The guy, eh, don't know. He looks like lots of guys. Can't say I've seen him, but can't say I haven't."

Jack gave the old man his card in case he thought of anything that might be of interest, walked to the end of the dock, and headed back toward the Motel 6. There were two groups of working girls, texting or playing games on their iPhones, but one woman with stringy blonde hair, standing alone, had her eyes peeled, and Jack chose her: she caught his eye and he nodded in her direction. Her languid sexuality hardened as he drew nearer.

"You a cop?"

"Retired."

"Me, too."

"Retired?"

"No, tired, been on my feet too long. You want to get comfortable?"

Her timing was impeccable and Jack laughed. "I'm good."

"I'm better. Help a girl out. I'm working my way through college."

"What's your major?"

"Sex education. Make the right moves, I'll give you an A."

Jack pulled out the photo of Roxy and Trent and handed it to her.

She had attitude but gave the photo a hard look. "You know,

all the activity lately is cutting into my bottom line. How's a girl supposed to earn a living?"

Jack pulled out a twenty and handed it to her. She flashed a withering *what the fuck* look. Jack relented, gave up another twenty that she snapped out of his hands.

"Are they in trouble?"

"Not yet."

"A couple days ago, it's possible. She wasn't a redhead. She was wearing a wig. Brunette."

"How do you know it was a wig?"

"I'm a hooker. It goes with the territory."

"Where did you see them?"

"They parked a car in the lot over there. And I noticed because when the doors swung open, I could hear them arguing. She was in his face, high-strung type, a little crazy, and he wore a smirk that set her off. I know lots of men like that. Passive-aggressive pricks. Don't take it personal."

"And the man in the photo, you're sure it was him, you could ID him if necessary?"

She nodded. "He looked like a towel head."

"Nice," Jack said.

"Oh, please, I get called worse twenty times a day. Big whoop. Yes, he looked like he was of terrorist descent. I could ID him."

Jack had just about enough of her but needed her ID. He flashed on the photo from LAX long-term parking. The man—it was assumed to be a man—wore a hoodie and dark glasses and averted his face from the camera.

It could've been Trent, but then again, it might have been Roxy. Worth taking a second look.

"What kind of car were they driving?"

"Something big. Coulda been an Explorer. They all look alike."

"My name's Jack Bertolino," and he proffered his hand.

"Cindy," and she shook with a firm bony grip. She saw Jack eyeball the track marks that makeup couldn't hide anymore. "We all have our demons."

"I'm not judging. Did you see where they went?"

"They walked past me like I was invisible, and kept walking down onto the dock. Then I lost track, or my phone rang, or I hooked up."

"If I need to get in contact with you, is there a way?"

"Jerry, who runs the 6, knows how to find me. This is my spot, though."

"Cindy, give me your cell number? If I call, it'll mean a financial windfall for you. You have my word." Jack pulled out two more twenties and again they disappeared before his fingers had spread.

Cindy dug in her purse, trading the money for a card: a nude selfie that could make a stripper blush, and a single phone number written in ballpoint. "If I don't pick up, it's because I'm working. If you call, I'll get back to you, and don't forget the windfall."

Jack gave her his card, thanked her, and headed up to the main drag, where he'd grab a cab and catch a flight home.

He made a stop at the parking lot and spoke with the attendant on duty. The lot did have a digital security camera, and after negotiations, Jack paid the man a hundred, under the table, for a download of the day in question. The video was emailed to his cell phone and forwarded to Cruz.

Jack was on a roll. Firing on all cylinders. This was the first potential break in the case. It was painting a circumstantial picture, but he could finally cobble together a conceivable scenario. A possible motive for Luke's death.

---

Jack and Nick were back at Hal's Bar & Grill. Arsinio placed a shot of Herradura Silver in front of Detective Nick Aprea, and topped off Jack's glass of cabernet, before disappearing.

"So you paid a hooker eighty dollars to identify the woman in the photograph as being Roxy, if not for the color of her hair."

"Right," Jack said, wanting to slap the silly grin off Nick's smug face.

Nick cackled. "The DA is going to have your ass."

Jack would've been loath to admit that he was second-guessing his case, but Nick had him on the ropes.

"He'd have your ass if—Oh, wait, did I tell you I had the DNA results of the illegally collected hair samples?"

Jack perked up, waiting on Nick.

"They just arrived on my computer this morning. Your call was perfect timing. I had to get out of the house, old lady's driving me nuts."

"Nick?" Jack's eyebrows were raised; he knew Nick was playing him, it was a love/hate brotherly kind of thing, and Nick understood it, too, and stifled a laugh and a not so subtle belch.

"The DA would have your ass if it weren't for the hair samples. The red hair was definitely Roxy's. The second was positive for Luke. And the third hair sample locks Trent in." Nick picked up the shot, air-toasted Jack, emptied it, and chased it with salt and citrus. Jack was doing a slow burn at this point: Nick was enjoying himself too much. "But," he finally blurted, "it turns out there was a fourth sample in the mix. It was brown but turned out to be nothing more than synthetic fiber."

"You motherfucker." But Jack's eyes were creasing into a grin. "Motherfucker."

"Yes, my friend. If the tape from the parking lot corroborates your theory, you might seriously be on to something."

*Bang.* Arsinio dropped off another shot, which Nick picked up with a flourish and drained.

Jack took a sip of his cab and savored the moment. He had a foothold. Now he needed to prove it. He had to deliver a solid enough case to stand up in a court of law.

Nick watched his good friend and felt compelled to take it a step further. "So, tell me, what do you think Luke stumbled upon to turn him into gray meat? What are they planning?"

"I don't know. But if there's radioactive material involved, potent enough to have killed the captain if not for the severed spine, what could it possibly be used for?"

"A dirty bomb?" Nick said.

"That's my thinking."

"Prove it."

"That's my plan." Jack took a sip of wine, his brain working overtime.

"What about calling in the feds?"

"They're already on it," Jack said. "They tore apart the trawler and were joined by Homeland Security, the CIA, the Coast Guard, and the cops. The FBI knows that Roxy and Trent are people of interest off the suspect list I submitted. They delivered research on both of them. Flannery fired me. They don't want my help."

"That's never stopped you before, my friend."

"And it won't stop me now."

# Twenty-four

*Day Fourteen*

Rusty Mannuzza looked worse for the wear as he stepped into Vincent Cardona's foyer. His silk suit was wrinkled, his skin pale, and he looked like he needed a shot of bourbon. Cardona was heading down the stairs as Rusty threw the deadbolt. "Hey, boss, got a minute?"

"Whadda you need?"

"So, I had a conversation with East Coast Mickey over on the yacht, and we talked about this and that, and he wouldn't have a problem with me laying into Bertolino and getting to the bottom of who the fuck he's working for. I hate the prick, and I blame him for getting popped. Out of respect, I wanted to run it by you."

Cardona spun, grabbed Rusty by the lapels, lifted him off his feet, and banged him against the gold-filigree wallpaper. The house shook like a 5.2 earthquake and his men came running out of the kitchen, guns at the ready.

"You went behind my back? You talked to the New York family before me?" Cardona delivered with deadly intention.

"I didn't mean no—"

"Shut the fuck up," he said with a strained whisper. "And youse"—he spun on his men—"get the fuck back in the kitchen."

"I'm sorry, boss," Rusty croaked, "I didn't mean no disrespect."

"Get the fuck out of my sight." And he tossed the slight man to the ground. "I'll handle Mickey myself."

Rusty scrambled to his feet and hustled down the hallway. The chastised gunman exited the back door without glancing at the men in the kitchen.

Frankie-the-Man stuck his melon head into the line of fire. "You okay, boss?"

"Shut the fuck up."

"No problem," and his head snapped back like a Warner Bros. cartoon. But no one on Cardona's crew was laughing.

---

Jack bumped fists with Mateo as he stepped off the dock and entered his boat's cabin. He placed a plastic bag on the galley counter. "I stopped by Target."

"A little upscale for you, El Jefe," Mateo said, entering the cabin.

Jack ignored him, eliciting a snort from Cruz. "Agent Hunter said Flannery was going up on our phones."

Cruz was set up at the small desk with the view of the *Bella Fortuna*. Jack handed him one burner and mugged as he handed Mateo the other.

"How was the trip?" Mateo had read Cruz's research and was up to speed.

"Someone cleaned the trawler. There were no prints, no trace of radioactivity, no sign of life."

"A ghost ship," Cruz said.

"A professional crew," Jack said. "It would've taken Roxy and Trent two weeks to clean that rusting hulk."

"They have to be connected to someone with juice," Mateo said, concerned.

"I'm going with Sukarno Lei. He's the man of the hour. He's got wealth and a solid connection to Trent.

"Mateo, I want you to stake out Sukarno and see how he spends his days. Who he rubs shoulders with. We know where he likes to spend his nights."

"I looked at the parking lot tape you sent," Cruz said. "It's definitely a Ford Explorer, rental plates; and it's a definite on Roxy and Trent, but it only puts them in the general area. It didn't carry them onto the dock. Circumstantial."

"Jesus," Jack said to Mateo. "He's starting to sound like a lawyer. I've got a positive ID from one of the local ladies of the night, works out of the Motel 6. She can take the pair onto the dock. Not onto the boat, but she did track them that far.

"And I got some interesting news from Nick last night. There was a positive DNA match for Roxy, Trent, and Luke from the samples I collected on the catamaran. But here's the kicker: there was also a hair sample that didn't match anyone."

Cruz, with youthful impatience, "And that's good because?"

"Because it wasn't human hair," Jack said. "It was synthetic. Brunette. The color of the wig Roxy wore in Oakland. So, with them dead to rights on tape and the hooker's ID, it loosely ties them to the trawler and a second possible victim. It's not enough for an arrest, but it's more than enough to keep us in the game.

"The question is, how do you bump up against radioactive material? How did Rafi get dosed? Where's the material being created?"

"So, I looked into it." Cruz never disappointed. "Let's say his gig was trafficking in nuclear material to foreign nations. The closest and only site generating nuclear power today, after San Onofre shut down, is the Diablo Canyon Power Plant. It's near Avila Beach in San Luis Obispo and the only operational facility in the state. Because the government stalled in opening a permanent storage site at Yucca Mountain in Nevada, Diablo stores spent uranium fuel rods on-site."

"You get the wrong man in the right position for a crazy price . . . ?" Jack posited.

"If they made the pickup in the boat," Mateo spun, "and things went sideways at Diablo, they could've killed the captain down there and dumped him in the ocean."

"And you're not gonna believe this," Cruz continued, "but twenty-four U.S. universities run nuclear reactors. On the West Coast, we've got Oregon State, Curtis Tech, and University of California, Irvine. All possible suppliers."

"What about hospitals and nuclear medicine?" Mateo asked.

"There are more than a few in the San Francisco area," Cruz answered.

That information silenced the crew. The case had just widened exponentially.

"One step at a time," Jack said, bringing his men back down to earth. "We know they had a Ford Explorer in Oakland, and they came home in an Uber ride. Three days on the road with only carry-on luggage and scuba gear. Where did they stop, where did they end up? Cruz, start with the Uber and work backward, it'll answer a few questions. We stay the course, tail Sukarno, Trent, and Roxy. The trio just moved to the head of the class. Rusty might want my ass, but he's not worth the time or the effort at this point. Let's do it. I've got a car to rent."

———

Vincent Cardona walked onto the bridge of the *Bella Fortuna*. It was empty except for Mickey, who was drinking an espresso, going over the abbreviated books caused by the recent storm, his reading glasses at half-mast. He looked over his cheaters and read Cardona's emotional state. Mickey, who'd been around the block and back, took the lead. "You're gonna be plenty mad when you hear what's up, but not about what you think."

"So, you're here for a week now, and you know how I think?"

"Vincent, whether you're in the loop or not is none of my concern, but in this matter, you're a blind man. Shut the fuck up and listen."

Cardona wanted to draw down on his brother-in-law but kept his counsel.

"Caroline!" Mickey shouted. "Get a cup of espresso and some biscotti for your boss. Sit down, Vincent, we got problems."

Cardona sat in one of the swiveling captain's chairs and waited for the real boss to talk.

"The Galanti brothers?"

"Yeah, so?"

"Both dead. Shot in the mouth."

"Rats?"

"Rats."

"I think we gotta find out if Jack's tied to the feds. If the brothers were dirty, it's a good bet Luke was."

Cardona rolled the potential implications around and came

up with nothing but a swirling shit storm and the onset of a migraine. He'd been played by Luke Donato, and that undermined his power base. He'd shared personal business with the rat; he'd expedited his move up the food chain. Luke made him look like a chump. He better be dead. If he wasn't, Cardona would fix it, but he still had to know where Jack's allegiance lay.

Jack was right about one thing—it was only a matter of time before the cops or the feds came snooping around looking for the body. And that was bad for business and bad for his personal safety. Cardona knew if he became a liability to the family, he was as good as dead. There was nothing on paper tying him or the family to the gambling enterprise. It was all in Caroline Boudreau's name. And their contract was written in blood.

There was no good way out of this situation. He immediately went into primal mode. Self-preservation.

"Can't blame Frankie, necessarily," Mickey said, breaking the silence, "but it deserves a conversation. No?"

Cardona's eyes narrowed, and the vein on his temple throbbed. He grabbed his cigarettes, slapped the hard pack against his meaty hand, and lipped a butt out of the pack. He lit a match and sucked in a third of the cigarette in one draw, letting the nicotine work its magic, and slowly exhaled a billowing cloud of smoke. "I need some time to think about this, Mickey. It's my crew we're talking about, here."

"Time's running out, my friend. You now got five families watching your every move. I can only do so much on your behalf. It may be time to clean house. It ain't personal. It's bottom-line, pure and simple."

"Knock, knock," Caroline said as she brought in a silver tray of espresso, biscotti, prosciutto, and melon. She put down the tray, gauged the temperature in the room, turned on her heel, and closed the door on her way out.

Cardona picked up his cell. "Frankie, yeah, I'm here with Mickey in Long Beach. C'mon down and have lunch with us. Now. I know it's early, get your ass moving."

Cardona clicked off and Mickey went back to the numbers. "Taste the biscotti," his brother-in-law said. "She buys from a good vendor."

Cardona wanted to shove the biscotti down his brother-in-law's throat. He took a cookie and said, "The vendor's mine." He dunked it in his coffee and bit his lip, breaking skin instead of cookie. "Caroline!" Cardona shouted. "Get Bertolino on the horn and tell him you've got a few things you want to run by him. *You* being the operative word. We'll all break bread together."

———

As Jack pulled into the *Bella Fortuna*'s parking lot in his rental car, a black Mustang GT coupe with blacked-out windows, his cell chirped. He parked and took the call. "Agent Hunter."

"The Boston connection. The Galanti brothers who vouched for Luke are no more."

"Both dead?"

"Bullets to the mouth. A few broken teeth, crater out the back of their skulls. The message was clear."

"Cheese eaters."

"You're a poet, Jack. It's time for you and your men to walk away."

Jack looked up from his throwaway phone. Frankie-the-Man was standing in front of his windshield, a 9mm trained on his face. Jack glanced into his rearview in time to catch Rusty's Jaguar snugged up tight, locking him in. Jack followed Frankie's dead eyes and silent nod; he was now shadowed on both sides of the rental by two of Mickey's soldiers blocking his egress. "It's too late, I've got company."

"Shit, where are you?"

Jack knew if the feds arrived on-scene, it would be a death sentence for him and his men. "I'll get back to you," he said, and he clicked off.

Frankie-the-Man gave the universal hand signal for lowering the window. Jack leaned forward, secreting his Glock under the front seat, and complied.

"Orders, Jack. Don't hold it against me."

———

Cruz watched from the safety of his perch on the cabin cruiser as Jack exited his rental and slid into the back of the Jaguar, crowded on both sides by Mickey's armed men.

Cruz leaped off the cushion and hit 999, texting Mateo. He ran up the dock, jumped into his Mini Cooper, and peeled out of the lot, talking on Bluetooth the entire way. The beep of the GPS on Rusty's Jaguar would allow him to follow at a discreet distance. Mateo was about ten minutes out, also locked into the system, heading in his direction. Cruz prayed he would arrive in time and provide sorely needed backup. He also prayed to God to give him the strength to take care of business. He was outmanned and out-gunned, and it was crazy to even think he could make a difference in the equation. But it wasn't a numbers game at play here, it was life and death. And it was Jack's life hanging in the balance.

———

The sound bleeding off Lincoln Boulevard, and the industrial businesses on either side of the body shop, masked the screams.

Jack had been hung from one of the pneumatic car lifts. Metal chains bound his wrists; wrapped with duct tape, his feet dangled off the oily concrete floor.

A single shaft of light cut through a dirt-encrusted window and lit Jack's tortured face. Pain-induced sweat dripped from his forehead and ran off his chin, drenching his shirt. Rusty would've been happy taping his big mouth shut, but they needed an answer.

Frankie-the-Man stilled Jack's body, which was spinning from the last kidney punch, and stepped back. "Let's stop this now, Jack. C'mon, man. Who the fuck is your client? Jack . . ."

Rusty got antsy, stepped in with a sawed-off piece of hose, and whipped it against the burns on Jack's shoulder. Jack's growl was pure animal, his breathing labored. "I'm gonna come looking for you, Rusty, and I'm gonna find you . . . and you won't like it."

"So, who's your contact with the FBI, big man? You were probably out there watching the day I got popped. Who's laughing now, shithead?"

"You're not smart enough to stay out of jail. And with your little hands and little feet, you'll be somebody's bitch your first night inside."

That elicited a snicker from one of Mickey's gunmen.

Rusty pulled back his arm, and the hose split Jack's skin. His scream was bloodcurdling.

Frankie slammed into Rusty with his ham hands. The slight man lost his balance and slid to one knee, staining his pant leg with black oil.

"You motherfucker," and Rusty started for Frankie while Mickey's two gunmen stood idly by, drinking from Starbucks cups.

"C'mon." Frankie's grin was deadly.

Rusty knew he couldn't go one-on-one with the big man. And if he shot Frankie, Cardona would shoot him dead. He spat on the oily floor at Frankie's feet and started toward Jack to punish him and try to save face.

"Hello! I'm here to pick up my car. Is anybody back there?" Cruz stepped into the depths of the body shop, staring at the violent tableau, freezing everyone in place.

Rusty dropped the hose, went for his gun, and was outdrawn by Cruz, who ordered, "Drop it!"

Mickey's soldiers spilled their coffee reaching for their weapons, but Mateo's appearance, ratcheting a shell into his Mossberg 500 shotgun, stopped them in their tracks. He waved Frankie back with the double barrels, ordered the men to drop their weapons, and moved across the slick floor to where Jack was hanging. He hit the red plastic button with his fist and the car lift edged down, compressed air hissing. Jack's feet touched the ground and he pulled loose from the chains, wincing as he unraveled the tape binding his ankles.

Rusty was slow to comply and Cruz fired one shot that whistled by his head. Rusty's tricked-out abalone-gripped Colt clattered to the floor.

"Frankie, we're going to need your gun," Jack said. Frankie looked relieved by this turn of events. He wheezed as he bent down and placed his 9mm on a clean spot of concrete. Jack gathered the weapons and ordered, "Everybody down, hands behind your backs."

"Bullshit, Jack," Rusty sputtered. "You're a dead man."

Jack cocked his head as if there must have been a misunderstanding, raised Rusty's Colt, and fired.

Rusty screamed and fell to the floor, a clean through-and-through thigh shot.

Mickey's men dropped to the ground and assumed the position next to Rusty, who was howling. Frankie made eye contact with Jack before lowering his 350 pounds to the cold floor. Jack read his contrition but wasn't in the mood to give absolution.

Mateo passed Jack his shotgun and bound the men's hands and ankles as if he were calf-roping.

Jack nodded a thank you to Cruz who stood as tall as his five-nine frame would allow. He looked like a giant to Jack.

One of Mickey's gunmen tried to negotiate: "You might want to give this a second—" Mateo slapped a piece of tape over his mouth and around his head before he could finish his thought.

Jack leaned toward Frankie and whispered, "Keys?"

"Back pocket," he answered sotto voce.

Jack grabbed his car keys out of Frankie's slacks, and Mateo taped his mouth.

With his torturers silenced, Jack pocketed Frankie's 9mm, dropped the rest of the weapons into a fifty-gallon drum of viscous waste oil, and led his team out of the dank body shop into the daylight.

———

Jack felt light-headed and steadied himself on the side of Mateo's BMW. He turned to his team and was at a loss for words. Every possible response felt trite. "Thank you" was all he could muster. "Cruz, head back to the boat and get your camera set up. There's going to be a lot of action the next few hours. I'll call when the dust settles."

"You've got to get to a doctor, Jack."

"One stop to make first."

Cruz slid into his Mini, powered up, and headed south.

Mateo opened the car door for Jack and waited until he eased his broken body in. "Where to, boss?"

"The *Bella Fortuna*. Time to face the lion."

Mateo peeled away from the curb.

———

Mateo pulled in to the *Bella Fortuna*'s lot and Jack was out of the car before it stopped moving. He was in obvious pain as he strode unevenly up the gangplank and passed Caroline in the main salon. She couldn't hide her horror at the bloodstains on the back of his shirt and the state he was in.

Jack sucked in a breath and glanced toward the bridge and she mouthed "Yes." He pulled Frankie's gun, took the stairs two at a time, and kicked the carved wood door open.

Cardona and Mickey turned on the intrusion and, confronted with a 9mm pointed at their heads, responded with their best studied dead eyes.

"What're you doing here, Jack?" Mickey asked.

"I'm supposed to be dead?"

"We had questions. We have a lot at stake, and you weren't forthcoming," Mickey stated as if it were business as usual.

Jack lowered his pistol, clear on who had ordered the beating. The information didn't let Cardona off the hook, and Jack decided to turn the knife some. "Your top-notch crew threw a bag over my head but didn't plug my ears. Rusty bragged that he always knew Luke was a rat, and said as much, but the bosses were too dim to listen."

That elicited the first twitch of emotion from the men.

"That's the first I heard about Luke being on the cops' payroll." Jack used *cops* instead of *feds* to cement the lie. "It still means nothing to me. I'm not interested in Luke's affiliations. I'm looking for his murderer. The rest isn't my concern."

"What do you want?" Mickey said without animus. As if talking to his gardener or pool man or the kid he paid to wash his Cadillac, not the man he'd ordered hung and beaten.

"Protection. I wouldn't talk to you, and your men couldn't beat it out of me. I won't spill to the cops. I think I'm on to something bigger than your gambling enterprise. I need some time, the run of the boat, until I get my answers. I've got enough information to shut down the *Bella Fortuna*, the Chop House, and you. Your business is safe with me as long as I stay alive and my men remain unharmed."

Jack gave them a moment to meditate on that. He knew the Mob didn't respond well to threats, but time was short and life was precious.

"I gave you my word, Cardona. You gave me yours. I came out on the short end."

Cardona bobbed his head like he was having a personal conversation with himself. He knew if Jack had made one phone call, the cops would've been all over the *Bella Fortuna* and his entire crew would be sitting in jail cells. It took some sand, he thought, comin' here like this. Cardona turned to the boss, who had the unblinking eyes of a great white. Mickey flicked three fingers and his eyebrows in a *whatever* gesture, and it was proclaimed.

Jack got to the door and turned back to the mobsters. "My guess is your boys are still at the body shop or I never would have made it onto the yacht." To Cardona he said, "You better call Peter and send him over, or Rusty's gonna bleed out."

Jack slid Frankie's 9mm into his belt and left the door swinging wide.

---

Jack found Mateo standing just inside the door of the salon cabin with his gun held at his thigh, on the ready. The two men exited and approached Caroline as they headed for the gangplank. She turned away from the security camera and whispered, "I didn't know, Jack. You've got to believe that."

Jack knew she was speaking more to Mateo than to him.

"They told me to invite you for lunch and a sit-down. I wasn't privy to anything else."

Jack had a feeling she would've made the call if she'd been in or out of the loop. For Caroline, business was business; you went along to get along in this world. He'd let Mateo sort out his own relationship with her. He trusted the man with his life.

Jack walked down the gangplank and headed for Saint John's Health Center and the verbal abuse he was in for when Dr. Stein saw his back.

# Twenty-five

Vincent Cardona watched his daughter exit the Lee Strasberg Institute in West Hollywood and jaywalk across Santa Monica Boulevard. "She's still a fuckin' New Yorker," he said to Frankie-the-Man as she ducked into the diner where they had agreed to meet. She'd sounded suspicious of the last-minute call, but that was to be expected. Trust never came easily in their relationship. She was a heartbreaker, he thought as he stepped out of the back of his limo and walked the half-block into the diner. This conversation would not help the cause.

She was seated and smiled when Cardona walked in. He bussed her cheek and slid heavily into the cracked Naugahyde booth.

"The cheeseburgers are worth eating, and the coffee is generally fresh," she said. "My scene-study class starts in a half hour, so we've got to chop-chop."

"Gimme both," Vincent said.

"Ronny, could we have two medium cheeseburgers and two cups of coffee, black, please. So, what's the occasion?"

"I just needed to talk. Some things came up, and well, so here I am."

"I'm all ears."

She wasn't going to make this easy, Cardona thought. Right down to it and all. "Okay, then."

That was as far as he got before Ronny, who worked the counter, dropped off two scalding mugs of coffee.

"Thanks, Ronny, I'm in a bit of a rush, so whatever you can do to help will be appreciated."

"Two burgers, make that cheeseburgers, on the quick!" he shouted into the kitchen as if auditioning for a part.

Cardona burned his lip on the coffee as he waited for some privacy. "Okay," he started again, and tried for a smile that came off tight. He chose his words carefully. "You're gonna hear some things that I had no control over. I hope you're old enough to understand, my business being what it is and all, that I stood up for him. After the fact, but I just wanted you to hear it from me."

The life and color drained from Angelica's face and hit Cardona like a two-by-four to the solar plexus.

"Are you talking about Jack?" she said with a cautious edge, her gaze shredding him. "Is Jack okay?"

"He'll be fine."

Angelica winced at the implication. "He'll be fine from what? What did you do to him?"

Cardona looked over the counter and saw Ronny fake-reading the newspaper. "We've got to keep our voices down. This is personal family business."

"What did you do to him?" Staccato.

"You know all about Luke Donato and his disappearance. Reason Jack's on the job." He waited for a response that didn't come. "Well, as it turns out, Luke was a rat. The guys in Boston who verified his résumé were working for the feds. We needed to find out if Jack was, you know, fronting for the feds. Because if he was, it could be very bad for business. Very detrimental for me personally. We could lose everything, and my life would be in mortal danger. So, we asked him, very polite and all, and he wasn't forthcoming."

"I'm going to ask you one more time, and I want a straight answer. What did you do to Jack?"

Cardona took another sip of coffee and welcomed the burn this time. He deserved it for what he was doing to his daughter. "A couple of my guys and a couple of Mickey's guys pulled him in to get some answers. They roughed him up a bit. And maybe Rusty got a little carried away."

Angelica's face remained frozen, but her eyes welled.

"I saw him after, and he's okay. He's all right. He's better than Rusty; Rusty took a slug to the thigh. We won't hold it against him."

A bell dinged, and Ronny appeared at the table and set the two plates of food down. "Your wish is my command." He looked at Angelica's face and rushed back behind the counter.

Angelica's gaze shifted from the cheeseburger and fries to her father. His face, blurred by her tears, appeared to melt. She looked a harsh question at him, stood, and walked out of the diner. The door jingled behind.

---

Jack wasn't surprised to see Angelica sitting in front of his door. Gossip spread at the speed of light. She had a basket on her lap. It contained a bottle of cabernet, a bottle of olive oil, and a dry aged salami. She stood as he approached, and he could read her pain and confusion.

He looked into her eyes and said, "This isn't on you. You must understand that. There are forces at work beyond your reach. You share no blame." He kissed her lightly, took the basket from her hand, keyed the door, and let her in.

"I couldn't make up my mind," she said, referring to the basket. "I didn't know what hospital you were in. I called all over town. I was so worried, I wanted to do something, and I just couldn't make up my mind."

"Thank you, I'm fine. I'm in pain, and the doctor read me the riot act, but I'm in one piece. Thank you for the care package." Jack opened the wine and poured two glasses. He swallowed a Vicodin with his; Angelica took a careful sip of hers.

"Let me see what they did to you."

"Not a good idea."

"Jack. I have to see."

Jack turned and carefully unbuttoned his shirt. Angelica pulled the shirttail up, exposing his brutal beating. His lower back was black and purpled. The dressing on his shoulder burns had been changed, but the bloodstains seeping through the bandages on his left side told a violent tale. Angelica lowered his shirt.

"What can I do for you, what can I do to help?"

"Don't slap me on the back, that'd be number one," Jack said, trying for humor, "and two, I have to sit down before I fall," he said, heading for his black leather chair. He gazed around the loft at his art and his few special possessions, thought about Mateo and Cruz, who had risked their lives to save him; his son, Chris; and then back at Angelica, who sat tentatively on the couch, fragile and beautiful. He did a quick accounting of what was important and meaningful in his life and decided he was grateful as hell to be alive.

"Is my father going down?" she asked.

"It won't be from my hand. We had an agreement in place. I stuck to my end of the bargain."

"And he turned on you."

Jack didn't deny it. "I can tell you this much. I know how these things play out. If Luke was working for the cops or the feds, and he was killed because of his affiliation . . ."

Angelica completed his thought. "My father is the first person they'll come after."

Jack nodded and took a sip of wine. His throat was dry from screaming this afternoon, and he tamped down the anger that the memory conjured in order to spare Angelica.

"He's also on a slippery slope with the New York family. Luke came in on Frankie's coattails. The Galanti brothers, out of Boston, vouched for him and already paid the price. But it was your father who elevated Luke to a position of trust. Meaning he cost the family money and reputation."

"He's been a good earner, always."

Jack didn't take offense at her familial concern. He knew she was trying to process the information. "It may not be enough. It depends how savvy he is and how he plays his hand moving forward."

"Do you think my father had Luke killed?"

"No, I don't. The cops might not see it that way. But when the money disappeared, it put your father in jeopardy. The info about the Galanti brothers just surfaced."

"Unless he discovered Luke's identity and set the brothers up."

The fragility had been replaced by strength and intellect.

"That move would have been sanctioned by the five families. A no-brainer. And the money wouldn't be in play."

"Then why is he on the hot seat?"

"Like I said, the cops probably won't see it my way. And if the feds dig in their heels, your father will spend more time in a courtroom than his restaurant. Even if the charge is tax evasion.

The pencil pushers and accountants will find a way to take him down or make his life a misery. And the New York family might worry he'll cut a deal."

Angelica took a sip of wine. Struggling with her emotions. "Why do I feel bad? Scared. Why do I care? You were brutalized today. My father and my fucking uncle were responsible for beating the man I love."

That was a first in their relationship. Jack sat a bit straighter and set off a wave of pain that nauseated him. He gripped the arms of the chair until it passed. "He's blood. You don't have to like him, or the life he leads, or what he's responsible for, but he's your father. And that complicates the picture."

Angelica walked over to the chair and gently put her hand on his cheek. It was warm and reassuring. "You shot Rusty?"

"I did."

"Good."

Jack didn't disagree. Some men deserved to get shot. Some men deserved to die.

"Let's jump on a plane, Jack. Disappear for a few years."

"Tempting. But I'm in too deep."

"And that, Jack Bertolino, is why I love you. Don't get all worried that I used the L word. You stay the course. If you hadn't, I wouldn't be alive. And if my father had killed you . . . I believe in my heart of hearts, I would have shot him myself."

"Not a comforting thought any way you play it. But thank you, I think."

Angelica's laugh was as soft and musical as rain, and it dislodged something in Jack's chest. As he tried to make sense of the feeling, the meds kicked in, and Jack fell into a deep sleep, but his dream state held no answers.

# Twenty-six

"Don't ever hang me up like that again, Jack," Agent Hunter shouted, angry as a thunderclap. "We're partnered on this. I didn't sleep last night. What happened? Where were you? Are you in one piece? What the hell?"

"Things got messy. And I'm lucky to be breathing, but here's the thing. We continue as if nothing happened. Time's running out, and if we don't get an answer soon, we never will. I want to keep pushing forward."

"You sound like hell."

"Been there and back."

"I want to see you."

It didn't sound like purely business to Jack, but he chalked it up to being groggy and suffering more than his normal pain quotient. "You already set the parameters, and things have escalated. If anyone makes us, your career is dead in the water, and Mateo and Cruz are as good as dead. The men saved my life yesterday. I'll keep you in the loop and run things by you as they turn up."

"I'm trusting you, Jack."

"Make sure your boss doesn't do an end run. If the feds come sniffing anywhere near the *Bella Fortuna* or the Chop House, it's over. And we'll never find out who killed your brother."

"Jack?"

"Christ! I'm not thinking straight. I'm sorry, Liz. That was— that was unacceptable."

All of Agent Hunter's anger dissipated upon hearing that one reality. "We're on the same page, Jack. You find my brother's killer, I'll run interference with Flannery. Whatever it takes."

"Okay, Liz."

"And Jack . . ." The hardened FBI agent kicked into gear. "Don't disappear on me again. I brought you into this game, and I can't lose anyone else on my watch."

Jack didn't know what was worse: the pain that was knifing down his spine from the burns on his shoulders, or the painful admission that he'd thoughtlessly shared.

———

"There's nobody from Cardona's gang on board," Cruz reported as Jack stepped into the cabin of his boat. "There was a constant flow yesterday, but all's quiet today except for the occasional vendor and the yacht's skeleton crew."

"I think they're going to make themselves scarce for the immediate future. They don't want anything that can tie them to the *Bella Fortuna.* I wonder where they went to get Rusty stitched up."

"Speaking of which, how are you feeling?"

"My arms are longer, my back's screaming for retribution, I'm happy to be alive, and I have you and Mateo to thank for that. Oh, and I want to exact revenge."

"The bullet to Rusty's leg didn't do it for you?"

"It was a good start. Back to you . . . how are you doing? You handled the situation like a pro, but when the high wears off, you've got to live with yourself."

"So, here's the deal," Cruz said. "I feel pretty good. I don't want to make a habit of having to save your *ass*"—eliciting a grin from Jack—"but all in all, we pulled it off. I felt like I was tested again and passed."

"With flying colors. I'll do what I can to lighten your load, but I was more than happy to see you arrive on-scene. And great entrance line—thinking on your feet—nobody knew what to make of you, and damn if you didn't show them what you were made of."

Cruz couldn't keep a smile from splitting his face. "Thanks, man. So, here's what I've got. I was able to trace Roxy and Trent's Uber van off of the date, time of drop-off, and license number from your notes. It took some fast talking—"

"Which you're a pro at."

"But I got the Uber driver on the phone, and he agreed to check his records."

"Okay?"

Cruz glanced at his yellow pad. "He picked up Trent and Roxy from an Enterprise rental agency on Venice, near Motor. I called, gave them the plate number and make I pulled off the digital tape from Oakland, and reserved the same Ford Explorer. If they didn't clean the GPS, and there's no reason to think they would, I should make short work of hacking the system, and we'll have their itinerary locked down."

"Let's head over."

Cruz fist-bumped Jack and was first off the cabin cruiser. Jack followed in his wake, feeling a sense of pride at witnessing his young associate's newly found swagger.

---

The Musso & Frank Grill was the oldest restaurant in Hollywood. It had been catering to the showbiz elite since 1919, and some of the waiters in their red tux jackets with black satin lapels and bow ties had been serving meals for thirty years.

It was why Sukarno Lei loved the place. He'd grown up on one of the two thousand islands that comprised Indonesia. His father was a white-collar worker who had provided the bare necessities, which included a public school education.

Young Sukarno's favorite recreation had been watching black-and-white Hollywood classics from the thirties and forties on a battered television set with tinfoil rabbit ears. The movies allowed the boy to spin dreams and escape into a glamorous world outside of his poor upbringing. Musso's was one of the last L.A. restaurants that kept the vibe alive.

Sukarno was ushered to a large red leather booth in the center of the smaller dining room and ordered a Grey Goose martini, dry. The walls and accent pieces around the booths were cut from dark mahogany and hammered home the old-world feel. Sukarno always requested the same booth because it offered privacy and the off chance of seeing the occasional star.

What he didn't see was Mateo walking in behind a party of four and grabbing a central stool at the well-stocked bar, where lunch could also be had. He was dressed in high-end workout clothes, a thick gold chain, and dark Persol glasses; his dark hair was gelled and pulled back tight against his scalp. He looked like a Hollywood hipster and not Mateo Vasquez.

A large beveled mirror hung behind the bar and made the room appear larger. It also allowed Mateo to capture photos with his iPhone of people sitting in the booths against the back wall, directly behind him, in the mirror's reflection.

Sukarno's drink arrived at the same time as his lunch partner, who slid into the side of the booth opposite Sukarno like a snake. The round lenses in Gregory's sunglasses were darker than his heart, and if asked to describe him, most people would draw a blank. Dark hair, darkish skin, no personal identifiers, an everyman.

There was no standing on ceremony, no warm hello; Sukarno was doing business with a stone-cold killer, and the less said the better. The less the shadow broker knew about his personal life, the more likely Sukarno was to come out of this experience alive. Alive and enriched.

Gregory was a man who could ransom a government and live to make another deal with the same country. He was known, respected, and feared in certain circles of the underworld and only took on multimillion-dollar contracts. He was already collecting a hefty retainer, Sukarno knew, because he was light two hundred K just for Gregory taking the meeting.

"You like chicken potpies? It's potpie Thursday," Sukarno said.

"No."

"So get the steak or the lamb chops."

Gregory nodded.

"You want a cocktail?"

"No."

"Iced tea's good here." Sukarno took a sip of his chilled vodka while Gregory looked at the menu.

Mateo ordered the prime rib sandwich, and when the bartender walked to the end of the bar to place the order, Mateo snapped a few digital shots of Sukarno's booth and then checked to see what he'd captured. Sukarno's guest kept his head tilted down as if he felt the presence of a security camera and didn't want a digital record of his existence.

As the waiter who'd taken their order walked away from the men's booth, Mateo went to work snapping pictures as if interested in the restaurant's architecture, until he had a series of shots that might provide a positive ID.

Sukarno started with the Caesar salad with extra anchovies, then the potpie. Gregory ordered a dozen oysters and the lamb chops, rare. They polished off their main courses, and when the coffee was poured, Sukarno pushed an iPad across the table and hit Play. The noise in the dining room had taken on a feverish pitch with the overbooked lunch crowd and became the silent movie's sound track.

The digital film that Sukarno had edited was the underwater GoPro footage Trent had shot at the nuclear waste depository, and his harvesting of the spent nuclear fuel rods. The next sequence was shot on dry land and featured the assembly of the two dirty bombs. No faces were shown, nothing site-specific, nothing that could be traced back to the team.

In all of sixty seconds Gregory could see that Sukarno had delivered as promised.

On Gregory's "We're good," the deal was struck, and the clock was ticking.

Mateo shot pictures as Gregory slid the iPad across the table and Sukarno gave his new partner a flash drive with the damning footage.

Gregory would deliver the footage to the television networks and the Chinese conglomerate he would be negotiating with.

When the hundred million was wired and the Bitcoins dropped, they would divert to the men's Bitcoin wallets, get tumbled, split, and delivered to new addresses that existed in an online world driven by mathematics and cryptographic protocols. And one of the largest terrorist attacks on U.S. soil would make history.

Mateo held the phone up and snapped one clean shot of Gregory as he pocketed the flash drive, rose from the table, and exited the restaurant.

A chill ran down Sukarno's spine as the enormity of the endeavor set in. He took a few faltering breaths, then ordered a crème brûlée, an American coffee, and the bill. He tried not to stare as Harrison Ford walked across the dining room floor, but couldn't help himself. He'd seen all the Jack Ryan films based on Tom Clancy's novels and was a huge fan.

Mateo finished his open-faced prime rib sandwich and ordered vodka rocks with lime. He went over the photo gallery and wondered what the iPad show-and-tell was all about. Yesterday's action had gotten his heart pounding; today it was all about finesse. Nothing boring about his life, he thought. He had enough money, a beautiful woman on his arm, and enough action to keep his heart rate elevated. He took a deep drink of his cocktail with satisfaction. His drink was dry and his demeanor drier. He laid cash with a healthy tip on the bar, waited until Sukarno exited onto Hollywood Boulevard, and slipped out behind him.

---

Jack and Cruz picked up the Ford Explorer at Enterprise, and it took Cruz all of thirty minutes to crack the GPS.

Cruz traced Trent and Roxy's trip from the rental company on Venice Boulevard, north to Oakland and the assisted-living facility, to a hotel, to the dock and the trawler, and then back down the coast.

They drove to the last GPS input and decided to drive into Playa Vista and fill their stomachs before trying to figure out why Roxy and Trent's last stop was on Jefferson Boulevard, in the midst of nondescript industrial buildings, because at first glance nothing caught their eyes.

———————

Vincent Cardona stared at Rusty Mannuzza, and if looks could kill, his soldier would be in a pine box instead of a hospital bed in an urgent-care facility that, for a hefty price, was happy to provide care and not file a police report for a gunshot wound.

Rusty's face was pale, and he looked diminished in size, if that was even possible, propped up with pillows and wrapped mummy-like in the hospital sheets. He was due to make a court appearance on his money-laundering charges in five days, and if it leaked that he'd been shot or been caught anywhere near a gun, his bail would be rescinded and he'd be remanded to lockup for the duration of his trial.

The incessant beeping of the monitors and fluids being pumped into the little man just irritated the boss.

"You brought this on yourself," Cardona said.

"You're fucking kidding me."

Peter was propped against the far wall and raised his eyebrows on Rusty's response. "It's the drugs talking," Peter said, trying to help.

"Ask yourself one question," Cardona said, ignoring Peter. "Did anybody else get shot?"

"No, because I was doing the heavy lifting." Rusty directed that jab at Frankie-the-Man, who was blocking the doorway. "Bertolino was ready to talk when his guys showed up."

"He was about to talk?"

"That's what I said."

"Frankie, you've been good in these circumstances. In your expert opinion, was Jack about to talk?"

"He would've gone to the grave first."

Rusty bolted up in his bed. "Fuck you. Son of a bitch," and the pain knocked him back against the pillows. One of the monitors set off a solid wail, and a nurse entered the room, gave the men the evil eye, and reset the monitor. "Time to run, gentlemen. The patient lost a lot of blood, and needs his rest," she told them.

"Two minutes," Cardona said through a tight smile.

"I'll give you all some room," Peter said, and exited with the nurse.

"You're becoming a liability, Rusty. I want you on your feet, and I don't want any more trouble. Are we clear?"

"It's my leg that's shot, not my ears."

Cardona leaned his big hand down on Rusty's bad leg and exerted pressure. Rusty bared his teeth. His face turned red as he fought the pain and stifled a groan. Cardona's big head hovered over his gunshot man. "You see, that's what I'm talking about." Cardona straightened, sucked in his gut, and left the room.

Frankie-the-Man started out and turned toward the bed. "You never know when to stop. But you're gonna learn one way or the other."

"Blow me," Rusty responded.

Frankie's eyes were lidded, his vibe deadly. "Guess it'll be the *other* way."

The big man let the intended threat fill the room like fog and joined the huddle in the hallway.

Cardona leaned into Peter and opened his stance to let Frankie in on the conversation. "Bertolino's being chased by persons unknown to us. He must be getting close to Donato or he wouldn't be on their radar screen. Take turns if you have to, but I want someone on him twenty-four/seven. I want to know who's following him and what their story is."

"What about retaliation against Jack's men?" Peter asked.

"They were just doing their job." Cardona flashed a look at Frankie that said he'd fallen short.

"And Mickey can't be too happy," Peter said.

"I'll handle Mickey. So far, he hasn't brought anything to the table except grief. Get the fuck out of here, both of ya."

# Twenty-seven

"I've got a couple things of interest," Mateo said to Jack while Cruz copied the photos from Musso & Frank off Mateo's iPhone. "Caroline suggested we look at the security tapes from the second night we were on the *Bella Fortuna*. She picked up a strange vibe from Roxy when you escorted Angelica across the gaming salon."

"The wolves are starting to eat their young," Jack said, eliciting a grin from Mateo, who'd been there and back when he was working for the Colombian drug cartels.

"Okay, here we go." Cruz started a slide show on his iPad of the photos Mateo had shot at lunch.

"Nothing of interest until now," Mateo narrated. "Any idea who the mystery man is?"

"Not a clue," Jack said.

The men watched Sukarno present something on his iPad to a dark-skinned man wearing black circular sunglasses. And then something small enough to be covered by Sukarno's hand was surreptitiously passed to the man. The only straight-on photograph that could provide a possible ID of the stranger was when lunch ended and he exited the restaurant.

"I followed Sukarno until he returned to his high-rise."

"I like their potpie," Cruz said as his stomach grumbled. "I'm picking up a heavy vibe from the dude."

"I'll forward the last shot to Agent Hunter," Jack said. "See if she can run it through their system on the QT."

"It was a wash over on Jefferson?" Mateo asked.

"The last GPS stop showed them parked on the street with Playa Vista on the left, near Whole Foods, the movie theater, and a thousand condos, and across Jefferson were a series of high-tech industrial buildings and two storage facilities. We paid Public Storage and Security Storage a visit and came up empty. No one could ID Trent or Roxy, and their names didn't match anyone renting space. I tell you what, let's print out a photo of Sukarno and run it by their desks. We might get lucky."

"I'll take care of that," Mateo said.

"Here's the digital tape Caroline wanted us to screen." The men crowded around the computer and Cruz hit Play. They could see Angelica grab a glass of champagne off a tray before giving Jack a kiss. The couple walked arm in arm past the bar, where Roxy was shaking a mixed drink. Her brow furrowed and her gaze followed the couple, which caused her to splash some of the alcohol onto the bar.

"She does look uptight," Jack mused.

"She spilled half the drink," Mateo said.

Roxy grabbed a bar towel, cleaned up, added another shot of vodka to the cocktail shaker, gave it a quick shake, and was back in command.

"Why would seeing you with Angelica rattle her?" Cruz asked.

"If she was up to something and learned for the first time I had an inside edge with the boss. I become a complication she wasn't expecting. Looks like it threw her. Good call from Caroline," Jack directed at Mateo, who nodded in agreement.

"So what are you thinking?" Mateo asked.

"Ring her up and find out who's staffed today. If Roxy's not on call, I'll pay her a visit and do some shit-stirring. I won't show my hand, just turn enough cards to put the fear of God into her."

"Let's hope she's a believer," Mateo said.

---

Jack pulled to a stop in Marina del Rey where Roxy and Trent's catamaran was docked. A colony of seagulls screamed overhead as they arced across the blue sky and landed noisily on a full Dumpster, scavenged, and fought each other for scraps. The warm sun and cool breeze made Jack forget his ever present pain. As he walked up to the security gate, he noticed movement inside the cabin of the cat. He dialed Roxy's cell number and could hear her ring tone as she picked up.

"Hello?"

"Roxy, how're you doing?"

"Not bad, Jack. Look, could we do this another time? I'm standing in line at Gelson's and—"

"Look out your window, Roxy."

Jack saw her face appear, and then, "Goddammit, Jack." Roxy stormed out of her cabin and stomped up the dock. "What the hell do you want?"

"With all the lies you've been telling, I'd think practice would make perfect. Not so much, huh? Let me in, I have a few things I want to clear up. Fifteen minutes and I'm out of your hair."

Roxy, pissed but caught off guard, turned the lock. Jack followed her onto the tight deck of the catamaran. He could almost see the heat radiating off her body.

"What?" she snapped.

Jack gazed into the cabin and took a seat on one of the plastic deck chairs. "Just wondering who you were visiting on Jefferson Boulevard."

"What the hell are you talking about?"

"I know you made a stop on Jefferson before you dropped off the Explorer after your trip north. Must have been important?"

"How so?"

"To make a stop after six hours on the road."

"Don't know what you're talking about."

"Stop fucking with me, Roxy. I know more than you think, and you're in over your head. I'm the only one who can get you out of the jam, but I need you to stop lying. You're digging yourself a deep hole."

"I'm going to the police department and filing a restraining order against you for harassment. I'm going to complain to Vincent Cardona and get you barred from the yacht."

"Good luck with that," and Jack decided to drop the bomb. "If I know you stopped on Jefferson, and I know your father's alive because I visited him at Rush Street Care"—he paused to let that sink in—"isn't it likely I'm aware of the stops you made in between?"

Roxy's pounding heart turned her face a dangerous shade of crimson. The news that Jack had been in her father's room was almost too much to bear. She couldn't talk, because she wouldn't be able to stop her voice from quavering.

Jack stepped through the opening: "You've been so busy, I'm not sure if you've stayed up on the local Oakland news?"

"Jack . . ." was all she could manage.

But Jack could see Roxy's face morphing back into the warrior. Her eyes stone-cold. The last time he'd seen that trick was when he'd arrested a crack-dealing sociopath in the Red Hook projects in Brooklyn. He decided to do a full-court press and keep her off balance.

"A ship's captain named Rafi was snagged in a fisherman's net out in the Pacific a few days after you left town. Stabbed to death."

"What's it to me?"

"He would've died anyway. Go on, ask me why."

"I'm not playing this game."

But Jack knew she would. He'd dropped enough iceberg tips to pique her interest. He stood and closed the distance, invading Roxy's personal space. "Ask me why." His tone demanding, dangerous. Roxy stood defiant. "Radiation poisoning. Interesting, huh?"

"You better have a good lawyer, Jack, because you're going to need one."

"Do I detect a chink in the armor? Don't let Trent take you down. How's your father going to survive without your visits and your infusions of cash? Do you want him to be moved to a county warehouse to die?"

"And you are aware that Trent got fired from the Jet Propulsion Lab and not that sweet coming-of-age and understanding his own limitations tale he spins?"

"I'm out of here, Jack." Roxy locked the door to the cabin, pushed past, and headed up the dock toward the parking lot.

Jack followed in her wake. "I know about the documents that went missing before JPL let Trent go."

Roxy spun and thought for a split second, then pushed the security gate open and strode out. She jumped into her Prius and silently tore out of the lot. The only sound the car made was from the spinning tires sending gravel pinging against other parked cars as she powered out of the lot.

Jack waited a few seconds and then smiled as Cruz's dark blue Mini drove past and followed Roxy.

———

Roxy pulled off Pacific Coast Highway into the south parking lot at the Annenberg Community Beach House. It was her destination of choice when she needed time and space to think things through.

She grabbed her yoga mat out of the rear of her car, bought a large coffee at Back on the Beach Café, and set off across the sand. It was late in the season for the pool crowd, and only two of the beach volleyball courts were in use.

What she didn't see was Cruz parking his Mini on the far side of the lot. After attaching a GPS locater in the wheel well of her Prius, he ordered a bacon, egg, and cheese burger, a Coke, and grabbed a seat on the view deck, where he watched Roxy kick up sand as she made her way to the ocean.

The beach house was five acres of oceanfront property that had been built in the twenties by William Randolph Hearst for Marion Davies. The wide expanse of sandy beach had views north to Malibu and south past the Santa Monica Pier all the way to the curved tip of the Palos Verdes Peninsula.

Roxy, a lone figure, sat cross-legged on her pink yoga mat and appeared to be floating on an expansive sea of white sand in front of a sky so blue it looked like a theater scrim. She felt alone and adrift in a plot that could be her ultimate undoing. She'd always been a forward-thinking woman who prided herself on having all the answers. A skill set that had allowed her to rise to the top of her platoon in the army. But at the moment, she was at a total loss.

Roxy didn't want to share what she was privy to with Trent or Sukarno until she was clear in her own mind how they should proceed. If they should proceed—or scuttle the operation.

Jack Bertolino had done a surgical mind-fuck on her. She couldn't stop the image of Jack in her father's room from replaying again and again like a scratched vinyl disc.

He'd said he had information as to why Trent was fired from JPL, and what was in the documents that had disappeared on his watch.

He'd tied the couple to the fishing trawler and knew that Rafi, the dead sea captain, would have died of radiation poisoning if the knife hadn't done the job.

If he was aware of the underwater nuclear waste depository from the JPL documents, and he suspected it was tied to the death of Rafi, and he could connect them to the trawler, why weren't they under arrest? Why hadn't Homeland Security kicked down their door and hauled them away?

He knew they'd stopped on Jefferson but didn't seem to have tied it to the storage facility.

Where is Bertolino getting his information? He's a PI and a retired inspector, she thought, answering the question herself. Roxy knew from her Google search that he had highly placed connections. Adding insult to the very real possibility of injury, he had a direct link to Vincent Cardona through Cardona's daughter. That was just about as many complications or known-unknowns needed to abort a mission.

Roxy sipped her coffee and watched a pod of porpoises break the dark whitecapped water, arcing upward, and knifing back below the surface without a splash. They looked playful. It had been years since she'd felt that free. She was fueled by hate and revenge, and it was killing her one cell at a time.

Roxy did believe her father would die without her presence, but she was ambivalent about his passing. He was already as good as dead. But she refused to allow him to be warehoused in an impersonal state-run facility.

After his first series of mini-strokes, she'd promised him that she would provide prescription opiates and help him take his own life if things ever became, well, the way they were now. In the end, she couldn't kill her own father. It was as simple and complex as that. She could not kill the man who'd brought her into the world and nurtured her. Couldn't do it.

What she could do was detonate a dirty nuclear weapon and give a hearty fuck you to the United States government for the incapacitated state her father found himself in, all the other veterans suffering from PTSD, and the emotional scars she and her fellow soldiers dealt with on a daily basis. That she could still do.

---

Jack received a call from Cruz on the road. As far as he could tell, Roxy hadn't placed any phone calls. He was on her tail, driving south on the 405, but with the Prius's tinted rear window, it was hard to tell if Roxy was even driving the car. He'd ring again when she landed. Jack pulled into the *Bella Fortuna*'s parking lot and boarded the yacht. He wanted to approach Trent before Roxy had time to muddy the waters.

Jack headed for the bridge to let Caroline know he was on board, but found Trent alone in the cabin, replacing one of the security monitors. He couldn't hide his disdain when he glanced over his shoulder and saw Jack. "Caroline's not here. She's due back at six."

"Man of the hour," Jack said, ignoring the attitude. "Were your ears burning?"

Trent finished unfastening one of the wires that attached the blown monitor to the multiscreen system. He set it down next to the opened box that contained the replacement screen. "What can I do for you, Jack? I'm on the clock."

"I guess it's the life we've chosen."

"What?"

"We're all in a hurry. All the time. Take me, for example. I'm trying to find out who killed Luke Donato. And now another body has dropped onto my radar screen.

"And what a shame about Roxy's father. I mean he's not dead, he's not the second body I'm talking about, but he is stroked out."

Trent's face remained placid as he tried to process the new information. Jack's discovery of Roxy's father wasn't a concern. But the second body? Could he have made the leap? "You know, Roxy's trouble dealing with her father's attempted suicide is none of your fucking business. It's personal, a family matter."

Jack had him on the ropes. "I tracked your route from Rush Street Care to the trawler." He thrust his hand up to stop the obvious question and give the knife a sharp turn: "I'm just good at what I do. And then I learned from Roxy that you hadn't been keeping up with your current events."

"You lost me, Jack."

"No, I've got you. They pulled Rafi's body out of the water a few days after you left Oakland. And the mystery, which Roxy indicated you might be able to solve, was how a man who died of a knife wound could end up with enough radiation poisoning in his system to kill him a second time."

Trent listened with a tight smirk. "Jack, I don't know a Rafi. I don't have a clue as to what you're talking about."

"Good one," Jack said, enjoying himself now. "Here's the thing, you won't be the first man to be taken down by a woman. But in the end, it'll hurt just as bad.

"I asked myself how you hooked up with Rafi. Came up empty until I read in the paper that he was Indonesian. And your mentor, Sukarno Lei, is . . . bam, that's right, Indonesian. Coincidence? I think not. Why don't you explain?" Jack's tone turned harsh.

"I've got work to do. I've wasted enough time listening to your shit."

"Roxy let it spill that you rent storage space at Security Storage on Jefferson. Do you mind if I take a look at your unit? I'm thinking of renting space there myself." Trent was about to respond, but Jack pressed, "I'd cut her some slack, she didn't mean to give up the location. She got flustered and couldn't answer why you'd make a stop on Jefferson after the drive from Oakland. Your rental drop-off was on Venice, just off the 405. Jefferson's obviously out of the way. Maybe you can make sense of it?"

Trent stood, grabbed the burned-out monitor, and started walking toward the door. Jack blocked his egress.

"Get out of my way," Trent challenged, the pulsing vein on his temple threatening to burst. "I'll knock you down, and you won't get up."

"Don't take this grin as a put-down, but really? I'm just getting warmed up."

Trent laid the monitor on the table and took a menacing step forward.

"Jack, you son of a bitch," said Frankie-the-Man, standing at the top of the stairs. "What the fuck're you doing on the yacht in the middle of the afternoon? And Trent, you should take a red. You look a little"—Frankie searched for a word—"out of your league?" and he entered the bridge.

"Getting behind on my work," Trent said, trying to appear in control. "I really don't have time to socialize, and Jack was just leaving."

"I'm sure he doesn't need any help getting off the boat. Are we clear?" Frankie-the-Man's eyes drilled Trent's.

"As a bell."

"Good, now get the fuck outta here. I like seeing the dedication of my, you know, employees. Don't let me stop you."

Trent picked up the blown monitor and headed out, avoiding eye contact.

Frankie looked at Jack and shook his head. "You should be, uh, takin' it easy. You gotta be in a world of pain."

"I've had better days. And you just happened to stop by . . . ?"

"Making the rounds. Protecting our interests."

"Good to know I made the cut."

"A man should only have to prove himself once. But hell, what do I know."

"More than you let on, it seems."

"Whatever," Frankie replied, brushing off the compliment. "So, you're done here for now?" The big man lowered his voice. "Is he dirty?" referring to Trent.

"As soon as I know, you'll all know. Oh." Jack pulled Frankie's 9mm from the back of his belt.

The big man's face creased into a rare grin. "I felt naked without it."

"I do what I can." And Jack headed out. He planned to set up shop on his boat and see if Trent hightailed it or had any surprise visitors.

# Twenty-eight

Jack had spent enough time with liars, killers, and thieves to last a lifetime. He knew he was closing in on an end game. Something major was going down, and he believed Luke had stumbled onto it and it had cost him his life. Jack felt he had some time to sort things out. He'd put the major players on notice, and that should reap rewards in the next few days.

Tonight he wanted to ease his back that was screaming with pain, his brain that was on overload, and spend time with someone he cared about.

There was no action on the *Bella Fortuna* except for Mateo's; he had just arrived with a bottle of wine in hand. Jack was fairly sure his friend winked before heading up the gangplank. He'd get a report in the morning. Jack locked the Cutwater 28, making sure Cruz would keep an eye on Roxy and Trent. He called Angelica, who said she'd stop by after a workshop she'd committed to, and he headed over to the Hinano Café for a one-on-one with Agent Hunter. It was time to set caution aside and use her resources to full advantage.

———

Agent Liz Hunter was dressed in civilian clothes—boots, jeans, a pale blue work shirt, mirrored sunglasses—and she still outclassed the café's clientele. A stone's throw from the pier, the Hinano was a comfortable dive that serviced Venice locals. Pitchers of beer and rolled eyes if you ordered anything fancier. Sawdust on the floors and the sound of pool balls colliding fought the aging jukebox for airtime. And the tables in the back provided just enough privacy for a clandestine conversation.

Liz, first to arrive, grabbed a table, ordered a pitcher of draft, and sat facing the door. When Jack walked in, she took notice of his wince as he lowered himself onto the straight-backed wooden chair.

"How bad is it?" she asked.

"It could've been worse. Mateo and Cruz changed the odds in the room."

"You've got a good team."

"They earned their paychecks."

Liz glanced at her surroundings. "You know how to spoil a girl."

"Only the best for the feds."

Liz poured two glasses of beer, pushed one in front of Jack, and settled in. "I'm running the head shot you texted me through ViCAP, and I'm waiting on results. If there's enough intel, we could do a network analysis, but then we're talking about alerting the troops, and I'm on Flannery's shit list. He suspects I'm crossing company lines but hasn't been able to nail me."

"Let's keep it that way. If it blows up on us, my men and I could be out of the play permanently. I've got scar tissue for my time in, but Cardona has granted me a short reprieve."

"Big of him."

"He's all heart. But the clock's ticking, and I need some answers. It's all tied to the *Bella Fortuna*. That's the nexus, and I can't exert pressure if I'm off the case or dead."

"Let's get down to it, Jack. It's all about trust now. We live or die together on this one. It's time to pony up."

Jack stared at his own reflection in Hunter's mirrored lenses. She read his expression and took off her shades. One less wall. He searched her eyes for the lie and came up empty.

"Paint me a scenario, Jack. Facts, gut feelings, the works. Maybe I can fill in some of the gaps."

Jack took a long pull of beer and a handful of popcorn. What Liz was asking for was an exercise in trust. But there were real lives at stake. He decided to leap off the high board and have faith there was water in the pool.

"Broad strokes," Jack said, and laid out the map as he saw it. "Luke had an affair with Roxy. I think he was taking one for the team, although he was well loved on the yacht. That was literally and figuratively. Your brother loved the ladies, and it was reciprocated."

That elicited a wistful smile from Hunter.

"The principal suspects at this point are Roxy, Trent, and Sukarno. I've caught Roxy and Trent in multiple lies, and they keep digging themselves deeper and deeper holes."

"What are they after?"

"I don't think money's the motive for Luke's disappearance, but it's still on the table. And if I'm correct, I think that lets the Russian off the hook. He was running a gambling scam, stealing from the Mob, but I don't think he killed Luke."

Jack took a sip of beer, getting his thoughts in order. "This is all speculation. I think the three of them are involved in a deal using radioactive material, or may be plotting an event utilizing or selling nuclear material of some sort, and Luke was on to them. He didn't have enough information to share his intel without jeopardizing the undercover operation, but when his suspicions were discovered, it was serious enough to take him out."

That sent an uncontrollable quiver through Hunter's body. She took a swallow of beer to wet her dry mouth. "How could they get their hands on fissionable materials?"

"Good question. And I can't prove they have." Jack took her through his trip to Baja and then to Oakland. "I tracked their movements off the coordinates you delivered." He went on, "Trent lied about their travel plans; Roxy lied about the affair, lied about Luke being on her catamaran, lied when she told me her father—a retired vet with PTSD—mustered out of the army, hit the skids, and committed suicide. I traced him to an advanced-care facility in Oakland. Her father's in a coma-like state after suffering a major stroke from the suicide attempt, but his heart's still beating. She blames the government and the army for his mistreatment and vegetative state. She said as much when I caught her in the lie about her affair with Luke. That gives her a possible motive if they're planning an attack. Her father's health care is astronomical, and that keeps money a strong second.

"I trailed the pair to a fishing trawler docked at a marina in Oakland. I can't put them on the boat, but I have them dead to rights walking toward the dock the night the boat went missing. Roxy's wearing a brown wig, and I found that same brown synthetic material along with Trent and Luke's hair in the catamaran.

"The captain of the trawler was pulled out of the water in a fishing net a few days after Roxy and Trent left town."

"How'd he die?"

"A knife wound to the neck. But the autopsy revealed an anomaly: if the stabbing hadn't killed him, the man would've died of radiation poisoning."

"Do we know where he got infected?"

"Not a clue."

"Where'd they find the boat?"

"Scuttled on the shore five miles south of Oakland."

"Huh." Hunter took a swig of beer, letting that information percolate. "I didn't get much of a feel for Trent off his bio," she finally said. "A Saudi national whose parents were killed in a terrorist attack when he was, I think, eight. Emigrated to the U.S., raised by his aunt and uncle in Philadelphia. Became a citizen when he turned eighteen and changed his name from Omar Khan to Trent Peters. Go figure. The kid was a fully assimilated high achiever, UCLA and then the Jet Propulsion Lab. No police record, no known mosque affiliations, no red flags. He's not on any FBI or international watch lists."

"He's intelligent and slick, and when I pushed him, he was ready to push back," Jack said. "He lied about his itinerary and lied to me about his history at JPL. He was let go under suspicious circumstances about the same time classified documents went missing. If he's not radicalized, who knows what his motive is. The documents might answer that. I could use your help."

"I'll try. I can't promise anything. It would be difficult even if Flannery were on board."

"Sukarno is the biggest mystery. Why would a man who seems to have it all get involved with the likes of Roxy and Trent?"

"Trent's an engineer. Technical expertise?"

"As in bomb building? Or connections to sell the nuclear material on the black market?"

"We're looking at possible prison time if this goes sideways on us," Hunter said.

"I'd be worried about not contacting Homeland Security at this point in the game, but by the time I arrived, they were all over the trawler, along with the feds, the cops, and the Coast Guard. They're already on the case. I'm surprised it hasn't crossed your desk. And Flannigan was copied on my initial interest in Roxy and Trent through you. I'm just an independent contractor trying to solve a murder."

"I just lost my appetite," Hunter said.

"Have some popcorn. I rattled Roxy's and Trent's cages today. Played one against the other. If I did my job, it should set something in motion."

"What are your plans?"

"We have surveillance on Roxy and Trent and a GPS locator on Roxy's Prius, the couple's only car. Trent Ubers it if the car's being used. Sukarno Lei flew up to Portland for a tech convention but scheduled a cabin on the *Bella Fortuna* for the weekend. I'll be on board, keeping an eye out. If anything goes down, I'll let you call in the troops and give you credit for building the case and the arrest."

---

Roxy and Trent walked on the granite-particle meandering path in the Pacific Palisades. The trees were old-growth and lush, the Pacific sparkled over their shoulders, and the passersby were multinational, multiethnic, and relaxed. The pair could have been discussing a Pilates class; instead, they were plotting a terrorist attack.

Sukarno had hatched the plan and then cut a side deal with

Trent, using his wealth, business savvy, and connections to alter the tactics and fulfill his own ambitions.

Trent, motivated by greed and anger, was all in.

Retribution and an unyielding burning in her gut that couldn't be vanquished drove Roxy.

They were better business partners than lovers, but their chemistry worked on both levels. Roxy coordinated logistics; Trent had the technical ability to make an abstraction a reality.

Trent devised a secret play for the *Bella Fortuna* on D-day. Payback for the wiseguys who treated him like a hired hand. Because of the potential loss of life, Roxy never would have signed on. Trent was unfazed. His surprise move would support their plot, guaranteeing his payday.

The warm spring air was spiked with salt and the pungent smell of eucalyptus. The proximity to other mortals forced civility, which was why Trent had chosen the location.

"When you ask a question worthy of a response," Roxy said, her eyes hidden behind dark sunglasses, "we can continue."

"My guess, and I won't hold it against you, is that Bertolino was fishing, it rattled you, and you gave up Security Storage."

"Don't be naive. He's a master of misdirection and used half-truths against us both. Divide and conquer. And he sucked you in."

"He made a good case."

"And you're a horse's ass who better get some backbone or you'll melt away."

A homeless man sitting on a soiled blanket near the path reached a dirty hand toward the couple. He mumbled something under his breath in a language only he understood, and they looked through him, rendering him invisible, as they passed.

"If Jack is sure about the underwater nukes from reading the

JPL docs he claimed you stole," Roxy said, "and he can link us to the trawler and through Sukarno to Rafi's death and radiation poisoning, why the hell aren't we under arrest? Why haven't the FBI and Homeland Security dragged us away?"

There was no easy answer, and Trent had to concentrate, because every word had life-and-death implications. "He has enough information to feel confident that he's headed in the right direction, and he's obviously building a case, but it's built on half-truths. You're right, he doesn't have enough to drop the hammer and call in the feds. His focus is split, trying to discover who killed Luke. By the time he works it out, we'll be on an island in Indonesia."

"I'll die if I have to," Roxy said, devoid of emotion. "But it's not my first choice."

"I don't plan on dying or letting you die. This isn't a suicide mission."

Roxy stopped, grabbed Trent by the shoulders, and stared into his eyes. "We could start the clock, we could delay, or we could walk away."

"Gregory is on board. Sukarno has everybody in place for our exit strategy. The clock is set. The plan is already in motion."

"No more questions, Trent. Trust is what keeps you alive on the battlefield."

"No more questions. I was wrong."

They continued walking until the foliage opened, revealing the sun-drenched Pacific reflecting shards of silver capping the dark blue chop.

Trent stopped and put his arms around Roxy. "Are we all in?"

Roxy gave that serious thought before answering. "There's nothing to tie us to the storage room, nothing to tie us to Rafi and the trawler except proximity; all the rest can be chalked up to conjecture and an active mind. It's not a crime in America to lie to a PI."

"Are we all in?"

"We're all in."

"Good girl."

"Don't call me *girl* or I'll cut your balls off."

"Let's make history."

Trent leaned in to kiss Roxy and she bit his lip and drew blood. Trent fought the urge to slap her, seeing his future swirl into the ether because of an ego-driven moment.

"You're my queen."

"Now you're talking. Let's make history."

# Twenty-nine

The four landlines in his loft were ringing as one when Jack opened his front door. He grabbed the closest phone moments before it went to voicemail and wished he'd been a few seconds late.

His ex-wife, Jeannine, was in a froth, and Jack asked her to hold the line. He placed the receiver on the kitchen island, popped a Vicodin and two Excedrin, and poured a healthy glass of wine. His body needed all the bolstering that chemistry, and the grape, could provide.

"Jeannine, how's Jeremy?"

"Oh, Jack, are you developing a sense of humor? I'd let it go, humor is something you're born with."

"As always, a pleasure to speak with you," and Jack could hear his ex-wife shouting as he held the receiver at arm's length, inching toward the cradle. Pay now, pay later. He second-guessed himself and continued the call. "What's up, Jeannine? I just got home."

"It's about your son. Do you have time for him?"

Jeannine called Chris Jack's son, in the singular, when she was worried.

"Okay, shoot."

"That's what I'm worried about."

Jeannine was the reigning queen of the non sequitur. "Let's bring the conversation into focus. What are you worried about?"

"I think our boy wants to quit Stanford, walk away from his baseball scholarship, and become a cop."

"Huh?"

"Deep, Jack. That's all you can come up with?"

Jack tamped down his reaction to his ex's sarcasm because no good could come from an emotional reaction. "Did he talk to you about changing majors?"

"Damn you, Jack. If you knew, why didn't you call me?"

"Because I thought stalking killers would be more uplifting." Maybe Jeannine was right and he wasn't funny. Can't kill a guy for trying, he thought.

"A cop!" she said, ignoring the dig. "What kind of life is that?"

Jack, who had spent twenty-five years on the NYPD, working his way up from undercover narcotics detective to inspector, took her attack in stride. "It paid for a nice house, food, good schools."

"Do I now have to spend my elder years worrying about my son? You weren't enough? Twenty-three years wondering when I'd get that knock on the door and learn you'd been shot dead in some crack house?"

Jack's plan had been to spend the night with someone he cared about and ease his load, and the gods were laughing.

But times like these, when Jeannine was wound tight worrying about their boy, evoked distant memories of the love they once shared and propelled him to higher ground. "He's been talking around an interest in criminal justice. I'm not sure how far it will go, but if we're not his support system, he'll do it to spite us. I think he's struggling with the team and might be looking for an excuse to walk away."

"Oh, no, Jack."

"I might be reading too much into the conversation I had with him, but pressure from his parents is the last thing he needs."

Jack could read the silence on the other end of the line. Jeannine was processing what she had just heard, and she generally came to a sane, thoughtful conclusion.

"It's so hard."

"I know."

"I want to help, but it will just drive him away."

"I agree with you."

"Are you saying that to placate me and get off the phone?"

"You're a good mother, and I agree with you. You raised a strong young man, and whatever his decision, he'll make the correct one and make us proud."

"Damn you, Jack. I promised myself I wouldn't cry. And Jeremy is a horse's ass, and he agrees with you. He learned his lesson trying to interfere in Chris's life."

"Send my best."

"Oh, Jack."

"Good night," and Jack hung up, so fatigued he hardly made it to the comfort of his black leather chair before his eyes closed and he drifted off.

*A beautiful woman's face appeared out of the gray and white fur of a massive, Gulliver-sized Irish wolfhound. She eased herself down the dog's side hand over hand, gripping the monster's thick hair, and dropped lightly to the ground.*

*She turned to Jack and said simply, "I'm a queen."*

*Jack agreed, "You are a queen."*

A sharp rap on the door woke him out of a disconcerting REM moment. He shook his head and groaned as he lifted himself out of the chair and opened the door for Angelica Marie Cardona. The strange dream lingered but disappeared with the touch of her lips.

"I brought Chinese," she said, handing the bags to Jack and shrugging out of her jacket. "I stopped at Twin Dragon on my way across town. Are you in pain?"

"Not anymore."

Angelica liked that answer, tossed him a set of chopsticks, and started pulling cartons out of the bags. Jack poured the wine, and they ate standing up at the kitchen island.

"How was the showcase?" he asked.

"Spotty. You ever get the feeling everyone in Hollywood thinks they can be a thespian? Oh, I could play that role. Right. It's not that easy, and tonight proved it. You can study and have all the technique in the world, but if acting isn't in your DNA, you should find a new way to earn a living, because talent can't be taught."

Maybe Jeannine was right about him and comedy, Jack thought. "Sorry I missed it."

Angelica swatted Jack in the shoulder and then, "Oh my God, I'm sorry."

"I'm good, pass me the Kung Pao?" Jack scooped a few pieces of chicken into his mouth and washed it down with cabernet. "I was hungry, I fell asleep without eating."

"I could tell. About the sleeping."

"How are you getting on in class?"

"It's as much about therapy as anything else. Inhabiting other characters and learning more about my emotional limitations and myself."

"I role-played out on the street when I was doing undercover narcotics work. You know, to get over on the dealers. They weren't the most trusting characters in the world, and it felt good when they bought my act and we executed a clean bust."

"I can relate. There are times when I'm in the moment, in the zone, and time stands still." She pierced a steamed dumpling, and it flipped off the chopsticks inches from her mouth, bouncing off the island onto the floor.

"Three points," Jack said, grimacing as he grabbed it and tossed it into the sink.

"My shrink thinks I should stop seeing you." She took a sip of wine, grinning shyly over the rim of the glass.

"Aren't you supposed to keep what you discuss in a session private?"

"He's not a priest, Jack."

"Good point."

"Have you ever been?" The grin was gone, and Jack knew it wasn't the time for a glib response. She'd probably spent the drive over trying to figure out how to approach this conversation, and Jack wasn't going to take it lightly.

"Shrink?"

"I know you've been to confession, Jack."

"Yeah, I went through mandatory counseling after an OIS. An officer-involved shooting. It was short-term, routine. They protected my confidentiality and I did what I had to do."

"Did it help?"

"They thought so."

Angelica took another sip of wine, and Jack took her lead, drained his, and refilled.

"Ever feel any guilt?"

"I live with guilt. About not being there for my son, mistakes I've made and wish I could undo. But not about the shootings.

The men I killed are better off dead. Or I found myself in a kill-or-be-killed situation."

"You know who you sound like?"

"Please don't go there. Or I'll be forced to put you over my knee, and with my back, you could probably take me."

"Hmmm," she said. "I only ask one thing from you."

"Lay it on me."

"Take a sip of wine."

"Oh, boy."

"No one knows what I've lived through better than you and my shrink. Trust is ephemeral. I had it, I lost it, I was afraid I'd never get it back. This is the first time, in what seems like forever, I've let anyone touch me. And I like it. All I ask of you in return is honesty. Don't lie to me. If I become too hot to handle, or too crazy, or too anything, respect me enough to be honest. Man up and tell me the truth. I have the strength to deal with that. I don't think I could handle a lie." They both sipped their wine. "A lie might be a shooting offense."

Jack's eyes narrowed but crinkled into a smile. He did look hard to see if it was black humor or a threat. Angelica's laugh, light, strong, and reassuring, put that question to rest.

"You've got my word," he said.

Other than putting himself in the line of fire opposite the full weight of the United States government, this might be the biggest challenge he'd ever faced. But the strength of this beautiful woman's honesty left him feeling light-headed, and lighthearted.

———

Peter Maniacci had grabbed a perfect parking spot in front of designer James Perse's corporate headquarters on Glencoe with a bird's-eye view of Jack's loft. He checked his watch and at midnight, straight up, saw a shadowed figure lowering the blinds.

Good to go, he thought. He pulled a bottle of wine out of the goodie bag his French girlfriend had prepared, unscrewed the top, and poured a healthy glass of red into a plastic cup. He took a long sip, savoring the flavor. No hurry, because he was in for the long haul. He pulled a piece off a baguette and wrapped it around a stick of provolone.

He'd cut cards with Frankie-the-Man, come up with a deuce, and drawn the night shift. He pulled out his phone, setting the alarm for six a.m. That would give him enough time to walk up the block for a cup of coffee and be back in time to catch Jack's movements.

He drank some more wine, pulled up Snapchat on his phone, and counted his blessings. His girl had sent a sext along with the care package to keep Peter entertained in the wee hours. Life was good.

With Rusty on the outs with Cardona and the New York family, Peter would now be stepping forward and getting a long-deserved promotion—if he didn't mess up. And with everything to live for, for the first time in his life, failure was not in his playbook.

# Thirty

Peter Maniacci's hair was greasy, and the long strands were haphazardly hand-combed off his face. His beard was dark, his eyes bloodshot, and the strong coffee tasted like the elixir of life. He was a hundred feet from his car when Jack drove out of the parking structure and made a left onto Glencoe.

"What the fuck, it's only—" Peter dropped the coffee, and as he sprinted toward his car, a gray government-issue sedan powered by, following in Jack's exhaust.

"Holy shit." Peter leaped into the car and tore after them. The gray sedan was two vehicles behind Jack and forced to stop as a car waited to make a left onto Beach Drive. Jack was the first to pull away and hung a right onto Washington Boulevard. Before the sedan could follow at a safe distance, Peter hit the gas, screamed dangerously fast up the turning lane, slammed on the brakes, and went into a power spin, coming to a chattering stop directly in front of the sedan, in the far lane, blocking their egress.

Peter popped the hood and leaped out of the car, staring at

his engine, as two burly men in suits walked menacingly in his direction.

"Son of a bitch, my car died and my wheel locked," Peter said, putting on his best act. "I hit the brakes, and holy shit! Are you guys all right? I think we just dodged a bullet." He wondered if that was the right choice of words.

"Move your car, now."

"Don't I wish?"

Cars were honking and traffic was stacking up with irate early morning commuters.

The men took another step closer. "Move your vehicle or you're under arrest."

Peter didn't doubt the men were feds or cops, and so, "I can't promise anything." He jumped into his car, made a show of pumping the gas, turned the key, and when it fired up, he raised his hands as if a miracle had just occurred. He backed up and waved to the feds as he pulled slowly to the curb.

The gray sedan sped down the half-block and executed a tire-squealing slide onto Washington.

Peter was breathing heavily as he uncapped the dregs of the wine and drained it. He pulled out his phone and dialed Jack.

"Yeah?"

"Trade in your rental."

"What?"

"Your shit list seems to be growing, Jack. You got some government boys on your tail. I slowed them down, but they're tearing up Washington. Who's your rental company?"

"Enterprise, on Venice. I owe you, Peter."

"Big-time," he said to a dial tone.

Jack swung a hard left onto Beethoven, heading for Avis.

---

Mateo struck out at Public Storage, but then he showed Sukarno's photo to the woman behind the desk at Security Storage. Joan was African-American, in her forties, with wedge-cut brown hair that sat just below her jawline. She gave him an appraising look, trusted what she saw, and gave him the nod.

"If I'm not mistaken, that's Mr. Setiawan."

"Really? Oh, good, I'm supposed to drop off a package, and I was worried I read his text wrong."

"Well, you certainly might have." The woman appeared happy to have someone to talk to. "Mr. Setiawan closed his account last night and moved out after hours. I wasn't on duty, but I saw the invoice this morning. Paid in full until the end of the month. You're not looking to rent a space yourself, are you?"

"You know, I was thinking about it," Mateo said, and Joan's eyes brightened. "Would it be possible for me to see the unit?"

"You may, and if you sign the lease today, I can give you a free month on top of the three weeks Mr. Setiawan paid for. That gives you plenty of time to move your things. We also have a truck at your disposal to help with the move if you need. I can coordinate everything."

"You are accommodating," Mateo said.

"I'll take you back there myself." Joan locked the front door and rotated the red hands on the paper clock that announced she'd return in fifteen minutes. Joan walked him through a door in the back of the lobby that led to the outside units. They were well maintained in neat rows, corrugated stainless-steel roll-up doors, large inset locks, and an eight-foot solid metal fence topped with concertina wire that enclosed the property, with night access to cardholders only.

"I'll make any excuse to get out of the office, the sun feels so warm." Joan walked a few steps with her eyes closed, but when she opened them, she was standing alone.

Mateo was behind her, looking at the roofline, where the security cameras were spaced every thirty feet or so. It looked as if four of the camera lenses providing video coverage for this row of units had been blacked out. He caught up with Joan, and when they arrived at unit 46, "Here it is," she said proudly. Mateo easily rolled the heavy door up. "I've never seen anything like it," Joan said.

The three-hundred-square-foot room was spotless. It smelled like bleach, and there was a new coat of white paint on the walls.

"It's so clean," she went on. "No one leaves a unit this clean. Well, what do you think?"

"I have a strange request."

"Really," she said, not sure where the conversation was headed.

"Could you please check the security tape for last night?"

"Why on earth?"

"I'm not sure, but it looks like someone tampered with the cameras."

"Oh my God, nobody reported anything missing, uh, I should call the manager first."

"Joan, just a peek. Then we'll know if there's any reason to worry the manager."

Joan hightailed it to the office and into the back room. Mateo stood by her desk until he heard Joan say, "Oh my God!"

Mateo stepped into the room in time to see a blacked-out

screen on one of the multiple monitors. "Could you roll it back to just before it goes to black, and maybe we can get some idea of how it happened?"

"Oh, I don't know."

"Joan, it'll make you look sharper with management if you've discovered how it occurred and can give a concise report."

"You think so?"

Mateo flashed his smoldering eyes, nodded with concern, and Joan complied, berating herself for being so damn easy. She rewound the tape for fifteen seconds, and a night shot appeared.

"Let's stop here and hit Play," he said casually.

Security spots created pools of amber light. The picture was still for a moment, and then a shadow seemed to enter the frame and a dark hooded figure made his way up the aisle. His face was obscured as he methodically blacked out the cameras with spray paint in Sukarno's row of storage spaces.

"We've never had a problem like this before."

"I'd report it, all right, but I wouldn't worry about it, Joan. It doesn't look like anything's out of place, and somebody saved the company some money in unit 46. The security company can change the lenses on the cameras, and insurance should cover the cost."

"Why on earth would somebody do such a thing?"

"They might have been planning a robbery, but you foiled their plot. I'd suggest you get a security guard for a few nights. And it would be smart to check the camera that covered the outside gate."

"Good idea." Joan switched to another screen, hit Rewind, and stopped when the night scene appeared. She hit Play and the same dark shadow entered the frame, and the screen went black. "My, my," she said, trying to make sense out of the situation.

Mateo knew the cleaning crew were professionals, probably the same team who cleaned the fishing trawler up in Oakland. "Could I have one of your cards?" he asked. "I'll call when I've made a decision about the unit."

Joan flipped a card out of her holder like a blackjack dealer.

Mateo felt a slight pang of guilt manipulating the woman, but it was for a worthy cause. Jack had been up to his neck in alligators on cases they'd worked in the past, but never from so many directions at once. The Mob, the feds, the men who'd tried to burn him alive, and this morning the guys in the government-issue sedan. It could've been Homeland Security or the cops or the CIA, for that matter.

Mateo was a loyal friend. Jack had saved his life, after all, kept him out of the big house for a twenty-year stretch, and that was money in the bank. As far as Mateo was concerned. He'd have Jack's back until they were too old to remember why.

"Thank you, Joan. I'll get back to you. Call your manager now, you might get a raise for being so observant."

Joan was all business. She grabbed the landline and was talking in hushed tones as Mateo stepped into the sunlight and called Jack's cell to relay Sukarno's alias and late-night housecleaning.

———

Agent Liz Hunter was in her office, printing a copy of the ViCAP report Jack had requested, when her phone rang and she was summoned. From the tone of Flannery's voice, she knew she was in deep trouble. She racked her brain to ascertain where she'd messed up and decided she'd been made in the café in Venice talking with Jack, consorting with the enemy.

Liz folded the report and slid it into her back pocket, checked her hair in a small mirror she kept in her desk, and mumbled "Shit" as she took the long walk down the hallway.

Special Agent Ted Flannery was seated at his desk and backlit by the California haze that streamed through his window on the seventeenth floor of the Federal Building. The shadows couldn't hide his physical state. He looked five years older; a patch of dry skin flaking over his eyebrow, hollowed bloodshot eyes, and a spot of beard under his chin missed with his morning shave spoke of a beleaguered civil servant.

Hunter paced in front of his desk, poised to cull her boss from the herd if she'd had the power.

"You're not a stupid woman."

"Ted! Don't go there."

Flannery tossed a photograph of Hunter and Jack, thick as thieves and leaning close at the Hinano Café in Venice. "What did you discuss?"

"We talked about the case. About Luke. Nothing more. Nothing that moved the case forward or backward. You've been copied on all the suspects. Nothing you're not fully aware of."

"What did I tell you?" Flannery hammered.

"Jack thinks my brother's dead. Okay? That's my new reality. I got to cry in my beer, so what? He has some leads but nothing to take to the bank."

"Do you know the position you've put me in? That you've put both of us in? My ass is on the line here because of your brother."

"You were all over the idea of sending him undercover. And you weren't fooling anyone. You thought he'd make you a star."

"I supported him with my reputation, which is now being called into question."

"Big fucking deal. My brother's probably dead, and there's

only one person besides me who gives a good goddamn, and that's Jack Bertolino."

"I ordered him to cease and desist."

"That had teeth." Her tone dripped sarcasm. "You're worried about your ass, I'm worried about Luke. I'm the one who has to tell my parents their only son is dead, and I'm supposed to walk away? You used to have balls."

Flannery leaped up and his chair banged against the wall, startling them both, his verbal attack a violent torrent: "I brought you up through the ranks when everybody thought you were a lightweight. And you have the temerity to disregard my orders? Washington's orders? Your brother knew the risk when he signed on. You did the risk-reward analysis, for Christ's sake. And now you've gone outside the department. Crossed company lines." Flannery faced the window, his eyes locked on the traffic on the 405 as he stilled his breathing. "I tried to bring your brother in. He defied me. And now you . . . you defy me."

Agent Hunter remained silent, waiting for the final edict.

Flannery turned. "Agent Hunter, you are now on your own. It's out of my hands. You've been suspended without pay for twenty days, at which time you'll meet with the Office of Professional Responsibility. If they recommend removal, you can appeal to the Disciplinary Review Board. We know how that usually plays out with their low threshold for misconduct."

Hunter's stomach churned and her head reeled, but she stood tall, tamping down her emotion and waiting to hear the rest.

"Washington wants a full written report on what was discussed with Bertolino, where the case stands to date, and I want it on my desk by five o'clock tomorrow. I'll do what I can to save your pension, but I wouldn't count on it.

"On a personal note, I couldn't feel any worse than I do about Luke."

Hunter refused to break eye contact. "But he's dead, and you've got a few years left before retirement. Given any more thought to buying that bar in Key West?"

"Close the door on your way out," he said, all the fight gone.

"Who's running with my brother's case?"

"It's no longer your concern. You're ordered to maintain strict silence until the case is disposed of, however it plays out."

Hunter turned to leave.

"Liz, your weapon, your badge."

Hunter pulled her badge off her leather belt and placed it faceup on the edge of Flannery's desk. She stared at the golden eagle that capped the badge, the source of pride and all that it stood for, and her anger erupted. She drew her 9mm and Flannery's eyes narrowed.

Hunter tossed her Glock on the desk's surface. It bounced once and knocked over Flannery's FBI mug. His face reddened as the dark liquid leached into his paperwork.

Agent Liz Hunter walked out the door, leaving behind years of success, struggle, and a career she profoundly loved.

———

Hunter made a stop at Gelson's on the way home from the office, loaded up on junk food, and was now dressed in her most comfortable sweats, sitting on her favorite couch, wearing her favorite slippers, her television set to the Travel Channel, working her way through her sweet acquisitions and trying to deaden the pain, when her safe phone rang.

"It's never easy," Jack said.

"You got my text."

"Are you drinking?"

"Hah!" exploded out of her. The first smile to pierce her melancholy in hours.

"Eating?"

"Entenmann's crumb cake."

"Good choice. Häagen-Dazs?"

"How'd you know?"

"A good match with the coffee cake."

"Chocolate peanut butter."

"One of my favorites."

"You're not going to make me feel better, although my esteem for your sleuthing skills just rose a few points. Which is a lot higher than my self-esteem."

"I get lucky once in a while. But there's more than one outcome at play here."

"Oh yeah?"

"My team is stretched thin. You have a few days when you can still call in favors before the rumor mill shuts you down. I think we're coming to a head one way or the other. I tell you what, sleep on it. I'm on my safe phone. I've moved onto my boat because of the feds, or Homeland Security, or whoever was on my tail this morning.

"If you want to stay active and be a part of taking down the scumbags who killed your brother, come on board. No strings. I'll take you through every move we've made, and I know you can bring something to the table."

Hunter chewed a piece of crumble off the top of the crumb cake while she thought.

"Cake, for example," Jack said.

"I'll call you."

"Fair enough."

"Jack," she said before he could click off. "Thanks."

Hunter wondered if accepting Jack's offer was just hammering the last nail in her coffin. And was that necessarily a bad outcome? As things stood, she didn't see a way forward at the agency. Even if she could prolong what seemed to be the inevitable end game, she'd bleed out slowly until retirement in some obscure outpost. Not what she had in mind when she signed on with the FBI.

It might be better to go out in flames. After all, she was the one who'd set the investigation into her brother's disappearance in motion. Jack Bertolino had been *her* choice. It seemed a little chickenshit to have engaged him and then let him risk his life without backup.

She'd never forgive Flannery for authorizing the arrest of Rusty Mannuzza without clearing it with her first. It had put Jack's life in danger, and he'd paid dearly for a move that hadn't advanced the case one iota.

And let's talk about loyalty, she thought, working up a head of self-righteous anger. Jack suffered a brutal beating and did not give up the Bureau. That should count for something to someone.

Hunter unfolded the ViCAP report and read about a man named Gregory, who piqued her interest. Why would Sukarno be meeting with an individual who traded in black-market contraband and acquired information he reportedly sold to the highest bidder? There was only one damn way to find out.

Hunter grabbed a fistful of crumb cake and polished it off in two angry mouthfuls. Hell, yes. Better to go out in flames.

# Thirty-one

Jack had picked up his second rental in as many days. He'd traded the Mustang for a matte-gray Camaro with dark-tinted windows and a dangerous 330-horsepower V8. If he got into another altercation on the highway, he wanted the power to blow his pursuers off the road. Jack checked twice to make sure he'd signed the collision damage waiver.

He stocked up on food and drink before heading to Long Beach and filling his galley. Jack was confident it had been Homeland Security tailing him earlier, and the last thing he needed was to spend a day in interrogation. The boat would more than serve his immediate needs.

Cruz was in the field tailing Roxy and Trent; Mateo was on his way back from Playa Vista, and the storage facilities. Jack pulled out his laptop and booted up. He hadn't heard from his contacts in Oakland, and he pulled up the *East Bay Times* to see if there were any stories of interest related to the case.

There was no mention of the fishing trawler or the death of the captain on the front page. Jack crawled down and, in the California section, skimmed an article about a thousand dead Pacific herring washing up on the shores of an island group about thirty miles west of the Golden Gate Bridge.

He was about to shut down when he read the article again, making note of the name. The Farallon Islands were a wildlife preserve. If Jack wasn't mistaken, the destination was one that Cruz had stumbled upon when doing research on the computer Luke frequently used. It hadn't rung any bells when it first surfaced. The search on Miranda's computer had targeted the Farallones, along with Baja, Hawaii, Indonesia, and a few other exotic destinations. They'd chalked it up to vacation travel destinations, but it was worth taking a second look.

Jack sent a text to Cruz, requesting a copy of the research related to the computer and a copy of the doodles Luke had inked on the margins of the magazine Jack had retrieved from Miranda's apartment.

Cruz's thought was if the numbers were listed in a specific configuration, they might've been maritime coordinates.

Jack went back through the photographs he'd taken when he broke-and-entered Roxy's boat. He'd snapped shots of different nautical charts stored in their cabin, and wanted to see if one of them referenced the Farallones.

Cruz forwarded the research and let Jack know that Roxy and Trent were lounging on their catamaran, and if they were planning a terrorist attack, they had ice water running through their veins.

Jack told him to stay put, knowing it might be the calm before the storm, and transferred the intel to his computer. He went to Luke's doodles, and if what looked to be a period was in fact a degree icon, then the coordinates did take them in the general area of the Farallones.

One of Roxy and Trent's nautical charts had the Farallones in a hundred-mile radius outside of San Francisco, but there were no markings to show intent or desired destination.

If the radioactive material had come from the Farallones, it could be responsible for the school of herring washing up on shore.

Jack decided to call in a favor from his friend Coast Guard Captain Deak Montrose. Pick his brain and see if there was any traction, or whether this was an exercise in coincidence and wishful thinking.

————

Captain Deak was in his early thirties, with a trim muscled physique, clear eyes, a square jaw, brown brush-cut hair, thick eyebrows, and an easygoing military bearing.

"Jack, you made the news again," Captain Deak said, sitting down behind his desk at the Coast Guard station in Marina del Rey. He gestured for Jack to grab the visitor's chair. "That was one cherry Mustang. Burned to the ground. Would've pissed me off."

"Trouble seems to be a close companion. You, my friend, look like life's treating you well."

"Life's been dull. I haven't seen any serious action since our last go-round." Their friendship, based on mutual respect, was battle-tested. It was the captain who'd first come to his aid in the waters off the Terranea Resort, in Rancho Palos Verdes, where Jack and Angelica Cardona had been locked in a heated boat-to-boat gun battle with an Iraqi gangster. Jack's Cutwater 28 had been blown to pieces, but because of Deak's timely arrival and decisive action, the pair came out of the water with mild hypothermia but alive to tell the story.

"What's your interest in the Farallones Marine Sanctuary?" Captain Deak asked, his tone thoughtful.

"I'm working a case, and here's the thing. There's only so much I can disclose without violating my client privilege. So, if we could talk in general terms, and if anything comes of it, I can protect you and my client."

"It's never easy, huh? Let 'er rip. If it gets too dicey, I'll shut you down."

That worked for Jack. "The case is a missing persons turned into body reclamation. A young man disappeared along with a half a million in cash. I was hired to find him, dead or alive. And, if dead, to run his killer to ground."

"Sounds reasonable."

"The trail took me from Baja to Oakland and a scuttled fishing trawler." From Deak's change in demeanor, Jack knew his friend was aware of the story. "The boat had been scrubbed clean. The captain turned up in a fisherman's net a few days later."

Deak finished the story. "He would have died of radiation poisoning if a knife hadn't done the job."

"There you go. And by the time I showed up, Homeland Security, the feds—"

"And my brothers in the Coast Guard were already on scene."

"Okay, so give it to me."

"We have to stop right here, Jack. I was briefed on their findings, and the information is protected. What I can do, since you asked a general question about a nature preserve, is fill you in on what is now a matter of public record under the Freedom of Information Act."

"Works for me."

"The Farallones were one of our government's dirty little secrets. The island chain is also known as the Farallon Islands Radioactive Waste Dump."

Deak had his attention. He was clearly in the hunt. Jack leaned forward and sat taller.

"Before you get ahead of yourself, the site was looked at and passed over. Between the late forties and early seventies, the government dumped thousands of metal drums containing radioactive waste in the Gulf of the Farallones. The drums were dropped at depths of three thousand and six thousand feet, respectively.

"There's no way a civilian could extract the drums at that depth, and whether the nuclear material was still viable is a debatable point. My opinion? No one has the answer."

"Huh," Jack said.

"Sorry to be the bearer of bad news."

"And the dead fish that washed ashore?"

"The herring? Could've been red tide, algae, El Niño effect. The marine biologists will run tests, but no one is fast-tracking a school of herring."

"Shit."

"But so much better than the alternative."

"Right," Jack said without enthusiasm.

"If you need anything, I'm set up and ready to lend a hand. On the water, in the air, you call me, text me, I'm there for you."

"As always, greatly appreciated."

---

The fast-food boxes had changed, but that was about it. Agent Hunter was in the same sweats, on the same couch, fighting for resolve. She took those fears, compartmentalized them, pulled up a number on her cell, and hit Dial, hoping she wasn't committing agency suicide.

"Jerry, Liz here, I need a favor."

"How's life treating you, Agent?"

"Full of surprises."

"You can say that again. Lay it on me. It's good to hear your voice."

"I'm working a murder investigation, and one of the persons of interest worked at JPL. He left under suspicious circumstances a few years back. Name's Trent Peters."

"Hold a second. Let me pull him up."

Hunter knew she was going to miss the badge, but the universe had given her a pass for a few days. She'd maximize her new reality and get to the bottom of her brother's disappearance if it took every ounce of blood and her reputation.

"Okay, got it, he was a class-two engineer with B-three clearance."

"We got word that some classifieds went missing, and I was wondering what that entailed."

"It'll take a few minutes to access the file. You want me to call you at the office?"

"I'm in the field." Hunter gave him the number of her safe phone. "I'll owe you one."

"Good. I love to have beautiful women in my debt."

"You're a hound dog, Jerry, but I love you, thanks."

Hunter thought it was time to shower and greet the world. She finished her Diet Coke and her buttered Eggo, walked the phone into the bathroom while the shower water warmed. She wrapped her hair in a towel, and as soon as the spray hit her back, the phone rang.

"Shit!" she said as she dried her hands and picked up the phone. "That was quick."

Jerry was all business. "It was considered strange because it didn't have anything to do with Trent's area of expertise. We partnered with the U.S. Geological Survey and began a cooperative survey of part of the Farallon Island Radioactive Waste Dump using sonar imaging. The government dropped forty-six thousand drums onto deep-water shelves, but it was an inexact science. The government wanted to know how many broke loose and landed in the shallows. It was too expensive for a hunt-and-peck, so we designed the side-scan sonar imaging system. They were able to detect waste drums more easily and to distinguish them from other targets with a high level of confidence."

"Did they find any in the shallows?"

"They retrieved a single fifty-five-gallon drum at a depth of about two hundred and fifty feet using a manned submersible. The lion's share was down in the six-thousand-foot range. I'm not sure what came of the study."

"And Trent Peters?"

"We couldn't make a case. He was questioned and released without prosecution. As I said, it had nothing to do with his specialty, and they gave him a pass. His career would have stalled because of the asterisk next to his name in his personnel file, and they let him go a few months later."

"Huh, thanks, Jerry. Not sure if it helps, but I'll run it up the pole."

"If you're in the area, give me a call, and lunch is on me."

"Will do, but I'll take you to lunch," and Hunter clicked off and jumped back in the shower. The case was starting to coalesce, and she felt her pulse tick up a notch. It was the juice that motivated her career and a feeling she would dearly miss if forced to go into the private sector.

---

Jack gathered his team on board his Cutwater 28. It was time to share intel and see where the case stood. Mateo was pouring a cup of coffee while Cruz pulled up his files on his computer, and Jack grabbed the notes he'd penned on his yellow pad.

"FBI!" Agent Hunter shouted. "Down on the ground!"

Three heads pivoted as a grinning Hunter walked into the cabin carrying a large pepperoni pizza. "I hate to arrive empty-handed."

"You had me going there for—No, you didn't," Cruz said, smiling.

"I hope I'm not spoiling the party?"

"Perfect timing," Jack said, "we're about to share notes. Bring everybody up to speed." He pulled plates out of the galley, and the team descended on the pizza.

Mateo went first and filled them in on Security Storage, Sukarno's alias, the security cameras spray-painted out of commission, and the fact that the unit had been cleaned, disinfected, and painted.

Hunter jumped in. "You said you rattled Roxy's and Trent's cages yesterday. It looks like you hit a nerve, and Sukarno cleaned house."

"The question being, what was he storing that could come back to bite him?" Jack asked. "Let's put a pin in that. Cruz?"

"I've got nothing. They looked like two lovebirds, getting some sun, grilling burgers, living the life. And then they showed up here, and it was business as usual. Roxy dealing with liquor vendors, and Trent doing some underwater work, and then he disappeared on board."

"I struck out," Jack said. "Worked up a head of steam, went to visit Captain Deak—my friend in the Coast Guard," he added for Hunter's benefit. "I went back over Luke's inked doodles in the margins of the magazines I got from his girlfriend. If you looked at them a certain way, they could be interpreted as nautical coordinates. I pulled up the charts from Roxy and Trent's cabin, and they encompassed an island chain called the Farallones, but not directly. And the kicker was a story I pulled off the computer today about a school of dead herring washing up on the shores of the Farallones. I put two and two and two together, got six. I ran my theory past Deak, and he filled me in on what he called the Farallon Island Radioactive Waste Dump, and I thought we'd hit pay dirt."

"So, what happened?" Mateo asked.

"Deak couldn't go into specifics but said the depth of the water precluded a civilian being able to access the steel drums that contained radioactive waste."

"Did you like the pizza?" Hunter asked, leading the men on.

No one smiled.

"Because I brought dessert. I spoke to a friend over at JPL. Where Trent Peters worked until they fired his butt."

"What do you have, Liz?" Jack said, knowing she was enjoying herself too much.

"I got a similar story. Where it veered off was the depth of the fifty-five-gallon drums. JPL did a joint venture with the USGS, the U.S. Geological Survey, and came up with a side-scan sonar-imaging device to track where the drums were dispersed. Forty-six thousand had been dropped in three areas of deep water, but a small number landed on a shelf that bottomed out at only two hundred and fifty feet. They pulled one of them out with a manned submersible. And so . . ."

Jack picked up the narrative. "It's possible Roxy and Trent, who's a scuba diver and had his scuba gear in Oakland when the boat went missing and the captain was killed, are now in possession of nuclear waste."

"And responsible for the deaths of two men," Hunter said, quieting the building excitement in the room.

"And responsible for the deaths of two men," Jack repeated in deference to Liz Hunter's brother, Luke, bringing a personal face to the forefront of their case.

"And Jack just put the fear of God into at least two of the principals and caused the third to react," Mateo said.

"The clock's ticking," Jack said. "I feel it in the muscle."

"I agree," Agent Hunter said. "I received the ViCAP report on Sukarno's lunch partner. He goes by the name Gregory, no last name, like Prince or Madonna." She pulled up Mateo's photograph on her cell.

"What's his story?" Jack asked.

"He's what they're calling a shadow broker. He's a fixer. An agent who operates in the underground economy. Never been arrested, but a person of interest in illegal oil deals in the Congo, arms deals in Syria, and blood diamonds in Angola. He also trades information to the highest bidder. This is the best photograph of him to date. Good work, Mateo. Gregory's a big question mark."

"So, why here, and why now, and what's the target? Where does he fit in?" Jack tossed out to the group.

"Unless it's all about the bottom line and he's brokering the deal. It goes with his résumé," Mateo said. "How much could you get on the black market for a dirty bomb?"

"Ten million, easy," Hunter said. "But that's not enough to change Sukarno's life."

"What if it was the beginning of a black-market pipeline? If this deal goes through, they've got a ready supply." But Jack didn't buy his own reasoning. He grabbed a slice of pizza and took a frustrated bite. "Liz, could you go back into Sukarno's file? See what I missed. There's got to be something.

"With Trent, maybe it is bottom line," Jack went on. "He likes the good life. I don't know how much he's making on the yacht, but I doubt it pays for the resort in Baja he frequents. And I'm not getting a political or radical bent from the guy."

"I'll get on Sukarno," Hunter said.

Mateo grabbed some pizza. "And I can get the pay grade on Trent. I'll talk to Caroline when we're done here."

"Well, that's it," Jack said. "Cruz, you stay on Roxy and Trent?"

"No problem."

"We have to be locked and loaded if they make a move to-night, tomorrow. I'm not going anywhere. I'm on my burner. I'm going to pick apart my case notes from the beginning and see if anything pops. Let's get this done."

---

Jack grilled a steak on the deck of his boat while two V-formations of pelicans flew silently past, looking like fighter jets on a bomb-ing sortie. Jack cobbled together a chunk salad of Persian cucum-bers, tomatoes, onion, and basil, poured a glass of red wine, and let the slight movement of his craft and the thick salt-laden breeze slow his heartbeat. But he couldn't silence his mind. He tented the steak with foil to let it rest, pulled a card from his wallet, and dialed a number.

Vasily Barinov sat hunched, inhaling a dish of blinis with cav-iar and sour cream, as a waiter set a pork kebab dinner and a fresh shot of chilled vodka in front of the hungry man. He was dining at Maxim on Fairfax, and the flashy room seemed the correct setting for the bearish Russian, who quickly dispelled that notion by wip-ing his greasy fingers on the edge of the pristine white tablecloth before answering his phone.

"Mr. Jack Bertolino. What can I do for you?" came out in a low growl.

"I need a moment of your time."

"I'm staring at a plate of food, so time is short."

Jack let that slide. "What's your take on Sukarno Lei?"

Barinov belted back the vodka and gave it some thought, signaling his waiter for another shot. "I took enough money off the man that I became curious and made a few calls. He's a rich man who hates to lose and so can't enjoy what wealth he's got. He hates the Chinese who were his business partners. This I know."

"How?"

"You know Dr. Chen? Silver hair, fair player. When he walked away from the table, well, I couldn't do the translation, but Sukarno's clucking and vengeful eyes told a story of animus.

"I took him for fifty grand later that night, and he left the table in a huff."

Jack wanted him to stay on message. "What did your friend have to say?"

"Sukarno lost a fortune on a stock-option deal. He's rich but not rich enough. It's understandable. He's also a man who holds a grudge. My pork is getting cold; call me again if there's anything I can help you with. I myself don't hold grudges, it's bad for the heart, and as you can see, I pay my debts."

"All right, Vasily." Jack clicked off, sliced his New York steak on the bias, served himself some salad, and dug in.

Tomorrow was the day. Jack felt it in his bones.

# Thirty-two

Rusty Mannuzza was being wheeled out of the urgent-care facility in Playa del Rey. His girlfriend pulled to a chirping stop in his Jag, threw the car into park, jumped out, and opened the door for her wounded warrior, who scowled dangerously as he limped to the car and eased himself in.

"Whatever you do, don't say thank you for getting out of bed at seven to pick your sorry ass up and take you to court," Cory said, twisting the emotional knife.

"Shut up. Make a right. Let's do the drive-through at Mickey D's. I'll need some protein before I kiss the judge's ass."

Cory slammed the door shut. If looks could kill, Rusty's bullet would've pierced her heart. The nurse enjoyed the schadenfreude moment and wheeled the chair back into the lobby. Rusty hadn't left a trail of fans at the clinic.

Cory snapped on Jack FM, turned up the volume on the rock station so she wouldn't have to listen to Rusty's sharp tongue, and headed for the exit.

A gray sedan made a tight turn into the lot, forcing her to slam on the brakes or get hit. "What the fuck?" she shrieked.

Two more cars swooped in, blocking the Jag.

"The feds," Rusty said. "This is not good."

"You think so?" Cory bitched, channeling her mother.

Special Agent Ted Flannery watched the proceedings from across the street as Rusty was cuffed, Mirandized, and roughly shoved into the back seat of the nearest sedan, while Cory stood there bewildered at first and then red-faced as she railed at the departing vehicles. "Motherfuckers! Goddamn motherfuckers."

———

Cardona had his cell phone plastered against his ear. He was sprawled on his overstuffed couch in the gym, a towel around his neck, blue velour Nike workout clothes, sweat pouring off his forehead. "What do you mean he's not there? He was due in court an hour ago. Find him. What the hell?"

Cardona clicked off and redialed. "Henry, Vincent here. Listen, anything going on I should know about? Anywhere? In regard to me?" he said, losing it. "I got a bad feeling is all. Rusty's MIA at the courthouse. This morning, goddammit! Hold!"

Cardona lowered the phone and watched Frankie-the-Man pound across the yard toward the pool house, followed by an FBI agent, as two sedans pulled up alongside the house and four suits joined the chase across the vast lawn.

"Henry, get your ass over here," all business now. "The feds are on my property, heading in my direction. Get your team on it. Find out what's what, and what the fuck they know. I ain't saying word one until you show."

Cardona hung up and dried the sweat off his furrowed brow.

He belched, rubbing his gut as he walked to the mini-fridge and grabbed a chilled water. He stretched to his full height and stood tall, an imposing figure, as the FBI pushed past Frankie and entered his world.

"You got papers?" he asked the first agent in, as if talking to a neighborhood punk.

Agent Flannery sauntered past his agents, search warrant in hand. "We'll be looking in the house, adjacent structures, place of employment, vehicles, electronic devices, and all safe-deposit boxes."

"Looking for buried treasure?"

Flannery ignored him, signaling two of his agents. They walked past Cardona and pushed over the first of the treadmills.

"Hey!" he snarled. "That's an eight-thousand-dollar machine."

The men came up empty. They tilted the second treadmill until it toppled silently onto the shag carpet. One of the agents pulled a locked metal security box out of a hidden compartment at the base of the machine and turned back to the room, holding it overhead as if he'd just won the U.S. Open.

Cardona's eyes cut toward Frankie and deadened. The communication was clear. There were rats on their crew, and blood was going to flow.

Frankie's gaze let him know he was on board, loyal, and he'd mete out the appropriate punishment.

Flannery couldn't hide his smug satisfaction. He lived for these moments. And if played correctly, this bust could resurrect his floundering career. He stepped up to Cardona and made a show of reading him his rights.

It took two men to cuff Cardona, who writhed like a python, sweat spraying off his feral brow wetting the FBI agents.

"Where you taking him?" Frankie demanded, taking a step forward.

"I ask the questions," Flannery said, staring up at Frankie as Cardona was led out of the pool house.

"Where the fuck is Henry?" Cardona asked Frankie over his shoulder.

A black Bentley pulled in tight against one of the feds' sedans. Henry Katz jumped out of his car in his three-thousand-dollar suit and strode across the lawn. "Cease and desist," Henry demanded in a demeaning tone that could diminish most men. It had no effect on Flannery, who handed him a copy of the search warrant.

Cardona walked past his lawyer and said, "Stay on it."

The arrest wasn't a surprise, Cardona thought as he was led past the manicured gardens and Olympic-size swimming pool. He'd had a good run, paid off the right people, provided steak dinners and women for the right cops and politicians. But hell, it still clenched his gut.

Jack had warned him it was only a matter of time before they'd come snooping around looking for Luke. Most of his life was in order. There was nothing on paper tying him to the *Bella Fortuna*. The second set of books the agents had found was related to the Chop House and could be problematic but not necessarily a game changer. His lawyers were killers. It was time for them to sharpen their knives and work off their retainer.

His fucking brother-in-law was in town exerting pressure, Rusty was AWOL, and if the feds grabbed him again, he might have turned state's evidence. How else would they have known about the second set of books under the treadmill? Luke was probably dead, and definitely on the feds' payroll, or the Boston rats never would've vouched for him. No, Vincent Cardona wasn't surprised, but heads would roll.

The first call he'd make would be to his daughter, Angelica. He wished he could keep her on the sidelines, but she'd have to run the Chop House while he was out of commission. Cardona knew if he didn't have a strong family presence in Beverly Hills, Mickey would be only too happy to take control of his cash cow. That would be over Cardona's dead body. Wasn't gonna happen. He'd cut a bloody swath through the New York family before he rolled over.

It was time for his daughter to step up to the plate and fulfill her birthright. He'd leave Frankie-the-Man as second in command to oversee and protect. Angelica Marie Cardona would keep the family name alive.

———

Jack slept like a baby on his boat, but the roaring pain he felt as soon as his eyes opened forced him to dry-chew two Excedrins, chased with black coffee and Vicodin. After a career in narcotics, the irony of being tied to prescription drugs was the ultimate bitter pill.

After three unsuccessful back operations, there was a very real possibility that if he went under the knife again, he'd be wheelchair-bound for the duration, and that wasn't a scenario he could live with.

So, Jack compartmentalized the pain and rationalized the treatment. The ringing cell phone thankfully dragged him out of introspection. And the sound of Angelica's voice planted the day's first smile.

"You're up early. I'm glad you called."

"Really?"

"I want you to stay off the *Bella Fortuna* tonight. Things are coming to a head, and if I'm right, I don't want you in harm's way."

"That won't be a problem."

"Good," Jack said, picking up an attitude and feeling that an explanation would follow.

"You haven't heard?"

"You're my first conversation of the day."

"My father was arrested by the FBI."

"Huh," Jack said. He'd known it was only a matter of time before Agent Flannery dropped the hammer to bail out his own career. "When?"

"An hour ago. Rusty got picked up first. Didn't make it to court. Dad was on the phone with his lawyer when the feds came calling. You didn't know?"

Jack let the implication of her veiled question slide. "I'm not surprised. I warned your father. He's been juggling too many balls. What were the charges?"

"A laundry list. Luke's disappearance and probable death . . . money laundering and running an illegal gambling boat."

"If my case plays out the way I think it's heading," Jack said, "he should be off the hook for Luke's disappearance."

"Well, that's a start."

"Does he think Rusty turned?"

"He's not saying. But if the feds have Rusty for half the crimes he's bragged about committing, then he has the most to gain from turning state's evidence."

"I can't believe we're having this conversation."

"Then you're not going to like this."

"Lord."

"I'm running the Chop House while the New York crew's in town. So that nobody gets any ideas what family is running the show until my father bails out. I'm at the restaurant now. The feds are here tearing the place apart. I know what you're thinking, but I couldn't say no."

Jack wasn't pleased but decided not to add to the pressure Angelica was already under. "How are you doing?" he asked instead.

"Confused. Messed up. I didn't sign on for this. But when he asked for help, I didn't think twice."

"All right. Okay. You take care of business. We'll talk later. Who's got your back?"

"Frankie-the-Man. Peter's on the *Bella Fortuna*. Uncle Mickey is nowhere to be found and not answering his phone."

"Okay. Call me if things get any crazier than they already are."

"Sorry to ruin your day."

"It's you I'm worried about."

"Thanks, Jack. Gotta run," and Angelica clicked off.

Jack exhaled an angry breath, contemplated taking another Vicodin, and vetoed that. He compartmentalized Angelica's troubles and the shit storm that would follow—an old cop trick—and readied himself to confront the day.

# Thirty-three

Roxy checked her makeup in the beveled mirror in her cabin on the *Queen Mary* and snugged down her brown wig. She felt as if she were in Afghanistan. Stepping into the unknown, praying she would make it back to camp alive. Her heart pounded against her chest.

She sucked in a few deep breaths and slid on her sunglasses and her wide-brimmed hat. Roxy Donnelly pictured her father lying in his long-term-care room, drifting between life and death, and it propelled her forward.

She conjured her commanding officer callously raping her, and the army's chain of command that had accepted his story over hers, turning a blind eye.

Payback was going to be a bitch. And when the *Queen Mary* was scuttled and the Port of Long Beach was shut down for six months, the United States government would pay dearly for their callousness and total disregard for their soldiers.

She harnessed all the rage and fury that lived just below her surface, and picked up the cell phone. Roxy fought to control the shaking of her hand as she carefully tapped in a number. She hit Send and heard a faint click emanate from the metal briefcase. Done!

The nuclear dirty bomb sitting on the floor of her cabin in the *Queen Mary* was now fully engaged.

She banged out a text to Trent and Sukarno.

Roxy hung a DO NOT DISTURB sign on the door to her suite and walked out into the sunlight. Adrenaline coursed through her body, and it took all of her military training to maintain the appearance of composure as she strolled down the gangplank.

Roxy glanced over her shoulder and, after judging it was all clear, tossed the cell phone into the water next to the ship and walked across the parking lot.

The bomb was set with a forty-five-minute delay to give the networks time to view the film, air the footage, and deploy the troops. It also gave the tourists and crew time to exit the *Queen*. Roxy had refused to sign on to needless collateral damage.

Tears welled, but her face remained placid. Her leg of the mission had been successfully completed, and the terrorist attack was now a go.

In the next few minutes, first responders would descend on the *Queen*, allowing the second leg of their attack to proceed unimpeded. Roxy jumped into her rental car and drove the speed limit toward the rendezvous point near the front gate of Long Beach Harbor. Once there, she would join the team to proceed with their exit strategy. Nothing could stop them now.

The nuclear clock was ticking.

———

Gregory, the shadow broker, sat in a dark room, round black glasses in place and three phones in play. One to the Chinese negotiator, one watching the Bitcoin Network, one to Sukarno Lei, who waited impatiently for news that the negotiations were completed and the money safely in his Bitcoin account.

---

Trent moved quickly in his perch fifteen stories above the wharf. He had to keep himself from grinning as he set his nuclear dirty bomb in the cabin of the crane, scheduled to off-load the Chinese conglomerate's tanker, *Hua Yong*. But he was giddy. High on adrenaline and the realization that their careful planning was coming to fruition, and the rich payoff was close at hand.

Trent had visualized this moment for years. From the time he'd first seen the classified documents at JPL and understood they were the key to his fortune. His dream was finally a reality. He felt no empathy as he stepped past the operator he had just killed. Sukarno's papers had opened the cabin door, and Trent led with his knife. The man bleeding out in his chair was his second victim of the day.

Trent propped the man up and started the dizzying climb down the metal stairway, game face on, all business. Like the authorized employee of the Port of Long Beach that his forged badge confirmed he was.

---

The negotiator for the Chinese conglomerate sat at the head of a large conference table surrounded by fifteen worried men in suits, watching Trent's underwater digital film reveal the nuclear dump site off the coast of San Francisco, the harvesting of the spent fuel rods, and the assembly of the dirty bombs.

The offer was simple. One hundred million U.S. dollars for the safe passage of the *Hua Yong*.

When Gregory was notified that the transaction had been confirmed by Bitcoin's network, the dirty bomb would be deactivated, and the conglomerate's container ship would dock and unload unharmed.

The digital tape was damning.

The clock was ticking.

———

The *Bella Fortuna* was two miles off the shore of Long Beach, heading for international waters when four gray government-issue sedans pulled to a skidding stop next to the yacht's empty berth. Eight men dismounted as the lead FBI agent slammed his fist against the roof of his car, grabbed his cell phone, and tapped in a number.

The mood on board the *Bella Fortuna* was festive. Late-afternoon sun spilled into the main salon. What wasn't to like? The yacht was beautiful, the day picture-perfect.

John Legend was piped into the room, silver dollars clanged heavily as they disappeared into the slot machines, muted bells sounded if someone pulled a winner. The poker tables were full, the players relaxed, the liquor flowing.

Caroline Boudreau stood next to Jack on the bridge while Mateo scanned the wall of security screens. Jack glanced over at one of the screens and noticed Ramón standing behind the bar.

"I parked next to Roxy's car when I arrived," Jack said.

"Trent must have used the car," Caroline answered. "Roxy called, oh, I'd say seven-thirtyish. She woke me. Stomach flu. She didn't want to leave me high and dry. I told her to stay in bed, no sense sharing the joy with my high rollers. Ramón was thrilled to take her place."

"Thoughtful," Jack said, hiding his concern.

Cruz had reported looking up from his laptop in the early-morning hours just in time to catch Roxy's Prius pulling out of the parking lot in Marina del Rey. The GPS tracker engaged, and he followed at a safe distance, peeling off only when he was sure her car was headed for the *Bella Fortuna*.

"It's a hell of a crew," Caroline said.

"What about Trent?" Jack asked.

"Here when I arrived, doing some work on the autopilot system."

"And Sukarno Lei?"

"My, you're full of questions this afternoon, Mr. Bertolino. Mr. Lei reserved the Presidential Suite. He's flying in at seven. Placed an order for Dom Pérignon to be delivered to his cabin upon arrival. He's bringing a guest."

"Lucky man," Jack said with attitude.

"I'm sure he hopes so," Caroline said, letting Jack's tone slide, not wanting to engage.

"Look at Peter," Mateo said, grinning.

Jack and Caroline glanced toward the security center as Peter Maniacci crossed from one screen to the next, moving through the room to ensure an honest game. Peter was wearing a tux. He thought it only proper for the man in charge.

"He's strutting like a rooster," Caroline drawled, enjoying the moment.

"He's the only one who made out like a bandit with Rusty and Cardona sitting in jail cells," Mateo said.

"He'd better get some résumés circulating."

"Is there something I should know, Jack?" Caroline snapped, not happy with Jack's inference.

"Sorry, I was thinking out loud. Don't mind me."

"Well, Lord. Pour yourself a drink. You're in a mood." She turned and looked at the mileage on the high-tech dashboard. "We're closing in on three miles, has anyone seen Carter?"

The captain would normally be on the bridge, switching out of autopilot, once the yacht had arrived in international waters.

"We crossed paths a few hours ago; he had some questions for Trent," Mateo said as he glanced at one of the lower screens. "I don't see anyone in the engine room."

"Would you be a dear and see if you can roust the pair?"

"My pleasure," Mateo said, and walked out.

"He is a keeper," Caroline said to Jack, who couldn't disagree.

---

Trent's digital tapes had arrived at the top three networks, along with a written statement directing law enforcement to the *Queen Mary*, where a dirty bomb had been secreted. The material was screened, vetted, and aired, setting off a flurry of activity.

NBC interrupted normal broadcasting for breaking news from Long Beach, California: "A nuclear dirty bomb has been planted on the iconic landmark the *Queen Mary*. No one has come forward claiming responsibility for the attack."

---

The Chinese, in their conference room, viewed on-scene cellphone video coverage on multiple screens, of terrified men and women fleeing the ship, running for their lives. The Chinese executives' voices rose in pitch as pictures of the panic surrounding the evacuation of the *Queen Mary* aired on all the major news outlets.

All hell was breaking loose in Long Beach as the Harbor Patrol, Long Beach Police Department, and Fire Department converged on the *Queen*. First responders ran against the flow of humanity fleeing the ship. Homeland Security, Coast Guard, Bomb Squad, SWAT teams, and the FBI were deployed and in transit.

———

On the *Bella Fortuna*, Mateo pounded up the stairs onto the bridge. His eyes raked from Jack to Caroline. "The engine room's locked, no one answered my knock. No one's seen the captain."

Caroline remained calm until she received a text. "Turn on the television."

"The report has now been corroborated by the Long Beach Police Department," Lester Holt said with gravitas. "A nuclear dirty bomb has been discovered on the *Queen Mary*, in Long Beach, California. Evacuations are under way . . ."

The *Bella Fortuna*, still running on autopilot, did a sweeping turn, heading back toward the mainland. The electricity snapped off. The security screens went dark. The music silenced.

"Trent," Jack said. And then to Caroline, "You said he worked on the system this morning. He's not on board. He's on dry land."

Jack phoned Captain Deak, who'd been deployed and agreed to pick him up.

Mateo moved up to Jack, his voice low. "I'll handle things here. Send help ASAP. I've got a bad feeling it's all tied together."

Jack had come to the same conclusion.

Caroline walked from the bridge and made an announcement to her guests. If she was panicked, she hid it well. "Hi, all, we're having some mild technical difficulties. Please bear with me. Order a drink. It's beautiful out on the decks, get some sun. We'll get the auxiliary power turned on in a few minutes and be good to go."

But a few of the patrons were listening to or reading reports on their cells, and fear rippled through the main salon.

Jack grabbed his cell; his phone rang before he could punch a number. Agent Hunter was on the line, working in Jack's cabin cruiser. Cruz was in the galley, pouring coffee.

Jack picked up on the first ring. "Liz, is your television on? It's going down."

"Shit," she said as she turned on the small flat-screen. Cruz stood behind her as they watched the terrorist attack unfold.

"I missed something in Sukarno's bio," she said. "He went public in 2012 and sold to a Chinese conglomerate the following year."

"I got that."

"The major share of the deal involved stock options."

"Okay?"

"I found an article in *Forbes*."

"He was on the list of wealthiest tech moguls that year," Jack said.

"Now jump five years."

"Not on the list?"

"Not even close. So I researched that and discovered Hua Yong Corp. The conglomerate that bought his company was accused of manipulating their stock price. The move cost Sukarno a fortune, and the deal was rumored to have been sanctioned by the Chinese government, who weren't fans. It's still in the courts, but Sukarno has spent millions litigating."

"I'm feeling motive," Jack said as he looked out the window of the *Bella Fortuna* and saw the bright orange-and-white body of the Coast Guard chopper descending.

"You got it," Hunter said as she looked past the *Queen Mary* to the port beyond. "The Chinese are big players in the Port of Long Beach, and a container ship owned by . . ."

"Hua Yong Corp."

"Is queued up and being towed into the harbor as we speak."

"He's doing a sleight of hand," Jack said. "Put a bomb on the *Queen Mary*, get all the government agencies targeting the ship, and blow up their real target."

"I'm headed over," Hunter said.

"Gotta run, my ride's here." Jack turned to Mateo. "I'll send help."

"Go get 'em."

——————

Captain Deak set his bird down on the bow of the *Bella Fortuna*. Jack jumped on board, pulling the door closed. The Coast Guard rescue chopper lifted off and headed nose-down for the mainland.

Deak's lieutenant, a young black officer with an open face, sat in the rear of the craft.

Jack filled Deak and his lieutenant in on the Chinese cargo container ship being a potential second target, and laid out *Bella Fortuna*'s troubles. He believed the gambling yacht, locked on autopilot, was headed for the *Queen Mary* to add misery to the mayhem, and he didn't want it shot out of the water.

Captain Deak called in a Mayday and asked for support. He gave the Coast Guard fleet the yacht's coordinates and signed off.

After a quick briefing, Captain Deak agreed to head north of the *Queen Mary* and execute a flyover of the Chinese tanker.

The chopper did a stomach-roiling pass over the massive

ship. Nothing out of the ordinary caught Jack's eye on the vessel, heavily laden with hundreds of multi-ton steel containers. Deak banked away, heading for the harbor, where the *Hua Yong* was minutes from docking.

In the distance, they could see the swarm of activity surrounding the *Queen Mary*. Choppers, boats, cars, and armored vehicles arrived en masse as throngs of terrified people spilled from the ship and ran through the parking lots toward safety.

———

Two Huey choppers set down, and heavily armed soldiers deployed and disappeared inside the *Queen*. Three F-16s came in low and streaked overhead, eliciting shrieks from the crowds.

———

Deak executed a flyover of the five red cranes, their long metal arms poised like sentinels to off-load the Chinese tanker. Jack signaled Deak toward the last rig, where an operator appeared to be slumped in his cabin seat.

As they circled the crane, it became clear that the operator was sitting in a pool of his own blood. The door to the cabin was open and flapping in the breeze. "They're here and gone. It may be too late. Get me onto the crane," Jack shouted over his headphones.

Deak knew Jack was battle-tested but was clearly uncomfortable bending the rules and putting a civilian in harm's way.

"It's a Hail Mary play, but time's running out, Deak. I know what to look for; I can do this."

"You better come out of this alive, Bertolino, or my ass is in a sling."

"If it blows . . . take off."

That didn't make Deak feel any better. Against his better judgment, he ordered his lieutenant to harness Jack in.

Deak hovered his craft over the cabin of the crane, which soared fifteen stories above the channel.

Jack sucked in a breath as he was lowered from the belly of the Sikorsky chopper. "Holy mother of God!" he shouted as he swung away from the bird.

"You sure about this, Captain?" his lieutenant shouted into the mouthpiece.

"Bertolino came to me and I shut him down. He called this. It's his play."

---

Jack's body, tethered by a thin nylon cord, started to gyrate wildly with the backwash of the massive rotary blades and the Santa Ana winds blowing across the mainland. Jack slowly stopped the spinning and swung his body toward the crane. On his first try, he missed the red metal support beam altogether, swung wide, and then whipped back into space.

On his second try, his body collided with the slick metal structure. His back screamed with pain. Jack gritted his teeth and grabbed for a handhold. His fingers peeled off before he could stabilize. "Shit!" he yelled. As if Deak could hear him, he adjusted the helicopter slightly, and Jack spun closer.

The third time was the charm. He reached out. The chopper inched him closer. Jack wrapped his arms around the crane, just above the cabin, and hugged the metal beam for all he was worth.

Jack caught his breath, carefully unsnapped the harness, and forced himself not to look down as he white-knuckled the dizzying descent to the trolley-mounted cabin hanging 140 feet off the ground. The cabin was where the controls were located that off-loaded the containers from the ships, and it was where Jack was confident he'd find the bomb.

Klaxons blared and echoed across the Port of Long Beach as Deak sent the alert and coordinates of a second potential nuclear attack and requested backup. The crane operators scrambled down to safety, while swarms of dockworkers ran for the gates.

---

Roxy strode up to Trent, who was standing just outside the Long Beach Harbor's gates. Sukarno was directly across the road, in front of the employee parking lot, with a cell phone plastered to his ear. Crazed workers clogged the street, running for their lives.

Roxy screamed, checking her watch, "My bomb didn't blow, Trent. What the fuck happened?"

"Motherfucker! I don't know," he said, checking his own watch, confused. "I just don't know. It should've . . ." Trent was distracted, more focused on Sukarno than Roxy as the crowd jostled past him.

"What are we standing here for? We should be moving. You engaged your bomb, didn't you?"

Trent didn't answer.

"Trent, talk to me."

"I'm waiting on Sukarno."

"What? Why! Do it now, Trent, engage. Engage, for Christ's sake!"

Trent waved her off while sirens wailed and swarms of frightened men and women sprinted through the gates toward their vehicles across the road.

"Why are you holding back?" she shouted. Her question fell

on deaf ears. She glanced at Sukarno talking on the phone. "Fuck Sukarno," she hissed, punching Trent in the shoulder. "Engage the bomb. Now!"

Trent had come too far to give up the prize. He shushed Roxy with a hand gesture and turned his back on her.

---

Sukarno spoke into his cell phone, fighting for civility, trying to keep the panic out of his voice amid the swirl of insanity playing out around him, exerting pressure on Gregory. "Has the money dropped? All hell is breaking loose."

---

Trent could feel Roxy unraveling. Afraid she'd have a panic attack, he turned back to her. "It's all under control," he said, trying to calm his partner in crime. He was shoved by a fleeing dockworker and almost dropped his cell phone but remained standing. He moved up to Roxy, exuding strength and composure. "Any second now, I swear," and then Trent spun on the sound of Sukarno's shouted voice. Their eyes locked.

"Now! Yes! Do it now!" Sukarno yelled.

Men and women, crazed and panicked, spilled through the main gates. Stumbling, tripping, stepping over fallen bodies, fearful for their lives.

Trent stood tall, his heart full, as he turned toward the crane, and tapped a number into his phone, and hit Send.

The bomb engaged.

"Ten minutes and counting!" he shouted at Roxy. "Let's go," and started walking toward Sukarno, pushing through the crowd.

Roxy caught up to Trent, gripped his arm, and in a low dark

voice, eyes blazing, asked, "Why was Sukarno waiting to engage the bomb?" But she already knew the answer. Trent yanked his arm away and kept moving. Roxy grabbed his bicep and spun him around. "What the hell did I miss here?" she screamed, spittle flying from her mouth.

Trent's eyes were wild. "We did it, Roxy. We're good. We're set for life. We can buy our own island."

And there it was. Roxy stopped in her tracks. Volcanic anger erupted as reality set in. Her bomb hadn't detonated. Trent and Sukarno had caused a delay that might have been the difference between success and failure. Between a successful mission and life in prison. Trent and Sukarno played her. They'd sold her out. Sold out her dying father.

---

Jack was close to the cabin now. Fifteen stories high. Not a big fan of heights, he held fast to the crane. Jack took a deep breath. Exhaled. And with his feet dangling, he swung and jumped through the open cabin door.

Jack landed hard. He regained his balance, heard a click, and his head snapped toward the metal briefcase on the cabin floor. He knew the bomb's timer had engaged and the clock was counting down. He fought to still his breathing as he dragged the dead operator out of his chair, sat in the man's blood, and started to manipulate the levers, trying to move the trolley-mounted cabin forward along the railings until it was suspended over the water.

---

On the *Bella Fortuna*, Mateo and Peter ran down a flight of stairs and stood outside the locked engine room. Peter pounded his shoulder against the metal door and bounced off. Mateo took a few steps back and ran, shoulder down, and threw his full weight against the door. It splintered open.

Carter, the captain of the *Bella Fortuna*, was lying in a pool of his own blood. Thick cables had been cut and were scattered haphazardly on the engine room floor.

It was immediately clear to Mateo that Trent had killed the captain and dismantled the diesel engine's override system. The coordinates were locked, and there was no way to stop the engine. The men ran back toward the bridge to deliver the bad news. The *Bella Fortuna* was on a collision course with the *Queen Mary*.

---

Outside the harbor gates, Sukarno and Trent fought their way through the crowds, heading past the parking lot toward their ride and a short trip to a waiting chopper.

Roxy lagged behind, losing control, afraid she was going to pass out, as the full weight of what had occurred crashed down on her tightly wound psyche. Understanding washed over her—the entire plan, from the very beginning, had been a lie.

Roxy bent over, hands on knees, to keep from puking. She started hyperventilating, her back bucking, her head reeling. In her panic, she relived what it felt like to be powerless. What it felt like to be raped.

Trent spun and ran back, frustrated, hands outstretched to nudge her along. "God is good," he shouted.

"But I'm not."

Roxy raised up, drew her .38, and shot Trent point-blank in the chest.

Trent straightened as he looked down at the dark blood blossoming on the front of his shirt. He staggered as men and women ran past. "What?" he asked, confused. Trent's eyes rolled back in his head, his knees buckled, and he dropped, dead before he hit the pavement.

Terrified men and women jumped over his prostrate body. No one of a mind to stop and help.

Roxy stood deadly still, oblivious to the mayhem that swirled around her. Sukarno turned at the sound of the gunshot, incredulous eyes locked with Roxy's, and then he disappeared amid the fleeing crowd.

---

Agent Hunter's car rocketed past the harbor gates, picked out Roxy, and braked to a gravel-spitting stop next to the chain-link security fence. She leaped from her vehicle and charged.

Roxy didn't hear but felt Hunter's approach. She turned the gun in the agent's direction, as she'd been army-trained to do. Hunter unleashed a punch to Roxy's jaw that dropped the soldier to her knees and sent her gun skittering into the gutter.

Roxy shook it off, reached up, and grabbed Hunter by the belt, dragging her to the pavement.

The women tore at each other. Throwing brutal punches. Fighting for their lives. Roxy muscled Hunter onto her back and straddled her; she cocked a fist, but before she could unload, Hunter flashed on her brother, Luke, and, filled with rage, fired a roundhouse to the side of Roxy's face, whiplashing her head at an unnatural angle. The blow knocked the warrior off balance and onto her back.

Hunter rolled, grabbed the .38 off the pavement, and leveled it at Roxy, who was bleeding profusely from the temple. Her dark blood ran down her neck, drenching her collar.

"Get up," Hunter shouted. But before Roxy could comply, Hunter yanked her to her feet, spun her around, and slammed her face-first against the chain-link fence.

Hunter slapped a single cuff onto one of Roxy's wrists and attached the second to the fence.

"It's too late," Roxy said as bile filled her mouth and she heaved.

---

The three F-16s had the *Bella Fortuna* locked on their radar screens. The pilot in the cockpit of the lead jet was on his radio. "Target on a direct line to the *Queen*. We're cocked and loaded. Please advise."

The sound of the fighter jets was deafening. Patrons shrieked, panicked, and ran onto the deck as they realized they were on a deadly collision course with the first responders' crafts surrounding the *Queen Mary*.

Caroline was in the main salon, handing out life jackets, ready to go down with her ship. The patrons were readying themselves to jump rather than go up in flames.

---

Jack glanced out the crane's cabin window, 150 feet off the deck. He could see the mayhem playing out around the *Queen Mary* and prayed the bomb would be disarmed.

But he was in the zone, hands flying over the instrument panel, with his own dirty bomb ready to detonate. Trying different configurations of the levers and coming up empty. The clock was ticking and Jack's heart was thumping. He tried one last succession and the motor kicked in.

Jack flashed a double thumbs-up to Deak, whose chopper was hovering a hundred feet beyond the cabin. Deak shouted "Yes!" as he watched the crane's cabin engage, lurch, and start rolling.

The behemoth Chinese container ship below cast a huge shadow over the channel, guided toward the docking space with the help of three tugboats.

The crane's cabin hovered over the deep-water channel.

Jack jumped from the seat and muscled the lead briefcase onto the ledge of the cabin's open window.

He sucked in a breath and shoved the heavy briefcase out and over the ledge.

The nuclear dirty bomb flipped end over end.

The metal case splashed down into the dark water. Expanding ripples of death marked the spot.

Jack ran to the cabin door as the *Hua Yong* slid to a silent stop over the bomb. The lieutenant lowered the harness. Jack snapped it on, tugged once to make sure he was secure, and swung off into thin air. Captain Deak banked the chopper up and away as Jack dangled twenty stories above the water, moving away from the Chinese tanker and the impending explosion.

---

The passengers on the *Bella Fortuna* were rushing to fasten their life jackets when two Coast Guard cutters closed in on either side of the yacht. Mateo and Peter ran forward, caught, and tied off heavy ropes to the bow of the yacht.

---

Deak sent a 911 radio call to the captain of the *Hua Yong* and the tugboat captains.

---

The sailors on the Chinese ship jumped dockside, sprinting for the exits.

---

The tugboat crews scrambled to untie and put distance between themselves and the ship as they powered, full-throttle, toward the open sea.

---

Only the high-pitched Klaxon could be heard echoing over acres of containers, and sixteen-wheelers, and docked ships waiting to be off-loaded.

---

The nuclear-laden dirty bomb exploded.

---

The sound was muted. The *Hua Yong* shuddered. A white funnel of water sprayed from beneath the tanker's midsection. The double steel hull had taken the bulk of the explosion. The ship creaked and slowly listed.

---

Jack was flying through the air, his life hanging by a thin nylon rope, trying not to heave as the lieutenant expertly winched him up and into the body of the chopper. Jack unbuckled the harness and strapped himself into a seat, happy to be on board. Happy to be alive.

---

The *Hua Yong* took on water, creaked, and groaned. As it tilted onto its side, hundreds of colorful multiton steel containers, filled with millions of dollars' worth of electronics, shuddered and scraped. Thick metal straps snapped. The upper stack of containers started to slide and then cascade, pulling down row after row, falling like stacked dominoes, splashing into the channel.

The three F-16 fighter jets streaked overhead and circled the carnage.

---

Jack reached Agent Hunter on the phone. He could see Trent on the ground and Roxy cuffed to the chain-link fence. "I need Sukarno's destination."

Hunter turned to Roxy. "I've got Bertolino on the phone; he's circling in that Coast Guard bird and needs some help." Roxy glanced at the orange and white Sikorsky chopper circling their position, wiped her mouth with the back of her free hand, and remained military-stoic.

Hunter got in Roxy's face. "Not the first time a woman's been taken down by male power brokers. You can still do some good. Something to make your father proud. Jack needs to know where Sukarno Lei is headed."

Roxy stood frozen with the realization that life as she knew it was over. That had always been a possibility, but damn, she'd believed they'd succeed. Roxy had signed on because she loved the symmetry of the plan. She'd gotten caught in the emotion and let herself be played like a fool.

"If Sukarno makes it to Indonesia," Hunter pressed, "there's no extradition treaty with the U.S. He'll be living large on his private island while you rot in prison."

Roxy spat blood as she glanced at Trent's body, bleeding out on the pavement, feeling little to nothing about ending his life. She saw the fleeing cars jammed bumper to bumper around the port. "Traffic's backed up," she shouted, fighting the blaring Klaxon and the beeping horns. "Jack can beat him there. Sukarno is driving to a chopper, headed for Santa Monica Airport. His private Learjet's waiting. Tell Jack to take the fucker down."

Agent Hunter turned her back on Roxy and raised the phone to her mouth. "Jack—"

"I heard her," he shouted over the thrumming of the chopper's rotors. Captain Deak pulled up and headed north.

Agent Liz Hunter looked at her phone, made a decision, and called her boss. Special Agent Flannery was in transit, not surprised Hunter was in the thick of it, and listened intently while she brought him up to speed.

---

Seven black-ops Huey Helicopters thundered across the parking lot and set down, blocking the port's entrance.

---

Agent Hunter, Roxy, and Trent's dead body were swept up and loaded into the belly of one of the black beasts. It lifted up and away as soldiers in hazmat suits, deployed, ran through the Long Beach Harbor gates toward the downed *Hua Yong*.

# Thirty-four

Captain Deak flew over Santa Monica Airport as Sukarno's red Bell chopper's rotors spun to a stop. Sukarno stepped onto the tarmac, gave a hefty tip to the pilot, and strode toward his Learjet sitting on the edge of the runway, waxed, fueled, and ready to fly. He was relieved to be free of Roxy and wasn't sure how to process the loss of Trent, but his blood pressure rose in excitement as he closed in on the finish line.

Sukarno was all but strutting by the time Captain Deak set his chopper down. The Coast Guard lieutenant approached the pilot of the Bell chopper and placed him in custody without incident.

Jack jumped to the tarmac and ran toward the Learjet just as the stairs powered up and slammed shut. Through the cabin window, Sukarno saw Jack running past the jet. His face was a mask of blind anger as he ordered the jet's pilot to take off.

Jack assumed a shooting stance thirty yards in front of the Learjet. He stared down the pilot as the two jet engines started to rev. Jack signaled with the barrel of his gun for the pilot to shut down.

Sukarno appeared in the cockpit window, red-faced with fury. "A million dollars says you don't have the balls to run him down," he challenged the pilot, who didn't like his tone but liked the sound of a million. "Gun it. He doesn't have the balls to shoot."

As if reading his mind, Jack fired one shot into the air.

Sukarno leaned over the pilot and nudged the joystick forward. The jet lurched toward Jack, who stood tall. "Back off," the pilot shouted as he braked, taking control of the craft as the engines started to whine. "Two million," he stated, making sure the stunt was worth the risk.

"Done!"

The whine of the jets revved to a deafening pitch. The burnished craft closed the distance to Jack in a heartbeat.

Jack fired and fired again.

The engine on the right side of the jet exploded. Followed by billowing smoke and the sound of metal tearing and grating.

The single powerful jet engine on the left side forced the plane into a violent spin. The right wing scraped the runway and snapped off, sending shrapnel flying.

Jack dove and rolled out of death's path.

One of the jet's tires exploded.

The plane jerked and flipped over, coming to a metal-wrenching, spark-flying rest, upside down. Fuel leaked and the second engine burst into flames.

The pilot shut off the power, unstrapped, and fell toward the roof of the cockpit, rapidly filling with smoke. He roused a dazed Sukarno and pulled the emergency lever on the fuselage door.

Sukarno pushed the pilot aside and was the first to lift himself onto the damaged fuselage.

Jack grabbed Sukarno by the collar and slid him off the scorched metal. The pilot jumped onto the runway and was immediately subdued by Captain Deak.

Sukarno got to his feet and swung a fist. Jack sidestepped the slim man and unloaded from the ankles. Sukarno's head snapped back, but he refused to go down. He threw a surprise side kick that connected with Jack's back. The pain rolled down Jack's spine, but a tight smile creased his face. "Bring it on," he said.

Sukarno might have been dojo-trained, but Jack was a street fighter. Sukarno calmed his breathing, took a spinning step in, and Jack hammered him with a solid right to the face, flattening the man's nose. The flow of blood choked him; his watering eyes momentarily blinded him.

Jack unloaded a thundering punch to the terrorist's gut. The blow knocked the wind out of the man's body and sent Sukarno down onto his hands and knees on the tarmac, crawling in a circle, gasping for breath.

The flames were building on the wrecked Learjet.

Jack dragged Sukarno away by his collar a second before the ten-million-dollar jet exploded in a brilliant flash of fire and fury.

———

An LAPD black-and-white rolled onto the scene, lights flashing, and the cop, brought up to speed by Captain Deak, cuffed Sukarno while he lay flat on the ground. The cop, who happened to be in the right place at the right time, read Sukarno Lei his rights. Since he was the cop of record, booking an international terrorist would make his career. Jack Bertolino and Captain Deak weren't glory hounds. They were more than happy to share the action.

———

Five gray sedans sped down the runway and surrounded the hangar as ten FBI agents deployed en masse.

After a few terse words with the uniformed officer, who made certain they spelled his name correctly, the feds grabbed Sukarno and secured him in the rear of a sedan with armed guards on either side.

Captain Deak fielded a call as Santa Monica fire trucks sped onto the runway, sirens blazing, light bars flashing. The first responders unspooled their hoses and blasted the conflagration with high-powered streams of water.

Special Agent Ted Flannery stepped out of the last government car, took in the carnage, and shook his head as he caught Jack's eye. He nodded acceptance, a wry smile creasing his face as he approached the men.

"You want to take a ride, Jack? That's not a question. We'll pick up something to eat on the way. You're going to be a while."

"Not until I find out what happened to the *Bella Fortuna*."

Deak, who'd just been briefed, spoke up. "Two Coast Guard cutters intercepted the yacht a hundred yards off the *Queen*, on a direct path. The F-16s were ready to blow her out of the water. Our men tied her off and changed her heading, and as soon as she runs out of fuel, she'll be towed to shore."

Jack nodded his appreciation. "And the *Queen*?" he asked Flannery.

"The bomb squad was able to disarm the device. Agent Hunter is already in transit. Her prisoner, Roxy Donnelly, requested an interview. With you personally. Any idea what that might be about?"

"Not a clue."

"She won't talk to anyone until you have a face-to-face. Go figure." Flannery glanced at Deak, "After you've checked in with your people, we'll want a go-round. Washington will need to get your story on record." Flannery handed him his card. "Good work, Captain."

Deak turned toward Jack, hand extended. The men shook, and then Deak pulled him into a bear hug. "You're the man, Jack Bertolino."

Jack looked at Deak and grinned, "We did good."

Jack shook the lieutenant's hand, turned, and walked toward Special Agent Ted Flannery's government-issue and his ride to FBI headquarters.

# Thirty-five

Jack sat in an FBI interrogation room. They all looked similar. No frills, the point being to make the suspects so uncomfortable they'd spill their guts. The rooms were generally wired for audio and video. This was no different. If Roxy wanted privacy, she was out of luck.

Jack looked up from the steam rising from his black coffee as the door opened and a handcuffed Roxy Donnelly was led into the room. Her face was ghostly white, bruised, and swollen; her red hair was matted and hung limply off her shoulders. The agent moved her to the chair opposite Jack and exited.

"Switch chairs with me, Jack?" she whispered.

———

"What did she say?" Flannery hissed, watching from his office on the seventeenth floor of FBI headquarters. Agent Hunter was sitting across the desk, but the monitor was turned so they both could view the interrogation. "What does she want?"

Hunter didn't think his question deserved an answer; she responded by pointing toward the monitor.

They watched as Jack nodded, stood, and changed places with Roxy. The camera was now trained on Jack's face.

"Son of a bitch," Flannery shouted.

"Maybe we can get it from Jack's side of the conversation."

"Son of a bitch."

---

Roxy looked like a woman in shock, but she was in total control. Her eyes were at half-mast, but she kept her head tilted and cupped her hand over her mouth like a defensive coach at a football game. No one on the other side of the camera could read her lips. "You signed on to find Luke Donato."

Jack understood where she was going. Roxy had a lot of blood on her hands, and he wasn't going to deal until he knew what she wanted. Then he'd make a determination. Jack was a strong believer in knowing when to give, to get. "I did," he said. Keep it simple, keep the prisoner talking.

"I can tell you where the body's buried."

Jack's gut twisted in a knot. He hoped Hunter hadn't heard the exchange. It would be a harsh way to have your worst fears validated. Jack gave away nothing. "What do you want?"

"Luke left behind a bag of cash. It's in an auto-pay account. Once a month a check is cut to Rush Street Care, and my father is guaranteed a clean bed and personal care until he dies. If there's a surplus, they can use it to pay for the lights and keep the facility open. It's a good operation."

---

"I'm stopping this," Flannery said rising to his feet. "I can't hear a word they're saying."

"Sit down, Ted. We have one opportunity to get information before she lawyers up. If you don't trust Jack, you're in the wrong business."

Flannery glared at Hunter, sat back down, and glanced at Jack's stony face.

———

"I can't promise," Jack said.

"Yes, you can. The Mob can't ask the feds for their bag of cash. It's dirty money. But my father won't know, and the government doesn't need it. Nobody else is privy to what I'm about to tell you."

"Did you kill Luke?"

"No."

Jack was feeling a lie. It was clear Trent had killed the captain of the *Bella Fortuna* and the crane operator. If Roxy pinned Luke's murder on Trent, and could also prove he'd killed the trawler captain, then the only death she'd be responsible for was Trent's. Her defense could claim emotional duress. With her role in the terrorist attack, she'd be looking at spending the rest of her life in a federal prison, but it might save her from the death penalty. Who was he to play God?

"Who killed Luke Donato?"

"Deal?"

Jack had no problem giving to get when it served the greater good. But he had no issues lying to a killer. Jack gave an almost imperceptible nod. Could've been a twitch. He wasn't going on record making a deal with a homegrown terrorist that could put him behind bars. But if he didn't sell it, Agent Hunter would never be the same. Some things in life needed closure. It wouldn't alter the result, but it might allow her to move on. Jack thought Hunter deserved that much. And while Jack would do what he could to protect Roxy's father, he wouldn't lie about the cash.

Roxy stared into Jack's eyes. Trying to discern if she could trust this ex-cop who had destroyed her life.

Jack hit her with his best poker face.

Roxy blinked first. She had no choice. "Trent killed Luke Donato. Luke was on to us, and Trent put him down. Bullet to the back of the head. We buried him at sea. The coordinates were plugged into the cat's GPS. If they're not there, I can find it on one of the charts on board. There's a key taped to the bottom of the engine hood."

Jack stood up, nodded to the camera. An agent who was standing by opened the door, and he left Roxy in the barren room with the nightmare she'd created. He felt no pity.

———————

Cruz jumped the fence at the dock in Marina del Rey where Roxy's catamaran was moored. He stepped on board as if he belonged. He pulled up the teak cover of the engine and grabbed the key.

No one dockside paid him any mind as he stood at the wheelhouse, turned on the power, and downloaded the GPS record onto his laptop and a small thumb drive.

Jack had coached Cruz on the need for speed. It was only a matter of time before the feds descended on the boat, and he didn't want the information, if it was valid, lost in bureaucratic wrangling.

Five minutes later, Cruz was cutting through traffic on Lincoln Boulevard in his Mini Cooper, giving Jack the lowdown. "The time and date are correct. The coordinates match Roxy's story. I left the charts on board; we can pull them up on the computer. She may be lying about who pulled the trigger, but this feels like the real deal. I'll text you the coordinates."

———

Jack's phone dinged, and he read Cruz's text. These conversations were the toughest part of the business. There was no good way to tell someone a loved one was dead. Most people knew on a primal level before the officer opened his mouth, but it was the spoken words that were life-altering.

Jack walked into Flannery's office and sat down next to Agent Liz Hunter. Her face was stoic, but her eyes filled before Jack shared what he knew. After Jack handed Flannery the coordinates of where Luke's body had been weighted down and lowered into the Pacific, the agent promised to immediately coordinate plans to retrieve Agent Luke Hunter's body, told Hunter how sorry he was, and exited his office.

Hunter and Jack sat in silence for a while.

"How did he die?" she finally asked.

"A single bullet to the back of the head. He never saw it coming."

Hunter gave that serious thought and then: "It's better than some."

Jack waited for her explanation.

"Ways to die. You know?"

"Yeah, I do, Liz. Our line of work and all."

"Thanks, Jack." And Agent Liz Hunter broke down and had a good cry. Jack gave her some time and then slid his arm around her shoulder.

The seventeenth floor was a flurry of activity. Orders shouted, men and women moving with concentrated purpose, but for Agent Hunter, it was all unfolding in slow motion.

———

Agents huddled around television sets in the conference room. The president was giving a news conference in the Oval Office with the most current information gathered by the FBI, CIA, NSA, Coast Guard, and local law enforcement.

He calmed the fears of the American public, assuring them that although the investigation was ongoing, the terrorists responsible for masterminding the attack in Long Beach, California, were either dead or in custody.

The bomb found in the *Queen Mary* had been disarmed, and the bomb detonated in the waters of Long Beach Harbor had leaked minimal amounts of radiation into the atmosphere. The double steel hull had absorbed the bomb's shock waves, dissipating the radiation, and the water had nullified the toxicity of the nuclear material. Cleanup of the site was under way, aided by the Santa Ana winds blowing the trace particulates in the atmosphere off shore. The northern quadrant of the Port of Long Beach would be shut down for months during the reclamation of the containers and the salvaging of the ship. The cleanup costs to the United States would run into the millions.

The president thanked the first responders who had risked their lives for the greater good, offered condolences to the families of the dead, and again assured the American public there was nothing left to fear.

# Thirty-six

Jack and Angelica were lounging poolside at the St. Regis Princeville Resort, with a spectacular view of Hanalei Bay. The resort was on the north shore of Kauai. The rain was abundant; the cliffs on the far side of the bay were a rich, verdant green.

Life had gotten too complicated for Jack in Marina del Rey, in the wake of the terrorist attack, and a secret escape had fit the bill.

The only thing more beautiful than the island was the woman lounging next to him, Jack thought. He was unwinding for the first time in recent memory and enjoying the moment.

"Where do you think the *Bella Fortuna* is right about now?" she asked, taking a slurp of her mai tai through the straw.

"Halfway through the Panama Canal."

Caroline had taken the hit from the feds for the gambling concession, since she couldn't very well ask the Mob to step up to the plate on her behalf. She was now serving eight of a sixteen-month prison sentence for her part in the illegal enterprise.

The upshot was: a gambling yacht on the West Coast was now a nonstarter.

Mateo had taken the lead in negotiating a settlement with

Vincent Cardona and the East Coast families. Caroline, with Mateo's financial help, ended up paying more than the boat's worth, but you couldn't put a price on freedom.

Mateo was presently motoring through the Canal in Central America while Caroline served her time. The *Bella Fortuna* would head up the coast, where a well-placed slip with a killer view of Miami was waiting. The *Bella Fortuna* would dock there, and on her release, Caroline would make a legitimate living running a luxury charter.

Cruz had earned a bonus. He'd put his own life in jeopardy to save Jack's. Jack told him to pick any destination in the world: he'd pick up the tab and fly him and a friend first class. Cruz's mother was Guatemalan, and being the great young man he was, he chose to take his mother back to the old country.

Agent Liz Hunter had been flown to Washington to speak before a Senate subcommittee on terrorism. She'd been reinstated, upped a pay grade, and given a promotion for exemplary conduct. Special Agent Flannery was not invited to the party.

With Trent taking the hit for Luke Hunter's death, Vincent Cardona was off the hook on the murder charge and made bail. So, Cardona was back, more notorious and more successful than ever while his money-laundering charges wended their way through the judicial system. Jack knew he was guilty as sin, and had ambivalent feelings about the pending outcome, but what the hell, with Cardona out on bail, it freed Angelica up.

"I got an email from Deak," he said.

"Oh?"

"He received a reprimand for letting a civilian use government property, and then they bounced him up to rear admiral."

"Well deserved," Angelica said. "Did you know they shot the

musical *South Pacific* in Hanalei Bay? Right across from where we're sitting."

"You are a fount of information."

"Am I bothering you?" she asked coyly.

"Not by half."

"Do you think Chris is going to quit baseball?"

"I hope not. But I'm behind him one hundred percent whatever he decides. I hope he understands that."

"Even if it means becoming a cop?"

"Hmmmm." Jack looked at Angelica and couldn't help but smile. "I'll have to give that some thought."

"You know there's one way to make me stop talking . . ."

Jack signed the tab and reached out a hand.

As the sun slipped behind the ridge of emerald across the bay, Jack and Angelica walked arm in arm up the garden path and disappeared into the hotel.

———

As Jack rinsed off in the shower, the hotel phone rang.

He turned off the water, shrugged into a terry-cloth robe and, towel-drying his hair, stepped out of the bathroom. Angelica was fully dressed, with her leather carry-on bag and suitcase open on the bed. Her makeup had been stripped from the top of the dresser, and she was emptying a drawer.

Angelica didn't look up. From her posture, the light tremor in her hands, and the tight set of her jaw, Jack could see she was wrestling with her emotions. "They arrested your father again," he intuited, the only scenario that made sense.

Angelica spun, her face incredulous, and then, realizing Jack wasn't the enemy, stepped into his arms and held on tight. Held on for dear life.

"Rusty's been busy," she said. "He implicated my father in the shooting death of a hijacked big-rig operator. Accessory to murder after the fact. Dad's been named the mastermind of the robbery. Add that to his money-laundering charges, and the judge revoked bail, calling him a flight risk."

"I'd ask you to think carefully before making a move, but it appears you've made up your mind."

Angelica took Jack's face in her hands and gave him a tender kiss on the lips. Jack took in the smell of sunscreen and sex, memorizing the worry lines on her young face and the gold rim around her green eyes, which searched Jack's for an answer.

"They picked up Peter and Frankie-the-Man," she said, and continued to pack. "There's no one to run the Chop House."

Jack wasn't good on his emotional feet in situations like this, and chose his words thoughtfully. "You've got a choice to make. This is not your problem," he said, knowing his words rang hollow. "It was only a matter of time before your father went down. You told me very convincingly that you were born into a situation beyond your control. You weren't a Mob princess, and you weren't a member of *that* family. You were your own person."

"Why didn't you just run away with me when I asked?"

"It never works. Life doesn't work that way. You've got a choice to make."

Angelica slammed the suitcase shut and snapped the locks with more force than necessary. "I need some time."

"It's complicated. But in your heart, you knew it couldn't last forever. And as hard as it is to accept, your father is where he deserves to be."

Angelica flushed, and her legs gave out. She lowered herself onto the edge of the bed. Shoulders back, military-straight, trying to make sense of an impossible situation.

"You've got all the right stuff," Jack said tenderly. "If you make the right moves."

Angelica was on emotional overload. She glanced at her watch and jumped to her feet.

"Let me throw on some clothes," Jack said. "I'll drive you to the airport."

There was a knock at the door. "Dad's lawyer sent a car . . . Give me a second!" she shouted, and then locked eyes with Jack. "Don't give up on me." Angelica didn't wait for an answer. She yanked the door open.

The bellhop stepped in. His smile faded as he picked up on the energy in the room; he grabbed her bags, slid them onto his brass cart, and wheeled it down the hallway toward the elevator, never looking back.

Angelica stood on her toes, gave Jack another kiss, and eased the door closed behind her.

The day hadn't ended as scripted. Jack was glad he was alone. His throat felt constricted, and his heart pounded in his chest. He gazed across Hanalei Bay to where *South Pacific* had been filmed, and all he could see was the beautiful face of Angelica Marie Cardona, etched in a pain he could do little to heal.

# Acknowledgments

Many thanks to my publisher, Karen Hunter, to my editor, Adam Wilson, for a masterful job, and to the entire team at Simon & Schuster for their continued support. Thanks to my attorney, Les Abell, and to my nephew, Lucas Detor, who was the inspiration for this book. Thanks to Micah Winkelspecht for his expertise on Bitcoin, Bruce Cervi for his understanding of physics, and Kathy Solorzano for her knowledge of criminal law. A heartfelt thanks to Vida Spears for being there every step of the way, lending her support and giving insightful notes. Diane Lansing, Deb Schwab, Annie George, and Bob Marinaccio all sacrificed their time and energy reading early drafts and sharing their ideas. And a special thank you to Gordon Dawson, whose creative notes kept me on the straight and narrow. I'm fortunate to be surrounded by so many talented friends.